KATHARINA, KATHARINA

EVERYONE HAS HEARD the phrase "making history come alive." *Katharina, Katharina* is a fruitfully accurate demonstration of that experience. Throughout the fictional narrative, the past is softened and enhanced by authentic atmosphere and culture. Farenhorst brings us into a world that not only was, but a world that is— warm, loving, true, and tragic—"the fabric of life," she reminds us.

Farenhorst's scrupulous historical research presents not so much her deep knowledge of the times but her rich perception of the humanity and the profundity of the Reformation— interactions not simply of characters but of sinful people who seek to know the Lord. *Katharina, Katharina* presents a commendable understanding of the Reformation itself, its impetus, its exigency, its biblical scholarship and the confusing heresies so long ingrained in the minds of sincere believers.

The familiar phrase "the heart of the Reformation" commonly refers to certain key scriptural truths. *Katharina, Katharina* effectively displays that heart, but beyond that, it personally brings twenty-first-century readers into the heart of the Reformation.

—NORM BOMER, *God's World News*, senior editor (retired) and author of *Sons of the River: A Nebraska Memoir*

WHILE THE STORY takes place in the distant past, it is really very relevant for our times. Katharina was a real person who experienced a spiritual struggle about her relationship with God. We all have the same questions to face, and that same message of being hidden in the righteousness of Christ is the only sufficient answer.

The book is well written, it flows smoothly and engages the mind and heart. It is suitable reading for teenagers and adults.

—BENJAMIN SHORT, lecturer at Gillespie Academy, Woodstock, ON

THIS IS THE very best way to learn—Christine Farenhorst uses historical fiction to pair an engaging storyline with an instructive setting. So yes, the day-to-day details of life among the Schütz family in sixteenth-century Strasbourg are made up (though based on good research) but all the big events in the story are entirely factual…and highly relevant for our day. So even as Luther never makes an appearance, he looms large, and in a very real way this is a Luther biography. I absolutely loved it.

—JON DYKSTRA, editor of *Reformed Perspective*

KATHARINA, KATHARINA

The story of Katharina Schütz Zell

Christine Farenhorst

joshua press

www.joshuapress.com

Publisher Joshua Press Inc., Kitchener, Ontario, Canada
Distributor Sola Scriptura Ministries International | www.sola-scriptura.ca

Scripture quotations, unless otherwise indicated, are from The Holy Bible, English Standard Version® (ESV®), copyright © 2001 by Crossway, a publishing ministry of Good News Publishers. Used by permission. All rights reserved.

Cover and book design Janice Van Eck
Cover illustration Keturah Wilkinson; coloured by Nathan Wilkinson

Library and Archives Canada Cataloguing in Publication

Farenhorst, Christine, 1948-, author
Katharina, Katharina : the story of Katharina Schütz Zell / Christine Farenhorst.

Includes bibliographical references.
Issued in print and electronic formats.
ISBN 978-1-894400-84-8 (softcover).—ISBN 978-1-894400-85-5 (HTML).—ISBN 978-1-894400-86-2 (EPUB)

1. Zell, Katharina, 1497 or 1498-1562—Fiction. I. Title.

PS8561.A68K38 2017   C813'.54   C2017-905858-4
                                            C2017-905859-2

Dedicated to my mother
Petronella Johanna Vlietstra
(1909–1988)

Part I

But the Lord answered her,
"Martha, Martha, you are anxious and troubled
about many things."
Luke 10:41

Weeping may tarry for the night...
Psalm 30:5

Preamble

"A generation goes," says the preacher in Ecclesiastes, "and
a generation comes, but the earth remains for ever. The sun
rises and the sun goes down and hastens to the place where
it rises."

The last decade of the year 1400 was the end of one generation on earth and the beginning of another. This particular
decade had a great many persons born into it. Dying, a
great many people stepped out of it as well. There was, for
example, Girolamo Savonarola, a Dominican monk and a man
who took God's mandate to honour him very seriously. He was,
however, burned at the stake for the courage of his conviction on
March 23, 1498, by the command of Pope Alexander VI. Pope
Alexander VI, the father of numerous illegitimate and wicked
children, was a man who did not honour God.

That same last decade of 1400 also saw Spain expel its
Jewish citizens and beheld Portugal massacring a great many of
Abraham's physical descendants.

"All things are full of weariness; a man cannot utter it; the
eye is not satisfied with seeing, nor the ear filled with hearing.
What has been is what will be and what has been done is
what will be done."

Columbus sailed from Spain looking for new countries; the explorer Ojeda proudly thought he was the first to have seen the sun shine on the mouth of the Amazon; and Turkish soldiers, without any thought of almighty God, conquered a large portion of Montenegro, murdering thousands in the process.

And, as if that were not enough excitement to fill a tumultuous decade, Vasco da Gama rounded the Cape of Good Hope; John Cabot discovered Newfoundland; and Amerigo Verspucci claimed to have reached the mainland of America before Columbus. France invaded Italy and captured Milan, but was afterward driven out by Ferdinand of Spain. Lust for power, desire to accumulate wealth and an inborn desire for fame ruled.

"...and there is nothing new under the sun."

But God lets his mercy shine throughout generations. And so it came about that a young boy in this same decade, a child by the name of Martin, travelled from Mansfeld to Magdeburg to attend the school of the Lollards. And the boy increased in knowledge, so that he might become wise.

Chapter I

Totally oblivious of the vast amount of vanity about them in the year 1498, two little girls sat on the stone steps of a tall four-storey house in the city of Strasbourg. Their arms entwined, their blue kerchiefs bright, they chattered together like springtime robins.

"I hope Vati and Mutti will be out soon with baby Kathe," said Elisabet, whose seven years gave her seniority.

"You are not to call the baby Kathe," the younger child responded, with a small pout, "She is to be baptized Katharina, you know that."

"Oh, hush, you baby," laughed her sister, not meaning it one bit, as she squeezed her sibling's hand, "Of course I may call her that. I call you Barba, don't I? And your name is Barbara."

"Well," the four-year-old answered with a shrug, "I suppose that is true, but she is not named yet, so perhaps we should not call her anything. Just baby."

The peaked roofs of the Strasbourg houses on the opposite side of the street dwarfed the children. The gables, with their numerous attic windows, ran up into the sky. They were all richly engrafted with wreathed work, stone carvings, leftovers of previous centuries.

"Look!"

Barbara pointed a small index finger toward the lace curtains hanging in front of the window on the second storey of the house directly across from them.

"Frau Bauer is watching us again. She is waiting for Mutti to come out with the baby. I think she is jealous that...."

"Hush, Barba," said her sister, pulling the accusing finger down hastily and putting her hand over Barbara's mouth, after quickly glancing up at a shadow figure standing motionless behind the curtains. "That is not kind to say. The priest would give you ten Hail Mary's as penance for thinking such a thought let alone saying it. It is not kind at all. Do you not wish that you could give a little baby to Frau Bauer?"

Elisabet took the hand away as Barbara made no reply, straightening her skirt, which had become rumpled by the impulsive motion. But once her sister's hand was far away, Barbara's little lips burst forth in a rush of words.

"The Virgin Mary has not blessed Frau Bauer with living children, so perhaps she has done something very bad. When your babies all die, all die before they are baptized...."

Barbara uttered her accusation breathlessly, taking no time for air, but Elisabet clapped a hand in front of Barbara's mouth again, not allowing her to finish. At the same time, Elisabet clucked disapproval in the same way her mother made short clicking sounds when she was upset about something.

"You ought not..." she began chiding but was interrupted when a small pebble suddenly bounced off the steps in front of her feet. She stood up, surprised, pulling Barbara up with her.

Above their heads, laughter pealed out, and as they craned their necks heavenward they detected the face of eight-year-old Lux disappearing behind the relative safety of the shutters on one of the second floor windows. Barbara grinned, shrieking out indignantly at the same time.

"Lux. We saw you. We know it's you and we'll tell...."

But she did not get to finish her sentence. Elisabet's hand effectively shut off the effusive flow of her words and her shrill cries. Behind them the heavy, double, oak doors of the house opened and Vati and Mutti stepped out. Mutti was carrying the baby and Vati held the hand of Jacob, their two-year-old brother. As Vati carefully closed the door, Mutti smiled at her daughters.

"Are you girls ready?"

Giving the second floor another cursory glance, Elisabet nodded, simultaneously taking Barbara's hand into her own.

"We are ready, Mutti."

"We've been waiting a long time," Barbara piped up, "and Lux...."

But Elisabet yanked her hand so hard that she stopped mid-sentence.

"Ow, you're hurting me, Elisabet. Mutti!"

The door opened again and Lux pranced out. He smirked at the girls, jumped down the steps ahead of his parents and began skipping down the street. Across the road, behind the window, the shadow figure of Frau Bauer disappeared.

Herr Schütz was dressed in a fur-collared, grey cape. A cloth beret rested on his dark, curly hair and a big black beard, trimmed neatly, hung down toward his broad chest.

"Vati! Vati!"

Barbara pulled loose from her sister's grasp and danced in front of her father, begging for his attention. But Vati shook his head, indicating she should move away. He stood next to his wife, supporting her with his right hand as she carefully made her way down to the street, all the while protectively cradling the bundle in her arms.

"Go back and hold Elisabet's hand, Barbara," he admonished, "and stay by her side because we have a long walk ahead of us."

It was February and still quite chilly outside. Elisabet could see her breath. Humming softly, she walked Barbara and herself a safe circle around a beggar on the first street corner—a man who sat in a small, wooden-wheeled cart. Often seen on Johanngasse, their street, he appeared to be a cripple, although Lux swore he had once seen the man get up out of his cart and walk. After they had passed, Barbara turned her head to stare at him. He boldly stared back, grinning and holding out a cracked cup, but then moved the cart with his hands as Herr and Frau Schütz approached, respectfully tipping his cap to them. Birds flew overhead. Elisabet followed their flight, her eyes also taking in the wide scope of Strasbourg's skyline—a skyline dominated by church spires.

The Schütz family, making good progress, passed the St.

Thomas' Church before turning left to head toward the centre of town. Vati, as he always did, pointed out the Chancellery, the office of the chief rulers of the city and said, as he always said, that their city was well structured and laid out. At that point, small Jacob began to tire of walking and started to whine. His legs, too short for the long walk, were giving way. Vati, with a flourish, lifted him high up into the air, seating him on his neck. Barbara cheered and Mutti smiled. She shifted the baby from one arm to the other and Vati asked her if he might also carry little Katharina for a while. She shook her head.

"No, no. You have Jacob. The child is light. She is no bother."

"Elisabet called her Kathe, Mutti," Barbara said in a clear voice, turning as she spoke and trying to walk backward but could not as Elisabet held her hand tightly, "but that is not her name, is it?"

"I think it's a very nice pet name," Mutti answered, winking at Elisabet over Barbara's head, "Indeed, I think we should all call her that."

Barbara turned her face toward her sister and stuck out her tongue. Elisabet ignored her.

"Are we almost there?"

Barbara, in spite of her playful skipping, was also finding it hard to keep up.

"There is the Pfalz," Vati said, pointing to the city hall, "the cathedral's only a bit further."

The church spire of Strasbourg's cathedral could be seen for miles and miles around Strasbourg. It was very much higher than any of the other church buildings in Strasbourg. Dwarfed by its magnificence, Elisabet felt very happy that their baby would be baptized there. The cathedral had two towers, the one but just recently completed. As well it had a single spire—a spire known to be the tallest in all of Europe in this year of our Lord 1498. Elisabet had heard Vati say this, so she knew it to be true, and it made her heart burst with pride. Strasbourg was a good city to live in. For besides having the cathedral, was it not also guarded by a circle of thick walls, high towers and strong bastions?

"There it is."

Barbara nudged Elisabet's arm and pointed. Barbara was

always pointing. Exasperated, Elisabet pushed her sister's hand down. The family had turned the last corner of their walk and, although they all knew it was coming, the thirteenth-century cathedral fell upon their vision like a giant. Everything else around them dwarfed into insignificance. Not at all in awe of its magnificence, however, baby Katharina began to fuss. Through the woollen blankets which Mutti had wrapped around her, they could all hear a soft whimpering.

"Never mind, little one," Mutti whispered, "we are here and soon you will receive the sacrament of baptism."

She was stopped in her murmurings by the chatter of a group of people who had evidently been waiting for them on the church steps. Smiling, she increased her pace. But Elisabet, even though she loved her beaming relatives, found it difficult to take her eyes off the cathedral. The huge stained glass window between the two towers was like a flower, she thought, and the rose-coloured stones around it were beautiful. She again felt happiness flow through her that Katharina, her very own new baby sister, would be baptized here—here in this very cathedral—a place so grand and so important. Surely it meant that Katharina would have a long and healthy life.

"Elisabeth! Jacob! We were worried that you would be late!"

Mutti laughed and shook her head at Vati's brother and her sister-in-law who had agreed to stand as godparents.

"Dr. Geiler is here already. He just stepped inside and said he would come back soon."

Everyone hugged and kissed and Tante Maria pulled aside the woollen blankets just a smidgin to steal a peek at the baby.

"She is small but very comely, Elisabeth. Is she drinking well?"

Tante Maria had a wart on her double chin, and her jowls shook when she spoke. The wart fascinated Barbara, but she had enough sense not to point at it, something for which Elisabet was truly thankful.

Horse-drawn carriages passed by on the street. There were, as well, some pedestrians about—some of them were out for morning strolls and others were on their way to work. There was also the occasional beggar such as the one they had passed. But begging, Elisabet knew, was actually not allowed in Strasbourg. But what if you owned nothing at all? However would you get food? She tried to imagine but could not. She looked at Mutti in her fine green, going-to-Mass dress. Mutti looked very much like a gentlewoman, and Vati was so handsome. Surely the good Lord had blessed their family very much!

Dr. Geiler von Kaysersberg suddenly stood next to them. An older man, he had been the Schütz family priest for a great many years. Everyone in Strasbourg liked and respected him because it was sensed that he truly cared for the people, unlike many of the other priests in town. Of course, nobody dared say this out loud in the vicinity of the church, but it was well-known that a great number of the priests were lazy and could not even read proper Latin text. At least, that is what Elisabet had heard Vati and Mutti say when they thought she was not listening.

Elisabet, Lux and Barbara now gathered next to their parents and watched with interest as Dr. Geiler began the baptism procedure by exorcising baby Katharina. He spoke in familiar German as they stood before the door of the great cathedral, directly under the wings, Elisabet keenly felt, of God.

"I cast out Satan from this newborn heir of Adam and Eve."

Dr. Geiler's voice boomed out over the church steps and Elisabet, Lux and Barbara shivered involuntarily. Jacob, still on his father's shoulders, was the only child who was not perturbed. Elisabet cautiously looked around to see if the devil was indeed running away. But, of course, she did not know what the devil looked like, so how would she know? Barbara tugged her hand.

"Where did Satan go, Elisabet?" she whispered, a tinge of fear in her voice, "Where is he?"

"I don't know, but far away, I think," her sister answered and squeezed Barbara's hand reassuringly.

The priest next made the sign of the cross on Katharina's forehead and chest. That was a good thing. Elisabet knew this for certain, for the blessed cross protected people from evil things.

"Open the baby's mouth, Frau Schütz."

Dr. Geiler spoke gently and as Mutti opened Katharina's rosebud lips, his long white fingers sprinkled some salt on the pink little tongue, praying as he did so. The salt, Elisabet had been told previously, was a salt which had been especially blessed for the baptism. Salt preserved, this she knew to be true. Katharina was not tremendously respectful of the blessing, for, upon tasting the salt, she crinkled her face terribly and let forth a protesting howl. Lux grinned and punched Elisabet. She gave him a look which meant, "Be quiet, or else!" and Vati swatted him on the head.

"Let us now enter the sanctuary," Dr. Geiler said to the family, and the entire group sedately followed him through the great cathedral doors. Vati lifted Jacob down to the ground before he entered. The church was massive, a place where your feet sounded both hollow and holy, Elisabet thought. She began walking on her tiptoes and Barbara mimicked her. Lux, on the other hand, began to stamp his feet for the sheer enjoyment of the echo, and Jacob copied him. Vati had to swat both of them on the head. A few people were present in the church, praying as they knelt down in the benches. Heads down, knees on the prie-dieux—the kneeling benches—they seemed oblivious to the clatter the Schütz family made as they passed by in the centre aisle. The exquisite stained glass windows on both sides of the sanctuary were awesome and matchless. Elisabet found herself holding her breath, the way she sometimes did during Mass, when she contemplated the sheer grandeur of her surroundings.

Stopping at the front, Dr. Geiler turned to the left, leading the way into a small narthex. It was here that the baptismal font was located. His long, flowing black robes impressed the children. He now appeared so severe and so wholly imposing, that even Lux lost his desire to make noise. Dr. Geiler waited until Frau Schütz had uncovered Katharina, handing over the woollen blankets to Elisabet. Underneath these blankets, the wide-eyed baby had been decked out in a long white robe. Elisabet contemplated the baptismal dress with great satisfaction. She had helped Mutti stitch some of the hem. It was baby Katharina's robe of innocence, Mutti had said, and the long, snowy folds fell beautifully around her tiny form. Would Dr. Geiler see how delicate and intricate the work on the gown was?

"Do you promise…"

Startled, Elisabet looked up from admiring the gown. Dr. Geiler was speaking to the godparents.

"...that when this small girl-child comes to the age of understanding, that you will teach her the Our Father, the Ave Maria and the Creed?"

They both promised solemnly, Tante Maria's chin, wart and jowls quivering with sincerity in the process.

"Do you," Dr. Geiler went on to say, now speaking to Vati and Mutti as well, "renounce the devil and do you confess the Father, Son and Holy Spirit in the name of this baby?"

"We do," the adults all intoned in a unison of voices.

At this point Dr. Geiler took out a small vial from a deep pocket in his black robe. The vial contained chrism, holy oil. He poured some of the oil onto the baby's head and then, as the thick liquid ran down the tiny baby's face, he turned to Vati.

"Do you, Jacob Schütz, want this child baptized?"

"Yes, I do."

Vati's voice boomed so loudly through the quiet of the church that it made Elisabet squirm a bit. His enthusiasm almost seemed like a desecration of the silence that, strangely enough, shouted from the vaulted ceiling. But Dr. Geiler did not seem perturbed by Vati's joyful answer. As a matter of fact, he smiled.

"Name the child."

"Katharina."

"Katharina Schütz," Dr. Geiler's voice rang heavy with solemnity, "I baptize you in the name of the Father, the Son and the Holy Spirit."

Elisabet felt there should have been a choir to accompany this moment. She knew that some of the wealthier families paid for choirs alongside baptismal services, but Vati had said that they really could not afford it and that Katharina would be just as baptized without a choir.

"You must know," he had said with a smile, chucking her under the chin, "that we are only a woodworker's family, Elisabet. Woodworking is a good trade, but it does not pay for jewels, child."

The ceremony was over and after thanking Dr. Geiler, the whole group walked back to Johanngasse. At home baby Katharina, after Mutti had fed her, was greatly admired, travelling from lap to lap. Next she was lulled to sleep in the cradle Vati had carved, the cradle in which they had all slept. After that, there was ale and pork sausage and white bread. Fleetingly, before going inside, Elisabet had again spied the thin figure of Frau Bauer across the road, a thin figure almost hidden behind the lace curtains. Mutti noted her as well and sent Elisabet over to bring their neighbour some of the white bread. It was no good telling Mutti that Marta, the servant girl, should bring the bread, for Mutti was of the strict opinion that every one in the household should share in doing good deeds.

"The smile on Frau Bauer's face," Mutti whispered in Elisabet's ear before she left the room, "will make your heart joyful."

With a last glance at Katharina sleeping peacefully in the cradle, Elisabet complied, both of her hands carefully sheltering the bread in a clean napkin. And the truth of it was that Frau Bauer's smile did indeed make her heart joyful.

Chapter II

I t was nearly three o'clock in the afternoon. Father Jacob Schütz was in his workshop. Lux was with him as it was the boy's job to sweep shavings off the floor and to run errands for his father, if errands needed to be run. Elisabet and Barbara and the other children were in the sitting-room with their mother and Marta. The day-girl was in the kitchen preparing the evening meal. Elisabet laboriously spelled out the letters of the alphabet. She went each morning to one of the *Lehrhäuser*, one of the private schools in Strasbourg, where an older man, well-versed in the classics and in grammar, taught young, middle-class children how to read and write.

A large west window let in the afternoon sun. Its panes were small and shaped like rectangles, soldered together by strips of lead. Elisabeth Schütz sat in a high-backed armchair and baby Katharina played on the floor at her feet with some wooden blocks which father Jacob had made when Lux was born. Little Jacob, the sibling closest to Katharina in age, sat by his sister and built towers. He endlessly constructed buildings some ten stories high and then permitted her chubby hands to knock down the structure amid loud squeals of delight. Then he began again with a patience and a zeal that surprised his mother.

"This is the cathedral," he stated in a very matter-of-fact voice, sitting back on his haunches contemplating his last masterpiece.

"Oh, you shouldn't make her think it's fine to knock down the cathedral," Barbara was quick to interfere.

"She doesn't understand and besides that," Elisabet said, looking up from her book, "it's not really the cathedral."

"Well," said Barbara, "I think...."

"Hush," Mutti said, "I think I heard the knocker. I wonder who might be calling today?"

The girls ran to the window and pressed their noses against the panes.

"It's the cousins, Mutti! It's the cousins, Ursula and Margred."

Mutti sighed and stood up.

"Well, so much for me reading to you from the new book Vati brought home yesterday—the one everyone is talking about."

"You mean the book with the fox in it, Reynard the Fox?"

Elisabet stood with her back against the window as she spoke, her eyes dark with disappointment.

"Yes, but I promise we'll get to it at another time, perhaps even tomorrow."

Marta knocked at the sitting-room door, before discreetly opening it and saying, "Frau Schütz, your cousins are in the hallway."

"Send them in, Marta and please prepare some repast for them."

"And hide the silverware," Barbara whispered, giggling at the same time.

"Hush, Barbara," Mutti said, eyeing her daughter angrily, "I'll not have you rude to visitors."

"Yes, Mutti."

Barbara hung her head in shame and took her place next to Elisabet who had resumed looking at her primer as she sat at the small oak table parallel to the window. And baby Katharina crowed in delight as she toppled yet another wooden-blocked structure.

The cousins were duly ushered in by Marta. Ursula was long-faced and severe of eye, but Margred was round, plump as a pudding and jolly in her face. She followed her sister like a dog follows its master, but her jollity was generally not displayed unless, by some remote chance, her sister was in another room.

"Well, cousins," Frau Schütz said, putting as much cordiality in her voice as she could muster, "what a pleasant surprise."

Cousin Ursula nodded, at the same time extending her hand to Elisabet, who was now standing by her chair. Elisabet came over, curtsied and then took the proffered hand for a moment before retreating back to the table. Barbara followed suit. Cousin Margred smiled and stood next to her sister.

"Please be seated."

Frau Schütz indicated two high-backed chairs close to the hearth. Their arms were carved boldly with floral designs and their high backs were almost at right angles with the seat. Both cousins primly took a seat, Margred's smile never leaving her genial face. Baby Katharina, after staring at them for a few moments, crawled over and took hold of cousin Ursula's robe. It was of a rich brown colour, but that was not what attracted the child. It was the gold chained crucifix glittering and dangling from her waist, reaching half-way down to the floor that had caught her attention. A handful of the wool cloth firmly held in her chubby hands, she tried to pull herself up to reach the shining cross. Cousin Ursula did not respond favourably to the baby's action but regarded the child with disdain.

"She is not well-behaved."

"She is a good baby."

Jacob suddenly stood next to his sister. Shyly he had hidden behind his mother's chair when the cousins came in, but such an insult to his Katharina was too much for him to bear, and his sturdy arms began to pull the baby away from cousin Ursula. Katharina, however, stubbornly refused to let go of the brown material, her eyes still fixed on the shining object which she regarded as a toy. The robe could stretch only so far and cousin Ursula's bony knees began to be outlined, even as her thin mouth pursed with disapproval.

"Oh, now, now," intoned cousin Margred, "The baby means no harm, sister. Indeed, look at her sweet blue eyes. She is quite taken with you."

"Taken, indeed." cousin Ursula snorted, "She is quite an ill-behaved little...."

"Stop it. You must not say such unkind words about Katharina."

Now it was Barbara who stood in the breach for her baby sister.

Frau Schütz stood up. There was a twinkle in her eye. She calmly walked over to the chairs, undid the child's fist full of cloth and picked her up.

"Go back to your building, Jacob," she instructed softly, "and Barbara, go to Marta in the kitchen and see that some cider is warmed for the cousins."

Then she returned to her place, taking Katharina on her lap.

There was quiet for a moment. Then cousin Ursula turned to Elisabet, whose head was studiously bent over her work at the table.

"What are you doing, child?"

"I am spelling out my letters," Elisabet replied, slightly discomfited.

"Letters?"

"Yes, the alphabet letters."

"Why do you need to learn letters?"

"She needs to learn how to read," Frau Schütz replied mildly, "Jacob and I decided it would be a good thing for her to have this skill. Lux can read and Barbara and Jacob will also learn to read and even little Katharina here, God willing, will learn in due time."

"Ah, yes, sister," cousin Margred mouthed, "we never learned, did we? And sure as my name is Margred, I know that you chafe each time the meisterin calls on sister Clara to read."

"You know no such thing," cousin Ursula responded icily, "I have never had any yearning to read nor do I need to read."

"Well, I would dearly like to know how to read," cousin Margred said, smiling at Elisabet as she did so.

Elisabet smiled back. Cousin Margred was not so bad.

"How are things at the beguinage? And how is it that you are out walking at this time of the day?"

Frau Schütz tried to change the subject.

"Well, ordinarily we would not be out but we would be working at our daily chores of mending," cousin Margred responded, "but meisterin had need of a message to be delivered to our priest and called for us to deliver it. As you know we can't be out alone and that is why the two of us came out together."

"Meisterin gave us permission to call on you as well," cousin Ursula added, "as she knew you lived close to the St. Thomas church, and she bid us greet you from Gotteshaus Zum Wolf."

"Well, please carry my greeting back to the meisterin and tell her I will be pleased to receive her for a visit as well if she happens to be in the neighbourhood."

Barbara opened the door and came back into the room, followed by Marta. Marta carried a wooden tray replete with two steaming cups of hot cider. At a sign from her mistress, the serving girl shyly approached the two visitors. Cousin Margred's eyes lit up, and she took one of the proffered cups with eagerness.

"That is something we do not often get," she said as she smiled at Marta, "Thank you."

"And well that is," cousin Ursula interjected, "for it is a virtue to be moderate in food and drink and to fast periodically."

Marta blushed and after curtsying, quickly left the room holding the empty tray at her side.

"Do you ever fast, Barbara?"

Cousin Ursula, hands around her cup, addressed the question to the child standing in front of her.

Barbara nodded.

"Yes, of course we do. Mutti makes us. But I do not like it one bit. And it seems to me it helps no one at all."

"Child!"

Shocked, cousin Ursula put down her cider on the small table next to her chair. She looked reproachfully at Frau Schütz.

"Are you not concerned about this child's eternal welfare? She could be snatched away from you at any time. There are many, indeed, in the flower of youth, such as this child standing here in front of me, who are alive one day and dead in the grave the next."

"No, I am not concerned."

Frau Schütz eyed her cousin calmly, all the while patting a thumb-sucking Katharina on the back.

"Dear Elisabeth, you ought to be concerned then and be so good as to let me warn you. Perhaps it would be wise as well to consider sending the child to the beguines to be taught what holiness is and...."

"I think, cousin Ursula, that I, as her mother, might teach her such virtues as holiness and patience myself. As well, I think that I can instruct her not to be idle or to gossip."

Cousin Margred smiled. It was not often that her sister was put in her place and rebuffed, but cousin Ursula was not to be put off.

"Child," she persisted, still looking at Barbara who had slowly retreated behind the larger table, away from cousin Ursula and who was now standing next to Elisabet, "can you recite 'Vater Unser'?

"*Ja*, yes," the girl replied, seeking Elisabet's hand under the table.

"Well, recite it for me," cousin Ursula said.

"*Nein*, no, I do not wish her to do so," Frau Schütz interposed, "It is a prayer to be spoken to God and not to be recited at will as if it were a poem or some other piece for entertainment."

She was red in the face from the exertion of speaking harshly and Katharina, sensing her mother's discomfort, took her thumb out of her mouth and began patting her mother's cheek.

"Well, it seems to me you are a trifle discomfited. And those who are discomfited usually have a conscience which speaks to them."

After these words, Ursula picked up her cup again and drank. For all her talk of moderation in food, she did seem to find the cider very tasty. Indeed, Elisabet noted that cousin Ursula licked her lips.

It was quiet for a long while. The sun shone through the panes of the window, and Frau Schütz stroked Katharina's blond hair. She was, even though she fought the vice, irritated. Another baby stirred within her, and suddenly she was quite tired as well.

"Have you heard," cousin Margred ventured at length, "that Father Geiler von Kaysersberg has taken it upon himself to defy the pope's authority by administering sacraments to a criminal on his way to execution?"

Elisabet sat up and looked at her mother. She knew that Father Geiler was much loved by her parents and very dear to their hearts.

"I had heard," Frau Schütz replied gravely.

"Well," cousin Ursula said, "I hope that he will be banished for it. Father Geiler is approaching the bounds of heresy by this conduct, and Strasbourg would be well rid of him."

"Your own priest, Balthazar Horst," Frau Schütz answered, her weariness making her throw caution to the wind, "is a drunkard. I have it on good authority that the man was seen tipsy last Tuesday while carrying the sacraments to a dying soul. That, dear cousins, is real heresy, it seems to me."

Cousin Ursula stood up.

"We will take our leave now," she said.

Cousin Margred, immediately following her sister's suit, stood up as well, all the while smiling apologetically at her cousin, Frau Schütz. Jacob's head peered out from underneath the table where he had taken refuge after his mother had taken Katharina on her lap. Frau Schütz also rose.

"I'm sorry you have to leave so soon," she said, "but I am sure, cousin Ursula, that it is your *keusch* and *demuetigs*, your chasteness and humility, which call you back to the beguinage."

Cousin Ursula did not deign to reply, but made for the door. Cousin Margred was her shadow. Frau Schütz, a quick step ahead of them, opened the door, preceding them into the hall. As the door closed behind the adults, Elisabet and Barbara breathed a sigh of relief, giggling at the same time. Jacob came out from under the table and balefully kicked his blocks. A moment later they heard the front door close. Running to the window, all three watched as cousin Ursula fairly ran down the Johanngasse. Cousin Margred's plump, little figure had quite a difficult time keeping up. But in spite of that she turned, looking up at their faces pressed against the panes and she smiled a broad smile, waving as she did so. They waved back. Elisabet felt an unaccountable pity for the squat little woman who was after all quite a bit younger than her sour sister. Would she herself ever enter such a place as a beguinage, choosing to have no home but a terraced house within a courtyard enclosed by nothing but walls on every side? But if cousin Ursula or cousin Margred ever chose to leave because of marriage, they would be free to do so. Beguines were not under vows such as the nuns were. But who would ever ask for either cousin Ursula's or cousin Margred's hand in marriage?

Chapter III

Jacob Schütz was a woodworker.

"It's a good trade," he told his children, "and one of which a man need never be ashamed."

Lux, however, was not as enthusiastic as his father was about the gouge or the burin, the plane, the awl or the saw. Lux was eager to go to school, anxious to use his head and not his hands. Consequently, he would occasionally complain about having to help out in his father's shop. Father Schütz was a patient man. Although he insisted Lux help, he did not insist the boy become his replica. Little Katharina, on the other hand, loved the workshop. Sometimes when she was underfoot in the house, Elisabeth would send the young child down to her father who always welcomed his small daughter's presence.

One afternoon, when he presumed Katharina had been sent down by her mother to keep him company, Jacob, who usually talked to his daughter while he was working, told her that there were many printing shops in Strasbourg—as a matter of fact, Strasbourg was a printing capital.

"Why are there so many printing shops?" Katharina asked, standing by her father's side as he was working on a design.

They were in the centre of the workshop, an area which was situated at the back of the house on the first floor. A large window made the shop bright and roomy. Katharina delighted in the smell of the wood shavings and often gathered the curls in her arms to deposit them in a pile in the corner. On busy days, after she had collected a large pile, she would sit in the middle of the pile together with her doll and settle down to watch her father as he worked. Jacob gently stroked his daughter's blond hair, before he stood up from his work stool, stretching his frame as he did so.

"Around fifty years ago," he began, as he picked up his gouge to continue a design in a block of wood, "movable type was invented."

"What's that?"

Katharina picked up the broom at her feet, and her five-year-old frame industriously began to sweep. Jacob regarded her with affection. Her sturdy figure and bouncing honey-coloured hair moved in perfect imitation of his wife.

"Movable type are individually carved letters that can be printed with the illustrations I cut on wood blocks."

"Oh," Katharina answered, looking up at her father, not at all understanding what he had said, but smiling.

She loved it when he talked to her. Looking with satisfaction at the small hill of shavings she had collected, she dropped the broom and skipped back to her father.

"What are you making today, Vati?"

Chucking her under the chin and pleased with her interest, he replied, "I'll show you, little one. It is only a small design today."

Standing on her toes, Katharina gazed with interest at the block of wood on the work table. It was covered with white background, and her father had almost dug out all the wood that was not part of the design.

"Is it Our Lady?" she asked softly.

"Yes," her father responded, "it is indeed, and a printer will be by later this week to pick it up."

"Can I watch you finish, Vati?"

Jacob picked the child up and set her right onto the work table next to him where, to her great delight, she was allowed to observe him closely as he finished the design. As he worked, she made music for him. She loved making music, humming gently and sometimes putting words into her melody.

"Oh, Our Lady is so beautiful, so beautiful, so beautiful."

Her father's fingers crafted even as his voice spoke.

"Do you love her, Katharina?"

"Oh, yes!" the child answered without any hesitation, "I do!"

"It is a good thing to love our Lady. She helps us, little maid. That is why on the banner of our city Strasbourg and on our coins, we have the words 'O Virgin Mary, please beg your Son to save our city and its people.'"

To persuade her father of her extreme love for the virgin, Katharina broke into fervent singing.

"I love Our Lady, I do! I do! I do!"

Katharina's thin treble filled the workshop. Looking at her father, she continued with a rush of affection, "and I love my Vati too!"

Jacob looked up and smiled at Katharina.

"And I love you and your singing, little maid. There's the truth of it."

He held up his work.

"Well, here it is. The design is finished, Katharina."

"Oh, may I, may I, please...."

Katharina did not finish her request. It was hardly ever that her father let her use the dabber on one of his designs. But it was such fun and this was such a beautiful design. Jacob relented upon seeing her pleading face.

"Yes, this once you may. But it is just this once, mind you and you are not to ask again. At least," he added, "not for a very long time."

"Yes, Vati, I promise."

Jacob took the dabber from a shelf. It was a leather-covered, round tool with a wooden handle. Carefully coating it with ink, he set it on the block he had just made and began rocking it over the design. After a few moments, he allowed Katharina to hold onto the dabber with him as the tool was moved back and forth.

"Now our Lady is black," Katharina said spontaneously.

Suddenly shocked that she might have uttered something blasphemous, she put her hand over her lips. The impetuous motion left a streak of ink on her small chin. Her father sighed when he saw it.

"Your Mutti will be upset if you come up like that, little one. Don't touch anything else until I wipe you up."

"Make a paper picture first, Vati!" Katharina begged, "Please!"

Jacob relented again and took a sheet of paper from another shelf. Placing the paper on the inked block, he next put a larger and heavier block of wood on top, applying even pressure as he did so. Katharina watched with bated breath. After a few minutes, her father carefully lifted the wood, peeled the paper off the block and handed Katharina the clear impression of the Lady imprinted on it. She held the paper gingerly, not wishing to crumple it.

"You must lay it down to air dry for a few minutes," her father said.

She painstakingly laid down her treasure on the table next to her and then begged him for a story.

"Well," her father hesitated, "I should be starting another design."

Seeing her eyes look with longing at one of his own favourite books, however, he relented once more and picked the little girl up off the work bench, carrying her in his arms to the window seat. He sat them both down with a sigh.

"What book is this?" he asked, as he picked up the volume which was lying next to them. She knew the answer.

"Dürer's," she said smoothly, but then tripped over the next word, "Dürer's acapo ... acapolypse."

Jacob smiled and corrected.

"Almost right, my Katharina. Almost! It's Dürer's *Apocalypse*."

"*Ja*—yes."

Satisfied that she would get a story, the small girl leaned her head against her father's shoulder, waiting to hear him intone John's Revelation. There were fifteen woodcuts in all, illustrating the last book of the New Testament. Katharina loved the words of the book, even though she understood very little of them. Some of the words frightened her and some made her happy—especially the ending. She also loved most of the woodcuts. The one of the apostle John kneeling down before the double doors of heaven she understood so well that she sometimes felt compelled to kneel in front of her bedroom door while knocking on it with her chubby fists pretending she was asking leave to enter heaven. And she was also very much impressed with the twenty-four elders, all in white, holding crowns in their hands, as they stood around the throne of

God in a semi-circle. She equally admired the face of the Lamb. But when her father read of the sun turning black and the moon becoming blood, she closed her eyes, tried not to listen to him and avoided looking at the woodcuts. As well, she very much disliked the scene where the avenging angels wielded their swords. But the picture she waited for most patiently, and the one which enthralled her more than any other, was the one in which a glowing angel with a sunburst face, cloud-body and feet like flaming columns, stood firmly as if nothing could move him. His right foot was on the sea, and his left was on the land. Yet for all her admiration, she dared not touch any of the pages of Dürer's book.

"Katharina!! Katharina!!"

Her mother's voice, as if searching for her, rang through the front hall. Jacob stopped reading and looked at Katharina.

"Doesn't Mutti know that you are here, Katharina? I thought that she sent you down to help me?"

"Well, she would have sent me if she had thought of it," Katharina answered and then blushed and softly went on, "I was supposed to rock baby Magdalene and play with Margaret, but they both fell asleep so I thought it was no harm to come and help you. I thought of it all by myself."

"Katharina!! Katharina!!"

Her mother's voice sang out again. Gravely Jacob closed the book and slid Katharina off his knees.

"You best go and explain, child."

"Yes, Vati."

Head bent, her entire little frame dejected, she trudged toward the door. Upon watching her, his heart melted somewhat and he called out to her.

"Kathe."

She turned.

"Yes, Vati?"

"Don't forget your picture."

She ran back and took the proffered sheet, grinning as she did so.

"Explaining to Mutti while I'm holding a picture of Our Lady will make it much easier, won't it, Vati?"

He hid a smile behind his hand. Waving the picture like a flag, she raced back to the door and opened it, disappearing into the hall with a flourish. And Jacob noted with regret at the last minute, that he had not wiped the black smudge off her chin.

Chapter IV

It was evening and candles were lit in the sitting-room. The Schütz family was comfortably gathered together in the soft gleam of their light. Father Jacob regarded the faces of his wife and older children with satisfaction. The younger ones were already in bed. How wonderful it was to sit thus! How marvellous to have healthy children when he knew full well that many, many of the children of his friends had died in childbirth and in infancy. He regarded young Katharina's face with especial love. That child, always in and out of the workshop, in and out of the kitchen and in and out of everything, most often with a torn stocking, tousled hair and a smudge on her face somewhere.

"You know," he said, "I have heard that in Italy, a small linen square called a pocket handkerchief has come into use."

"What is it, father?" said Barbara, as she smoothed the pleats of her dress with her hands, "What is a pocket handkerchief?"

"Well, it is a piece of cloth which you can keep in your pocket in case you have to... well, for example, sneeze. Then you can use it to wipe yourself instead of using...."

He stopped and smiled at Katharina. The child was regarding him with such big eyes.

"Can you have three of them in your pocket at the same time?" she asked.

"Why would you want three, Katharina, child?"

"Well, in case I sneezed three times," she said, "or I might use one of them to carry some shiny pebbles, or," she went on with increasing enthusiasm, "I might use another to wave like a flag, or...."

Her mother interrupted.

"Enough, little girl, do not speak so much in company. It is not becoming."

"But," responded the child, "what if I have to say something that takes many sentences, Mutti? What then?"

"Then you have to swallow your words and keep them inside," her mother said, "and that is that."

"But...."

"Shh, Katharina."

Lux, who sat next to Katharina poked her in the ribs.

"Ouch!" she said and gave him a shove.

"I have heard a story," Lux said, seemingly not minding the shove at all and looking at her in a teasing way. "At Hammel in Saxony, on the 20th of June in 1484, which is not that many years ago, the devil, in the likeness of a pied piper, carried away 130 children."

But it was his sister Barbara and not Katharina, who responded.

"The devil!" she cried, nervously, stopping the incessant smoothing of the pleats of her skirt and tightly clasping her hands in her lap.

"Oh, he is teasing," Elisabet interjected, putting her arm around Barbara, "isn't he, Vati?"

"Well," Jacob said, "I have heard the story as well, but I wouldn't put too much stock in it."

"Probably," Lux went on, "the children in Hammel behaved badly. Perhaps," and here he eyed Katharina again with a grin, "they talked too much, or perhaps," and here he eyed Elisabet and winked, "they were just a little too critical of good brothers."

"Oh, pshaw," Elisabet said, "as if you are good."

"Well, the truth is," replied Lux, "that those children were never seen again."

"Well, I wish that pied piper would come and pipe some of the monks away," Katharina said.

"Katharina!"

Her mother was about to reach over and give the child a swat, but Jacob, who sat next to his wife, put an arm about her, forestalling the move.

"Why would you say that, child?"

"Well," Katharina said, "yesterday, when I went to get a bolt of cloth from Frau Schel, I saw a monk take some money from a blind beggar's box close to the Blatterhaus, the new hospital built by Herr Hoffmeister. And...."

"What were you doing there, Katharina, by the Blatterhaus?" her mother interrupted, "Frau Schel's house is not...."

"Well, you see," Katharina was quick to interrupt and explain, "I heard the tower bells ringing, and the music was so beautiful that I thought it might be angels ringing them. So I...."

"Katharina," her mother sighed, "can't I trust you to go where I send you?"

"Oh, yes, you can, mother. Did I not come back quickly?"

Lux, once more grinning at his sister, intervened because he thought the conversation was rapidly turning into Katharina's disadvantage.

"I have heard talk at the school lately, about a monk named Savonarola," he said, "and about his death in Florence in 1498. That was actually," he turned to Katharina, "the year you were born, Kathe."

"Who was Sanorovala?" she asked.

"Not Sanorovala, you goose, but Savonarola."

"He was an Italian monk, Katharina," her father answered, "and not the kind you would want a pied piper to lead away, I think. I have only heard good things about this Savonarola."

"Tell us, father," Elisabet pleaded, hoping for a story.

"Well, mother, what do you think?" Jacob said, eyeing his wife's face.

"Go ahead," she conceded with a smile, "not that I can stop you if you have a mind to tell a story."

"Well, I do believe," Jacob began, crossing his legs and stretching himself as he began his tale, "that Savonarola was born in the year 1452, in Ferrara in Italy. That was actually a year before I was born. The man could have been my brother."

Jacob said the last sentence rather speculatively and very slowly, stretching his legs again as he said it.

"Your brother, father?" Katharina interjected, "but how could that be if he was Italian. You are not Italian but German."

"Yes, but there are more ways than one in which men can be brothers."

"Be quiet, goose," Lux said, "I want to hear what father has to say."

"Savonarola felt that God wanted him to be a monk when he was only a young boy."

"How...?" Katharina began but was poked by Lux.

"Whether his parents were against him becoming a monk or not, I don't know, but the fact is that when he was twenty-two years old, he secretly left home and joined the Dominicans at their monastery in Bologna."

"You mean his mother and father didn't know where he was and it was all right?" Katharina interjected, and the words spilled out quickly for she didn't want to be poked by Lux again.

Her mother gave her a long look mingled with severity and love, causing Katharina to look down rather shamefacedly at her lap. It was true. She had asked the question to alert her mother to the fact that sometimes children find it necessary to leave home without saying where they are going.

"Shh, Katharina. Let Vati tell the story please."

This time it was Barbara who hushed her.

"Savonarola stayed with the Dominicans for seven years—years in which he reportedly lived a good life. He prayed much; he gave away what he had to the poor; he studied the Bible, and he read about the lives of saints. After these seven years, the Dominican monks sent him back to Ferrara to preach."

"I wonder if his mother and father were happy to see him again," said Elisabet, "after all, he had snuck out of the house, and they didn't know where he was all that time, did they? Or did they?"

"Well, I heard that the people in Ferrara, and I'm not sure about his mother and father, were not too happy to have him come back. So he didn't stay in that city very long but moved on to Florence and preached there."

"Were they happy to have him come to Florence?" little Jacob piped up, seated on Katharina's other side.

"Well, some of the people in Florence were happy to have him and others were not." Jacob senior answered his young son.

"Why?" the child said.

His father did not answer directly but went on talking.

"Florence is a beautiful city. It is in a valley and has a beautiful river running through it called the Arno. On either side of the river are olive and cypress groves. I have heard tell it is a wonderful sight to behold as the sun is setting in that place. Yes, I have heard tell that by many."

"Would you like to make a picture of that city, father?" Katharina threw in impulsively, "Would you like to make a picture of the olive groves?"

"I think I might," her father answered with a smile, "There are many things there, for a fact, that I would like to behold—many works and monuments of art, things built with marble and not with wood. In any case," he went on, sitting up, "this was the city where Savonarola came to preach, a city which was the centre of intellectual and literary learning. As a matter of fact, he preached there for ten years. He was, I think, quite popular and much more liked than he had been in Ferrara."

"Why?" Jacob asked again.

"He preached maybe just like our Dr. Geiler?" Barbara asked, who had a great respect for their priest.

"Yes, Barbara," her father answered, "I think that in many respects this was true. Many people came to hear Savonarola preach. As a matter of fact, thousands of people came from all over Italy and other places to hear the monk."

"But why?"

This time it was not Jacob who asked but Frau Schütz.

"Because, dear wife, Savonarola addressed all those things which also bother us. He addressed the evils of the day; he was not afraid to attack the corruption of the church, even drawing attention to monks from his own monastery; he compared the sumptuousness of their lodgings with the poverty of the Lord; he criticized the silks and velvets that the church leaders wore; and he deplored the fatness of the tables at which they ate while there were so many poor in the city who went hungry."

"It seems he was a brave man," Lux said and Katharina poked him this time and said 'Shh,' much to the amusement of little Jacob.

"After about ten years of preaching," Jacob went on, "Savonarola was made prior of the monastery, and better yet, in 1492, he was made manager of the city, instead of the Lorenzo family, the ruling family. And that is how Florence, for a short while, became a republic with a reforming preacher at its head. And things began to change in the city—good things began to happen."

"What sort of things, father?" Barbara asked.

"Well, things like the monks not being allowed to take advantage of the poor, things like good preaching being accessible to all and virtues like love and compassion being stressed as being virtues that our good Lord and Saviour desired in all people. But...."

He stopped and looked at them all. Everyone looked back at him.

"But what, father?" Katharina finally interjected when, in her estimation, he was not quick enough in answering.

"But there were people in the city who did not like to give up their wicked practices; they did not like to see the true words of the Lord Jesus preached out loud to the people of the city; they did not like to hear that men are saved, not by good works, but by the suffering of our Lord Jesus Christ."

"But it is good, is it not, father, to do good works. Surely...." Barbara began, in a bewildered voice.

"Yes, it is child. Of course it behooves us to do good works."

"Well, then," she said, "perhaps this Savonarola ...."

She stopped again.

"Yes," her father said slowly, "I have thought on it. Not as much as I fear I should think on it. And in my small amount of thinking, I have not come to a clear conclusion. But this is what he preached: that men are saved only by the suffering of the Lord Jesus Christ."

"What happened to him, father? What happened to Savonarola?"

"Well, the pope at that time, Alexander VI, a pope who was not known for his piety....Yes, yes, I know," he nodded to his wife who eyed him rather reproachfully, "the man has died, and I should not speak ill of the dead for God will judge—well, this pope was not too pleased by Savonarola's preaching. He first offered Savonarola a bribe—he offered him a cardinal's hat."

"A hat?" Katharina called out, "The pope offered Saranovola a hat?"

"Savonarola, you child," Elisabet corrected her.

"Well," Katharina said, "it seems to me that a hat is not a very good bribe at all. I shouldn't think that I could be bribed with a hat and...."

"Shh," Lux poked his sister again as she spoke.

"A cardinal's hat, Kathe," her father went on, "is not just a hat, although, mind you, cardinals do wear very red hats. No, a cardinal's hat is a position, an office in the church, which gives you a great deal of authority and money."

"Oh," Katharina said, shamefaced that she had not known such a thing.

The rest of the children snickered.

"But Savonarola would not be bribed. Indeed, he was angry to receive such a bribe from the pope. So the pope excommunicated him, and as a result, many people, afraid of the pope and his power, turned away from Savonarola, although they had rather liked the way he preached at the beginning."

"Well, you shouldn't turn away from friends," Barbara said, her cheeks red and eyes flaming.

"No, you shouldn't, Barbara," her father rejoined, "but these people in Florence did. And the result was that Savonarola, who would not change his mind about what he believed and kept preaching it, was arrested by agents of the pope and thrown into prison. He wrote much while he was in prison. He wrote down everything he believed. Then he was tried and found guilty of heresy, and shortly afterward he was hanged, and his body was burnt at the stake on the Piazza della Gran' Ducca—burnt in front of a group of people who previously had listened to him, had cheered him and had been his friends."

"That's ...." Katharina began but could not finish.

"Were there people left behind who believed what Savonarola

said?" Lux asked.

"I... I don't know, son," Jacob Schütz answered.

"It is dangerous not to believe what the pope says," little Jacob said, "so I suppose we must all believe what the pope says if we do not want to hang and burn."

"But what if what the pope says is not true?" Elisabet threw out.

"Well, this I know," Barbara said to no one in particular, "that we must do good works, or we will spend a long time in purgatory."

"Yes," Katharina agreed, "I think that this is true. But," she went on, "what if it is not true?"

"You are a silly goose," Lux said, patting her on the shoulder. "You say one thing and then you say another."

"It is time for the children to go to bed, Jacob," Mutti interjected, "and I hope they can go to sleep."

"Well, let us have our prayers then, before we all go to sleep, wife."

Jacob knelt down in front of his chair. Everyone followed suit, kneeling down, and then he intoned, with great sincerity, the Lord's Prayer, afterward committing everyone to the care of God the Father in heaven.

Chapter V

Katharina was seated at the kitchen table. Together with Marta, the day-help, she had been busy polishing a number of gilded decorated cups, as well as articles belonging to the family table service. The table service included a beautiful *silberin schal*, a silver platter. Katharina greatly enjoyed polishing and often held things up in order to see her own round face reflected in the shining surface. When her mother entered the kitchen with baby Andreas on her hip, she stood up, curtsied and walked over to stroke Andreas' fat cheek. The baby cooed contentedly and then burped, much to Katharina's and Marta's delight. Elisabeth sat down, eyeing her third daughter reflectively before beginning to speak.

"It is time for you, Katharina," Elisabeth began, sternly regarding her fifth child, who was standing in front of her with a solemn face, "to become more adept in things which might stand you in good stead later in life."

"Yes, Mutti," Katharina dutifully replied, for often her mother held such speeches which culminated in her being sent out for an errand or being dealt a special task, such as cleaning off a shelf or airing out blankets.

It was best to listen and wait.

"Your father and I have spoken at length, and we feel that you might benefit in learning the craft of *heidnischwerck*, the art of weaving picture tapestries."

"*Heidnischwerck?*" Katharina repeated softly.

"Yes," Mutti said, stroking Andreas' soft, downy hair as she continued, "for you know that the cities of Basel and Strasbourg have been important centres of this craft since the fourteenth century and many women practice it. Women have no access to guilds in the city of Strasbourg. But because tapestry weaving is not a guild in Strasbourg, women can make tapestry weaving a respectable occupation here in the city. It can be and is, an independent profession for many women. So your father and I think it would be a fine craft for you to learn. "

She bent over now and chucked Katharina, who was staring at her wide-eyed, under her chin.

"Would you like to learn how to weave, Kathe?"

"I think I would," Katharina answered slowly and rather gravely, not quite having understood everything Mutti had said, but certainly grasping that this was an important moment, "but I don't want to go away from home. I don't want to leave you...."

"Of course you would not leave us, you silly goose," her mother interrupted, a twinkle in her eye. "Have no fear of that! You are too young, much too young! Only seven years old."

She clucked her tongue after she spoke and then kept on talking.

"But you are not too young to begin to learn this craft. So twice every week you will go to a cousin of Frau Bauer, a cousin who lives not too many streets away, and you will spend some hours learning the art. She is a widow and her name is Frau Stoffler. She has an atelier and makes tapestries for some of the local churches and for some of the wealthier families here in Strasbourg. These churches have, in times past and present, commissioned her to weave simple patterns and pictures. Although I have heard tell that possibly some of her tapestries also hang in the court of the emperor."

"The emperor?" breathed Katharina, "you mean Emperor Charles V?"

"Yes, so I have heard," Mutti smiled at her daughter's earnest face. "But I do not know if it is true. Frau Stoffler's husband was a banker. She is well settled financially, but she takes great pride in tapestry weaving and enjoys passing the craft along to her daughters and some other young girls. In any case, on Wednesday afternoon Barbara will accompany you to Frau Stoffler's home. You will make her acquaintance, and perhaps you will also meet her two daughters, Johanna and Annalein."

"I'm seven, Mutti. Does Barbara have to walk me over there?"

"Well," Elisabeth could not help it but her smile grew broader at the independent, determined face staring at her—a face that but one moment ago had showed worry that she might be leaving home and that now registered upset because she would be accompanied by her older sister.

"Well," she repeated, "the truth is that you have been known, Kathe, to leave the path you were sent on for an errand, in order to visit another place. Something as simple as the ringing of church bells, for example, often tempts you to stray from where you are supposed to go. But," she added, moved by the downcast face in front of her, "I will tell you what I will allow. Barbara will walk you over to Frau Stoffler's house. But after she makes sure you are at the correct address, she will come back here. You can knock and enter the home by yourself. How is that, Kathe?"

Satisfied, Katharina smiled.

So it happened that on Wednesday after the noon meal, Barbara and Katharina, hand in hand, walked past the St. Thomas Church. Keeping north they turned right, crossing the bridge over the River Ill, toward the Butcher's Gate. After their feet had pattered over another bridge straddling a canal, they turned left toward the eastern, and the somewhat newer but poorer, section of Strasbourg.

To many people, Strasbourg seemed to be the metropolis of the Upper Rhine. It lay on a plain, just below where the River Ill met the River Breusch before it ran down to the Rhine. The city's impressive walls encompassed close to 620 acres, and these acres were home to about 20,000 people. The walls held towers and bastions and had ten pedestrian gates as well as a massive water gate through which both the Ill and Breusch flowed into the city's numerous canals. Besides the cathedral in which Katharina had been baptized by Dr. Geiler, six other parish church spires graced the skyline. There were nine male religious orders, nine women's convents and several dozen chapels. As well there was a great hospital, several hospices, the *Blatterhaus* for syphilitics, the Good People's House—albeit outside the city walls—for the lepers, a poorhouse, an orphanage and a dozen or so public bath-houses. Over all these people and institutions, there were secular and temporal authorities, civic magistrates and a bishop. There were four *stettmeisters*, or city rulers, chosen by a council and there was also an *ammeister*, or mayor.

Strasbourg was a busy metropolis. It collected and exported wine and grain from both sides of the Upper Rhine. As well it traded in meat, salt, oil, sheets, metals and furs. The canals were used to transport these goods. Strasbourg was also a centre of crafts and banking. A thriving city, it was a city which had room for what could be termed "the little people"—people who were trades-men, shopkeepers and artisans—artisans such as Frau Stoffler. It was true, as Katharina's mother had told her, that in Strasbourg, women were not permitted to belong to the guilds. As a matter of fact, a law had been passed when Katharina was but a toddler, which required all single women to have male guardians. It was a law which had been protested against by Dr. Geiler but to no avail. However women *were* allowed to practice the craft of *heidnischwerck* —a craft of weaving passed along in some families from mother to daughter or aunt to niece, or taught by one friend to another.

Big merchant families, smaller merchant families and patrician families, all walked the streets of Strasbourg every day. That is not to say that there were no lines of separation delineating the various families of aristocrats from the merchants and separat-ing the merchants from the smaller business people. There were those lines. But on a daily basis, gardeners, fishermen, butchers, metalworkers, goldsmiths, tinsmiths, coopers, furriers, painters, printers and stonemasons all mixed in the routine of daily living.

It was a fine day to be out. Katharina and Barbara breathed in the sweet smell of spring as the sunshine warmed their cheeks. Upon reaching the destination where she was to drop off her sister, and standing under its gables, Barbara spoke decisively.

"Look, Kathe. This is Frau Stoffler's house. Now you must re-member to be polite. You must remember to do exactly what you are told and you must never question...."

"Yes, I know," Katharina interrupted her sister rather impatiently, "Mutti told me, and I promised her I would be good."

Her rebellious heart whispered to her that she would have known how to get here on her own, for it still stung her vanity that Barbara, even though she was four years older and all of eleven, had been asked to supervise her.

"I will be here at four to take you home," Barbara went on, never minding the tug on her hand and holding her smaller sister's fingers tightly between her own. "And do not leave by yourself, because Mutti said you ought not."

With this last admonition, she finally let go of Katharina's hand.

"Knock at the door and wait until the day-girl lets you in."

"I know that, Barbara."

Katharina's cap, under which her blond hair had been neatly tucked when she left home, showed a few escaped stray strands. But when Barbara tried to slide these in with the back of her hand, Katharina pulled away.

"I'm not a baby, Barbara."

"Well, goodbye then. And remember, do what you are told."

"Yes, I will."

KATHARINA WAITED UNTIL Barbara was well down the street, before she lifted her hand to knock at the great door. It was a rather imposing door, heavy and dark. No one must have heard her knock, because a few minutes later she was forced to lift her hand again. When that as well did not produce results, she used both fists and banged on the door rather vehemently.

"Yes, yes, I heard you. No need to break the house down."

A rather thickset older women suddenly peered through a half-open door, staring straight down at Katharina who nervously blinked into the not unkind face. Then the door opened wider.

"Are you the new girl who is supposed to come to Frau Stoffler's for lessons in weaving?"

Katharina nodded, suddenly shy and at a loss for words, something that rarely occurred at home. The woman's black skirt, which was protected by a white apron, moved aside. Her hands made a sweeping motion, indicating that she expected Katharina to enter.

"Well, you better come in then, hadn't you and mind, wipe your feet on the mat."

Katharina stepped over the threshhold, wiped her feet thoroughly and timidly looked around the hall.

"Frau Stoffler is expecting you in her sitting room. It's this way. Follow me."

THE SITTING ROOM was a bright and cheery place. It reminded Katharina a great deal of her father's workshop. There was a wonderfully big window facing east with the light of the early afternoon sun streaming in. Her father often told her that light was vitally important and that it must fall into a room with great splendour in order for thoughts to hatch, even as a chick hatches from an egg. She had seen baby birds hatch in her window sill and....

"You are Katharina Schütz?"

Katharina was startled. She had been concentrating so hard on the window and on the thoughts that it engendered, that she had forgotten to look for people in the room.

"Yes, I am."

She curtsied formally and then walked forward to take the outstretched hand of the woman standing in the centre of the room. Anna Stoffler was wearing a grey, fur-lined gown with turned-back sleeves over a blue kirtle. She had a soft sash at her waist and a sheer partlet over a square-necked chemise. All in all, she was an impressive and a very well-dressed person.

"I am Frau Stoffler."

"I am very happy to make your acquaintance, Frau Stoffler," Katharina responded softly, very much in awe of the quiet dignity with which the woman stood.

"And I am happy to make yours, Katharina Schütz."

Katharina curtsied again, not because good manners dictated that she should, but because she felt that another curtsy might make her more acceptable. Everything was so clean and so neat in this room. Instinctively her hand flew up to her little cap to try and tuck in the few strands of hair, which she had not let Barbara touch. She wished now that she had. Frau Stoffler smiled at her.

"It was good of you to come, Katharina. Please sit down by me, and we can talk."

She pointed toward the window seat—a seat generously padded with pillows—and as she spoke she walked toward it. Taking her place gracefully, she waited for her visitor to follow suit. Katharina did so, awkwardly plumping a pillow before she sat down.

"So you would like to become my pupil and learn how to make a tapestry?"

Frau Stoffler's voice was cultured and well-modulated. Katharina nodded.

"Well, child, why is it that you would like to learn this craft?"

It was on the tip of Katharina's tongue to say that her mother and father had decided that it would be a good craft for her to learn, but she thought the wiser of it and let the words starve in her mouth. It was quiet for a long while. Frau Stoffler did not make the silence uncomfortable. And Katharina pondered the question as she looked about. She admired the tapestries decorating the walls of the room. They were rich and warm in both their colours and in their thickness.

"I like," she began at last and her words came hesitantly, "colours —colours that I see outside in the fields and in the sunset."

"Yes," Frau Stoffler encouraged.

"I stop sometimes, when I see flowers in a convent garden, because the colours on the flowers are almost good enough to eat —to eat with my eyes, I mean."

She halted, closed her eyes and continued.

"And I love to feel the texture of leaves on the trees, or on hedges. I like to rub a leaf between my fingers, and I also love to feel the smoothness of a chestnut. So sometimes I put chestnuts in the pocket of my cape and then in church...."

She stopped abruptly, opened her eyes and blushed before she added, "Oh, not in church, of course."

Frau Stoffler slightly shifted her position next to Katharina.

"Yes, I think you had better not let Dr. Geiler hear you say that, Katharina Schütz."

"Oh, no, Frau Stoffler!"

Wide-eyed and apologetic, Katharina turned to look at her

hostess, only to find that Frau Stoffler's eyes were crinkled with laughter. Relieved she smiled.

"No, indeed. And now," Frau Stoffler said, "I think I shall take you to my atelier, and we shall have a small lesson to begin with— just to give you an idea of what weaving is all about."

She stood up and Katharina followed suit. Holding out a slender right hand of which Katharina timidly took hold, they walked toward the door.

"You will not meet my daughters today," she said, as she opened the door with her left hand, "as they are out visiting relatives, but you will surely meet them another time."

A stairway took them up to the second floor. Frau Stoffler, letting go of Katharina's hand at the top of the flight, indicated a door a little to the right of the stairs.

"This is where my housekeeper, Dorothea, will bring you each time you come," she said, "and when she goes back downstairs, you must knock at the door and wait to hear me say 'Enter.' Do you understand?"

"Yes," Katharina answered.

"Good," Frau Stoffler said, and she took a key from the metal chain hanging from her waist.

She inserted it into the keyhole of the door, turning it. Then she took hold of the door handle and opened the door.

"Welcome into my atelier, Katharina Schütz," she smiled as she spoke, "I hope you can come often and learn much."

Walking a few steps into the atelier behind Frau Stoffler, Katharina suddenly stood still to take in the cosy room in front of her. Within the long stone outer wall, a large window boasting a good-sized sill cast afternoon sunlight onto a rug-covered floor. The other walls of the room were covered with colourful tapestries. Colourful flowers, human and animal figures, as well as landscapes, all hung side by side. Next to the window, in a shaft of light, stood a wooden frame of sorts. Frau Stoffler, after a moment, walked ahead of her toward the wooden frame. Katharina followed suit.

"This," Frau Stoffler said in a rather solemn voice, as she stood by the frame, "is my loom."

"Oh," replied Katharina in an equally solemn voice, slowly

coming over to stand next to the frame, not daring to touch the thing which very likely had produced the wonderful range of pictures on the walls.

"It is called a high-warp loom," Frau Stoffler continued, "and those words will be some of the first new words you will learn here."

"High-warp loom." Katharina repeated.

"There is also a low-warp loom, but it is used mostly in France. High-warp looms are more common in cities such as Strasbourg and Basel."

"Yes," said Katharina in a positive tone, as if she had studied the matter her whole life.

"In weaving," Frau Stoffler went on, "two types of fibre are usually used together. One is the warp string," and here she touched some of the vertical strings on the frame, "and the other is the weft, or filling material. The warp is the fibre that runs up and down and the weft is the material that is woven across, into the warp."

Katharina sighed. Weaving presently seemed to her to be both a beautiful and difficult thing to learn, and she was full of admiration for Frau Stoffler who had very likely made all the wall hangings in the room and who had, as Mutti had told her, possibly made one for the emperor.

"The warp and the weft," Frau Stoffler's voice continued, "can be made of the same type of fibre, but very often, they are not. The warp is usually a strong thread in a light colour, but the weft can be almost any colour you want."

Katharina sighed again. She could picture herself on the chair she saw placed in front of the loom, turning out one magnificent tapestry after another. She could see herself weaving the Virgin Mary onto a wall hanging made of light and dark blue colours and she could see....

"Katharina?"

Frau Stoffler's voice called her back from her reveries.

"Yes, Frau Stoffler?"

"You were day-dreaming," her hostess remarked.

Katharina hung her head and dug her flat shoes with the broad square toes into the rug.

"What were you day-dreaming about?"

It was kindly asked and Katharina's self-confidence flooded back.

"About making tapestries of...of our Lady, the Virgin Mary. And about perhaps...perhaps giving one to the emperor."

The crinkles of a smile appeared once more around the edges of Frau Stoffler's eyes.

"For the emperor? And a tapestry of our Lady?"

Katharina nodded, blushing again at the sheer audacity of such thoughts.

"Well, who knows?" Frau Stoffler smiled. "But for now, I think we will set our sights a little lower. To begin with, your father has been kind enough to design and make you a small loom—a hand loom."

She walked over to a great, oaken cabinet standing behind a table at the far side of the room. A prayer stool had been placed alongside the cabinet, and on the wall above, a crucifix hung. On top of the cabinet itself stood a stone cruse filled with flowering hawthorn and apple blossom branches. Opening one of the doors, Frau Stoffler took out a wooden frame. Turning back to face Katharina, she held the frame toward her.

"This is yours," she said, "your own small hand loom."

Katharina, quite disappointed at the size of the frame, slowly reached out to take the frame from Frau Stoffler's hand.

They spent the next few hours at the table, warping the loom. Frau Stoffler carefully showed her small apprentice how to tie one end of a wool thread in a double knot around the bottom crosspiece of the loom and then loop that thread over the top crosspiece of the loom, bringing it down to the bottom again to repeat the procedure.

"The thread must be kept tight, but not so tight that you can't lift the warps up with one finger."

When Katharina sighed because her fingers seemed determined to slip and lose hold of the thread and to crumple it, Frau Stoffler laughed.

"Weaving," she said, "is a slow process and is composed of many steps each of which requires different skills. This can be frightening. You are doing well, Katharina. Better to get started on this small loom than on a large one. Do you understand that?"

"Oh, yes," Katharina breathed as she laboriously wound the last of the thread over the bottom crosspiece.

"You are doing quite well," the older woman praised again.

"Thank you," Katharina answered, inadvertently looking at all the fine pieces on the wall, pieces that she most likely, considering her progress these past hours, would never create. She sighed again.

"Child," Frau Stoffler said softly, "you should know that in the large ateliers in France, apprentices serve for three years before being allowed to try their hands at a finished work."

"Three years?"

"Yes, but I think perhaps we might move a little quicker than the apprentices in France. What do you think?"

Katharina smiled. She liked Frau Stoffler. She wiped her hands on the sides of her dress, thinking that a pocket handkerchief, such as her father had described, might be very handy to have when one was weaving.

"I think," Frau Stoffler went on, "that it is time for you to go home again. Shall we look out the window to see if your sister is on her way here?"

Companionably walking over to the window together and leaning into the sill, they could see Barbara walking up the street toward the house.

"Well, that was good timing," Frau Stoffler said.

"Next time," Katharina told her, "I shall come alone. I shall not need my sister to show me the way."

"I see. But do you not like to have her with you, perhaps to talk a bit on the way?"

"Well," Katharina answered slowly, "sometimes I do. But you see, often Barbara will want to walk quickly—to get to places. She does not let me stop and look at flowers. Now Jacob...."

She stopped, afraid that she had overstepped her boundaries. Mutti always told her not to talk too much.

"Jacob is your brother, is he not?"

"Yes, he is. He is next to me in age. He is nine, and he is so good and kind. He likes the same things I do and...but," she went on in haphazard fashion, "he is at school and is learning many things."

"You must bring him to visit me sometime," Frau Stoffler kindly offered. "But now you must go downstairs because I am sure that Barbara will be at the door by this time."

"Yes, Frau Stoffler. Thank you, Frau Stoffler."

"*Auf wiedersehen*, Katharina."

Katharina curtsied and walked toward the door.

"*Auf wiedersehen*, Frau Stoffler."

Chapter VI

The evening of that same afternoon with Frau Stoffler, Katharina sat down to eat at the kitchen table with her family. A wooden trencher stood in front of her. It was a piece of wood with a large depression hollowed out for food and a smaller one hollowed out in the upper right hand corner for salt. Marta, as she always did prior to each evening meal, walked around the table with a pitcher of water for cleaning hands. She also offered a towel for drying. Mutti helped the younger children wash their fingers and when this was done, Vati stood up to recite the mealtime prayer. He spoke slowly and meticulously.

"O heavenly Father, Fountain and Treasure of all goodness, we ask You to bestow Your mercies upon us Your children. Help us to remember continually not only to seek food for our bodies but also the spiritual food of Your Word, wherewith our souls may be nourished everlastingly, through Jesus Christ, who is the true Bread of Life, which came down from heaven, of whom whosoever eats shall live forever and reign with him in glory, world without end. So be it."

"So be it," they all echoed.

Vati had a napkin draped across one shoulder, as men were wont to have at mealtimes, whereas Mutti and the girls had their napkins on their laps. Katharina crumpled hers even as her fingers moved again as they had at the hand loom, tying knots and looping the wool thread. She had a difficult time concentrating on the meal in front of her. Her thoughts were still in the atelier with Frau Stoffler.

"You are dreaming, Katharina."

Jacob, next to her, playfully poked her with his wooden spoon. She smiled at him.

"I had a fine time this afternoon, Jacob," she whispered. "I learned so much today at Frau Stoffler's house. I'll tell you all about it later when we...."

"Katharina!"

Mutti's voice was strict. There was a rule that there was to be no small talk at the table while the food was waiting to be eaten. There was bread, cheese and some smoked sausage. She sighed and reached for her bread.

"Yes, Mutti."

"After you finish your bread, Katharina," Vati said kindly, "you may, just this once, speak and tell us all about your first visit with Frau Stoffler."

Katharina smiled broadly and nodded. Her cheeks flushed as her jaws were beginning to work double speed at the mouthful of bread she was chewing.

"Frau Bauer came in today," Mutti said a few moments later, eyeing Vati across the table, "to tell me that her niece's boy, Erich, you remember that fine little fellow who visited here last week, fell into one of the canals this morning."

Katharina stopped chewing as did the other children.

"Was he all right, Mutti?"

This time it was Elisabet who spoke. Elisabet was fourteen now, almost fifteen, and often permitted to speak at table.

"No," Mutti went on softly, "although enough seems to have been done to try to help the child. A crowd gathered almost immediately at the edge of the canal. But after he went under they did not see him come up again. It was not until a few hours later that some men pulled him out with an iron hook. They suspended him by his feet...."

Her voice grew louder and more agitated as she spoke, but then she suddenly stopped, aware of everyone's eyes on her.

"Yes," she continued, a trifle calmer, "and that is why I always warn all of you not to walk too close to the edge of the canals and that is why I always like it if you walk together, so that one can warn and protect the other."

Barbara, across from Katharina shuddered. Making the sign of the cross, she pushed her trencher with the half-eaten bread on it away from herself.

"I have seen children pulled up from the canal," Lux said soberly.

He was the oldest boy and considered a man now as he was getting ready to go to university.

"I have seen them suspended," Lux went on, "just as you say, Mutti. Often rescuers will put something in the drowned person's mouth to hold it open so that the water can run out. Sometimes that will revive a body."

"They should have called on the Virgin Mary," Barbara said, "for then perhaps there might have been a miracle."

"Frau Bauer told me that the boy's mother did call on the blessed Mary," Mutti went on, all the while stroking Andreas' fine baby hair, "and she also vowed to give a silver thread the length of her son, to the St. Thomas Church, should he survive."

"But he did not survive?" little Jacob asked, even though Mutti had already indirectly implied that the boy had died.

"No," she repeated, her eyes far away, "and it was her only child."

"Oh," he whispered, even as he reached under the table for Katharina's hand.

Katharina held it in her own, squeezing it hard to comfort him. She and little Jacob had a special bond. If she had a sore, such as a scraped knee or elbow, it was more likely that Jacob would bind it up and speak sweetly to her, than would Mutti, Elisabet or Barbara. Only two years her senior, they often sat on the stairs together in the evening and shared secrets.

"Well," little Jacob breathed out softly, his voice tremulous, "I think then that she must be very sad, his mother, I mean."

Katharina squeezed his hand again.

"We are blessed," Vati commented to no one in particular, "to have lost none at all."

"Yes," Katharina said, "many families lose children, do they not, Vati? But we have nine children."

"Yes, Katharina, that is so. We have been very blessed," Vati responded and, wishing to change the subject, he added, "and if you are done eating, why don't you tell us something now about your first lesson in tapestry weaving."

"Well," Katharina began, her mind retreating back into the warmth of the atelier, "a tapestry is a wall hanging. I knew that, of course. Frau Stoffler had a lot of them hanging up on her walls, and she showed them to me. And, tapestries are either woven with the warp stretched out on a vertical loom, called high-warp tapestry weaving, or horizontally on a low-warp loom."

She stopped for breath and then added, "Thank you for making me the hand loom, Vati. First I thought it was quite small. Frau Stoffler has such a large loom. But it is quite lovely."

Her father laughed at her.

"You are very welcome, my Katharina. It sounds like you've learned quite a bit already, little maid."

"Yes, I have," Katharina responded only to be reprimanded by her mother for having a boastful spirit.

She blushed and fell silent. Jacob was still holding her hand under table.

"There is a story," Vati said, taking pity on Katharina's red face, "about a tapestry called *The Two Riddles of the Queen of Sheba*. This tapestry was made only a few years ago right here in Strasbourg. On this tapestry the Queen of Sheba asks King Solomon two riddles. One of the riddles is how to tell a boy from a girl in a look-alike pair of children and the other riddle asks how to tell a real flower from an artificial flower."

"Are the riddles answered?" Elisabet asked.

"Yes," Vati said, "King Solomon told the Queen of Sheba that the girl, who is standing under an apple tree in the tapestry, will catch an apple in her lap. And he tells her that a bee will only go to a real flower."

"Was that a good answer, Vati?" Margaret questioned shyly.

"Yes, I think that was a good answer, Margaret."

Margaret was almost six, a sturdy, shy girl and she always sat next to Vati during the evening meal.

"Vati?"

"Yes, Katharina."

"Vati, drawings are made by famous artists and such drawings are often copied by a weaver. So perhaps you could make a drawing sometime for Frau Stoffler and then she can copy it."

"Did she ask you to ask me that?"

"Oh, no, Vati. She did not. I just thought that maybe you...."

She stopped and looked at him imploringly.

"If everyone is done eating, I think we should have our thanksgiving prayer, Jacob."

Mutti looked at Vati, and he stood up. Everyone bowed their heads.

"Glory, praise and honour be to you, most merciful and omnipotent Father, who hast fed us again from your bountiful hand. Grant that as you have nourished our mortal bodies with this food, so you would replenish our souls with the perfect knowledge of the beloved Son Jesus Christ; to whom be praise, glory and honour, for ever. So be it."

"So be it," they all intoned.

"Katharina, please help Barbara and Elisabet carry the trenchers and the cups to Marta in the kitchen. And after that, ready yourself for bed."

Katharina nodded. She pulled her fingers out of little Jacob's hand and stood up.

LATER THAT EVENING, after she and Margaret, Magdalene and Ursula had all been tucked into bed by Mutti, she pushed back the covers and stole out, careful not to awaken her younger sisters as she did so. Jacob was waiting for her on the stairs. She slid down and sat next to him, immediately beginning to whisper about her day, her fine day. He listened—listened to her excited voice and then grinned at her.

"You will be a famous weaver someday, Kathe and I...."

He stopped.

"You will what, Jacob?"

"Well," he playfully poked her in the ribs as he spoke, "well, I will shoe your horses. For surely when you are a famous weaver and everyone asks for your tapestries, you will have lots of horses."

"What do you mean you will shoe my horses?"

"Well, I mean that I will become a blacksmith."

"A blacksmith?"

Jacob nodded vigorously.

"Yes, a blacksmith. Every chance I get, Kathe, I go down to the blacksmith's shop and watch him work. There's nothing you can compare to doing a blacksmith's job, nothing at all in the whole world."

"But Vati wants you to go to school—to go to school like Lux is doing."

She took hold of his hand and went on.

"Isn't it dangerous, Jacob? I always walk around the blacksmith shop in a circle. I do not like the large horses and the fire... and...."

He laughed softly.

"You silly goose. Someone has to do work at these jobs. How else would they get done?"

She was not too sure that she wanted Jacob to be the one to do what she considered "dangerous things." But she took pity on his enthusiasm. After all, he so often encouraged her.

"And," he went on, whispering into her ear, "I do not know if Vati can afford to send two sons to university anyway. So it works out just fine that I happen to like becoming a blacksmith."

"But you will have to work very hard and...do you think that you will leave home soon? That you will go and live with...."

"I don't know," Jacob replied, chewing his bottom lip thoughtfully. "I know that I am only nine, but soon I will be ten. Albrecht, my friend at the blacksmith shop, he is twelve, and he has already been apprenticed for two years he told me. So I think that perhaps I might...."

"Oh, Jacob, you would have to work very hard. Would you not rather go and be apprenticed to a printer? Strasbourg has so many printers, so I'm sure you could...."

Jacob interrupted.

"No, Kathe. I want to be a blacksmith. I truly do. I will help a farmer make his tools—and I will help soldiers with their weapons of war and with their armour."

"You will have to work very hard," she repeated stubbornly,

"and you will get your hands very, very dirty. I know this, for I have seen how black, how very black and smudgy the people are at the smithy."

He laughed softly.

"Yes, that is true, Kathe, and you know what I will do when I see you? When I am working at the shop, I mean?"

"No, what?"

"Well, I will grab you and give you a great big kiss. And then you will be black too."

They both convulsed with laughter at the thought and made such a commotion that Mutti, alerted by the sounds, suddenly appeared at the bottom of the stairs.

"Away to bed, away with the both of you, or...."

They did not wait to hear, but scurried like two frightened little mice, to their bedrooms. Snugly back under her blankets, Katharina thought to herself how nice it was to have Jacob in whom she could confide and how wonderful it was to have such a brother to love.

Chapter VII

t was a beautiful day. Marta was singing a song at the top of her lungs in the kitchen. Margaret and Andreas heartily joined her whenever she reached the refrain which had to do with flowers and sunshine. Katharina could hear their cheerful voices grow fainter as she was descending the stone steps of their house. Together with Barbara, she was leaving for their morning lessons at the *lehrhaus*, for their time of elementary instruction in the basics of the German language. She was not keen on the lessons; she had no great appetite for umlauting, for transforming the back rounded vowels of 'u' and 'o' into the front rounded vowels 'ü' and 'ö.'

"Purse your lips, child," the *lehrmeister* admonished her again and again, "and you will hear how the word is to be spelled."

And so Katharina pursed her lips, even as she was walking down the street.

"What are you doing, Kathe?" Barbara asked, "Whatever it is, stop it. You look silly."

"I'm practicing spelling," she answered, "and that is a good thing, isn't it."

"You practice spelling at the school and not here in the street, you goose."

"Vati says you can learn wherever you are."

"Well, not if you look silly," Barbara replied, pulling Katharina's hand hard. "Stop it right now! You are making people look at us."

"Barbara, let's walk past the smithy."

"The smithy?"

"Yes, let's do it! It's only a block or so out of the way."

"Why?"

'Well, because...because there might be some horses there. And horses are beautiful creatures and...."

"No, Kathe, we are not going out of our way to look at some horses. And besides we are already late for class. The *lehrmeister* will be upset."

Katharina fell silent. She had dreamt about the smithy. She had dreamt that little Jacob had turned all black and that a knight had come in with a huge sword for him to sharpen. Although he tried, he had not been able to lift the massive weapon and the knight had been angry, so angry that he had turned the sword on Jacob. That's when she had woken up. But she knew it was a dream and dreams, Vati always said, were deceitful.

"Come on, Kathe, walk faster. You're dragging your feet. And besides that your cap is on crooked. Here, stand still for a moment."

Katharina stood still. She willingly let Barbara adjust her cap before her sister took her hand again, pulling her along at twice the speed at which they had been moving.

"Ow, you're hurting my hand, Barbara!"

"Well, come on then. Run a little faster."

They arrived, red-cheeked, at the *lehrhaus*, just as the teacher was beginning to ring the bell.

ACTUALLY, KATHARINA QUITE enjoyed her German lessons that morning. The *lehrmeister* allowed her to read for a while, together with Adel Borg, a girl her own age, from Herr Sebastian Brant's German translation of a book called *Aesop's Fables*. Herr Brant was from Strasbourg, and that made the book, the *lehrmeister* said, extra special. Although the reading was slow and careful, the girls enjoyed the stories. Katharina almost forgot that she was in school and was sorry when it was time to go home.

"I think," she told Barbara, as they walked back, "that perhaps instead of a famous tapestry weaver, I shall become a famous writer."

"You will certainly not become a famous saint," Barbara retorted.

"You are much too proud. You know that Mutti says you must not boast."

Katharina knew her sister was right, and she hung her head contemplating how proud she was.

"Well," she conceded, after about twenty steps, "perhaps I shall become famous after I become more humble."

"You are a silly goose," Barbara answered.

"Everyone calls me a silly goose. I don't know why," Katharina responded dolefully. "We certainly don't think geese are silly when we eat them."

"Well, maybe sometime when we are really hungry, we will eat you."

Barbara squeezed Katharina's hand and smiled at her sister. Katharina smiled back. They had rounded the last corner on their way home and, in the distance, could see their home. It seemed that there was a large group of people gathered close to their house. It even seemed as if they were grouped in front of their steps. Straining her eyes, Katharina wondered if Vati was having a meeting, or if perhaps he was showing some of his work to visitors. Sometimes this happened, and that was good because it meant he might be commissioned to do some important work.

"Let's walk faster, Barbara. I wonder who is standing by our steps."

The girls began to increase their pace, and as they came closer to their home, Katharina was struck by an awful apprehension. Shivering, she remembered her dream about the knight who had turned his sword on Jacob. But of course, dreams were deceptive. Yet the crowd of people did not look as if they were visiting Vati; they did not look at all like people interested in wood carving. Rather, it looked as if people were idling about because something had happened within their home.

With trepidation the girls made their way through the small clump of people and climbed the front steps. An almost eerie silence had begun when they came within earshot of the folks clustered about. No one spoke to them as they passed through to get to their front door. Not letting go of Katharina's hand, Barbara opened the door and stepped in, pulling her sister behind her. Then she shut the door with a bang. When the echoes of that sound died down, all they could hear was the silence of the house.

"I'm afraid," Katharina whimpered.

"There's nothing to be afraid of," Barbara whispered in her ear, although she herself looked rather shaken, "I'm sure everything is fine. Come on, let's go and find Mutti."

They walked toward the kitchen. Mutti was frequently in the kitchen with Marta at this time of day, preparing the noon meal. Mutti, however, was not to be found in the kitchen. There was only Marta, and she was seated at the table, hands supporting her chin, looking melancholy.

"Marta."

Both girls spoke simultaneously, and the servant girl rose and stretched out her arms.

"Oh, my dear lambs."

"Where's Mutti?"

"She's gone. She...." Marta hesitated and then stopped.

"She's gone where?" Katharina asked, "and what about Vati? Is he in the workshop?"

Not waiting to hear the answer, she turned and ran out of the kitchen. Reaching the workshop, she flung open the door, at the same time calling out, "Vati? Vati? Are you here?"

But there was only silence. Vati's tools lay on the counter. There was no one in the workshop. Lux was not sweeping the floor and, she noted quickly, had not done so for quite some time, as there were shavings everywhere. For a moment she was struck with a great desire to shut the door behind her and to begin sweeping up those wood curls. It would perhaps ease the appalling fear that had crept up into the bottom of her stomach. But then she turned and went back to the kitchen. When she entered the second time, both Marta and Barbara were seated at the table. And Barbara was crying, sobbing as if her heart would break.

"What is it? What is the matter with Barbara?"

Marta looked at her rather helplessly.

"It's Jacob...your brother."

"What of Jacob? Where is he?"

Before Marta could answer, there was a commotion in the front hall. Katharina could hear people entering by the Johanngasse door. She turned and ran out of the kitchen again. But before reaching the front door, she stopped. Vati, Mutti and Lux were in the hallway. Vati was carrying something—a body, a limp body, Jacob's body—in his arms. A raw cry rose from Katharina's throat. It was a sound that cut like the wind on an icy day. And then Katharina was at her father's side, pulling at his arms, whining like a sick puppy, until her mother's hands took hold.

"Shh, my Katharina, shh. It will do no good."

"My Jacob," she cried and again, "my little Jacob. What has happened to my Jacob?"

Behind her Barbara stood in the kitchen door, Marta by her side. Vati carried Jacob upstairs. Katharina followed, Mutti holding her hand. Vati walked into the boys' bedroom and laid Jacob on the bed.

"Mutti?"

Katharina barely had enough breath to whisper. There was no answer. Looking up, she saw tears coursing down her mother's cheeks. Vati had knelt down by the bed. And her Jacob? Why, little Jacob was gone, was dead. She knew it even without seeing the awful wound on the side of his head, without touching the blood that had congealed on his cheek.

IT WAS LATER, much later, that she was told that Jacob had been at the smithy's, as was his wont whenever he had a free moment. Standing behind a courier's horse, that animal had reared. It was said that the rider had suddenly applied his spurs. The horse had kicked his legs up with such force that the blow which Jacob had received, had driven the boy's head against the nearby stone wall. It was thought at first that he was merely unconscious for his chest seemed to still be moving up and down. They had carried him inside the smithy's house, but it was not long before he had stopped breathing. Even though his friend Albrecht had immediately run to fetch a doctor, it had been too late. And then Albrecht had run to their house on Johanngasse. Mutti had immediately sent Elisabet to Frau Bauer's house with the little ones—with Margaret, Magdalene, Ursula and Andreas. And then she and Vati and Lux had gone to the smithy to carry Jacob home.

Mutti, Elisabet and Tante Maria, who had come over to help, washed Jacob's body and then wrapped him in a shroud, or winding sheet. Katharina, who was forbidden entrance while they were thus engaged, sat outside the bedroom on the steps of the stairs. There they had sat yesterday, she and Jacob, talking about tapestries and horses, and Jacob had said that he would kiss her when he was all sooty and black. Here her thoughts faltered, and she asked herself, over and over, if she could have done anything to prevent this sadness. Truly, she knew at this moment that she hated death, hated it with a passion, for it took. It took what you loved and made you feel all queasy and sick and lonely, so lonely.

"Katharina?"

It was Barbara at the bottom of the stairs. The little ones were still at Frau Bauer's house across the road.

"Katharina?"

She looked into Barbara's red-swollen eyes. Barbara had loved Jacob too.

"Do you think, Kathe, that...." Barbara hesitated, "that it was my fault that Jacob...."

"Your fault?"

"Well, I have not said my Hail Mary's properly the last few days, and I did not show proper respect to...."

She stopped and began to sob. Katharina scooted down the stairs on her bum and put her arms around her sister's waist.

"No, you are so good Barbara. It surely would not be your fault. But it might be mine. You know how proud I am, you even said so yourself this morning. I...."

She did not get any further. There was a knock on the front door.

"Who...?" Barbara began and did not finish.

Katharina stood up and took her sister's hand. Together they approached the front door. Barbara swung open the oak door. There was a priest on the steps. Katharina recoiled a little. She had noted him at the beguinage, while she was visiting the cousins. He was also someone whom she had observed more than once berating beggars for sitting at the side of the road, and she had even seen him take money from their begging bowls. Instinctively she mistrusted him. He was fat and had an oily face.

"I heard there was a death in the family."

The girls said nothing.

"I have come to offer condolences and," he continued in an unctuous, smooth voice, "my help."

They still said nothing. He eyed the empty hall behind them.

"We don't....," began Barbara softly, but the man did not let her finish.

"You need spiritual succour, prayers and masses said and for a small sum...."

His speech was interrupted. Unbeknownst to the girls, their father had appeared in the hallway and stood behind them.

"We have our own priest," Jacob Schütz interrupted, stopping for a moment and swallowing with difficulty before adding, "and have no need of your...your spiritual succour. Thank you for stopping by, but there really is no need."

He shut the door in the man's face and Katharina was glad.

"Have my two little girls eaten any supper yet?"

"Oh, Vati, I am not hungry," Katharina said, looking up at him, tears brimming under her lids.

"Neither am I," Barbara lisped.

He knelt down in the hallway and put an arm around each of them.

"You must be brave, little ones, you must be brave. Will you promise me that, for your mother's sake?"

They both nodded.

"Your mother, Elisabet and Tante Maria have finished washing Jacob's body. You may go upstairs and see how peacefully indeed, little Jacob is resting."

His last words sounded very much like a sob and without a word the two girls left their father's arms and held one another's hands again as they began to climb the stairs. Passing the spot where Katharina had sat with Jacob just the day before, she shivered. Barbara noted it and let go of Katharina's hand, instead putting her arm around her younger sister.

"It is alright, Kathe. I'm here with you."

"And I'm with you, Barba," Katharina responded, unwittingly using Barbara's childhood pet name.

Barbara knocked before entering the boys' bedroom. It seemed proper to her to knock. After all, death was inside and death would answer. But it was not death but mother who opened the door. She smiled a slow smile to see the two girls standing side by side at the threshold.

"Come in, my sweet ones," she said, "come in and see your brother and how he is resting."

"Is he, Mutti?" Katharina asked, remembering the limp figure she had seen carried in by her father.

"Yes, he is, my moppet," her mother responded, running a hand through Katharina's tousled hair, "Jacob is resting eternally."

They tiptoed, both of them, toward the bed. Elisabet was standing with her back toward them, by the window and Tante Maria was sitting in a chair by the side of the bed. Jacob was lying on his back. Katharina remembered how he hated to sleep on his back and how he was wont to curl up into a ball on his right side. That is how he liked to sleep. But she durst not tell her mother that Jacob was lying wrong. Barbara squeezed her hand so tightly that it hurt.

"You see," Mutti continued in a strained voice, "that he is resting peaceably."

Katharina and Barbara both nodded. Katharina felt that her neck was stiff, and she had trouble moving her head up and down. She longed with all her heart to lie down next to Jacob and cuddle him in her arms. But the winding sheet, it separated him from her. Also the whiteness of the sheet, she felt, contrasted hugely with her own dirty skin. For a moment she had to look down at her left hand, the hand not held within Barbara's hand. It looked red and rough, not at all clean like the winding sheet was clean. Jacob had a huge bruise on the left side of his head. She could not see it clearly as she was standing on the other side of the bed. Was that where the horse had kicked him? Or was it perhaps where he had been knocked against the wall? Oh, if only he had not wanted to be a blacksmith!

"Tante Maria and Elisabet will watch the body tonight."

Mutti still spoke in a strained and rather monotone voice, a voice that did not appear to be her own. Katharina scarcely dared look at her, but her small face automatically tilted away from her dead brother's figure to the one who directed so much of her living. She saw that tears were coursing down Mutti's face even as she spoke. Mutti seemed unaware of them, as if the tears were a normal part of her facial features.

"Oh, Mutti!"

Forgotten was her father's admonition to be brave. Katharina let go of Barbara's hand and hurled herself at her mother's white kirtle.

"Oh, Mutti!" she repeated in a muffled sound, as her sobs were absorbed by the fabric. "It's all right," her mother said, stroking her hair, "little Kathe, it's all right."

But now that she had started sobbing, Katharina seemed unable to stop, and in the end, Elisabet had to tear her away from her mother's embrace.

"Come on, Kathe, I'll take you to our room."

And she went, not actually seeing where she was going, for the tears were blinding her, choking her, as if she were drowning in a sea of misery and darkness.

Chapter VIII

Funerals were often held in Strasbourg. They were part of the fabric of life, strange as that sounded. For Katharina, passing a church meant passing through or by a cemetery—a place marked by wooden crosses and the sometimes open pits of common graves. She often heard the great bell of the cathedral, the *Totenglocke*, the bell of the dead, resound loudly and dolefully as she walked on her errands or was on her way to a friend's house. It had never meant much to her until now—now when her beloved Jacob was gone, was dead and had to be laid to rest in the cold earth.

There had been many times during services inside the cathedral that Katharina had stared at the numerous monuments surrounding her. There were memorial tablets on the walls, brass tomb slabs under her feet and the large sepulchres of the very wealthy buried under the aisles close to the altar, close to the rose-coloured stained glass window, or close to the elaborately sculpted pulpit. Sometimes she wondered, as she sat in the pew leaning against either Barbara or Elisabet, who it was that lay beneath her feet. Perhaps, she pondered, it was another little girl like herself, who had also sat here—a little girl who had been seized with the fever, or with the plague and then, suddenly, her mother could not hold her any longer because death had taken her. And the very idea would bring tears to her eyes, and she would inadvertently glance at Mutti sitting only a few places away from her.

But it would not be within the cathedral that Jacob's body would come to rest. That area, Vati had explained very clearly to her, was only for the very wealthy, and they were not very wealthy. Little Jacob's grave would be an outside plot and a wooden cross would mark the spot. But, Vati had added, seeing the dismay in Katharina's eyes, it would be in hallowed ground that he would lie, ground that their priest, Father Geiler himself, had blessed.

THERE WAS A plain coffin. Little Jacob, not dressed in any finery but simply pinned into the winding sheet, was placed inside its wooden frame. The coffin remained in the house for two days. Elisabet did not like it. She had an innate aversion to it, and although she was the oldest, Barbara and Katharina had to constantly remind her that it was but a box, only a container and could do her no harm.

Tante Maria kindly shared in the home wake and cousin Ursula and cousin Margred had come to help as well from the beguinage of Gotteshaus zum Wolf. The two sisters offered to sit by Jacob's corpse the afternoon of the second day. Mutti was tired and was actually happy to have them stay. Katharina was ordered to sit with the cousins during the afternoon.

"I have heard," cousin Ursula began, after the three had sat quietly for some time, "that you, Katharina, have begun to take up the craft of *heidnischwerck*?"

"Yes, cousin," Katharina replied dutifully.

She was not up to much conversation. Most of the time she simply stared at the pale wood of the coffin. Her height did not permit her to look inside, and for that she was glad, for she did not wish to see Jacob's face as he lay in the casket. It was so different, so very different from when he had been alive. His face had often been impish; usually been glowing with enthusiasm as he had told her things. And now it was so still, so very still.

"Why, Katharina," cousin Ursula continued, "are you taking up that craft?"

Katharina did not answer immediately. She felt rather far away, removed from the situation directly around her.

"Katharina?"

Cousin Ursula's voice was growing louder.

"Ursula," cousin Margred's voice cut in, "Ursula, it is not the time to engage the child in conversation, I think."

"Nonsense," cousin Ursula answered, "there is no reason why she should not speak civilly to her relatives."

"But the child is very sad and preoccupied right now. Can you not see that?"

"It's all right, cousin Margred," Katharina said with a small smile, "I can speak for all that. I am sad, it is true. But it is no matter to tell you that my mother and father think it wise that I should learn the craft of weaving tapestries."

She fell quiet again and reflected that it would be difficult not to be able to tell Jacob what she was doing and what she was learning at Frau Stoffler's house.

"I think, child," cousin Ursula's voice had dropped to a confidential, almost friendly tone, "that you should think about joining us at the beguinage."

Katharina's gaze left the coffin and met cousin Ursula's grey eyes. Those eyes shone with a particular intensity.

"Join you—at the beguinage?"

Katharina repeated cousin Ursula's words in a perplexed tone.

"Yes, exactly."

Cousin Ursula leaned forward in her chair, tilting toward Katharina.

"Don't you see that it would be a gesture of humility and that this gesture would greatly benefit your living family, as well as...," and she paused for effect leaning over even more and repeating, "as well as Jacob here who is most certainly in purgatory where...."

"Ursula!"

Cousin Margred placed a plump hand on her sister's knee.

"Ursula!" she repeated and went on, "you ought not to be saying such things."

"Hush, Margred!"

Margred fell back, an aggrieved look on her round face. Katharina felt cold and hot at the same time.

"Do you not wonder, child," Ursula went on, "why such a young boy, such a fine boy as Jacob, was taken from this life? Surely you must be thinking about it?"

Katharina had thought of it. And she had blamed herself although she was not sure about the mechanics of why some people lived and others died. Father Geiler von Kaysersberg's preaching did mention that it was very important to live a holy life—that God wanted holiness, good works and a clean conscience. Was she holy? Did she do enough good works? Did she have a clean conscience? Slowly, almost imperceptibly, she nodded to cousin Ursula.

"Well, there you are," cousin Ursula smiled. "Of course you have thought about it. You are a clever young girl. I have always thought it."

"But," Katharina faltered, as her feet began to swing back and forth nervously, "but how?"

She stopped. She did not really know what she wanted to say. There were so many mixed up emotions roiling about within her that nothing seemed to make any sense. But she was sure of one thing—and that was that her life was lacking, severely lacking in goodness and that perhaps, just perhaps, God might be holding this against her.

"You see, child," cousin Ursula bent forward again, chucking her under the chin, "we are here to help you. And I will tell you a story now—a story which might help you better understand why it would be beneficial for you to join the beguinage."

Cousin Margred clucked disapprovingly and was shot a baleful glance by Ursula before she continued to speak.

"You may have heard, Katharina," she began her story, "of Saint Douceline."

Katharina shook her head. She had never heard of this saint.

"Well, Saint Douceline was a wonderful model for women. And you are a woman, Katharina. Never be in doubt about that. You are a young woman!"

She spoke the words emphatically, meaning to encourage the girl. But Katharina, staring at her, only saw the long, thin face with the sharp eyes boring into her own and consequently, missed the first part of the story.

"...in secret Douceline wore a shirt of pigskin," cousin Ursula intoned, "hard and rough and when this shirt was taken off, it left her body all torn and covered with sores. It befell one day that this shirt was so ingrown into her flesh that she could not take it off. A handmaid had to draw off the shirt, tearing her flesh."

Cousin Ursula stopped for breath. Katharina blinked uncomfortably. She did not like the story, and she felt as if cousin Ursula's brown robe was floating toward her, slowly encompassing her with its coarse fabric, eating into her own flesh. She missed the next part of the sentence, honing in again a bit later.

"...Douceline also girded her waist so straitly with a knotted cord, that worms would oftentimes breed where the knots entered her flesh. She lay, for penance sake, on a little bit of straw in the corner of her room. And lest she should rest in her sleep, she bound a cord above her bed with one end and with the other end round her own waist; so that whensoever she stirred, the cord would drag and awake her. Then she would rise and say her matins...."

"Why?" Katharina interrupted.

"Why?" cousin Ursula repeated, as if the question were absurd, "Why what?"

"Why did she do those awful things to herself?"

"I think, Ursula," cousin Margred interposed softly, "that such a story is quite too descriptive and too hideous...."

"Be quiet, Margred," Ursula commanded, "you do not know what you are saying. The stories of the saints are there for our benefit and for young Katharina's benefit. They are not hideous...."

"But Ursula," Margred continued, for once not put out by Ursula's bossiness and moved with compassion by Katharina's pale face, "they never benefit me, I think. They just make me...."

"Be quiet, Margred," Ursula repeated firmly, "and now I will continue."

She shifted her position and went on in a softer tone.

"Saint Douceline ordered the avoidance not only of all familiarity with men, but also of all speech and interchange of glances. And this was not only for herself, but also for all who would live under her direction. For you see, she was the head of a beguinage such as where we live."

"You are not allowed to look at a man?" Katharina questioned, her interest piqued by this information.

"Well, yes, we are," cousin Ursula answered, "but Saint Douceline's beguinage was a little stricter than we are and so...."

"So the women in St. Douceline's beguinage could not speak with their brothers? Or their fathers?"

"No, Saint Douceline knew no man's face. And if she saw one of the sisterhood, one of those who lived with her, look at a man, she would rebuke her sharply."

"Why?"

Katharina could not comprehend that a girl might not want to speak with her father or with her brother or that this could be wrong. She gazed at the coffin again. She wished with all her heart that she might speak again with Jacob. What a strange and seemingly wicked thing not to want to speak with your family.

"Because of humility," cousin Ursula firmly answered, "And humility pleases God, of course, and earns much favour—both for the dead and for the living."

"Well, I think it would be wicked not to want to speak with your father...."

"Child," cousin Ursula interrupted, "mind what you say. Remember that Jacob is in...."

But she got no further than that. Cousin Margred again put her hand on her sister's knee.

"Really, Ursula. You must stop and remember where you are and why we are here. It would befit us all much more to say *Vater Unser* or to recite...."

Katharina stood up. She cared not that she had been told to stay all of three hours with the cousins and to wake with Jacob. She felt sure that Jacob would understand were it so that she could tell him.

"I bid you good afternoon," she said, as she curtsied and left the room.

And out in the hallway, after the door was shut, she could again hear cousin Margred berate cousin Ursula for speaking of Saint Douceline.

"Kathe?"

Katharina turned to see her five-year-old sister Margaret standing behind to her.

"Margaret, what are you doing here? You are supposed to be staying with Frau Bauer until after the funeral ceremony tomorrow."

"I missed you."

Touched, Katharina bent over her sister's small frame and hugged her.

"Come on. Frau Bauer is probably worried about you. She won't know where you are."

"Can I stay with you for just a little while?"

"Well, for a little while. Come on, we'll sit at the top of the stairs together."

Margaret followed her sister to the stair edge, and as they sat down, she nestled her small frame against her sister's. They sat in silence for a while. Katharina had put her arm around her sibling.

"Is this where you sat with Jacob in the evening?"

"Yes, how did you know that?"

"Because I sometimes followed you when you left the bed."

In spite of herself, Margaret giggled and Katharina smiled.

"Can I sit here with you sometime in the evening too?"

Katharina did not know whether to be angry or not. She could not discern whether to feel gladness or sadness.

"Maybe."

"Kathe?"

"What, Margaret?"

"Kathe, is Jacob in heaven now with angels? And can he fly?"

Katharina did not answer. For a moment it all overwhelmed her. And then she began to cry.

"Don't cry, Kathe."

But Katharina kept on sobbing. She could not stop herself. Her sister's arms tightened around her, and a small voice whispered in her ear.

"I will say extra Hail Marys, I promise. And the Virgin Mary will hear. That's what Frau Bauer said. She said I must say a lot of them and then it will be all right. Please don't cry, Kathe."

"It's true, Margaret," Katharina whispered back into her sister's ears, even as the tears ran down her cheeks, "it's true. We must say Hail Marys, and we must make sure we do many good deeds."

"Yes, I know," Margaret smiled, happy that her sister was talking to her, "and I promise that I will do very many good deeds. We can do them together, Kathe, can't we?"

Katharina nodded and then resolutely stood up.

"But now you need to go back to Frau Bauer. That will be your first good deed then. Being obedient and doing what she tells you."

Margaret stood up too.

"All right, Kathe," she said, "watch me walk down the stairs. Watch me start my first good deed."

Katharina watched as her little sister marched down. And at the bottom of the stairs Margaret turned, waved and blew her sister a kiss.

THE FUNERAL CEREMONY began early the next morning with the removal, the carrying out, of Jacob's body from the house on Johanngasse. Although family, close friends and good neighbours gathered by the Schütz's front door, the procession accompanying the little corpse to the church was a ritual in which the whole community was permitted to participate. Vati had arranged for a crier to ride through their neighbourhood, announcing Jacob's death. At the same time, the crier requested prayers on Jacob's behalf and told everyone to be ready to assemble for the funeral.

"The prayers of the poor," Lux had told Katharina, "are especially beneficial, because the poor have little else to offer."

"But will they do it? I mean will they really pray for Jacob and will they come to the funeral?" Katharina had asked her brother.

"Yes, indeed, why should they not? For we will give them alms at the church ceremony. We will do that on behalf of Jacob as it is a chance for Jacob to demonstrate Christian charity one last time."

He stopped and swallowed before he went on.

"It will add to his good works and lessen..." he hesitated, but then went on in a lower tone of voice, "lessen his time in purgatory."

"But I have no money," Katharina faltered.

"Vati will give you alms to hand out," Lux said, "You need not worry."

Everyone in the family wore black. Katharina continually plucked so nervously at the folds of her dark skirt with both hands that, as if by common consent, Barbara suddenly took one of them and Elisabet the other. The church bells rang and echoed over the cobblestones. Katharina, who often stood still to listen to the many bells of Strasbourg on her way to errands, now wished to put her hands over her ears to shut the sound away, to blot the doleful clanging out of her heart. But she could not pull her hands away from her sisters' hands. Margaret was walking in front of them, holding onto Vati's hand. Little Ursula and Magdalene held Mutti's hands and baby Andreas was being carried by Lux. Solemnly they all walked through the streets, following the six neighbours who were carrying the coffin. Every now and then, Katharina peered ahead, trying to see past her parents in order to make sure that the coffin was still upright and a part of their procession. A priest, one whom Katharina did not know, had sprinkled the coffin with holy water just before it left their home. He was at the head of the procession. And now they were leading Jacob to the cathedral for his very last attendance in that great big church. Every now and then, the girls would toss some coins to the people they passed on the sidewalk. There were not many of them. But every time she tossed some coins, Katharina felt she was helping Jacob—helping him escape from that terrible place of gloom called purgatory. A harsh wind blew about her face, and she closed her eyes to shield them from its sting.

Once inside the church, the coffin was carried to the middle of the sanctuary. At that place there was a hearse, a metal stand, with several candles arranged around it, on which the coffin was placed. The huge sanctuary was quiet, save for the echoing sound of shuffling feet and throats clearing. Vati moved forward and carefully covered the coffin with a pall, a cloth on which the words *Orate pro Jacob Schütz* had been embroidered.

The candles around the bier were lit. A second priest joined the first who had led the procession. Katharina did not know him either. She wished Father Geiler were there. She trusted him and knew him, but Vati had told her that Father Geiler was gone from Strasbourg right now, that he was attending to some important business in another town. The second priest walked around the pall, spraying it with incense. Each time he passed the cross stationed at the head of the coffin, he bowed to it before continuing, his thurible dangling from his hands. And all the time the first priest continued praying, continued praying prayers for the dead. Katharina could not hear all of the words, and she was not listening to them either. Rather, she concentrated on the stained glass windows, the windows with the saints on them, the windows with the colour and light. She loved the windows and had often told Jacob so.

Here inside the church she could not hear the wind which had blown so harshly outside. There was a story which Vati had told them, a story about the wind. It had to do with the statues of the foolish virgins outside in the forecourt of the church. Next to the statues of the virgins was a statue of the devil in the shape of a handsome man. When the real devil had flown by the church, he had been flattered to see a statue of himself. Pride made him enter the church to see if there were more sculptures that had been made in his likeness. But once inside the holy sanctuary, he was held prisoner and could not get out. That was why, Vati had told them, the wind often wailed outside the cathedral. It was waiting for the devil to come out and was screaming with impatience. Katharina shivered. The story made her uneasy even though Vati had laughed and had told her that it was only a story, only a make-believe tale.

The priest reciting the prayers stopped speaking and lifted his hand to make the sign of the cross. The white flared sleeves of his surplice moved with the gesture, moved rather like the wings of a bird, Katharina thought. He then took the stoup, a stone basin, from the hands of the second priest and circled the bier with it, all the while sprinkling holy water on the wood, bowing profoundly when he passed the cross. Giving the stoup back to the second priest, he next, in a sing-song voice, began to recite the *Pater Noster*. In her heart, Katharina said it with him. And the words echoed around them all. When the *Pater Noster* ended, the Prayer of Absolution was begun.

"O God, whose attribute it is always to have mercy and to spare, we humbly present our prayers to Thee for the soul of Thy servant Jacob Schütz which Thou has called out of this world, beseeching Thee not to deliver it into the hands of the enemy, not to forget it forever, but to command Thy holy angels to receive it and to bear it into Paradise, that as it has believed and hoped in Thee it may be delivered from the pains of hell and inherit eternal life through Christ our Lord. Amen."

Chapter IX

King Maximilian and Queen Bianca visited Strasbourg the same year that Jacob died. The royal Austrian party entered the city by torchlight. They attended an evening service at the cathedral and heard Dr. Geiler preach but left again the next day. It was not because they did not like Dr. Geiler's preaching that they left, as some people were heard saying, but because they did not have the time to visit Strasbourg for very long. Indeed Katharina had heard her father say that Dr. Geiler had preached very well that evening. His words from the pulpit had pointed to reform —had proclaimed the fact that fat monks should pay more attention to good deeds than to food and that they should become better acquainted with the Word of God rather than sing bawdy songs. Vati said Dr. Geiler had not been afraid to say that if the pope, bishops, emperor and king did not work to change the unspiritual, insane, godless way of life that was being lived within the church, then surely God would raise up someone who would change it, someone who would restore the fallen religion.

"Did our religion fall down, Vati?"

Jacob Schütz sighed, looking perturbed at his young daughter's question.

"Don't bother your father with silly statements, Katharina." Elisabeth, bent over some embroidery, admonished the child.

But Vati had replied to the question as if it had not been silly.

"Perhaps it did fall, child," he had said. "Perhaps it did. And Dr. Geiler said that he wished he could see the day when our church would stand up again and that he wished he could be the disciple of the man who would restore the faith.

"Who will that man be, Vati?"

"Hush, child. Hush!!"

Katharina had stopped asking questions and instead she had listened as other people related that King Maximilian's and Queen Bianca's retinue had been such a wonderful, such a magnificent sight. Stately horses' hooves had clattered down their streets, lances had flashed and the royal couple had been so regal and impressive in their bejewelled gowns and crowns that they had stirred awe in everyone. Katharina wished with all her heart that she could have seen them. It was known that the king often visited Strasbourg with regard to his many debts. Katharina logically supposed that he must stop in to visit Mr. Fugger's bank, the same Mr. Fugger who's first name was Jacob like Vati. Unlike Vati, however, people called Mr. Fugger "Jacob the Rich." Vati was not rich. As for King Maximilian, she had never met him on the streets of Strasbourg, but perhaps if he had passed her she would not have recognized him, as she was quite certain that he would be wearing neither his royal robes nor his crown when he called on the banker. For people who have debts, Vati explained, are often a little ashamed that they owe money, and they do not want other people to know.

IT SO HAPPENED that Count William von Honstein was elected as the new bishop of Strasbourg in September 1506, when Katharina was eight years old. Again, she missed a very solemn city occasion as she was ill with a fever at the time, and her head ached terribly. Mutti had, with the help of Frau Bauer, their neighbour, who knew the healing power of herbs, mixed up a salve. There were radish, garlic, bishopwort and some other herbs in the salve, and it had been smeared on Katharina's forehead. Elisabet and Barbara, who both felt very sorry for their sick sister, told her a great deal of Count von Honstein's solemn entry into the city and how he had been escorted into their cathedral. The streets had been filled with people and all the windows of the houses on the way were crowded with men, women and children alike. It had been a very grand entry, indeed, for a great parade followed the count. The man had taken 600 mounted dignitaries with him, as well as some 400 mounted soldiers. In all, close to 1,000 men thronged before and behind his person. It had been very impressive. But the magistrates of Strasbourg, not liking the idea that so many armed strangers would enter their city, had refused the count permission to enter until he had sworn to protect Strasbourg's liberties.

"What did the count look like?" Katharina asked as she lay in her bed, her head propped up by pillows, her cheeks red with the fever, but her ears anxious to hear of the excitement.

"Well," Barbara said, "I did not see him long, but I think he looked like a proud young man. He did not smile overmuch and wore a black coat, a white choir robe and..." she paused to think, "I do believe that on his head there was a black beret."

"Our lords of Strasbourg were there as well and the *ammeister*. All the officials bared their heads in honour of the count, but they only bared them for a moment," Elisabet added, "and all the bells rang out. It was noisy but good. I think the bells quite startled the count. We were by the steps of the church, you see, and we could make out his form quite well."

IT WAS THE last Strasbourg expected to see of their new count bishop. For if he were at all like the last few bishops they had known, he would not be visiting very often. However, during Lent the following year, everyone was surprised. Count von Honstein returned to Strasbourg to be consecrated in the great cathedral. No bishop of Strasbourg had been consecrated there for over 200 years. It was rumoured that the consecration was going to be a richly elaborate church gathering, one which Katharina passionately begged permission to attend. In the end, her mother relented and let Elisabet take her younger sister. The glittering jewels which hung around the necks of the ladies of the count's entourage amazed Katharina. Her eyes bulged at the colours and at the fine brocade of the dresses that rustled and swished as they walked into the cathedral. Tightly holding onto Elisabet's hand and wedged into the back pews with other common folk, she gaped at the men and women of the count's court who seemed not to walk but to fairly glide down the aisle. The sisters were seated on the very corner of a pew and had a good view of those passing. Katharina hardly dared breathe as she gaped at the people, for fear that she would be reprimanded and that Elisabet would desire to go home.

Although it was dark within the cathedral, there were splashes of sunlight breaking through the stained glass windows. Each time a dress paraded past through a patch of such light, Katharina caught her breath at the brilliance of the personage.

She could not help but think, "There, where that gown stopped for a moment, that is where I, Katharina Schütz, also walked at one time and will walk again."

She knew within herself that probably this feeling was pride, was a raising up of herself to think more highly of herself than she ought to think, but she could not help it.

Dr. Geiler, after he mounted his high carved stone pulpit, did not seem the least intimidated by the splendour of the men and women gazing up at him. Katharina was quite proud of him. He was, after all, her family's priest, her city's preacher and her very own beloved pastor. As always Dr. Geiler, after he had mounted the high pulpit steps, removed his hat, knelt down to pray and then rose. Upon rising he put his hat back on and made the sign of the cross. The royal party was seated on the benches directly in front of the pulpit. Dr. Geiler, in a clear and authoritative voice, spoke.

"The unfathomable mercy of God our heavenly Father, the precious merit of the painful passion of our Lord Jesus Christ, must appear to you and to me in our final hour of need. Whoever seeks that, no matter their station in life, let them say: 'Amen.'"

Katharina, along with all the other folk who had gathered for the consecration mass, said: "Amen."

"I now have spoken," it briefly passed through Katharina's mind, "at the same time as Count von Honstein and I have said the same word he spoke."

There was within the pit of her stomach a lump, which she vaguely identified as pride and a bit of shame crept into her heart, especially when Dr. Geiler went on to speak in his sonorous voice.

"I cannot instruct you without the special grace of God, which it is always necessary to obtain through the advocacy of the heavenly Queen Mary. Let us greet her now with the angelic salutation, saying: 'Hail Mary, full of grace.'"

He took off his hat again, knelt down and began reciting the "Ave Maria," adding an 'Amen' at the end. Then he stood up once more, put his hat back on and made his way down the steps. Reaching the bottom, he strode over to the altar, his server following him. Latin words now began in a recited cadence. The words swelled and diminished and their echoes ran down the stone church floor. They ran past everyone, also past Katharina and Elisabet, fading out at the door. Katharina shivered with the importance, with the very seriousness of the occasion.

Suddenly, however, Dr. Geiler stopped speaking. The doors to the cathedral were flung open and some people walked in. Everyone in the church turned their heads and strained their necks to find out who would be so bold as to interrupt this important consecration mass. Eyes bulged with surprise when they perceived that it was King Maximilian himself who had strode in, surrounded by several other nobles. Looking neither to the right nor to the left, he stepped grandly past the back pew where Katharina and Elisabet were sitting, eyes agog. He was dressed in black, because, as Elisabet whispered to Katharina, after he passed them, his son, who had been known as Philip the Handsome, had died in Spain just a little while ago.

"I think the Emperor Maximilian is not so handsome," Katharina whispered back, "for his nose is exceedingly long and it is also crooked."

Elisabet grinned, but then poked her to be quiet. Katharina, however, continued in a tiny voice behind her hands, informing her sister that surely the emperor did not need his index finger to point, he could use his nose. Elisabet turned beet red, turning her head to see if anyone appeared to have heard what Katharina had said, before stepping on her sibling's toe.

"Ow!"

But Katharina said no more after that.

After Emperor Maximilian was seated, Dr. Geiler continued

Mass. Bowing and kissing the altar, he began reciting the very special words that always transfixed Katharina. Those words were spoken after the bell rang and Dr. Geiler's hands were raised high. Katharina had been told that at this point a mystery happened: what had been just ordinary bread a moment before, was transformed into Christ's body. Together with the entire church, she fell to her knees to adore that piece of bread, that holy body. Peering past the crowd, she tried to see Dr. Geiler as she knew he would at that moment eat of the host and drink of the cup. But there were too many people, and no matter how she craned her neck, she could not see. Then Elisabet pulled her hand, warning her without words to be still and not fidget.

Later, when they were outside, Elisabet scolded a bit, but soon forgot her irritation as they watched the courtly retinue down in the street ahead of them mount horses and enter carriages.

"Would you like to be a lady, such as the ladies we saw, Elisabet?"

"No, certainly not."

"Why not?"

"I should be tempted to forget all that Mutti and Vati taught us about doing good and helping others," her sister answered.

"Well," Katharina said, "I should not forget, and I should give half of what I had to the poor. That would be good, would it not?"

Elisabet laughed.

"And what would you do with the other half, you goose?"

"Well, I should...."

She stopped before continuing.

"Well, I don't know yet what I would do with it."

DURING THE DINNER hour, the girls described all that they had seen to the rest of the family. But it was not until later, much later, that Katharina suddenly knew what she would do with the other half of the money. Indeed, it was past the hour of midnight in the dark of their bedroom that Katharina shook Elisabet, who slept next to her, awake.

"I think I know what I would do, Bet, with the other half of the money, should I ever be a rich lady."

"Well, what would you do," Elisabet sleepily answered, only half awake.

"I should buy prayers for the dead. I should buy prayers for the soul of little Jacob so that he might not linger in...."

She could not bring herself to say the word. Elisabet did not answer, and Katharina folded her hands in the dark and lay them on the blanket in a mute appeal to God to not to be too harsh on her beloved brother who now dwelt in purgatory.

Chapter X

A few weeks after the consecration mass, on their way home from a tapestry lesson, Barbara and Katharina saw a group of priests entering St. Thomas Church. They had heard its church bells suddenly begin tolling loudly as they passed the yellowed brick building, and the striking, trembling tones caused them to stop and gape at the church door. It was draped in black. A sombre mood hung about the whole area. The two girls could sense it as they stood still, watching for what they knew not.

"Is it a funeral, Barbara? Perhaps a priest's funeral?" Katharina whispered, shivering as she spoke, even though the sun was shining and it was not at all chilly.

"No, I think not," Barbara answered as they stood very quietly, just near the stone walk that led up to the church steps.

"What then?"

"I know not."

"Well then," Katharina said, "let us go in and see, Barbara."

"No," her sister answered in a half-firm and half-persuaded tone of voice, "I think we should go on. Vati and Mutti know I have gone to pick you up from Frau Stoffler and...."

But Katharina intuitively sensed that a good part of Barbara also wanted to go in and see what was happening in the sanctuary. Tugging at her sister's hand, she turned onto the walk toward the church entrance and Barbara gave way.

Inside the large foyer, the girls could see that the priests they had observed outside were now gathered together in the nave. The pews, like the door they had just passed through, were also draped in black. A portly figure, a prelate very likely, surrounded by the others, stood in the centre chancel. Each of the robed priests was carrying a candle. In spite of the fear in her stomach, Katharina was plagued by a great curiosity to find out what was happening, and she pulled Barbara with her to sit in one of the side benches —a bench behind a column that almost, but not quite, hid them from view. The moment they sat down, shouting began at the front. It was done by the prelate, the portly prelate, and he had a thunderous voice. His words made the girls cringe.

"Let Simon Bauman be cursed in the city and cursed in the field; cursed in his granary, his harvest and his children; as Dathan and Abiram were swallowed up by the earth, so may hell swallow him. And even as today we quench these torches in our hands, so may the light of his life be quenched for all eternity, unless he repent."

Katharina gripped Barbara's hand hard and noted that her sister returned the squeeze—so much so that she winced in pain.

"Let's leave, Barbara."

"I think we better wait," Barbara responded softly, "until we are sure no one will watch us."

The next moment they witnessed, with mounting apprehension, that the priests flung down their candles, stamping them out as they did so. As the priests bent over, the girls beheld a man within the tight circle, a common man, possibly their father's age. He did not seem to be a priest, for he was wearing a pilgrim's robe. As they watched the man fell to his knees, covering his face with his hands. The priests, after they finished putting out their candles, now picked up clubs and began to beat the man. At every blow they dealt him, the victim cried out, his voice ringing pitiably throughout the sanctuary.

"Just are Thy judgements, O Lord."

Barbara, overcoming her almost paralytic fear, now hissed at Katharina to move from her spot and when the younger girl, mesmerized, did not move, she pulled her off the bench and dragged her back to the door. Fumbling at the latch, the girls were grateful to see the sun once more. They half-ran, half-walked down the stone walk. And, as if by unspoken agreement, during dinner hour, it was only of the tapestry lesson that Katharina spoke and Barbara's comments were totally restricted to the fine weather they were having.

Yet it was Jacob Schütz who later, when the family had finished eating, spoke of the event at the Thomas Church.

"I have heard tell," he said, as he eyed his children and his wife, "that the ever-hungry stomach of the church has richly feasted once again at the expense of some poor noble."

"What mean you?" Elisabeth asked, as she held the smiling and drooling baby Andreas on her lap.

"Well, some unknown baron, drunk and unhappy after the death of his wife, in a fit of who knows what, took it into his head to steal a chalice from St. Thomas Church a few weeks ago. Perhaps he thought it holy, possessing properties to ward of disease. In any case, he was seen with the chalice as he made away with it on his horse. Later he was caught and he was brought to justice this afternoon."

"How...how was he brought to justice?" Barbara asked softly, "And it is a heinous crime, is it not Vati, to steal from the church?"

"Yes, stealing is a crime," Jacob Schütz answered, "There can be no doubt about that. It just seems to me that the church takes advantage of crimes; that they are not as interested in the repentance of a soul, as they are in search of money. And they punish hard, as well. I have heard tell that the man was forced to donate his entire fortune to the church, at the pain of having his soul condemned to hell. Then he was forced to appear barefoot in St. Thomas Church, wearing a pilgrim's robe. For twenty-four hours he had to lie prostrate before the church's high altar, praying and fasting. Then, having already paid for his soul, the fellow was clubbed by a bevy of angry priests until most of his bones were broken. At that point, the bishop absolved him and gave him the kiss of peace. It is thought the man might die of his injuries."

It was quiet in the room. Elisabeth held the baby tightly, kissing his head, before looking up at her husband almost reproachfully.

"If thievery goes unpunished, then perhaps we would have an

unruly city," she said softly.

"Surely God is more merciful than the church was on this occasion," her husband retorted, although not unkindly.

"Yes, yes, I think father is right," Katharina piped up and then blushed and looked down quickly, for she knew she was not to speak unless spoken to when her parents were engaged in conversation.

A FEW DAYS later, Katharina waited in the pew of the church after Mass. She had told Elisabet, who had attended Mass with her, to leave for home, she had some special prayers to say. Elisabet had looked kindly at her small sister, patted her on the head and admonished her not to be overly long and to be careful coming home. Crouched down on the kneeling bench, Katharina peered through her fingers to mark when Dr. Geiler would walk by. She knew it was sometimes his wont to pray for a while in the church after he conducted Mass before leaving for his home, and this is what he seemed to be doing this day. She hoped with all her heart that she might speak with him. Indeed, she was not disappointed, for after some ten minutes of prayer, Dr. Geiler arose from his place at the front of the church and walked down the aisle past the very spot where she was hunched over on the kneeling bench close to the aisle. When he passed, she stretched out her hand and pulled at his cassock. Later, she did not remember how she had dared. He stopped his stride and glanced down at her.

"Yes?"

Though he spoke sternly, his voice was not unkind, which gave her much courage, "and what is it you want, child?"

"Oh," she said and then, much to her mortification, she burst into tears.

"Yes," he repeated, gazing down from what appeared to her to be a great height, for he was a tall man, "do not be afraid, child. Is there some sin you want to confess?"

"No," Katharina sobbed, trying hard to stand up and to stop crying, while clutching at the bench in front of her.

He held out his right hand to help and she took it. Raising her up, he gazed at her tear-stained face and smiled.

"Such big blue eyes," he said, in a kindly manner, "like a sky dropping rain. Such big eyes and surely you have prayed for something big also, I think?"

"I," she began and then remembered that Mutti always told her never to start with 'I.'

It was too impertinent, too proud.

"That is," she continued, "Jacob, my brother...."

"Yes," he encouraged.

"Well, Jacob died, you see and I....."

He patted her hand.

"It was perhaps my fault that he died."

There. It was out now and she stopped, looking away from Dr. Geiler's kindly and sympathetic face, waiting. Surely he would be horrified and send her away.

"Your fault, child?"

His voice was encouraging and she took heart and continued her story.

"He wanted to be a blacksmith, you see. He wanted to work in the smithy, and I did not tell him not to work there. That is, I could have been more disapproving. I could have told my parents that he often went to the smithy. But I did not, and then a horse kicked him, kicked him on his head. So you see, it was my fault. So you see," and the words ended in a sob, "I killed him, my brother."

"Ah," Dr. Geiler responded softly, "so you carry a weight of guilt within you?"

Katharina thought of the hard lump in her stomach, indeed, the hard lump within her heart, a lump that had grown bigger even though it had been a good year since Jacob had died, a lump that threatened to carry her down, pull her into despair at times. She nodded.

"It is natural," he began, "indeed, it is quite normal to feel a great loss at a death, child. And tell me first, what is your name?"

"Katharina," she answered and swallowed at the same time, making her voice seem thick and unnatural.

"Katharina," he said, his left hand stroking his chin as he spoke. "Well, that is a beautiful name. Now perhaps we should sit down, Katharina, and you can tell me exactly what happened to Jacob at the smithy."

"He was kicked by a horse," she repeated, even as she sat, sliding sideways down the pew to make room for Dr. Geiler who came to sit next to her.

"Oh," he answered, staring down at the kneeling bench in front of them before he looked up at her again, "kicked by a horse?"

"Yes," she continued, "and his head hit the wall behind him and he…he never…and the night before, you see, he had spoken to me about it…about wanting to be a blacksmith and about wanting to help farmers to make their sickles sharp and about wanting to help make other farm implements and such…. He was so excited."

Katharina spoke in spurts and starts.

"Jacob sounds like he was a fine brother."

"Oh, he was and I loved…I loved him so, you see."

"How shall you not cry at the death of a brother, Katharina? That is only natural. Even Christ himself wept at the death of his special friend Lazarus. Do you know that story, child?"

Katharina nodded again.

"Listen to me carefully," Dr. Geiler went on, taking Katharina's right hand into his own, patting it as he went on, "because this is important. Death is a friend. You should weep, that is a normal thing, but you should not weep overly much."

"A friend?" Katharina interrupted, "But what about…what about purgatory? He will be in pain now, I think and I am not," she stumbled again over her words, "I am not in pain."

"But think ahead, dear child. Think ahead. Is it not better in the long run to suffer for a little while if that is what it takes to come to a beautiful place? And that is where he will be—in a very beautiful place."

Katharina sighed deeply. There were still traces of tears on her cheeks.

"A beautiful place?" she repeated.

"Yes, more beautiful than any place here on earth," Dr. Geiler added.

"And what should I…?"

"Ah," Dr. Geiler said softly, "you want to know what you should do to help lessen his time in purgatory?"

"Yes," her answer came softly.

"Well, do you attend Mass regularly?"

"Oh, yes," she eagerly responded.

"Do you obey your parents and keep the commandments?"

She nodded.

"Do you say your *Pater Nosters*, your *Aves* and your *Vater Unser?*"

Her neck could now barely keep up with the bobbing of her head.

"And do you strive to love your neighbour by doing good works?"

She nodded a little slower now. It came to her that her zeal in answering Dr. Geiler's questions was perhaps just a trifle dishonest. For was it not so that she often took a longer path than errands for mother required, that she frequently teased Barbara and that she avoided visiting Frau Bauer if she could help it. And she knew for a fact that she had made fun of the cousins innumerable times.

"Maybe," she conceded softly, "maybe I don't obey quite as well as I ought to obey. But," and here she sighed again, "I surely do want to."

He again patted the hand still enclosed in his own and smiled.

"The desire is good, child. Pray for more desire and pray for the ability to repent of sin. God never abandons those who repent of sin and you must do penance by...."

"By what?" she questioned eagerly.

"*Facientibus quod in se est Deus non denegat gratiam.*"

Seeing Katharina's puzzled face, he translated the Latin to say, "Do your best, God will do the rest."

And then, as she sat looking at him in a somewhat bewildered way, he added, "By your good works, child. By your good works."

Chapter XI

It was difficult for Katharina, who liked to laugh a great deal and who also, at times, delighted in wiling away her hours in pensive thought, to actively pursue obedience in all matters. When her mother, for example, sent her on errands, whether it was to the market or to deliver something for her father, she had to constantly remind herself not to stand still and dawdle. Trying to remember, however, that by obeying she was truly helping Jacob come to a beautiful place, that she was helping him enter eternal heaven, made it a bit easier. Most days Mutti did not have to remind her it was time to get ready to go to school anymore; she did not have to call out that Barbara (and Margaret now also) was waiting for her, because the case was now often reversed. It would be Katharina who was waiting for them out on the stone steps of the house, and not they waiting for Katharina. As well, she took great pains not to interrupt at meal times, to be very quiet when others were speaking and to rise immediately when the meal was over to help Mutti and Marta clear away the dishes.

"KATHARINA IS GROWING up," Elisabeth remarked to Jacob one evening as they sat together after the children had been sent to bed.

"Why do you say that?"

"I don't know, really," Elisabeth responded, "it is just that she seems so changed. Have you not marked it?"

"What do you mean by changed?"

"She is so helpful. I mean, she goes out of her way to play with Margaret, Magdalene and Ursula. And she is very patient with Andreas, even when he is grumpy."

Jacob smiled.

"I should think that would make you very happy."

"It does, husband," Elisabeth smiled back at Jacob, "it does. But sometimes I miss the spontaneity that she still had but a year and a half ago. I think of how she blurted out whatever came to mind and how we often laughed at what she said?"

"I do remember," Jacob said, "but regardless, I am glad that she is becoming more mature. But I fully understand what you mean. You will be glad of her help, though, when this next baby comes, I think. With Elisabet engaged to be married shortly and with Barbara helping Elisabet prepare for her household, you are often short-handed. And our little Katharina will be twelve soon."

Elisabeth smiled.

"She has told me that," and she stopped, beginning to imitate Katharina's voice, "Although I do not disapprove of Bet's marrying, I will never marry myself."

"She has not!" Jacob responded, laughing out loud.

"Yes, indeed, she has. And she has vowed to be dedicated to a religious life of good works."

"She has never struck me as being impressed with cousins Ursula and Margred."

"Oh, I know," and again Elisabeth mimicked her daughter, "I am not drawn to be a beguin, Mutti, but I do think that marriage would keep me from thinking about holier things."

Jacob grinned.

"Well, just wait for the right man to come along, wife. As," and he grinned even more broadly, "he did for you."

Elisabeth blushed and then spoke.

"I think this next baby will be a boy, Jacob. And...."

"What?"

Jacob looked at his wife. Hands folded on the rounded belly, she appeared pale in the glow of the candles set on the sideboard and her eyes were half-closed. She was a beautiful woman and a good woman, and he had never regretted for one moment that he had married her.

"What?" he repeated, but softer.

She opened her eyes fully and sat up straight.

"Well, I have been thinking about a name. If it is a boy and I do think it might be and do not ask me why, I would like to call him Jacob again."

Her husband did not respond for a long time. Folding his long, tapered fingers over one another, he vividly recalled his first little Jacob—the child who had wanted to be a smithy's apprentice. He had not known. The boy had been so quiet, such a good boy and now, now he was gone. Moving his fingers, he suddenly yearned for the touch of wood, the feel of some solid object to carve into a thing of beauty.

"It is all right," he heard himself saying eventually, "If you so wish to call this child, if it is a boy, Jacob, that is all right."

"Katharina," Elisabeth responded, "may not like it. She doted on her brother. But perhaps this will make her forget."

"She will not forget."

There was quiet for a long while. Then Jacob spoke again.

"It is said that Julius II, our present pope," he spoke softly, almost as if to himself, "is the greatest patron of the arts of all the popes who have ever lived."

Elisabeth stirred in her chair. She had been almost asleep.

"He is friends with Michelangelo and Raphael...."

Jacob stopped. He contemplated the ceiling. He had heard tell of how the frescoes in the Sistine Chapel were masterpieces. And he had recently listened to a printer who had told him that the ceiling of the Chapel was to be painted by Michelangelo. Of course, he himself, even if he lived in Rome, would never be commissioned for any such grand project. He was not good enough. His fingers began to tingle, to itch to work, and he stretched them, impatient for the morning light in his workshop.

"This pope," Elisabeth, now awake, suddenly added to his thoughts, "needs more money for all his projects, so says Dr. Geiler, and I have heard that there has been a commissary appointed to Strasbourg and the surrounding area to get more money through the selling of indulgences."

"That could be," Jacob answered as he yawned widely, adding, "but I do not hold much with the sale of these indulgences."

"Dr. Geiler is not at all well," Elisabeth continued, "and he may not live much longer."

"I pray that he will live for a long time yet," her husband said, "for who knows what sort of priest we will get after him."

NOT AWARE OF her parents' conversation, Katharina was on her way to Frau Stoffler's the following afternoon, softly singing to herself as she walked along the cobbled streets. She often sang. Sometimes the songs were wordless and she just hummed and hummed; at other times she made up words and often the wondrous Virgin Mary appeared in her rhymes. After a few streets of soft singing, she stopped. Singing was good, but it did interfere with her thoughts. She was worried about Dr. Geiler von Kaysersberg for he had not been in good health lately. His legs were sore. She had heard Mutti say that the dropsy plagued him and that his legs were frightfully swollen. No wonder he was in pain. Perhaps if she stopped in to pray for him at the cathedral, this might give him some relief; or if she recited some extra 'hail Mary's'; and perhaps she could even begin a novena to Mary requesting her to pray to Jesus for Dr. Geiler. Mary's intercession, because she was the mother of God and the special saint of Strasbourg, would be so helpful. Her lips began to lisp softly.

"Please, Mary, mother of God. Intercede for me and ask Jesus to heal Dr. Geiler."

Automatically she continued.

"Hail Mary, full of grace. The Lord is with thee. Blessed art thou among women and blessed is the fruit of thy womb, Jesus. Holy Mary, mother of God, pray for us sinners, now and at the hour of our death. Amen."

Pausing in her litany, she pondered on the matter of stopping at the cathedral as she kicked a stone toward the side of the road. There was not really much time for stopping in at the church today. As well, Frau Stoffler was very particular about not being late. Besides that, it would not be a good thing to go somewhere else when she had told Mutti she was going directly to Frau Stoffler's house. And most importantly, she was working very hard on a pillow—a pillow with a beautiful floral design—a pillow which she hoped to give to Mutti when the next baby was born, and that day was not so far away. Her musings had carried her to the Stoffler house and her feet, energetic and youthful, climbed the stone steps. Rather guiltily she remembered the novena she had begun. She would pray more for Dr. Geiler tonight. Coming to the top of the steps, she reached for the knocker. But before she had a chance to use them, the door opened and Annalein Stoffler, a year older than herself, stood in front of her.

"Katharina, I saw you coming down the street through the window. Come in."

Katharina smiled and entered.

"Are you also doing tapestry today, Annalein? Are we to work together?"

"*Nein*, no, I am not. You see, Mutti is gone and there is to be no lesson. It is Dorothea's afternoon off so I was to stay and tell you."

"No lesson?"

"Yes, no lesson. That is because Mutti has gone to the cathedral today. There was a procession this morning—a procession going to the cathedral with the new Strasbourg commissioner who was appointed by the pope, leading it."

"A procession?"

"Yes, a beautiful procession. I saw it as I was running an errand for Mutti and had to pass by the cathedral. But I had to stand aside for there were so many people crowding about and everyone pushed everyone else so they might see the procession."

"What did you see?"

"Well," and Annalein grinned at Katharina, "I did push like everyone else, and I got a good spot right at the edge of the crowd. At the head of the procession I saw a great red cross carried by a monk—a rather fat monk with a hood thrown back over his shoulders. He had a very round face and piercing eyes. I could not look at his eyes for long. They seemed to burn. Also, someone close by the monk carried a velvet cushion and on this cushion there was a manuscript, I think."

"Yes," curiously Katharina prodded Annalein on, "and what did the monk want? Why was there a procession?"

"Well, behind him came several mules all laden with papers of sorts. I found out later, after I talked to Mutti, that these papers were pardons, to be given to those who could pay for them. They are called indulgences."

"Indulgences," Katharina repeated slowly, "I have heard tell of them. I think Vati has mentioned them and so has Lux."

"Well, that is why Mutti is not here. She has gone to buy one. For my father, you see, who has been dead quite a few years now. For it is said by the monk that such a pardon can purchase a soul out of purgatory and lead him straight into heaven."

"It can?" Katharina breathed softly and out of nowhere a pain appeared in her chest, "I think I had heard tell that indulgences were for the living."

"Yes," Annalein said, concurring solemnly, "they are for the living, but they can also help the dead. So it is said, anyway."

"How much do you have to pay for one?"

"I do not know, Katharina. But I would expect, from the size of the procession, because you see there were a lot of important people walking behind the mules, that buying one might cost a lot of money. There were many monks, priests and councilmen from Strasbourg in the procession, as well as singing women and children. They were holding flags."

Annalein paused for breath and then continued as an afterthought. "They were holding candles as well. The bells of the cathedral were tolling very loudly. Did you not hear them?"

"No...at least I cannot remember. But I would like to go to the cathedral," Katharina said with a catch in her voice, "I have no money with me though. I was thinking of Ja...."

She could not finish the name. Her hands felt empty. They held no money to pay for an indulgence. Her eyes filled with tears. Annalein eyed her sympathetically.

"Maybe I can loan you some money, Katharina. But only if you promise that you will give me the money back later."

"How much can you loan me?"

Katharina's voice was eager.

"A few guilders only. I have them in my room. Mutti will not mind, I think, if I do that."

Annalein turned and left Katharina standing in the hallway. Her heart was racing. If she could purchase a pardon for Jacob, how wonderful that would be! He could come out of purgatory and enter into the beautiful place Dr. Geiler had told her about. He would go to heaven and not suffer any longer. She could hardly breathe for thinking of it. Annalein came back.

"I have three guilders, Katharina."

"Three," she repeated, "Do you think that will be enough?"

"I don't know. But you can try. For whom do you want to buy a pardon, Katharina?"

"For Jacob. For my brother who died some time ago."

"Oh."

Annalein's face was kind.

"Perhaps three guilders will be enough. It seems to me that for a younger person, you should not have to pay as much as for an older one. Because it seems to me that a younger person would not have committed as many sins as an older person. Don't you think so?"

"I don't know."

Annalein pressed the coins into Katharina's hand.

"Here is the money. Are you going to the church now?"

"Yes, I suppose I am."

"Do you want me to come with you?"

"No, that's all right. I think I can manage."

"Well, if you're sure."

"Yes and *danke*, thank you, Annalein."

When the Stoffler door shut behind her, Katharina descended the steps and began to walk rapidly, almost breaking into a run, in the direction of the cathedral. She began to notice, after a while, that there were many others walking the streets as well and that they were all walking in the same direction—the direction of the cathedral. As she came nearer, her heart became heavier and her feet slowed down. For after all, she had but three guilders and very likely, such a pardon as would take a person out of purgatory would cost many guilders, or many crowns. She walked up the steps of the cathedral slowly, following some other folk into the great church. Immediately, upon entering the sanctuary, she saw the red cross which Annalein had mentioned. It was set up in front of the high altar, close to the pulpit. What appeared to be a strong, iron box, had been placed on a table next to it and a monk appeared to be standing guard behind that table. Another Dominican had mounted the pulpit, the beautiful pulpit that had been carved especially for Dr. Geiler by a great carver named Hammerer. The Dominican was speaking in a very loud voice, a hammer-voice. She shook her head at herself. Her thoughts wandered so easily and so strangely. But this Dominican's voice was not at all like their own Dr. Geiler's voice. As she took her place in one of the pews, the Dominican's loud voice echoed and rebounded through the sanctuary.

"What are you people of Strasbourg thinking about? Do you not fear your sins? Why don't you confess them to us, the vicars of the pope? Remember the example of Stephen and other saints who gladly gave up their lives and suffered horrible deaths for the salvation of their souls...."

Uncomfortable, Katharina glanced at the folk about her. Their eyes were all riveted on the round little monk. He surely had a voice like a bell, and he was ringing it hammer-hard.

"Others have given their bodies to be burned, but you people in Strasbourg delight in living well without any thought of hell. You are in a raging sea of storm and danger and you do not know if you will reach the harbour of salvation...."

Katharina shivered. She felt for the guilders in the pocket of her coat. Picking them up, they lay round and flat in the palm of her hand. Surely Jacob, her beloved brother, was burning in purgatory, longing for the harbuor of safety, the harbour of salvation. The voice of the monk hammered on.

"Do you not hear the voices of your wailing parents and others who say, 'Have mercy upon us, because we are in severe punishment and pain. From this you can redeem us with small alms and yet you do not want to do so....'"

Katharina could hear Jacob's voice calling out to her as the monk's voice pounded the rafters and ran down the aisle. In front of her she saw a woman sobbing and next to her a thin man gripping the wooden railing of the pew.

"Press in now, people of Strasbourg. Come and buy while the market lasts. Should that cross in front of me be taken down, the market will close. And mark well, heaven will close then also. And then you will knock and knock and you will bewail your folly in neglecting to avail yourselves of blessings which shall then have gone beyond your reach...."

Katharina could see herself knocking on Frau Stoffler's door that very first time she had gone to visit her. She remembered the slight feeling of panic when, after her initial knocking, no one had answered. She had knocked again. And after that, she had used both fists to bang on the door.

"This cross," the monk spoke vehemently, almost spitting in his earnestness, repeating, "this cross has as much power as the very cross of Christ. Come and I will give you pardons in the forms of letters, all properly sealed, by which the sins of yourself and your dead loved ones will be forgiven."

Katharina's hands were sweaty, and the coins in her hand slipped from her fingers sliding down, one after another, past the lining of her coat pocket. Her fingers, anxious to feel them, retrieved them, coaxing them back into her palm. Strange to think that inside her pocket lay remission of sins for Jacob—indeed, remission lay within her palm. It seemed to her, suddenly, that this was exceedingly strange. But she pushed the thought away. She pushed the thought into to the ground, pushed it under the pew in front of her, past the weeping woman who was sobbing uncontrollably now.

"*Wenn die Münze im Kästlein klingt, die Seele in den Himmel springt....* As soon as a coin in the coffer rings, the soul from purgatory springs. Go to the confessional stalls which have been put up against the walls of this cathedral. Confess and be shriven. Then come to the counter where I will take the sum you have gathered for the souls of your loved ones. You yourself will drop the money into the coffer."

Katharina stood up woodenly. She felt like a puppet whose strings were being pulled by the voice on the pulpit. She walked out into the aisle behind a rather corpulent man. His heavy breathing persistently interrupted the volume of the monk's continued words flowing around them. The man drumbled toward the confessionals and Katharina stayed in his shadow. Edging along the back of the sanctuary, they approached the booths. The man hesitated a moment, stopping abruptly, and Katharina almost bumped into him. Then he plodded on, making his way painfully and slowly in the direction of the third booth. It was empty. At least, peeping around the man's girth, Katharina could see no one lined up waiting to get in. What would her parents say if they could see her here? She did not know. Surely they would, given a chance, gladly pay for Jacob to leave purgatory and enter heaven. The man disappeared into the booth. She stood a few feet away, respectful of the privacy to which she felt he was entitled. When he reappeared a few moments later, pushing aside the curtains of the stall, he smiled at her before walking away in the direction of the counter. She smiled back a rather timid smile and hesitantly entered the booth herself. Later on she could not remember exactly what it was that she confessed, but did recall that she had wept openly and had begged that Jacob, her brother Jacob, might be taken from purgatory. The shrift was a short one with a small penance of ten Hail Mary's to be said that very day.

After Katharina exited the booth, she walked toward the front, toward the monk guarding the iron box. She waited in line behind several other folks until it was her turn to be addressed.

"What pardon do you need?"

The sentence was a recitation. She had heard the monk say it a number of times to those preceding her.

"I need to take my brother Jacob, Jacob Schütz, from...from purgatory."

Her voice was soft and her eyes somehow could not meet his.

"How much money do you have?" the monk's voice asked.

"Three guilders," she whispered back.

He scrutinized her sharply, running his eyes up and down her clothes, her face and the hand in her pocket.

"It is enough," he replied at length, but when she presented the sweaty guilders to him on her open palm, he shook his head.

"No," he spoke rather sharply, "don't you know that the hand which will give you the pardon, may not receive the money? Drop the money into the box yourself. After that I will give you the pardon."

She took a few steps toward the box, lifted her hand and gingerly dropped the coins into the slot. Then she retraced her steps to the monk. He had a scrolled letter ready and handed it to her.

"Thank you."

It was a customary politeness. But he did not appear to have heard her and was already speaking to the next one in line.

"What pardon do you need?"

She turned, holding the letter cautiously, afraid she might break it. Were these the very words of God himself then that she was carrying now? How passing strange! She walked quicker now. Down the centre aisle, past the pew where she had sat a while back, past a host of people who were also eager to save relatives, friends, children, husbands and wives.

Outside, the sun shone and the grass seemed greener than it had been when she had entered the cathedral. Now, this very moment, she should go home. But there was a vaguely troubled feeling within her that did not let up as she came closer and closer to her home. Questions churned about inside her. Was Jacob in heaven now—right now at this very minute? Had he just arrived there? Was someone attending to his wounds from purgatory? Was it really true what the monk had said? What did the letter say? Should she let Mutti and Vati read it?

"Kathe, oh, Kathe!"

It was Margaret running toward her as fast as she could.

"What is the matter, Margaret. You're all out of breath. Slow down."

"Oh, Kathe," the child sobbed, "It's Mutti. The new baby came. But he's sick. Frau Bauer has come to help, but she sent me to fetch you. So I came to meet you coming from your lesson."

"It's all right, Margaret."

Katharina bent down and put her arms around her younger sister.

"Where are the little ones?"

"In the kitchen with Marta."

"It will be alright, Margaret. I'm here now."

"Yes," the little girl sobbed, "I know. And Barbara and Elisabet were gone away on a visit. So I'm so glad you're here."

Taking Margaret's hand, Katharina stood up again. The letter in her hand had been crumpled by the weight of the child leaning against her. She loosed her hold on the child and smoothed the paper carefully. Margaret looked on with interest.

"What is that, Kathe?"

"It is," Katharina began and then stopped before she went on, "I suppose it is a letter."

"Who is the letter from?"

"From...from God," she slowly answered her sister.

"From God?"

Margaret's voice, still quavering with tears, was incredulous.

"How did you get it?" she demanded next and then added, "I thought that God only wrote in the Bible. That is what Vati has said."

Katharina nodded. It was true. That was exactly what Vati had told them on several occasions. But Dr. Geiler did not encourage personal Bible reading very much—not by the common people in the church, that is. This was, as he himself had told her, because ordinary people without any learning might read the Bible in the wrong way. Therefore, they should be guided in Bible reading by monks. But the monks with whom the Schütz family was acquainted, were not always living in the manner in which Mutti and Vati said you should live and a number of them could not read. And Mutti and Vati always said that the manner in which you should live was according to the rules taught in the Bible. This was another strange thing, that the monks....

"So how did you get it?" Margaret repeated, interruping Katharina's thoughts and taking hold of Katharina's hand, the one not holding the letter.

"Well, from a monk at the cathedral," Katharina spoke haltingly.

She was herself actually growing bewildered by the letter she held in her other hand, by the fact that this letter spoke for God, for was not that what the speaker in Dr. Geiler's pulpit had said?

"Is it a holy letter then, Kathe?"

"I will ask Vati," Katharina answered.

Then they were home and Margaret stopped asking questions because she suddenly remembered that Mutti had given birth to another baby and that the baby was sickly.

Chapter XII

Katharina loved the baby the moment she first laid eyes on the wee bundle in the cradle. It was so tiny. She did not recall Andreas, or Annder as he was called by the family, being so tiny. But she did deem it troubling that the shrivelled, old-mannish-looking face peeking out from between the swaddling clothes, was very pale, almost bluish, in colour.

"Well?" Mutti questioned from the big bed, looking from Katharina to the cradle, "What think you, daughter? Will he do?"

"Oh, yes!" she fervently answered, "he will."

"I'm glad to hear it," Mutti spoke very quietly, "for I don't think I can give him back."

Katharina smiled and was about to reply when she saw that Mutti's eyes had closed. She must be very tired. Kneeling down next to the cradle, she stroked the baby's cheek. It was so soft, so beautifully soft. An almost imperceptible knock at the door made her look up. It opened just a bit and Frau Bauer's head peered in.

"Ah," she said softly, stepping into the room, "you have met small Jacob."

"Jacob?" Katharina said, louder than she meant to and again, "Jacob? Is he to be named Jacob?"

"Yes, did not your mother say?"

"No, she did not."

Inadvertently Katharina turned her face back toward the bed. Her mother's eyes were open now, and they were regarding her with a mixture of something akin to love and sympathy.

"Do you mind, little Kathe," she murmured, "that the name of this little one will be the same as that of the dear Jacob that we lost?"

Katharina did not reply. Her hand, still on the baby's cheek, continued stroking.

"It is also your father's name," her mother went on, "and I do believe, he would like to have someone carry that name on."

Closing the door behind her, Frau Bauer came toward the bed.

"I think you should try and feed little Jacob," she said to Mutti, "The more he eats, the more he stands to have a chance at life."

Reaching over, she helped Mutti sit up, plumping pillows behind her back. Then she walked over to the cradle, brushing past Katharina. Very gently and very tenderly, she picked up the small bundle that was the new Jacob. Frau Bauer had no children—none at all. Katharina reflected briefly on this as she saw the neighbour sweetly shelter the baby. She realized that Frau Bauer was, after all, a good neighbour and a kind one. Carefully she lay the baby into Mutti's waiting arms. Little Jacob, small and bluish though he was, lost no time in finding the nipple and suckling noisily.

Katharina and Frau Bauer both laughed.

"Katharina," Mutti spoke softly, "will you go down and tell the others that they have a little brother named Jacob?"

"Yes, Mutti."

LATER THAT EVENING, when the younger children were in bed and Elisabet, Barbara and Katharina were sitting in the great room with their father, Katharina took out the letter from between the folds of her skirt. Lux was away at school.

"What have you there, child?"

"A letter, Vati."

"Who is it from?"

"Well," she responded hesitantly, "it was given me...that is to say," she corrected herself, "I bought it from a priest at the cathedral today."

"You bought a letter?"

Jacob Schütz sat up in his chair and regarded his daughter curiously even as he began to fire off a series of questions.

"What were you doing at the cathedral? Were you not to go to Frau Stoffler's this afternoon for your lesson in...."

He did not get to finish his sentence. Yet it was not Katharina who interrupted him but Elisabet.

"There was a procession, father. Barbara and I saw it. It was very impressive and...."

"Elisabet," her father said, "I know it is true that you are going to be married to Michael Schwencker sometime in the near future and that you will live in your own home and be mistress of that home. But I do not want you to interrupt me here in my home. Now, Katharina, tell me in your own words what you were doing at the cathedral."

"Well," she began slowly, "when I arrived at Frau Stoffler's, she was not home, and Annalein told me that she had gone to the cathedral because pardons for sins, that is, indulgences, were going to be sold there. So I thought that I would go to the cathedral as well. I thought that it would be a fine thing to purchase a pardon for our Jacob—for the Jacob that died, not the new little...."

Here she stopped because her throat filled with tears, and she knew that if she would keep on speaking she would weep in front of them all.

"I see," Vati said and again, "I see."

Katharina fingered the parchment and then got up from her chair and gave it to her father.

"Could you," she asked, "could you read it?"

Vati nodded and unrolled the small white scroll. Katharina returned to her seat in between Barbara and Elisabet, who both took hold of one of her hands as soon as she sat down. The three of them watched their father as he scrutinized the writing in front of him.

"Will you not read it out loud for us?" Elisabet said at length.

"Yes, I think I will."

Vati nodded as he spoke. His clear, strong tenor voice filled the room.

May our Lord Jesus Christ have pity on thee, Jacob Schütz and absolve thee by the merits of his most holy passion. And

I, by virtue of the apostolic power which has been confided to me, do absolve thee from all ecclesiastical censures, judgements and penalties which thou mayest have merited and from all excesses, sins and crimes which thou mayest have committed, however great or enormous they may be and for whatsoever cause, even though they had been reserved to our most Holy Father the Pope and the Apostolic See.

Jacob Schütz stopped for a breath and regarded his daughters sitting in front of him, all ears, all leaning forward not to miss a word. He sighed and then continued.

I efface all attainders of unfitness and all marks of infamy thou mayest have drawn on thee on this occasion; I remit the punishment thou shouldest endure in purgatory....

Here Katharina let loose such a big sigh, that her father stopped again.

"Have you been in such agony, child," he asked kindly, "that you must needs have bought this piece of paper from a priest about whom we know nothing?"

"Oh, yes, yes," Katharina threw out, "for I do...or rather, did, so worry about Jacob's suffering."

Her father frowned.

"And now you will not worry anymore?"

She shook her head, but inside her heart she was not at all sure. For there lay a piece of paper and only a crumpled piece of paper it was indeed, in the hand of her father. Such a piece onto which her father might press the dabber. And whatever father had carved would leave its imprint. So perhaps whatever the priest, or the pope, had written on that paper would leave its imprint onto something in eternity. But then again, perhaps it wouldn't. The truth was that she did not want to think any further. It just was not possible that the words written on the paper were not true. It just could not be. Her father picked up the scroll again and continued his reading.

I reinstate thee in the innocence and purity in which thou wast at the hour of thy baptism so that the gate through which is the entrance to the place of torments and punishments shall be closed against thee and that gate which leads to the Paradise of joy shall be open. In the name of the Father, of the Son and of the Holy Ghost. Amen.
Brother John Tetzel, Commissioner.

It was quiet in the room. Katharina could hear her heart beating against her smock. Barbara squeezed Katharina's hand hard.

"I know you bought the letter to help Jacob," she whispered softly.

"What did you pay, child and where did you get the money?" her father asked.

"I borrowed the money from Annalein when I came to Frau Stoffler's house," Katharina answered meekly.

"How much money did you borrow?"

"Three guilders."

Barbara squeezed Katharina's hand again.

"I see," her father said.

He stroked the parchment on his lap. Then he sighed.

"I have heard of this Tetzel, whose name, according to some of the more learned persons of this city, is Diezel, not Tetzel. He was, some time ago, a Dominican monk, born the son of a goldsmith in Leipzig. It is said that Diezel was an inquisitor—that he interrogated people to see if they were true Catholics. He did not have a good reputation. Then he was convicted of a shameful crime. I don't know what the crime was, but it occurred in the city of Innsbruck, and he was sentenced to be put into a sack and drowned."

The girls gaped at him and he went on.

"I am not sure, but someone or some people in the church, interceded for him and he was reprieved. And now he is a commissioner for the church, so it seems, and is selling these indulgences."

Katharina said nothing. She alternately gazed from the floor to her father. Was he going to punish her for having bought this letter from someone who was probably not to be trusted?

"I do believe," her father said at length, "that you purchased this indulgence with the sincere motive of helping your brother."

She nodded fervently.

"The truth of whether or not the indulgence has the virtues you were told," he soberly stated, "is dubious. I will tell you a story," he went on to say, "one that will make you think."

Everyone nodded, for they all usually loved Vati's tales.

"A Saxon gentleman," he began, "was shocked by Tetzel's indulgences and went to him to ask him if it was true that he was authorized to pardon sins which were about to be committed, as well as sins that had already been committed. Tetzel replied that he had full power to do so. The gentleman consequently told Tetzel that he wanted to take a small revenge on one of his enemies, without actually killing the man. Could he purchase an indulgence that would render his action harmless? Tetzel, smelling money, I think, told him that he could certainly buy an indulgence for this. They settled, I am told, on thirty crowns. The gentleman, after having secured this indulgence in his pocket, set out to follow Tetzel, beat him thoroughly with the help of some of his servants and robbed him of the chest of money that he was carrying. Tetzel, when he recovered, brought an action against him in court. But the gentleman was able to show the judge the letter of indulgence, signed by Tetzel himself, which exempted him from all responsibility. He was, therefore, acquitted."

Vati stopped and gazed at the daughters sitting wide-eyed before him. Katharina had been much impressed with his narrative, he could tell. He half-smiled at her.

"As I said before, Katharina, I believe you purchased the indulgence with good intentions. I will allow you to earn the three guilders you borrowed by sweeping my workshop every day for the next three weeks, so that you can pay Annalein back."

She nodded again.

"And," he was smiling now, "let us not tell your mother any of these things. It would perhaps spoil her joy in the birth of this new little baby."

And all three vigorously chorused, "No, we will not, Vati."

LATER ON, UNDER the soft covers of the bed, as she snuggled next to Margaret's curled up body, Katharina reflected on the afternoon. Her thoughts took her back to the cathedral.

"Come in now," the Dominican had shouted from the pulpit, "Come and buy while you can. Never before has the door of Paradise been open so wide. Should this red cross be taken down, you will no longer be able to buy."

She, Katharina Schütz, had bought an indulgence from the Dominican and his helpers. Even if the indulgence paper did not work, would it have been right to take a chance? Just in case?

Chapter XIII

Katharina had been confirmed and had become a member of the Roman Catholic Church at the great cathedral when she was ten years old. She had very much wanted to be confirmed when she was nine. There had been a tremendous longing within her to truly belong to God, and she deemed that confirmation would satisfy that longing. Vati and Mutti, however, had thought that being nine years old was just a trifle early. When she was confirmed a year later at age ten, Tante Maria and Uncle Peter had stood as godmother and godfather, even as they had stood as godparents at her baptism. Dr. Geiler, the officiating priest, had worn red vestments. The red, she was told, symbolized the glowing tongues of fire seen hovering over the heads of the apostles at Pentecost.

Even though it was several years ago and she was at this moment sitting on the edge of her bed, Katharina remembered the confirmation ceremony vividly. She knew she would never forget kneeling in front of Dr. Geiler in the sanctuary of the cathedral. At the moment of confirmation, he had laid his hand on her shoulder.

"Katharina."

Even though he had only murmured her name, it had seemed to her at that moment, that the very voice of God had called out to her and she had quivered inside—quivered with both fear and awe. Dr. Geiler had then dabbed chrism oil on her forehead. The oil was very smooth. A few rivulets ran just a little down her face but she had not minded.

"Be sealed with the Holy Spirit."

"Amen," Katharina had replied.

"Peace be with you."

"And with your spirit," she had again responded before standing up.

Tante Maria and Uncle Peter had kindly given her, as a confirmation gift, her very own string of coral beads, her very own rosary. It held fifty coral beads. Katharina had been ecstatic with joy. Later, in the privacy of the girls' bedroom, she had counted the beads very carefully, slowly caressing the large carnelian hanging as pendant just below the cross. Truthfully, the rosary had become Katharina's most prized possession. Besides the coral beads, the string was ornamented with two unusual and valuable decorations, decorations for which both Barbara and Elisabet envied her. Halfway along the string of beads was a *krotten stein* and the *krotten stein* had an elk's hoof dangling next to it. The *krotten stein* was a special stone—a stone believed to have been produced by a toad—a stone endowed with special properties, although no one was able to define exactly what these properties might be. There was no doubt, though, that it was special to have such a stone. Very few people possessed one. The elk's hoof was also very valuable. Everyone said so and Katharina believed it. Silky soft, she often fingered the beautiful fur on the hoof during mass.

Shifting her position on the bed, she thought of Mass and all the chanting and singing during that time. She did not know all the 150 Psalms by heart, and this sometimes made her feel guilty during church attendance. She did so very much want to be holy and good, a desire, it seemed, that after Jacob's death had become more important to her. Reciting the seven penitential Psalms which she did have memorized, made her feel proud. But when a person felt pride, there was reason to be on guard. Pride was, after all, a sin. She sighed. Life was difficult and it was well-nigh impossible to be good all the time.

Sometimes, sitting in the pew during Mass and fingering the beads, she began praying the *Vater Unser*, the Lord's Prayer. Her small fingers carefully touched and counted out the smooth beads, even as they counted and touched them now as she was sitting on the bed, moving ahead one bead for each time she prayed. It was difficult to always pay attention during Mass. The people around her were usually taller than she was, blocking out the view at the front. It was quite difficult to see the priest standing by the altar and it was hard to understand what he was doing. The Latin words he chanted danced around her like a familiar song, but she could not comprehend a great many of the words. She heard people around her murmuring, repeating the words. At times, wanting badly to be part of the chanting, she would whisper the Ave Maria to herself. Very softly, she would whisper it. She whispered it now, dangling her feet over the edge of the bed.

Ave Maria, gratia plena,
Dominus tecum
Benedicta tu in mulieribus,
   et benedictus fructus ventris tui, Jesus
Sancta Maria, Mater Dei
   ora pro nobis peccatoribus,
   nunc, et in hora mortis nostrae.
Amen

In church she often bent her lithe body sideways to peer around those in front of her. That is to say, she bent it only if she was not caught by her sisters and pulled back. Sometimes she glimpsed the priest bowing and kissing the altar. This fascinated her. Then she would hear him say some special words and a little bell would ring. She knew that at the precise moment in which the bell rang, the consecrated host at the front of the church changed into Christ's body. What had only been a piece of bread a moment before, was now God. Wondering greatly, she would fall to her knees alongside everyone else in the great church and she would worship. The priest then ate and drank, while everyone else waited. And within her heart, Katharina would, while fingering her precious beads, at such times say another prayer—the *Gloria Patri*. Her lips moved even now as her feet dangled over the edge of the bed. She did love praying and she hoped dearly that God heard her words.

Gloria Patri
  et Filii
  et Spiritui Sancto.
Sicut erat in principio
  et nunc et semper
  et in saecula saeculorum. Amen

THE NEW LITTLE Jacob was baptized at the cathedral in the same way that Katharina had been baptized. But the baptism had not happened until he was a few months old. This was because both Mutti and baby Jacob had not been feeling well. And it had not been Dr. Geiler who had performed the baptism but another priest. There was talk that Dr. Geiler, who continued ailing and who was feeling more poorly each day, would not live much longer. But Katharina faithfully prayed a novena for him every day and continued to pray for him now. She felt quite sure that her prayers would be heard even in her bedroom. Indeed, she felt it must be God's will that Dr. Geiler be healed, for he had been such a help to her and to so many others, and she loved him. But then Jacob had been a help to her too and she had surely loved him— and Jacob had died. Her thoughts stopped here and she began to doubt—doubt in the efficacy of her prayers and her works and... and then she remembered that Dr. Geiler had encouraged her for this very reason to be confirmed into the church.

"Your confirmation into the church," Dr. Geiler had told her when she had confided her worries to him about not being good enough to belong to the church, "builds on the foundation which was begun in your baptism when you were a baby. You don't remember that, do you Katharina? You don't remember, I am sure, being baptized?

She had shaken her head. No, she did not remember. Who could remember being a baby and being carried in the arms of one's mother?

"The Holy Spirit," Dr. Geiler went on, "was first introduced to you at that time, child. When you were a babe held up for baptism."

Sometimes visitors came to the house to see father. Very occasionally, if Katharina happened to be in the shop when they came, father would introduce her to them.

"This is my daughter, Katharina," he would say and often he would smile when he said it, as if to add, "I am very proud of her and I love her."

Katharina smiled at the remembrance of her father's introductions even as she remembered what else Dr. Geiler had said.

"Well, during confirmation, Katharina, God the Holy Spirit will truly come upon you, accompanied by God the Father and God the Son. This is what happened to the apostles and other believers at Pentecost. Confirmation completes the process of your initiation into the Catholic community, and it will mature you for the work in that community that lies in the years ahead of you, Katharina."

Her eyes wide, Katharina had listened to the old man speak, only comprehending part of which he said.

"But I am not such a good person, Dr. Geiler," she had whispered, "So how can I work in the community?"

"That is why it is good to be confirmed, child," he had answered, "You know what the twelve fruits of the Holy Spirit are, do you not?"

"Yes, they are charity, joy, peace, patience, kindness, goodness, generosity, gentleness, faithfulness, modesty, self-control and chastity."

He had raised his eyebrows at her in a comical way as she rattled them off, non-stop.

"That is good, child. And can you also tell me what the seven gifts of the Holy Spirit are?

"Yes," she had murmured, answering quickly as well, "they are wisdom, understanding, counsel, fortitude, knowledge, piety and fear of the Lord."

Dr. Geiler put his hand on her shoulder.

"Excellent," he had said. "Well done. Just remember that these gifts are supernatural graces given to the soul. At your confirmation, Katharina, you will be equipped with these fruits and gifts so that you can be a beautiful and useful member of the community."

"Truly, Dr. Geiler?"

"Truly, child."

Such a yearning arose in Katharina now, as she sat on the edge of her bed, such a yearning as she had never known before. It was a great desire to be holy, to be true and to do what was right. Confirmation was supposed to have helped her. Dr. Geiler had told her so, and he would not tell an untruth. And indeed, she did sometimes feel that confirmation had helped her. These were the times when she was happy and busy bringing soup to someone in need, soup that Marta had helped her make; or when she was cheerfully helping Mutti with the little ones; or when she unstintingly gave alms to a poor beggar on the street. Surely, Katharina thought, these were good works, and maybe because of these good works, God would now allow her prayers for Dr. Geiler to be heard. Dr. Geiler was such a godly man. She needed him. He was so good, and he always seemed to know the answers to her questions. But these last weeks she had waited in vain for him after Mass. He was not there.

She knew how to pray the rosary properly now. She had not known the way of it in the beginning when she had first received the beads from Tante Maria and Uncle Peter. But she did know now. To pray properly, you always began at the crucifix and you began by saying the Apostles' Creed. She fingered the crucifix thoughtfully. On the following bead, *Vater Unser* was recited. Her fingers moved up. On the next three beads, three *Aves* were prayed. Then the *Gloria Patri* ... and so it went on.

"KATHARINA. KATHARINA."

The door to the girls' bedroom was shut. The quiet helped Katharina think.

"Katharina!"

It was Mutti. Katharina got up and walked toward the door. Just as she was about to reach for the handle, her mother opened the door.

"Katharina, child, I've been looking for you. I need you in the kitchen."

"Yes, Mutti."

"Cousin Margred just came by to tell us that cousin Ursula is ill. I've begun to make some broth and as soon as it's ready, you are to take it over to Gotteshaus zum Wolf for me."

"Yes, Mutti."

Katharina followed her mother down the stairs.

"What is the matter with cousin Ursula?"

"I'm not quite sure. But cousin Margred was quite upset."

Marta was in the kitchen with Annder sitting on her lap. The little boy was playing with some spoons and looked up to smile at his sister. Mutti walked over to the fireplace.

"We've boiled a pot of water and have added five beaten egg yolks with some white wine. A little salt has already been added and Marta has stirred it well. Remember that we made this remedy for Frau Vugler last month? I want you to keep a watch on it now and when it is well boiled together, take it off the fire. Then pour some of the broth into a container and take it to cousin Ursula."

"Yes, Mutti."

Katharina took her place by the fire.

"Kathe! Kathe!"

She turned to see that Annder, deposited onto the floor by Marta, was crawling out from under the table toward her. He was a lovely toddler—round and chubby of cheek, dimpling when he smiled and of an agreeable temper. She reached down to pick him up. Mutti had left the kitchen.

"Better be careful not to let the broth burn, Kathe," Marta warned.

Diligently Katharina turned again, dandling Annder on her hip, stirring the broth religiously so that it would not stick to the bottom of the pot. Marta began sweeping the kitchen floor, singing as she did so, and it came to Katharina that Marta was a good girl, much better than herself. She was always cheerful and agreeable. Now how was it that Marta was a servant and she, Katharina was not? How was it that God had made her, Katharina, to be born into the Schütz household? She shook her head at herself—what strange thoughts! Annder poked her ear.

"Kathe!"

Laughing at him, she kissed his soft, round cheek.

"Yes, Annder, my lovely boy, I see you. But Kathe has to stir the broth for cousin Ursula."

"La, la, la," the child cooed and she laughed again.

"Indeed, la, la, la," she said, "and soon I shall have to go and see cousin Ursula la la."

The broth was thickening, and she put Annder down in a far corner of the kitchen before taking the pot, which hung over the fire, off its chain.

"I think it's ready, Marta. Will you help me pour it out into a little pail for cousin Ursula?"

Marta obliged and within ten minutes Katharina was on her way to Gotteshaus zum Wolf.

Chapter XIV

Sister Isabella, the resident doorkeeper at Gotteshaus zum Wolf, opened the door to the main entrance of the beguinage. Katharina had been standing in the courtyard, a courtyard surrounded by several small buildings. The courtyard and the beguinage itself were secluded from Strasbourg proper by a stone gate, a gate which was rarely locked in the daytime. If it had been locked, Katharina would also have had to ring the bronze bell that hung by the gate entrance. As it was, she did not have to wait in the wet March wind which almost took her breath away, her numb hand clinging to the little pail that she carried. Now, she simply had to lift the knocker and let it fall. The door opened almost immediately.

"You're here to see Sister Ursula."

Knowing Katharina to be Ursula's niece, Sister Isabella made her sentence a statement rather than a question.

"Yes, how is she?"

Sister Isabella shook her head doubtfully and then beckoned Katharina to enter.

"Not good, I think. Not good at all. As a matter of fact, I do believe the meisterin has deemed it necessary to send for a priest."

"A priest?"

Katharina was taken aback. She had not expected cousin Ursula to be really sick. After all, she more often than not pretended some sort of ailment simply for attention.

"Yes, a priest."

"Has cousin Margred gone to fetch one?"

"No, the meisterin offered to go."

"Oh," Katharina answered.

They were walking down the hollow-sounding, stone corridor toward the room where the two cousins lived. There were some sixty-five women who lived in the complex of buildings and rooms of the beguinage. The door to cousin Ursula's and cousin Margred's room was half-open. Sister Isabella turned, nodded her head at Katharina and walked back to her post. Nervously, Katharina took a deep breath before she entered.

There was a foul odour present in the room. Although it had been lurking faintly in the corridor, Katharina was hardly prepared for the stench that flew into her nostrils upon stepping into the chamber. Cousin Margred was seated before the double bed in the right hand corner of the room but she rose when she saw Katharina.

"Ah, Katharina," she murmured, as she padded over, the small plump form pathetically forlorn, "how good of you to come."

Katharina nodded. She was quite ill at ease. Her eyes were transfixed on the bed. Cousin Ursula lay quiet. Her mouth was half-open and her large hands twitched on the bedspread.

"Has there been," Katharina began haltingly, "a physician?"

"Indeed," cousin Margred answered, "and Ursula has been bled with the leeches twice. But it has not...it has not helped, as you can see."

Cousin Margred had come to stand next to Katharina. Katharina deposited the pail with the broth onto the small wooden table set in front of the right wall.

"Here is some broth Mutti has made. Perhaps it will ease the... ease the.... What actually is it, cousin Margred, that ails cousin Ursula?"

"Indeed, I do not know what ails Ursula except that she has the dysentery and has not much strength left. But I do thank you and your mother for the broth."

They spoke in whispers. Ursula made a slight moaning noise and Margred quickly padded back to her place in front of the bed.

Katharina followed. She knew not what else to do. Inadvertently her right hand brought up the sleeve of her gown to cover her nose. The smell was that bad.

"Has the priest come?"

Cousin Ursula pushed out the words, and they were but just audible. Margred shook her head.

"No, dear sister, he is not yet here."

"When he comes, make sure that you give him...."

Although cousin Ursula's voice was hoarse and weak, her eyes unexpectedly opened wide. They stared at Margred with a sharp look, a compelling look and a look which made Katharina uncomfortable.

"I'll..." Margred faltered, glancing over her shoulder at Katharina, "I'll make sure when the time comes that prayers are said on your behalf, Ursula. Rest assured."

Cousin Ursula's hands, fidgety and restless on the coverlet, suddenly shot out and grasped her sister's hands. Katharina could see cousin Margred wince at the force.

"You must promise me...you must swear...on your soul...about the money."

The words were almost hissed, and Katharina took a step backward. What was it cousin Margred had to promise? There was a noise behind her and she turned to see the meisterin, followed by a priest, enter the room. At that very moment she was transported back to the day that Jacob had died for she knew with a great certainty that this was the very same priest who had come to Johanngasse that day. She was sure of it. His face was just as smooth and greedy as it had been at that time. Instinctively, she now took a step to the side, out of his path.

"*Pax huic domui*"—"Peace to this house."

Katharina was relieved to see that the man took no trouble to notice her. His eyes were solely fixed on cousin Ursula, and he concentrated on nothing else.

"*Et omnibus habitantibus in ea.*"—"And all who dwell in it."

The priest chanted as he approached the bed. The meisterin smiled at both cousin Margred and Katharina, before nodding her head and mouthing, "If you need me, just send Sister Isabella."

Katharina curtsied politely in response, as did cousin Margred. The priest paid no attention but dug his pudgy hands into the burse hanging from a cord around his neck. Taking out the pyx, the communion container, he placed it on the table, right next to Katharina's little pail of broth. After he had genuflected to the pyx, he took another container out of his cassock. It held water, holy water, and he began sprinkling it around the room before returning to the bedside. Neither cousin Margred nor cousin Ursula spoke. The eyes of both were on the priest and on every movement he made.

As the priest planted himself at the sick woman's bedside, he took one of cousin Ursula's hands. At the same time, he began to speak, introducing himself.

"Sister Ursula, I think you will remember that I am Father Balthazar Horst, the priest confessor of the beguinage. I have come to administer extreme unction to you in your hour of need. Do you want to confess, daughter?"

His words rolled out smoothly, but rapidly, as if he were in a hurry to administer the sacrament. Katharina stood very still. She had not moved since the meisterin had left. Margred seemingly faded into the background, taking a few silent steps away from the bed. She also stood very quietly. Cousin Ursula's eyes remained wide open. Her breathing was very laboured. The coverlet on the bed moved up and down, up and down. But her focus was not on the priest. Her focus was still on her sister.

"Margred."

The voice was subdued but gritty.

"Margred."

It was almost an order for her sister to come back to the bedside. But it was crystal clear to Katharina that cousin Margred was loath to retrace her steps and stand directly in front of her sister. In a rush of compassion, she moved forward and stood beside her, taking cousin Margred's right hand in her left hand.

"It's all right," she whispered, "It's all right, cousin Margred, you can stay here. Just let the priest administer the rites to your sister."

Margred nodded, relieved that she was not alone. But still cousin Ursula's voice would not rest.

"The money," she rasped, "the money...Margred, give him the money for the...."

At the mention of money, the priest twisted his enormous neck to look at Margred, his jowls a quivering mass of greed.

"You must not deny your dying sister," he admonished and turning his gaze back on Ursula's form, went on, "in the hour of her need. And where is the money you are asking for, dear woman? Can I help?"

"In the wall...."

It was all cousin Ursula could manage before closing her eyes once more.

"In the wall?" puzzled the priest, turning back to Margred, before repeating, "In the wall?"

Cousin Margred now grasped Katharina's hand hard even as she answered the priest.

"She is addled with the fever, brother priest, please give her the last rites, even as the meisterin asked you."

Katharina squeezed cousin Margred's hand back reassuringly, hoping that her cousin would understand that the squeeze meant to say, 'You have spoken well to this money-hungry fellow.'

The priest's eyes turned to slits before he gave his concentration back to cousin Ursula, his lips pursing disapproval.

"Do you want to confess to me, daughter?"

Cousin Ursula, however, now seemed beyond speaking. There remained only the hard, laboured breathing. The priest stared at her for several moments, moments which lapsed into minutes, but she neither opened her eyes nor spoke again.

"Since you say she is addled with the fever, it would be wrong of me to put the host on her lips. I do not know if she would be able to swallow."

He skilfully maneuvered sideways, so that his back was not to the host. It was a sin, Katharina knew, to turn one's back on the host. He malevolently glared at Margred once more, before he continued speaking.

"It is an evil thing to withhold money from a dying woman who wishes, no doubt, to pay the church to say prayers for her. Surely you know that anyone who commits such a wicked sin, for wicked sin it is, will have to pay a severe penance."

Katharina could feel cousin Margred shiver violently next to her. But she replied not a word to the priest.

"Very well, then," the priest continued, surveying both women with one more damning glance before he turned back to cousin Ursula, "but note that I have warned you."

Reaching into his cassock, he took out a vial containing some liquid. Katharina knew the liquid was *oleum infirmorum*—a specially mixed oil which had been blessed by the bishop for those who needed supernatural assistance in dying. Frau Bauer had been anointed with such oil a number of times, and this was permissible. Father Geiler had told her that if it appeared as if one was dying, the oil should be administered. Frau Bauer had almost died during childbirth several times. Mutti had not. Katharina's right hand instinctively felt for the rosary in her skirt pocket. She fingered the elk's foot. How soft it was! Balthazar Horst...what a harsh sounding name. She watched him, even as her right hand held the rosary and her left kept holding on to cousin Margred's hand.

The liquid in the vial was thick, very thick and poured slowly onto the priest's thumb as he held the tube sideways. Leaning over, he put his bedaubed thumb onto cousin Ursula's forehead, tracing the sign of the cross.

"Through this holy anointing may the Lord in his love and mercy help You with the grace of the Holy Spirit."

The viscous oil slowly dribbled down cousin Ursula's face and Katharina had an inordinate desire to go and wipe it away for her. Surely it teased and offended the skin. But no, she had to remember that it was a holy oil, an oil blessed by the bishop himself, so it probably should not be wiped away. The priest let some more oil fall onto his thumb and anointed cousin Ursula's palms.

"May the Lord who frees you from your sins, save you and raise you up."

Now cousin Ursula's sins were absolved. Katharina heaved a slow, deep sigh. Cousin Ursula, miserable as she looked, was to be envied somehow, even as she helplessly lay there in the bed, her eyes closed, having difficulty breathing. The priest was finished. He carefully put the vial back into his cassock and then walked toward the table. After genuflecting to it, he lifted the pyx back into the burse around his neck. Then he once more tried to persuade the two women of his good will.

"Perhaps we ought to have a little talk," he began.

"No," Katharina heard herself saying, "that is not necessary. Cousin Ursula has been absolved and now her sister would like to stay at her bedside to comfort her as well as she can. It is a private time and...later we can...we can always call on Dr. Geiler."

She stopped. Who was she to talk? What would cousin Margred think of her?

"My cousin is right."

The words were soft but they were firm and they continued.

"I thank you for coming. But you have done that which was asked of you by the meisterin. No more is necessary for the present."

Balthazar Horst ran his eyes along the wall opposite the bed. Was that where the money was? It almost appeared, Katharina thought, as if the priest's eyes were fingers, groping along the cracks and fissures of the wall to see if there was an opening—an opening behind which he might find a treasure.

Cousin Margred let go of Katharina's hand and moved toward the door. She made the slightest motion of a curtsy as the priest made his way toward her, her face down. But when he reached cousin Margred, Balthazar Horst stopped, forcing the small woman to look up at him.

"I think it my duty to tell you, sad as I am to be the bearer of this news, that Dr. Geiler died early this morning."

And then he was gone. For a moment they listened to his footsteps retreating down the hall before cousin Margred closed the door. Weakly she made her way over to the table and sat down on one of the wooden chairs. Out of the corner of her eye, Katharina saw that cousin Ursula's chest still heaved up and down, up and down. Shaken with the news about Dr. Geiler, she walked over to the table as well and sat down on the other chair. Cousin Margred seemed not to have taken in the information that had just been passed on to them about their bishop. For sighing heavily, she began to speak of something else, of something totally different.

"Our father," cousin Margred began, "Ursula's father and mine, gave a dowry to this beguinage when we were admitted many years ago. It was to ensure that we would have a good, if rather plain life, when he was gone."

Katharina stared at her. In spite of the heaviness in her chest about Dr. Geiler's death, cousin Margred startled her. Not one for talk, she was generally quiet and had never, to Katharina's knowledge, passed along much information.

"He also gave both of us some money...money for private use. Just in case," she swallowed nervously, casting a quick look at the bed where her sister was lying, "there might be an emergency. Or in case we might change our mind and... and...."

She stopped.

"And?" Katharina encouraged, leaning her chin on her elbows, trying to pull words out of cousin Margred's lips.

"And get married," cousin Margred concluded, a blush beginning on her round cheeks.

"Get married?"

Repeating the words was all Katharina could manage.

"Ursula wanted, that is to say, now wants, my share of the money father gave me. She wants to use it to have prayers said for her. She says that this is what father would have wanted me to do."

"And what do you want to do?"

Katharina was intensely curious.

"I," cousin Margred began, her blush deepening, "I....Well, you see, there is a man...."

"A man?"

"Yes, a printer. I met him quite by chance at the market a few months ago. His housekeeper was ill, and he had to buy...to buy some essentials. I helped him. He is a widower and has some children. He has been calling...calling regularly."

"Oh, cousin Margred!"

"I don't know, truly I don't know, Katharina, what to do. Ursula does not like him one bit. She is envious, I think, for his interest in me, and she puts this interest in a ridiculous light. Perhaps she is right. For who in his right mind would like me? I am not a handsome woman. I know this, Katharina, I know I am not beautiful. And he is a printer and I cannot even read. And it is a fact that printers usually marry within their own guild and acquaintance. But I am of such an age that I will not...that I will probably not bear him children. So I am not really a threat to any inheritance. His son will inherit and I will simply run his household. Truly, he is so kind to me."

"Oh, cousin Margred. You are a very dear woman, and I cannot think of anyone who would be a better mother for young children than yourself."

Katharina threw out the words spontaneously.

"Think you?"

"Indeed, I do. And I also think you are handsome. And...and you can surely learn to read."

Cousin Margred's face was by now a deep, deep red, but there was a sweet smile both in her eyes and on her lips, and indeed, looking thus, she was handsome as she looked back at Katharina.

"Thank you, Katharina. And now would you do something for me? Would you carry away my portion of the money father gave us and would you keep it for me until...until such time as I might need it?"

"Surely," Katharina answered readily, "but I scarcely think that cousin Ursula is in a position to take it from you at this time."

Cousin Margred shrugged and then slowly rose from her chair. Walking over toward the wall opposite the bed, she placed her fingers on the edge of one of the bricks and pulled it out of its place. A niche was revealed—a large hollow space behind the brick. Cousin Margred reached her hand into the hollow and drew out a small linen bag. This she carried over to Katharina, handing it over to her.

"Please keep it safe."

"Can I give it to Vati?"

"Yes, I think that you can. Your Vati is a good man, and I trust him."

Chapter XV

A few days later, cousin Ursula's life came to an abrupt end. A convulsion, seemingly caused by the dysentery, suddenly caused her laboured breathing to halt forever. The sisters at the beguinage deemed this a violent death. Their priest, Balthazar Horst, lost no time in saying that countless prayers ought to be offered and that many candles ought to be lit. A violent death meant time in purgatory would be long. Katharina had not known what to expect; she had not known whether or not cousin Ursula would live. It might have been better, Katharina speculated, if cousin Ursula had died the moment the priest had absolved her. For if she had died at that precise moment, would she not have died with all her sins forgiven? But it seemed, somehow, that everyone must spend some time in purgatory.

Vati had shown her a small booklet called *Buchlein von den Peinen* (*Little Book of Pain*) sometime ago. He had received the little volume as payment from one of the publishers in Strasbourg for doing some work. The booklet had twenty-seven woodcuts, but these woodcuts had not been done by Vati. They depicted purgatory and the bad things people would suffer there. She had seen a picture in this book of someone being boiled in a cauldron above a roaring fire and another where some people had coins thrust down into their mouths. Katharina presumed that these people had been greedy for money during their lives. She could not imagine though, what someone might have done to warrant being boiled in a cauldron. Those were the only two pictures she had seen, for after this she had shut the booklet and had resumed sweeping the shop where the book had lain in the window sill.

And now there were two deaths to digest. Dr. Geiler von Kayserberg had died a few days before cousin Ursula. His funeral, unlike cousin Ursula's, had been attended by a host of people, many of whom were the very elite and important people of Strasbourg. Vati pointed some of them out to her as their family sat in a back pew in the cathedral.

"That man over there, the one wearing the very fine fur on his collar, that is Sebastian Brant. He was a very close friend of our Dr. Geiler," he had whispered in Katharina's ear. "He is a learned man, a lawyer, an author and Strasbourg's clerk."

"Oh," she had whispered back, "I remember that he translated a book of fables we read in school."

Her father nodded.

"Yes, he did. And," he added, raising his eyebrows at her with a twinkle in his eye, "I've had woodcuts in one of his books."

She proudly smiled back at him, lifting her eyebrows as well. Then, a little while later, he nudged her again.

"Those two men who just walked in and who are seated in the corner over there? They are Dr. Brunfels, who is an excellent doctor of medicine and Jakob Wimpfeling, one of the most important citizens of Strasbourg."

"Why is he so important, Vati?"

"Because he is taking such an interest in the education of the young people of the city. And," Vati added, "he has also written many books."

"Have you put woodcuts into any of his books, Vati?"

Vati had smiled and nodded at her.

"Just a few, little maid, just a few."

Monks carried Dr. Geiler's body into the cathedral for a Requiem Mass. It was said that he had died well and had been absolved of all his sins. The priest who led the Requiem Mass also led the funeral procession into the cathedral. A cross was carried alongside the bier, and there was continual chanting by all the monks, both Franciscans and Dominicans, in prayer and song. And through it all, the church bells tolled and tolled. These bells, Katharina knew, banned the devil, and they also reminded all the people of Strasbourg to offer up intercessory prayers for Dr. Geiler. Dr. Geiler was buried inside the cathedral, in the vault reserved for important and rich people. Cousin Ursula, on the other hand, was buried outside the cathedral in a common grave, neither were there any bells rung when she was buried. You had to pay the church to have the bells rung and not much money had been left in the hollow behind the brick.

KATHARINA HAD HANDED over the little linen bag cousin Margred had given her to Vati and had told him what had happened. He had nodded gravely and told her that she had done what was right and that he would speak with cousin Margred when the time came. Katharina had given out some alms to the poor when they followed cousin Ursula's body to the graveyard. She had also sat for hours with Mutti and with Barbara by the corpse's bed for the wake, just as they had done with Jacob. Cousin Ursula's body had been dressed in her coarse brown robe. Her gold crucifix had been fixed between the fingers of both her hands. It truly looked as if she was holding onto it, holding onto it tightly. Her rosary trailed down the brown robe off the side of the bed. There was still a bad smell in the chamber, a smell which made Mutti sprinkle rose water around the room and which bade her tell the others not to breathe in too deeply.

"Why don't you come and stay with us for a while, cousin Margred?" Mutti had asked while they were sitting by the bed.

Margred had flushed. Since her sister had died, she had been sleeping in one of the guest rooms of the beguinage.

"I know not…" she had faltered her answer and, "I do not want to inconvenience…."

"You are most welcome," Mutti had smiled at her. "Jacob and I would be most pleased to have you stay."

So cousin Margred had come and she had stayed.

THE PRINTER OF whom cousin Margred had spoken came to call on her in the house on Johanngasse. He was a short, rotund man, not at all impressive looking, but very jovial. As a matter of fact, Katharina thought he quite resembled cousin Margred. Round and jolly, he smiled easily and readily accepted the teasing and familiarity of the younger Schütz children. He spent time with Vati, closeted away in the workshop; it seemed that the terms of a nuptial agreement were being reached. Wolfgang Schott, for that was his name, also took cousin Margred to his own home at times, to meet with his children. It was clear to all that the printer would be a good match for cousin Margred.

After the nuptial agreement was complete, a wedding notice was posted on the door of the church. It was put up to ensure that there were no grounds for prohibiting the marriage. Cousin Margred confided to Katharina that she had been afraid that the priest, Balathazar Horst, might come forward and that he might want to claim her dowry and give it to the church. The dowry was, of course, to go to Wolfgang Schott. But as the months passed, he did not come forward, and cousin Margred was increasingly relieved. It was agreed that cousin Margred and Wolfgang Schott would marry in the summer. This would give her time to learn some household duties from her cousin Elizabeth as well as giving her some time to mourn the death of her sister Ursula. Indeed, she felt it would not be seemly to have a wedding so close after a funeral. Besides that, it was Lent and no couple could be married during a time of fasting.

Mutti, Barbara and Elisabet all helped cousin Margred prepare for the wedding. Together they sewed some tablecloths, some bed linen and some undergarments. As well, Katharina spent time in teaching her how to read.

"You are doing well, cousin Margred," she said to her one afternoon as they sat by the table and as Mutti worked with Marta in the kitchen, "and Wolfgang will be very proud of you."

"It is going to be my gift to him," cousin Margred answered, a blush deepening her cheeks, "and I hope that he will be happy. For what is a printer if he has a wife who cannot read?"

"Wolfgang Schott is one printer who will be delighted with you because of your generous character," Katharina answered quickly. "I know that even if you could not read, he would still love you."

"You are so kind, Katharina, much kinder," she continued softer, "than my sister was wont to be. I...."

She stopped and turned very red.

"I must not say such things," she then stammered, "for it is unkind to speak ill of the dead."

"Well, never mind," Katharina soothed, "we all know that cousin Ursula had a harsh tongue in her mouth. But we know also that she was a hard worker...."

She also stopped, for she knew not what else to say about cousin Ursula. There was silence for a long time. Margred bent over the primer, seemingly studying the page as if her life depended on it. Mutti and Marta left to do some work in the garden. Before leaving, Mutti walked over and stroked Katharina's braided hair.

"You are a good girl, Katharina," she murmured.

After they left, Margred finally looked up and smiled at Katharina.

"What your Mutti said is true," she haltingly began. "You have been such a help to me, Katharina. Thank you."

She continued, in small sentences, to speak of her Wolfgang.

"I never thought," she said, "that I would marry. I always thought I would finish my days at the beguinage. Ursula always... always made decisions for me, and that was right as she was my older sister and so knew best."

Katharina was about to interrupt, but looking at cousin Margred's intent face, which was now fixed on some spot on the wall behind her, thought better of it.

"I know that even had someone shown interest in me when father was still alive, I would not have been allowed to choose freely. And yet..." she paused and met Katharina's eyes with a smile on her face, repeating, "and yet here is a man, Wolfgang Schott, so many years later who...."

She stopped and looked down for a moment before continuing, "I had given up all dreams of marriage, but he truly wants me to run his household and mind his children."

"I think," Katharina said softly, "that God must have had you wait just for this time, cousin Margred."

"I know, Katharina," Margred went on, "that Wolfgang does not love me as…well, as a passionate wooer, as someone who dreams of me constantly. But I think he values my friendship. And I think that from friendship perhaps love can grow?"

She ended on a questioning note, and her smile became somewhat troubled and tremulous.

"He's a ninny, if he doesn't begin to love you," Katharina burst out before she had time to think, "and you such a treasure as I can't begin to describe."

Cousin Margred now grinned.

"Ah, Katharina, you are an optimist."

"No, cousin Margred, I am not. Indeed, I am not. Sometimes I worry a great deal too much about things."

"Worry? What do you worry abou? Look at you, girl. Two fat, glossy braids hanging about your neck. You have a fine complexion. Your blue eyes shine. You have such a winning way with you. Why I met three people the other day, who told me that they were all taken with you because you had helped them in one way or another."

"Oh, hush, cousin Margred," Katharina began, but she could not stop the flow of warm praise coming from her cousin's mouth as she ticked off tributes with the index finger of her right hand on her left.

"There was Anna, the butcher's wife. She told me of the herbs you had brought when she was brought to bed last fall with the ague. And then there was Frau Bocker whose children you watched several days because she had to visit her ill mother in the country. And then there was little Hans to whom you told a story when he fell and scraped his knee."

She stopped and began tapping the table with the same index finger.

"You know I could go on. People like you."

"But it doesn't mean anything," Katharine replied, hating the blush that crept up into her cheekbones.

"What do you mean, it doesn't mean anything?"

"Well, it doesn't guarantee…it doesn't guarantee…."

"It doesn't guarantee what?" Margred impatiently repeated.

"Your salvation…or the salvation of others."

"Oh."

It was all cousin Margred said and for a while they sat in silence again, cousin Margred now chewing her fingernails.

"You know," she eventually said, "it seems to me that if you do things like helping other people, then our Lord surely loves you and you love him."

"Oh, I do," Katharina answered fervently and then she wept.

It was not something she had planned and she was so ashamed, but she wept nonetheless. She could not help it. Cousin Margred became all tenderness. Pushing back her chair, she walked over to her cousin, and her arms crept around Katharina's sobbing body.

"There, there," she whispered. "It's all right. And don't I thank our Lady each night for the goodness shown to me by yourself and your sweet mother and father."

Comforted, at least physically, by cousin Margred's affection, Katharina slowly relaxed. Eventually she was able to look up and smile at Margred.

"There now," Margred said, smiling in return, "and isn't that the sun breaking out from behind the clouds?"

Chapter XVI

Cousin Margred was married to Wolfgang Schott on a beautiful summer day. The sky was blue and the birds were singing as the couple pledged their vows in answer to a priest's questions at the door of the cathedral. Their separate families stood around them in a half circle. After the vows, Wolfgang presented Margred with a fine gold ring which she shyly put on the fourth finger of her left hand. This was, everyone knew, because a vein from this fourth finger led directly to the heart, mirroring the emotional union of the couple. As well, the unending circle of the ring represented the indissolubility of the marriage. Margred gave Wolfgang a ring as well, which he solemnly put on the fourth finger of his left hand. After that, it seemed to all the onlookers that the happy couple could not leave off smiling. Afterward they all entered the cathedral for the early morning mass, after which they companionably walked back to the Schütz home for a good meal.

Cousin Margred wore a blue satin gown, specially designed for her by Mutti, although Elisabet, Barbara, Katharina and Margaret had all helped with the fine stitching. Blue was the colour of purity and, as such, Mutti had deemed it necessary to obtain blue material. Herr Bauer, who was a merchant, had been unable to supply her and after she had seemingly scoured the whole city, she finally had been able to buy some from a travelling merchant who just happened to have a small bolt of fine, sky-blue satin in his large satchel.

"It is a good thing," she confided to the girls as they sat sewing one afternoon, "that cousin Margred is short, or I should not have enough material."

They had all laughed, but it had been a good sort of laughter. Everyone was fond of cousin Margred, and all were glad she should have a good home.

The nuptial meal at the Schütz home was a jovial affair. Wolfgang and Margred drank from the same cup, ate from the same bowl and joined hands to symbolize their union. From time to time, Margred touched the ring Wolfgang had given her and, when she caught Katharina's or Margaret's eye, she blushed most becomingly. At one point Wolfgang stood up, cup in hand. Everyone hushed as it soon became obvious that he was about to speak. And speak he did, as he looked down at Margred by his side and beamed at his children gathered across from them at the table.

"I am of the comfortable hope," he began, his face flushed with happiness and contentment, "that Margred, my bride, will faithfully help me bring up my children."

Margred, to the amusement of all, did not quite know where to look and turned quite scarlet.

"I am sure," Wolfgang continued, as the group all raised their cups as well, ready to salute the bride, "that she will also profit my nourishment and be a helpmeet in my craft. For some of you may know and some may not and therefore I say this for your benefit, that Margred has mastered the art of reading these last few months."

He paused and let his gaze fall upon his stout little bride, who put her hands up to her cheeks in an effort to cool them down.

"She is the most wonderful of women," Wolfgang ended, "and I drink to her health."

"To Margred's health," all echoed.

ELISABET WAS ALSO married that spring, albeit it a month earlier than cousin Margred, to a young man whose name was Michael Schwencker. Her wedding had taken a great deal of preparation as well. Indeed, Mutti was wont to exclaim that she wished she were two people instead of one so that she would have more time for sewing. But every time she exclaimed this, Vati would laugh and say that he would not be able to live with two Muttis. Michael Schwencker was some six years older than Elisabet and had been born in Gernsbach. After attending Heidelberg University, he worked as the city's administrator in the Franciscan Cloister of St. Clara. Elisabet had met him through a mutual friend. He was a hardworking man, looking to acquire citizenship in Strasbourg, and her parents were pleased with both his lifestyle and his work ethic. He purchased a house on Rossmarkt Strasse. This was a small street close to his work and very close to the cathedral, and it was an exceedingly fine two storey house for a young couple just beginning life together.

"You will be too rich to come and visit us, Frau Schwencker," Margaret would tease her older sister, who would instantly deny it and chase her around the room, all the while both of them squealing with laughter.

The day on which Michael formally called to ask for Elisabet's hand, she was very agitated and stayed closeted in the bedroom, until Vati and Mutti called her to come down. The matter of marriage terms had been agreed upon between them. Vati and Mutti were waiting for Elisabet at the bottom of the stairs and led her by the hand into the room where Michael was waiting. Both Vati and Mutti judged Michael to be a moral man from a good family and felt that Elisabet would be well provided for and loved.

Even as Margred would do a month later, Elisabet presented her fiancée with a wreath at their engagement. She wore this same wreath in her hair during the procession to their church. It symbolized her virginity. She looked so beautiful and so very happy that her sisters, Barbara, Katharina and Margaret, had felt they were escorting a princess to the cathedral. As part of the dower, Elisabet brought a marriage bed into the Schwencker household. Its large frame had been made by her father, Jacob, and he had painstakingly carved wonderful flower motifs into the wood. Layered with mattresses, feather quilts, square pillows and bolsters, it looked grand. As well, it was covered with some of the linen Elisabet had collected over the course of her maidenhood for her trousseau. These items were all part of the household goods she was contributing.

Katharina missed both Elisabet and Margred in the weeks and months that followed, but there were always so many chores and so many errands to run that the hours and days flew by.

"Katharina is my right hand," Mutti was wont to say, and it made Katharina proud.

She still regularly attended her tapestry weaving lessons and had taken great joy in presenting her sister with a pillow she had made as a wedding gift.

"Oh, Katharina," Elisabet exclaimed, and the great delight in her eyes at the gift was enough to make up for all the painstakingly hard hours Katharina had put into the making of it.

WHILE KATHARINA MOVED through time helping her mother, running errands and creating *heidnisch werk*, the world around her also turned. New ideas were brought to the fore; new inventions were worked on; and new books were written causing people to think deeply. The world actually turned, Mikołaj Kopernik, a Polish physician and astronomer, boldly asserted. In a short manuscript published when Katharina was sixteen, Kopernik concluded that the earth rotated on its own axis and orbited around the sun. Yet, was it not so, other people reasoned, at least those who knew Bible stories, that Joshua had commanded the sun to stand still and not the earth? Then there was the artist Leonardo Da Vinci, the illegitimate son of an Italian country girl, who dissected cadavers and who penciled intricate drawings of the human body, the body made in the image of God, even writing a book about it. Was this proper? He invented a great many things and everything he wrote down was in mirror script— script that could only be read by holding it up to a looking glass. "Was this not devilish?" people said. Certainly the pope, Pope Leo X, thought so. Da Vinci was called to give account and consequently left Italy for the court of France, where he died a few years later. Many books were published during these times, and scores of these volumes criticized the church. A number of men quarrelled about indisputable "truths" for which the Roman Catholic Church stood and also dared to condemn the immoral lives of many priests. Pamphlets were distributed, also in Strasbourg, concerning all these new ideas and views, pamphlets which people read and discussed. It was whispered that the pope spent money like water on art projects. Should he do so while ordinary people starved? A man called Desiderius Erasmus even went so far as to write that Pope Julius II, who had been pope from 1503 to 1513, would not be allowed into heaven because of the many sins he had committed. Who was to say? Certainly people talked and argued; certainly people began to seriously question the validity of what they had always been taught.

Katharina pondered much as she walked the distance to her lessons with Frau Stoffler; as she helped her Mutti about the house in caring for her siblings; as she cleaned her Vati's workshop; and as she followed the bier carrying two of her little sisters, Ursula and Magdalene, both of them stricken dead of the *kinderpocken*, of the chickenpox, in one day.

One particular priest, a man called Brother Martin by the general populace, was often in Strasbourg's news. Brother Martin, whose surname was Luther, and who lived elsewhere, in Wittenberg, Germany, where he was a teacher, wrote pamphlets which found their way into the hands of many sincere Strasbourg citizens. In them, more than any other, he boldly attacked those evils of which Katharina so often heard her Vati speak: the draining of German money for Rome's building projects and the selling of indulgences. Also—and here Katharina shivered with an apprehensive worry—Brother Martin publicly wrote that the Mass was idolatry and that to bow down to a piece of bread was wrong. He also insisted that the offices of monks and nuns were an invention of humans and that monks or nuns could not be found anywhere in the Bible. He asserted that all Christians were free—they were free and yet they were servants. His pamphlets were distributed widely throughout Strasbourg. What did their words mean? Katharina wished that like Dr. Geiler, Brother Martin might be available to her so that she could speak with him and ask him questions. She had so many questions. They burned her up at times. Was Brother Martin a heretic? Certainly a lot of priests spit when they spoke of him.

"KATHARINA! KATHARINA!"

It was Margaret. She was red-faced and eager to get her sister's attention. Katharina smiled as she took the kettle off its hook and placed it on the table.

"What is it?"

Katharina turned to her younger sister who was impatiently tugging at her kirtle trying to get her attention.

"You were daydreaming again, Katharina. And Mutti said that you were to take me to visit cousin Margred. Do you not remember?"

"Yes, I remember."

"Well, then, are you ready to take me?"

"Yes, little one, as soon as I've finished this ointment for cousin Margred."

"I'm not so little any more. What is the ointment?"

"It is some wheat flour mixed with vinegar. Cousin Margred asked that Mutti make some for her a while back for sunburn."

A little later, as the girls strolled side by side toward the street where cousin Margred lived with her dear Wolfgang and her stepchildren, the sound of chanting fell on their ears. It appeared to be coming from one of the side streets. Peering down a partially cobbled and dirt road, they perceived a group of about six or seven men walking toward them. The first man carried some sort of banner with a cross emblazoned on it. All the men, Katharina noted, were stripped down to the waist although their faces were covered with cloth containing peepholes for their eyes. Strangely enough, as they were chanting, the girls saw that they struck themselves on their bare torsos with leather thongs. It was disconcerting and both Katharina and Margaret turned their faces away from the sight. The chanted words could quite easily be made out.

Nu tret herzuo der bössen welle:
Fliehen wir die haissun helle.
Lucifer ist bös geselle.
Wen er behapt, mit bech er lapt:
Dez fliehen wir in,
Hab wir den sin.

Come here for penance good and well,
Thus we escape from burning hell.
Lucifer's a wicked wight;
His prey he sets with pitch alight.

"Come, Kathe, I like this not."

Margaret's fingers pulled at her sleeve, but Katharina, perplexed, had turned her eyes back toward the group and stood transfixed. The banner cross undulated slightly as the first man carried it. As the motley collection neared the intersection at which the sisters stood, the leader turned and signalled to his followers, who were still intoning. He spoke to them in a loud voice.

"Jesus was refreshed with gall. We, therefore, on our cross now fall."

Stopping abruptly, the six men following him prostrated themselves on the stone and dirt road. Three lay on their backs, another on his side while holding up three fingers and two more fell on their faces. Then the leader, walking around them, a leather thong dangling from his right hand, commenced beating them. Margaret shuddered.

"Come on, Katharina. Please, Kathe, come away."

"These are flagellants," Katharina whispered, "and not seen often. Vati has told me of them. I know the pope does not approve, but I have heard it said that they intercede with the Virgin Mary for the grievous sins of the world."

Margaret, not listening to her sister, let go of Katharina's hand and bolted up the street. Not once did she look back at the bleeding bodies of the men lying on the ground. Other streetgoers gathered in a semi-circle, standing by Katharina. No one spoke. They all stared. At length, having finished the scourging, the master of the group took a letter out of his white mantle pocket. He proceeded to read it aloud as the men rose back to their feet.

"These words I am about to read," he began, "have been sent by an angel from heaven. And Christ, angry at the sins of the world, has threatened to destroy the world."

Katharina suddenly felt oppressed. She saw that the white gowns of the men were stained with blood, dirt and offal. She started to slowly edge her way backward through the crowd of on-lookers which had hemmed her in. One of the men in the group seemed to Katharina to have the eyes of her lost Jacob and she could barely tear her eyes away from him. *Guilt! So much guilt!!* It still gripped her. Why did it follow her and weigh her down?

"We pray for the intercession of the Bleeding Virgin, whose city Strasbourg is."

The man's voice rang down the street and vibrated up to the gables.

"Our blood which freely flows onto the dirt and cobbled stones of this street, mingles with the blood of Christ. This is our pen-ance to preserve the world from perishing."

Katharina was finally free of the crowd and broke into a half-run.

"For thirty-three-and-a-half days," the voice intoned to her re-treating form, "we will flagellate ourselves, for it was thirty-three-and-a-half years that our blessed Lord lived on this earth."

The voice faded. Katharina was out of its reach. Two corners further, Margaret was waiting.

"How could you stay and watch, Kathe?" her sister asked, "It was horrible!"

Katharina didn't answer. She saw Jacob's eyes again and beheld his limp body in the bed before it was buried. Christians are free, Brother Martin had written in his pamphlets. Were they? Were they indeed? These were guilt chains which bound her, were they not? Surely these men whose blood flowed so freely into the dirt and cobblestones on the road, surely these were men who desired to serve God with all their hearts, men who were doing penance for her. And this was good, was it not?

LATER, AS THEY sat in the kitchen with cousin Margred and her stepchildren, some of the anxiety in Katharina's heart dissolved. Cousin Margred cheerfully bustled about the room. She was so obviously glad to see them that Katharina could not help but smile and feel better. Her happiness was contagious. A large kettle hung over the fireplace. Stew simmered there for the supper meal. Its pungent smell permeated the room with comfort and cousin Margred chattered incessantly.

"I am going to make some soap tomorrow, Margaret. If you like, you can come and help us. I have some tallow, ash and mutton fat, and we are in need of some extra hands."

Margaret nodded eagerly.

"I will ask Mutti if I can come."

Margaret enjoyed being in the Schott household, for Ernestine, cousin Margred's stepdaughter, was the same age she was.

"As well," cousin Margred went on, "my neighbour, Anna Weiss, has told me that the buds of the black poplar make one's hair thick and...."

Katharina laughed out loud before she could finish her sentence.

"Your hair is already thick, cousin Margred. You don't need a recipe to make it thicker. Surely Wolfgang can lose himself in your tresses the way they are."

Cousin Margred blushed and Katharina felt some remorse. It was so easy to make cousin Margred blush.

"Well, Wolfgang does like my hair, it is true, but...."

"No buts, cousin Margred. You don't need your neighbour's tricks or connivances here."

"She has told me as well," cousin Margred persisted, as she put cups of steaming ale in front of them on the wooden table, "that wearing an opal necklace protects fair hair, such as your own, Katharina, from fading."

"Your neighbour sounds like a knowledgeable lady," Katharina commented, wrapping her hands around the warm cup of ale.

"She does not know, however," cousin Margred continued, raising quizzical eyebrows at Katharina, "how to make one's breath sweet. My Wolfgang...."

She stopped, blushed anew and gazed down at the table, before continuing.

"My Wolfgang sometimes has sour breath."

"Chew anise and fennel leaves," both Katharina and Margaret automatically answered and then laughed at each other.

"Mutti's special remedy," Katharina added, "and our Mutti learned much from her Mutti and she again from hers."

"I am much obliged to your Mutti," cousin Margred answered with a smile, "and, indeed, to you all."

"And we are obliged to you also. It is good ale, cousin Margred," Margaret added the last sentence sweetly, all the while smiling at Ernestine.

"Thank you."

Cousin Margred blushed again, but this time with pleasure, reflecting fleetingly how drastically her life had changed since Ursula had died.

LATER THAT EVENING, Katharina spoke with her parents about the flagellants.

"Perhaps they were pilgrims," her father said, "who left Strasbourg again before the city gates closed. Had they stayed they might have been apprehended by city officials."

"Why so, Vati?"

"They teach that there is no priesthood, and this does not sit well with the church or the magistrates."

Katharina nodded. She understood this.

"Also," her father went on, "they say no one can become a Christian unless he scourges himself and is baptized in his own blood."

"In his own...?"

Katharina did not finish. She again visualized Jacob's face as he lay limp against Vati's chest, blood on his face.

"Thirdly," her father added another bit of information, "these flagellants say it is better for a man to die with scourged skin than if priests were to anoint him with a whole pound of oil."

"I think," Katharina responded, "that were I the church, or the magistrates, then, indeed, I also might run them out of the city. But," she went on, "I am not. And I do wonder whether or not they can contribute to their own salvation, whether or not they can contribute by their own blood."

"I think not," her father said.

"I know not," Katharina concluded, "but I wish that I did know."

Part II

"...one thing is needful."
—Luke 10:42

...but joy comes with the morning
Psalm 30:5

Preamble

The preacher tells us in no uncertain terms, in the third chapter of his book of Ecclesiastes, "For everything there is a season, and a time for every matter under heaven."

So it has always been and so it was in the second and third decades of the fifteen hundreds. During these decades there was

a time to be born, and a time to die;
a time to plant, and a time to pluck up what is planted;
a time to kill, and a time to heal;
a time to break down, and a time to build up;
a time to weep, and a time to laugh;
a time to mourn, and a time to dance;
a time to cast away stones, and a time to gather stones together;
a time to embrace, and a time to refrain from embracing;
a time to seek, and a time to lose;
a time to keep, and a time to cast away;
a time to tear, and a time to sew;
a time to keep silence, and a time to speak;
a time to love, and a time to hate;
a time for war, and a time for peace (Ecclesiastes 3:2–8).

These years saw the Turks defeat Syria in the Battle of Aleppo. They felt the strokes of the hammer as Martin Luther's *Ninety-Five Theses* were nailed to the door of the Wittenberg church. They experienced the heat of the first burning of the Protestants in the Netherlands. They blushed as Charles V granted a Flemish courtier permission to import 4,000 slaves into New Spain, and from then on thousands of slaves were sent into the New World each year. They winced as three out of every ten people died in Zurich, Switzerland, of the plague. They blinked disbelievingly as Henry VIII, king of England, began to tire of Katharine of Aragon, his lawful Spanish wife, looking elsewhere for an English queen. They listened carefully as the pontifical ambassador interrogated Luther, and they smiled as Luther burned the papal edict demanding he recant. For, after all, the years were God's creation and in his hand.

That which is, already has been; that which is to be, already has been; and God seeks what has been driven away (Ecclesiastes 3:15).

Luther was excommunicated. His books were banned. But he continued to preach God's Word. And people listened.

...whatever God does endures forever; nothing can be added to it, nor anything taken from it. God has done it, so that people fear before him (Ecclesiastes 3:14).

Chapter XVII

Through the small gabled windows of the girls' bedroom, Katharina often stared up at the stars. It was well past the hour of midnight and she knew that she ought to be resting snug and content under the covers next to Margaret. But the bed seemed so much bigger and roomier since little Ursula and Magdalene had died two years ago of the *kinderpocken*, of the chickenpox. As well, Barbara had also left home to wed a faithful husband, even as Elisabet had wed, and now there were just the two of them left in the huge bed. Even though Katharina closed her eyes and willed her tired body to relax, she was not able to fall asleep. There was a small seat underneath the window sill and that is where she eventually sought refuge. Carefully opening the wooden shutters so as not to waken Margaret, she snuggled onto the seat, sitting on her knees, chin resting in her hands as she scanned the sky. It was a clear night and the vast, overpowering grandeur of the panorama directly above Strasbourg was overwhelming. The distance between her own small person and the innumerable constellations shining over the city was incomprehensible and yet, and here she smiled impishly to herself in the relative darkness of the bedroom, if she held her tiny thumb before the image of the moon, she could blot out its light. She wondered if such a thought and action was blasphemous, for the stellar vastness appeared so tremendously immense within her line of vision! God, after all, had made everything in the space of a brief six days, so Dr. Geiler had told his congregation again and again, simply by the Word of his mouth.

"Star," she whispered, following up with the word, "moon."

She did not understand that mere words, yes, mere words, could have created the world. It was beyond her ability to even come close to understanding this. But so it had been told her by Dr. Geiler and by her parents, and deep within herself she knew and believed it to be true.

ALL THROUGHOUT THE various cities and villages of surrounding Strasbourg, St. John's Day festivities had been celebrated earlier on in the month. Fires had been lit on mountains and hilltops. Frau Bauer, their neighbour, always insisted that this was the time of year when herbs had special powers of healing, especially if you could get a priest to bless them. Dr. Geiler had not held this belief, calling it superstition, and Katharina tended to doubt the truth of it herself even though she had to concede that Frau Bauer, who was getting older, was very knowledgeable about herbs. But then common sense told her that, after all, a herb was a herb. Again she felt the faint pang of sadness that Dr. Geiler's death had brought, even though it had been eight years since he had died.

Vati had given her a Bible earlier this year, on her twentieth birthday. It was a Mentelin Bible and had been a valuable gift indeed. She had begun to read it, though with the reading there was also a smattering of guilt. Her admiration for Dr. Geiler had been very great, but he had actually warned his flock that the reading of Scripture should be left to the church leaders. Yet, she had such a hunger to both know and understand what the Word of God said about everything that in this one matter she did not agree with her former priest. When she began reading the actual text, however, she had to admit to herself that it was difficult to always grasp what Bible verses meant. Oh, to have a teacher who would explain all things properly! She was now twenty years of age and a woman. Old enough so that she ought to be sure of things—so that she ought to know things. From her perch in the window seat, she sighed up at the stars and shook her head. No one knew better than herself just how little she was and how little she knew.

It seemed like a thousand years had passed since she had attended the *Lehrhaus* each day and since she had received instruction in the basics of the German language; it seemed like a hundred years since she had sat on Vati's lap in his studio and he had read to her; and it seemed like fifty years since Jacob, her first beloved Jacob, had died. Where did time go when it left you? Did God have a pocket bulging with hours, days and years and ages?

Katharina's mind wandered to the present controversy in Strasbourg, a controversy between the Dominicans and the Franciscans. Even though the two orders lived within a few blocks of one another, with only the Penny Tower Treasury separating them, they were at extreme loggerheads. Theirs was a heated disagreement with regard to the Virgin Mary. Katharina sighed again. Quarrels could make life so very complicated. The question that the Dominicans and Franciscans were debating seemed to be important: Was Mary without sin even as Jesus had been without sin? Or had she been born with sin? Everyone in Strasbourg was taking sides. From the children who played on the street, to the matrons who visited the market, to the artisans who ran shops—all cared and all argued. And why should they not? After all, Strasbourg's banner and coins both carried the motto: "O Virgin Mary, please beg your Son to save our city and its people." Katharina's right hand left off supporting her chin and began drumming its slim fingers on the sill. Mary was Strasbourg's patron saint, after all, and everyone loved her. Katharina vividly recalled how she herself, as a child, used to make up songs about Mary and sing them for her father in the workshop. Those had been such special times. But those times were gone now. She was not a child any longer. Katharina simultaneously yawned and shivered. Carefully closing the wooden shutters again and manipulating her cramped legs off the window seat, she tiptoed back to bed. Crawling under the covers, she revelled in the warmth which Margaret's body exuded and closed her eyes. This time sleep was not long in coming.

The next day, just before noon, little Jacob, as he was still called, raced in from the hallway into the kitchen. He was all of eight years old now and a sturdy boy. Katharina was glad of it for she loved him dearly. Often red of face and dishevelled, he was a good student though sometimes distracted by other things as he walked, or rather explored, on his way to and from school. He did this, as Mutti often reminded her, even as she had done. Katharina, who was helping Marta set the utensils for the noon meal, laughed to see him.

"What mischief have you been up to, little brother, and where is Annder? Did you not meet him as he walked home from the printer?"

She grabbed hold of Jacob, as he hopped by, to straighten his white shirt, adding, "It must be very warm outside for your cheeks are as hot as the flames on the hearth in the winter time."

The shirt's neckline drawstring on the boy was loose and dangled haphazardly on his heaving chest.

"Stand still a moment," she admonished, as he attempted to pull away from her ministrations. "Let me just make you a tiny bit neater before Mutti sees you and cuffs you over the head. And where is Annder?"

"Mutti never cuffs me, and I don't know where Annder went," he protested and then grinned up at her, before he went on to tell her his news. "Katharina, you'll never guess what I saw on my way home from the Lehrmeister's house."

"Three blue geese," she answered.

"No, you silly."

"What then," she asked, concentrating on pulling the drawstring through the narrow band of the neckline on his shirt, thereby creating tiny ruffles.

"Well, I saw a woman dancing on the street."

"Dancing?"

Katharina's answer was absent-minded. She was not really listening as she looked downward contemplating the obvious stains on little Jacob's hose, stains which were clearly visible next to his brown jerkin.

"Where have you been playing, Jacob? Just look at your stockings!"

Jacob glanced down guiltily, stepping backward, momentarily forgetting the story he was telling.

"Oh, I was by the stables...."

"The stables!"

Katharina's voice was horrified.

"But I was only passing, Katharina," Jacob explained quickly, well aware of his sister's special antipathy toward the stables, "and then Hans Kopfeld threw a stone at...and I...."

"Yes, yes," Katharina sighed, "I know. Now come back here so I can clean you somewhat before Mutti...."

"Before Mutti what?"

Frau Schütz had walked into the kitchen behind them. In one glance she saw Jacob's state and sighed.

"Let Katharina clean you up, Jacob, before we sit down and eat. And afterward, we better have a chat, you and I."

Little Jacob became all contrition.

"I am sorry, Mutti. Truly, I am! But I can tell you...."

"Later," Katharina whispered, "Later, Jacob."

IT WAS NOT until later, after Annder had arrived from his morning apprentice work with a Strasbourg printer and the whole family was seated around the table that Jacob once more began to talk about what he had seen.

"You'll never guess what I saw on the street," he said with the important air of someone who knows something no one else does.

"A dancing woman?" Katharina asked, smiling as she spoke, even though her mouth was filled with stew.

"Yes," Jacob answered, first looking mystified that someone should know and then rather upset that she should give it away, "but you knew, Katharina, so you shouldn't have answered at all."

"A woman dancing?" Annder piped up, pushing his trencher to the side.

"Eat your stew, Annder," Mutti admonished. "We are very privileged in that we have enough to eat. There are many who go hungry."

"Your mother is right," his father interposed. "Food prices have risen drastically and" he went on, his voice growing louder, "the harvest has failed three years in succession. And yet there is enough food in this kitchen for all of you to eat."

He tapped his fingers on the table. No one responded. They had all heard him make this speech many times before in these last months.

"You all know that the city opened its granaries to the poor this summer. Hopefully, God willing, we will have a better harvest next year, but for now we will cheerfully eat whatever Mutti puts on this table. What's more, we will be thankful for it."

He gave Annder a stern look as he spoke his last words, and the boy nodded, pulling his trencher back in front of himself.

"Have you children not noted the increase of beggars on the street?" Mutti took over. "These past years, as Vati said, have been lean years for the people in Strasbourg, but we have always eaten. I would have no one here waste a single bite."

"The clergy," Vati went on in a sombre voice, "are not helping the poor, because they say they suspect the poor of leaning toward the new Lutheran learnings. Heresy, they call these new learnings. I rather suspect the real reason they do not want to help is because they want to hang on to their own food stores. And I further suspect they make the poor out to be heretics on purpose. Ah, well," he went on philosophically, winding down, "I, for one, am happy and thankful that we can still feed our family."

Annder grimaced as he took another bite.

"The stew tastes strange," he said.

"No doubt," commented his mother, "as we have had to thin it down a bit. But I would not have you any less thankful. Eat, child!"

"You know," Jacob tried again, "I saw a...."

"Woman dancing in the street?" Katharina interrupted and then laughed, as did all the others at the table, breaking the tension.

"You are a tease, Katharina," Jacob retorted, "and because you are a tease I won't tell anyone what I saw."

"All right," Katharina responded and took another spoonful of her stew.

Everyone was quiet. Little Jacob looked down at his trencher. He had so desperately wanted to tell his story. Sighing deeply, he disconsolately moved his spoon back and forth through the watery stew. After a long moment, Katharina spoke.

"I'm sorry I spoiled your story, my little Jacob. Please tell us about the dancing woman."

"Was it Barbara?" Annder asked with a grin. "She has been very happy since she got married, and I daresay she would dance in the street."

"Eat your stew, Annder," Mutti admonished again, "or I daresay you will not be very happy before too long."

"Yes, Mutti," Annder muttered.

"Well," Jacob began again, his spoon suspended above his food, "I was coming home from the Lehrmeister's and stopped to... well, to speak to Klaus who lives by the stables."

"Go on," Katharina said, eyes intent upon her small brother.

"And while I was standing by the steps of his house, this woman ran out of the home next to where Klaus lives, and she started to dance."

"Did she dance alone, Jacob?" Vati asked, "Or were there musicians with her? Perhaps there was there a celebration of some sort?"

"No, Vati, she was dancing alone," Jacob eagerly went on, glad of his father's sudden interest, "and she was dancing funny. She was stiff, as if she was made out of wood."

"Wood?" Mutti questioned, her eyebrows raised.

"Yes and I got dirty, Mutti, because Hans Kopfeld, you know the stableboy, he picked up stones to throw at the woman, and I jumped at him before he could throw them," and here Jacob looked at Katharina, "and that is when I got dirty."

Katharina smiled at him.

"That was kind of you, Jacob, to want to protect her. Was the woman grateful?"

"No, she kept on dancing. I don't think she even noticed me or anyone else. She didn't even notice her husband who came out of the house after a while and tried to stop her from dancing."

"How did he try to stop her?" Vati asked.

"He pulled her arms. He pulled wherever he could to...to catch her, because she was moving about a lot," Jacob answered, "but her eyes were strange. And I think she did not notice him at all either."

THE NEXT DAY at noon, Jacob reported with gusto that the woman was still dancing.

"And," he added, proud to have the attention of all at the noon-table on him once more, "she was not the only one. There were many others dancing with her. I could barely get through that part of the street where she lived. And some of them were falling down on top of one another. It was quite funny really!"

"You are not to go there again, Jacob," Mutti immediately said, alarm visible on her face, "until your Vati has looked into this. Unless," she added, "you are making this story up and it is an untruth."

"Oh no, Mutti."

Jacob was offended.

"I have some work that I must attend to in the shop," Jacob Schütz responded to his wife's imploring look, "and cannot get away this afternoon. But tomorrow...."

"You are not to go near the stables again, Jacob," Mutti reiterated firmly. "Do you hear me?"

"Yes," Jacob replied in a small voice.

"Do you suppose she danced all night?" Margaret asked.

"Yes," Jacob supplied the information eagerly, "Hans Kopfeld said that she did dance all night, and a priest came this morning and sprinkled her with holy water but it did not help. And then other people came, and all of them danced and danced and danced."

"I have heard tell of a dancing disease. It was described somewhat like the situation of which little Jacob speaks."

Vati spoke slowly and thoughtfully, and all eyes were on him now.

"I might even have seen it illustrated on a woodcut made by a man named Wolgemuth—yes, a Michael Wolgemuth. The woodcut shows people dancing in fine clothes and wearing pointed shoes. There are also musicians at the site who seem to be standing on a gravestone or gravestones, if I am recalling correctly."

Margaret swallowed audibly. She disliked cemeteries.

"There is a copper plate engraving of such dancing as well. I think it too has musicians and people dancing," Vati continued, adding "in a graveyard."

"A graveyard?" Mutti echoed.

Vati nodded.

"I believe this disease was called St. Vitus Dance—a compulsive sort of dance in which people cannot stop moving about."

THE NEXT MORNING, at the insistence of Mutti, Katharina accompanied her father to the stables so that they could ascertain for themselves if the story Jacob had brought home was true. It was already humid and warm, even though it was early.

"Do you believe this to be some sort of illness, Vati?" Katharina asked.

Her father often knew stories. He read much and often told her tales of the past.

"I will have to see it first to be able to judge, daughter," he answered sensibly.

His feet measured calm and sure steps as they walked along the street toward that section of the city where the stables were. Katharina felt secure by his side.

"I have heard tell, however, that in Kölbigk," he went on, "in Saxony, many hundreds of years ago, there was a dance episode around Christmas time."

"A dance episode such as might be here in Strasbourg?"

"I do not know. But I know that it was said that the devil himself urged a few men and women to dance madly in the churchyard in Kölbigk. Some say the dancers even jumped about in the porch of the church itself."

"Yes?" Katharina urged her father on, as he had left off talking.

"Well, the story goes that these people sang, stamped their feet on the ground and leapt into the air. Hearing their commotion outside of the sanctuary, the priest came out of the church. He told them to stop but they would not listen. Then he bade someone try and pull the dancers out of the group, one by one. When this did not work, he excommunicated the dancers. But it is said they danced for months."

"But how is that possible, Vati?"

"Well, it is only a story after all, Katharina, even if it is purported to be written down. But there is always a kernel of truth in these old stories. As it is, I have it only by the word of someone else's mouth, and of course, I have seen the woodcut and the engravings of such things."

"Do you know what eventually happened to these people in Kölbigk?"

"Some of them apparently fell into a deep sleep which lasted for several days. When they awoke, they seemed to be restored. Others died before they awoke."

Katharina fell quiet at his side and contemplated what her father said. What had happened to those who had not fallen asleep? Had they kept on dancing? Had they died while they were dancing? The road was dusty, and it was particularly hot in the sun. She lifted her skirt carefully to avoid some horse droppings.

Katharina did not often pass by the stables. As a matter of fact, she studiously avoided the stable area if she could. However, sometimes there were errands; sometimes there were those in need that Mutti asked her to go and see. It became obvious, the closer they came to their destination, that there was, indeed, a great commotion in Stable Street. They could not tell if the people milling about were just witnessing something or if they were actually participating in some sort of riot. There was a great deal of shouting, and it seemed as if many folks were pushing one another. Slowly Herr Schütz made his way toward the group, his arm protectively around Katharina.

"If," he murmured softly to his daughter, "it appears that this is a dangerous place to be, you are to leave upon my say-so and return home immediately. Do you understand?"

She nodded.

"Yes, Vati."

The noise and shouting grew louder. The closer they approached, the more clamorous the sound. It discomfited Katharina. But, at the same time, she was curious. Why would a woman dance by herself, and why would others begin to dance with her? They had reached the perimeter of the crowd at this point. Now they could clearly see that these were only spectators and not participants in whatever lay beyond the pale of the rows of people. Vati spoke to one of the men loitering about.

"What is happening?"

"Some woman, they say her name is Frau Troffea, began to

dance a day or so ago. That is, I'm not sure she is dancing. It seems to me and to others I have spoken with, that she is afflicted with some urge to move."

"I see," Vati replied.

The man, eager to disseminate information, went on.

"The magistrates are involved now because others as well, have begun this strange dance and cannot be persuaded to move away from this spot."

"How are the magistrates involved?"

"Well, I have heard say that the guilds have been encouraged by the magistrates to open their doors to these dancers. Just so that they will be off the street. The guild halls are large. Here, as you can see, carriage and horse traffic is hampered and the whole issue is a hindrance to passersby."

Vati and Katharina strained their necks to see past the people directly in their purview, but could not, for the numbers in front of them were too many.

"I have heard tell," the man volunteered, "that later today the magistrates will attempt to lead those afflicted with movement to the Grain Market and to two of the nearby guild halls."

"Why so?"

"Well, as I said, the halls are large, and there is room there to dance and move about. There is also talk about constructing a platform. On the whole, that area is much greater than the area here in the street and will not cause as much of a disturbance as it does here."

Vati and Katharina nodded at him and then looked at one another. Vati shrugged and made as if to turn around and go back.

"We can do nothing here," he said, "so we may as well go home, daughter. Thank you for your information, sir."

He turned and Katharina was about to turn with him. Casting a last glance toward the melee of people in front of them, her eye caught sight of a figure that somehow seemed familiar. It was a woman bravely wading her way through the crowd toward their side of the street. Katharina stared fixedly at the figure. Vati, following her eyes and also recognizing the person, halted in his tracks. It was Frau Stoffler and when she at long last reached their

171

side, she was dishevelled, tired-looking and trembling. Realizing suddenly that she had come face to face with the Schütz family, tears formed in her eyes.

"Oh, thank God," she cried out. "Thank God, that I have found some who are my friends. Please, you must help me! Please."

Then she began to weep, to weep very earnestly.

Chapter XVIII

The snood fastened around Frau Stoffler's still dark coiffeur was coming dangerously close to sliding off. Wisps, as well as whole strands of hair, had escaped from the net, falling in unruly and straggly strings down her back, messily framing the sides of her face. The unkempt appearance made her seem much older than she was. Her front-laced grayish gown displayed traces of dirt, and her hands, ever deft and capable as they worked on the loom, were now clasping and unclasping. The raucous cries of the crowd behind her mixed with her incoherent weeping. It was difficult for Katharina and her father to make out what she was saying. Moved by pity, Katharina stepped forward, putting her arms about her former teacher's shoulders.

"Shh," she whispered, "Shh. It's all right. Whatever has happened, it's all right. Vati and I will take you home."

"No," Frau Stoffler, sobbed, "not home. I cannot go home. Annalein...."

"What is the matter with Annalein?" Katharina asked.

"She is...."

She could not finish, for such torrents of weeping broke out anew that her benefactors did not know what to make of it. They still could not understand what Frau Stoffler's problem was. Vati at length indicated with his hand that Katharina should lead the woman away from the turbulent crowd in the direction of their house. Katharina did so. Frau Stoffler seemed not to notice that she was walking. As her feet moved with a halting gait, she murmured her daughter's name unceasingly. Over and over she repeated it. Two blocks or so past the noise of the people, Vati stopped, surveying her person. Although dazed, Frau Stoffler seemed somewhat calmer, and she had left off both the weeping and the talking.

"We'll take you to our home, Frau Stoffler," he said kindly, "and my wife will give you something to soothe your nerves, and then perhaps we can talk about what has happened to upset you so."

This time she accepted the directive quietly, obediently stepping alongside Katharina, with Katharina still deeming it safer to hold a right arm about her former teacher's shoulder. At length they reached Johanngasse, Frau Stoffler limping rather badly all the while, and turned toward the Schütz home. At the steps of the house Frau Stoffler's emotions suddenly took the upper hand again.

"Annalein," she said, louder than before and again, "Annalein!"

"Yes," Katharina said, "we will speak of her, but first you must come in and sit down for a while, so that you can rest."

"No, I cannot," Frau Stoffler protested, "I must find someone who will help her."

"Yes," Katharina said again, all the while soothingly rubbing her shoulders, "we will find someone to help Annalein."

They climbed the steps, and Herr Schütz opened the front door. Without further words, Frau Stoffler entered the hall, and from there they walked her through to the kitchen. Mutti, Margaret and Marta were seated at the table polishing some silverware. They all rose, starting at the sight of the disorderly and untidy Frau Stoffler.

"Wife, here is someone in need of your aid."

"Indeed," Elisabeth Schütz responded immediately, moving to help Katharina as she guided Frau Stoffler to a chair.

"Annalein," the woman again lamented, as she sat down, "I must tell you what happened to Annalein."

Herr Schütz sat down as well, as did Katharina and her mother. Marta busied herself at the hearth stirring some simmering stew. Margaret just stared.

"What has happened to Annalein?"

Elisabeth, who had seated herself next to Frau Stoffler, took hold of her hand and held it within her own.

"She is ill, I think," the woman replied, "Annalein is ill, and I do not know what has come over her."

She stopped and swallowed. Elisabeth turned her head, signaling Marta to bring some ale for Frau Stoffler, and the girl left to go to the cellar.

"She had of late," Frau Stoffler continued hesitantly but clearly, "been visiting some friends in the country. It was quite safe. I knew the family. They are good and upright people. They have some land on the Alsatian plains and grow wheat and barley and rye. The crops have not been.... "

She broke off, looking about in a bewildered sort of way before she continued.

"But when Annalein came back about...about four days ago, she complained about pain, about cramps in her legs."

She stopped and pulling her hand out of Frau Schütz's grasp, once more began the act of nervously clasping and unclasping her long white fingers.

"Yes?" Herr Schütz's voice urged her to continue.

"She began weeping first, perhaps because of the cramping pain in her legs and then she began to... well, I know this sounds strange, but then she began to hop about into the air. She began to hum and sing as well, although there did not appear to be any words to her song."

"What did you do?" Katharina asked, staring at Frau Stoffler and literally seeing Annalein, her friend, leaping into the air.

"Well, I tried to hold her down," Frau Stoffler continued, "as it did seem a most unnatural thing the way she jumped about. Not decent actually. But she pushed me away, and she pushed so strongly that I fell down. She did not even notice that she had hurt me."

Here she stopped and tears began to flow again. Elisabeth Schütz gave her a cloth to wipe her eyes. It took a few moments before she was able to pick up the thread of the story.

"We were upstairs in her room at this time, and she left her room, wriggling and moving in a very strange way all the while. She made for the top of the stairs. I was so frightened that she would fall down. But I was not quick enough to stop her. I had been knocked down by her, you see. And indeed, it was a miracle that she did not fall down the stairs as she scampered down the steps in such a…in such a stilted manner."

"Indeed," Frau Schütz commented, a rather horrified look on her face.

"My maidservant, Dorothea, stood in the hall at the bottom of the steps. I suppose she had heard the commotion and came to see what was happening. I signalled from the top of the stairs that she should try and stop Annalein, but she could not. Even though Dorothea is strong, Annalein was…well, she was stronger."

Again Frau Stoffler stopped, wiping her eyes at the recollection.

"Then what happened?"

It was Margaret who threw out the question, impatient to know.

"The child moved toward the street door. She wanted to go outside. She moved woodenly. Truly, that is how she moved. Stiffly, as if she were made of wood. I did not want her out on the street, but by the time I got to the bottom of the stairs, she had gone—she had disappeared through the door."

"Did you follow her?" Herr Schütz asked.

"Yes, indeed. And so did Dorothea. We tried to follow her together. But my leg had been bruised and I was slower. I could not walk as fast as I would have liked to walk. Dorothea supported me. Annalein had begun that strange sort of dancing again. And I was so afraid all the while that she might inadvertently reach the edge of the canal and fall into it."

She stopped once more, wiping her eyes vigorously.

"At the same time, I was exceedingly thankful that Johanna, her sister, was not visiting as she is wont to do from time to time. She could have been hurt. As you know she is heavy with child and only lives some fifteen minutes away from us."

"So where did Annalein go?"

"At first we could not see her anymore," Frau Stoffler went on in a tremulous voice, "but then we thought we saw her. Or at least, we thought we saw someone in the distance that moved about in the same strange manner in which she had moved. So we began to run as fast as we could toward that person. But when we reached that person, it was not Annalein at all but someone who was afflicted with the same...."

Here she stopped, totally at a loss for words before continuing a moment later.

"There were more. And then there were even more. I cannot tell you where they came from."

"More?" Katharina and her mother asked simultaneously.

"Yes, more people who were skipping about. More people who were moving in the same curious manner that Annalein was moving."

"Where were they coming from?" Herr Schütz questioned.

"From houses, some of them. Others appeared from side streets. Truly, I know not where they came from or what motivated them to come. But there were many. I think I counted at least eight who were proceeding us. And we followed, for we thought that perhaps they would lead us to Annalein, of whom we had lost sight."

"And you ended your journey by the stables?"

"Yes, we did. And there, there were some ten people dancing in the street. More came later."

"Did you see Annalein among them?"

"Yes, after a few moments we did. And by the time we saw her, I had spoken with others who had gathered; because there were others who had relatives among these...these dancers. The same sort of thing happened to these people as happened to Annalein. And we knew not what it was."

"Was it yesterday, or the day before? Or was it today that Annalein became...became unwell?" Elisabeth interposed.

"It was yesterday, yesterday afternoon. I stood outside all night. Dorothea went home at my request, for I did not deem that it lay within the realm of her duties to stay with me and watch. She is, after all, my housekeeper, and she is older than I am. But I do not pay her to be a nursemaid to Annalein."

It was quiet in the kitchen for a long time. Marta returned with a flagon of ale and placed it in front of Frau Stoffler.

"Drink," Elisabeth urged, "you must drink something or you

will be of no use to Annalein at all."

"What shall I do?" Frau Stoffler murmured helplessly, even as she lifted the ale to her lips, "I have heard that the group will be herded over to the guild halls later, for where they are now they are holding up traffic and making a public spectacle of themselves."

No one knew what to say, and they all watched as Frau Stoffler sipped sparingly from the earthen cup. Katharina felt a great pity for her friend's mother. She had never seen this woman bewildered and unsure. She was always teaching; always composed; and always neat and graciously garbed. How humiliating this must be for her!

"I have also seen a priest come twice and sprinkle holy water on the dancers. He walked around the group, sprinkling the ground, and then he walked between them and sprinkled the people as well. But there was no abatement in the movement. None at all."

The kitchen door opened and Andreas, or Annder as he was called by his family, walked in. He was a big strapping boy of almost twelve years. He wore tan breeches and a brown apron. Apprenticed by a printer, he often came home for the noon meal. There was a good relationship between Herr Schütz and Annder's employer, and so it was that he was often allowed to come home to eat the noon meal. It saved his master from having to feed him, and Elisabeth was happy to see her son each day and to hear how he was doing.

"Hello," he cried out in a jovial voice, stopping short when he saw that Frau Stoffler was present.

"It is said that two people are needed for each dancer," Frau Stoffler said, not even noting that Annder had come in, "to help guide them to a guild hall. And that is why I left. I left to look for someone to help me guide Annalein. One of the priests said he would watch over her until I came back."

She looked around the table.

"What is the matter with Annalein?" Annder asked, as he walked over to where Marta stood at a small side table, "Why does she need help?"

His mother put her finger on her lips, looking at him sternly.

"Oh, I see," he muttered, embarrassed that he seemed to be

intruding.

"I can go," Katharina volunteered. "I am strong and I love Annalein. Perhaps she will hear my voice and walk with me."

"I can go too," Annder added, although he did not know what he was offering to do. But he surmised that if his sister wanted to help, he certainly could as well.

At this, Frau Stoffler put down her ale, lay her head on the table and began to weep again, this time in great racking sobs that shook her entire body. Annder was taken back. Had he said something wrong that Frau Stoffler should so take offense?

"I am sorry," he began, but was silenced by another look from his mother.

"Frau Stoffler," Herr Schütz spoke softly, increasing his voice as the sobbing totally drowned out his words, "Frau Stoffler, we will help you. But you will have to compose yourself a bit, I think. Perhaps it would be wise if you were to have a small rest, a bit of a sleep, while Katharina, Annder and I go back to the Stable Road to see what is happening."

"Jacob is right," Elisabeth underlined her husband's plea for needed rest, "you need to have a small nap before you can go back to see Annalein. You were up all night and cannot keep on. And the children and Jacob will go and see if they can help her. Now drink a bit more for I think that you are thirsty and exhausted. And in that state you are of no help to anyone at all, least of all to Annalein."

Frau Stoffler raised her head, wiped her eyes and obediently drank some more ale.

"So you will go and find her?"

"They will," Elisabeth answered for all, repeating, "They will and in the meantime you are to come with me and I will put you to bed for a much needed rest. Come now."

Frau Stoffler sat up straight. The hair graying at the temples and stringing about her forehead emphasized both her vulnerability and her age.

"Come now," Elisabeth repeated, holding out her arm.

Frau Stoffler pushed back her chair and stood up, taking the proffered arm.

"Thank you all," she whispered, "Thank you."

After the noon meal, which was eaten quickly, Katharina, Annder and Herr Schütz left for Annder's place of employment. The printers in Strasbourg were located in three main areas: one was in little stalls clustered around the base of the huge cathedral and its adjoining streets; another was in the square near the Dominican monastery; and the third was in the area around the city hall and the law courts. Annder worked in one of the smaller shops in a side street by the cathedral. Katharina often envied him for being so close to the greatest church in the city.

"Are you quite certain you can spare the time, Annder?" Katharina questioned her younger brother. "Will not Herr Kurtz be angry if you are not available after the noon meal hour?"

"Well, if I explain things to him," Annder said, "he will understand. I think he will be agreeable and I know he was not overly busy today."

"That is because Herr Kurtz," his father added, for Katharina's benefit, "runs his own small shop. He is dependent on the work which comes to him. When it does, he has to do it straightaway and," he added a moment later, "economic conditions in the printing trade are never stable."

"He teaches well and is always kind to me," Annder said, "and I am learning much."

"I would as soon have had you apprenticed to a successful printer," his father replied, "but am grateful this position was offered. Herr Kurtz is a fine man."

"He has no sons," Annder said, "and I think he might...."

"But he has a daughter," Katharina interrupted, punching Annder playfully in the side, "and I have heard she is very pretty."

Her brother blushed.

"Annder is much too young to consider any such a match, although," Herr Schütz said thoughtfully, "often one becomes a member of the printing industry by marriage. Printing is, after all, a family industry."

Annder shrugged, kicking a stone into oblivion. He did not like this talk about himself and about marriage.

"A printer's daughter," Herr Schütz went on, oblivious of his son's embarrassment, "not only brings useful connections but specific skills which are useful for a printer husband."

"It is very hot today," Annder offered, as a change of subject.

"You look warm, indeed. I think you can tell Herr Kurtz we will not be gone long," Katharina offered, winking at him, "but if help is needed to guide Annalein to another place, then you will be a most welcome addition, I am sure."

She smiled at her brother, and he flexed his muscles.

"Yes, yes," Katharina smiled, "we all know you are strong."

"Here is the printer shop," Vati noted, "I think I'll go in and speak with Herr Kurtz for a moment as well."

"Can I walk on by myself, Vati?"

Katharina half expected to hear him to say "No," but he nodded, and she walked on.

"I think things will have quieted down in Stable Road, but if I am wrong and there is still a great deal of shouting and pushing, daughter," he called after her, "be sure that you stay back and do not involve yourself in any unnecessary danger. Just wait for us."

Katharina nodded acquiescently and turned right, heading toward Stable Road.

Upon reaching Stable Road, she noted that, indeed, a great number of the people she had seen earlier that morning had dispersed. Very likely, Katharina reasoned within herself, these people would have returned to work. The folks who were still standing about, and there were only some fifteen or so as far as she could judge, were probably day labourers, men and women with no permanent jobs who had to find work on a day-to-day basis. She was glad that Vati was a respectable woodworker and that Lux, after completing university, was now a lecturer at the University of Ingolstadt. They were all proud of him, Vati especially so. Katharina was walking more slowly now, apprehensive as she approached the blacksmith shop. She did not know what to expect. Stepping past the few loiterers still present in the street, she could not detect any dancing or strangely moving people. It was oppressively warm. She waved her hand past her face to create some air flow. At the smithy, a small knot formed in the pit of her stomach. This is where it had been, yes, here it had been that her Jacob.... She willed herself to stop thinking about it. It had, after all, been so many years ago, and she had only been a child. Taking a deep breath, she walked into the smithy. The forge was heated, and the flames by the hearth made the area twice as warm as outside. The blacksmith, as well as two of his men, were stripped to the waist and sweating profusely. One of the men operated a bellows, and she watched for a moment, fascinated as the fire swept upward. So Jacob had watched. And then.... She pushed back her memories again and spoke.

"Excuse me."

Her voice, unusually high and squeaky, almost evaporated in the oppressive heat of the area. None appeared to have heard her, but as she stepped closer one of them saw her. A young man whom she guessed to be only a few years older than Annder, nudged the others.

"Could you tell me," she continued, as all three now eyed her curiously, "what happened to the people outside in the street? The people who were...who were dancing?"

"They were taken to the guild hall by the Horse Market—the Clothmakers' Guild Hall."

It was the blacksmith who answered, momentarily stopping the beating of the iron at his forge, briefly scanning her appearance as he spoke and not finding her at all interesting.

The young man, the one who had alerted the others to her coming into the smithy, now piped up as well.

"I have also heard that a platform is to be erected in the Horse and Corn Market, a platform for dancing, and that certain persons will be appointed to dance with...with these people and that there will be others appointed who will play music for them."

He stopped as suddenly as he had started, embarrassed by his own loquacity and went back to his work on the forge.

"Thank you."

Ingesting the information and seeing no reason to stay, Katharina half curtsied before turning quickly and making her way back to the door, back to the street. Once outside, she breathed in the warm air deeply. Then, lifting her skirts, she retraced her steps. The Horse Market was not far from where she was. And it was likely that she would meet Vati and Annder on her way there. She knew the location of the Clothmakers' Guild Hall, so that is where she would go. Surrounded by stately half-timbered homes, it was situated in the area of Strasbourg where the wealthy resided and where even the pigeons soundlessly strutted and primped their feathers, as if they were too fancy to coo.

Katharina found Jews Street without much effort. The Clothesmakers' Guild Hall was at its centre. Supporting arches in front of the building, as well as its small peaked tower, made it uniquely stand out from the other structures surrounding it. There were a number of people out on the road, restlessly pacing in front of the great double door. She approached them with alacrity. Surely some of these men and women would know who had gone in and out of the guild hall. But no one paid much attention to her. Walking between them, hesitant about speaking, she noted that the doors of the hall were half-open. No wonder! With the heat outside, the temperature inside must be stifling. Lively music drifted down the steps. Glancing around at the small crowd, she summoned all her courage and slowly climbed up the stone stairs, peering through the open doors.

Much closer now to the source of the melody, the music grew louder, and she inadvertently lifted her hands to her ears. The noise was almost painful. She noted drummers and pipers lined up against the great walls of the hall, playing with gusto for what seemed to be a distressing mix of drunken men and women—all of them swaying, kicking arms and legs in a disoriented but determined manner. Her first impulse was to leave—to put this cacophony behind her and go home. The horrible clamour and the uncontrolled sounds which broke forth from some of the throats of those dancing about, were almost inhuman. She longed for the quiet of her mother's kitchen and the sweet repose of her evening prayers. But then she spotted Annalein—gentle Annalein—her friend. Leaning hard on the arm of a sturdy priest, the girl seemed to have a kink in her neck. Her head was twisted in an unnatural angle to the right. With her mouth half-open, it appeared as if she was crying out in pain. Katharina's heart stood still for a moment and then beat convulsively with compassion.

"Annalein!" she whispered and again, "Oh, Annalein!"

Slowly she made her way toward the pair, suddenly not minding the ruckus and hullabaloo of the pipes and drums, nor the mindless singing of the afflicted. In one moment, her heart became focused solely on helping her friend. She carefully approached the side the priest was not supporting. Nodding encouragingly at him, she put an arm around Annalein's waist. Annalein gave no indication whatsoever that she noticed Katharina's presence. She continued to jerk and flail about in a manner that required all the priest's, and now all of Katharina's, strength.

"Thank you for helping. I vow that she is tiring," the priest remarked loudly to Katharina after a few moments, "I mark it well for her movements grow less violent than an hour ago."

He had to half-yell, half-speak to make his words audible, and she nodded to relay to him that she had heard what he said. It was difficult to believe that he had walked with Annalein for such a length of time. She had not been here for even five minutes and already her body was weary.

"Why," she called out loudly to the priest behind Annalein's back, "do you suppose this has happened?"

He shrugged.

"I do not know. Some have said it is a condemnation on the heresy which is spreading throughout Strasbourg."

"What heresy?"

Katharina did not understand what the priest meant, and she could scarcely make out his words in all the hubbub around them. Then she wished she had not asked for she saw that the question troubled him greatly, that this heresy was on his mind. She could detect, however, that it was true what the priest had said prior to that—that Annalein was tiring. But considering that the girl had danced, or rather had moved about in this convulsive manner for an extremely long time now—she would venture to guess that it had been for more than two days—was this not to be expected? Annalein would have to be beyond weary at this point. Glancing around the great hall, Katharina could see that a man had dropped not four feet from where they were and that several people were pulling him, feet first, toward the west side of the room. Was he dead? Annalein stumbled, and Katharina almost buckled at the full weight the girl deposited on her. Her limbs relapsed somewhat, and she seemed to be giving way to exhaustion. She surely must be extremely tired. The priest, leaning over, indicated with a shake of his head, that they should move toward the nearest wall. Between them they directed, half-pulled Annalein's body toward an empty section. The music, which had been slowing down as the players needed a break, petered out, even as they reached the wall. Annalein now collapsed so heavily she almost took Katharina down with her. The girl's breathing was very shallow. Indeed, Katharina wondered if she were breathing at all.

"*Danse macabre!*" the priest whispered, panting heavily on Annalein's other side.

His scalp, surrounded by his tonsure, was shining and wet with sweat.

"A dance of death," he interpreted, his tone hoarse, but quite understandable.

"Of death?" Katharina whispered back.

All around them many dancers were falling to the ground. It seemed as if the hushed music had robbed their limbs of the need to move erratically. A few moments later a man entered the hall, carrying a clarinet. He began to play almost immediately. Plaintively at first, the notes soon followed one another, faster and faster, in rapid succession. Several of the limp bodies strewn about the room started to twitch again. Half-sitting up in a stiff manner, they rose to their feet rather like wooden soldiers who have received marching orders while still quite asleep.

"I think it begins again," the priest called through the notes, "are you up to it, child?"

Katharina eyed Annalein who, as yet, had not made any motion to rise, but only jerked her limbs about. She stroked her friend's hand.

"Will she die?" she asked timidly, almost not daring to say the words.

In reply the priest began to half-chant, half-sing through the clarinet's melody.

Alas! O dearest friend, O dear!
A black man drags me far from here,
Why wilt thou let me go from thee,
I cannot walk, no, dance for me.

Katharina felt shivers slide down her spine. She did not like what the priest sang. She liked it not at all.

Chapter XIX

I t was not long after the priest's mournful dirge, that Vati and Annder arrived at the guild hall, spelling Katharina's watch with Annalein. Concerned for her safety, they sent her home with instructions to tell Frau Stoffler that they would stay the remainder of the day and the evening as well. As he sent her back to Johanngasse, Vati told Katharina that Sebastian Brant, the secretary of the council of Strasbourg, was seeing to it that people would be especially appointed to dance with those who had been afflicted and that neither she nor Annalein's mother need concern themselves that the girl would be left on her own.

Katharina walked home in somewhat of a daze. In more than a few side streets she marked one or two people with this new illness, this dancing mania. It filled her with both misgiving and sadness. What evil had Strasbourg committed that God should so visit the people living here? Was it the controversy over the Virgin Mary? Was that the evil which had brought down God's wrath? But was this dancing epidemic actually a sign of God's anger? Might there perhaps be a natural explanation? Even so, did God ever use natural means to punish a city, to punish anyone? She did not know the answers. Her walk was slow. Her footsteps trailed over the cobblestones without a purpose. It was so very hot. Sweat trickled down her face while thoughts trickled about in her mind. She wiped her forehead clean, but it was more difficult, if not impossible, to wipe her mind. The priest had mentioned heresy.

She had not thought of it right away, but now wondered if he had been referring to the tracts being printed and freely distributed throughout Strasbourg—tracts by the priest, Brother Martin Luther from Wittenberg. They were being nailed to church doors, fastened to cemetery gates and pasted to shop windows in a number of cities, including Strasbourg. All the people of Strasbourg had access to these documents; and, truth be told, most liked the priest's honesty. The ideas he put forth had taken hold of most of the population. And that was a fact.

The shadow of the cathedral fell on her. It was a few degrees cooler in its shade. Should she go in for prayer?—say some *Hail Marys* asking for Annalein's returned health? Or should she invoke St. Vitus? Vati had said more than once that the illness was referred to as St. Vitus' dance. There was a chapel dedicated to St. Vitus in Zabern just south of Strasbourg. Zabern was located in a particularly spectacular section of Alsace. Grim and foreboding, it abounded with cliffs and rocky crags, but it did hold a special beauty of its own. She remembered travelling through it a long time ago when Vati had taken her along on a trip. A beggar sitting at the curb now pulled at her skirt. She had not noticed him and was startled.

"Alms, lady, alms!!"

Katharina had no purse with her and shook her head.

"I have nothing," she murmured to the man.

He let go of her skirt, and she observed that he had but one leg and that his face was covered with running pustules. She walked on, casting a backward glance over her shoulder, but there was really nothing she could do.

"Katharina."

She stopped and turned again, surprised to see her sister Margaret running down the steps of the cathedral.

"Katharina," Margaret called out again, "Wait, please!"

Katharina smiled and held out her hands to her younger sister. The beggar grimaced at her from his position at the curb, as if to say, "You wait upon her, but not upon me."

"Kathe," Margaret gasped, reaching her side, "have you seen Annalein?"

As her sister nodded, she halted her words for a moment to catch her breath, before continuing with, "How is she? Is she all right?"

"She was...she was, when I last saw her, lying down on the floor of the guild hall. It was weariness from dancing that caused her to lie down...to lie down and even to sleep for a while. But her body was still twitching as she slept—at times still moving as if in dance."

"Why, Katharina?"

"I know not, Margaret. Indeed, I know not. How was Frau Stoffler when you left?"

The girls had resumed walking as they spoke.

"She was sleeping, Kathe," Margaret answered, "when I left for the cathedral, and sleeping soundly. Mutti gave her a sleeping draught in the ale to help her rest."

They walked home together, and Katharina was glad of her sister's company. Arriving at Johanngasse, Mutti told them that Frau Stoffler, though groggy, had just left to return home in the hope that Felix Rothmuller, her son-in-law, would be willing to help with Annalein. She thought he might, and she was much improved in her state of mind even after her short rest.

"Though not long, she had a good sleep," Mutti repeated, as she poured Margaret and Katharina a drink of ale and served them some bread, before asking Katharina how Annalein was doing. After Katharina had recounted all that she knew, Mutti sighed deeply.

"It is the same for many families," she said softly, "I have no idea as to why such a thing is happening. It is not just women that are affected, but there are men and children involved as well. I have sent Marta home to inquire as to how her family is doing. The poor girl was so worried!"

SOMEONE KNOCKED AT the door. Mutti went to answer and it was Frau Bauer. It was nigh evening now and unusual for her to be calling at such a time. After being ushered through to the kitchen, she asked about Annalein, who was, after all, a relative. Frau Bauer had no children. There was only Herr Bauer, and he was often gone on business trips as he was a merchant. But how the woman's arms would have loved to hold her own child, Katharina reflected as she watched her neighbour sitting across from her at the table. Perhaps God had something different in mind for her. She did, after all, help so many people with her knowledge of herbs.

"The city authorities," Frau Bauer told them, "have issued stricter regulations than heretofore. The guilds must take charge of their own sick and take care they do not run about the streets. Or they must send them on to St. Vitus."

"Send them to St. Vitus?" Margaret echoed, "But how?"

No one answered and they sat quietly for some time.

"I think," Mutti eventually spoke, "that you girls ought to go up to bed. It has been a long day for you, Katharina, and you must be bone weary."

Katharina nodded. Indeed, she was extremely tired. Again and again, she felt the jerking motions of Annalein's body, as if the girl were glued to her side and had become a part of her own body. Inadvertently she jerked her own body as she rose from her chair at the table. A startled look appeared on her mother's face. Katharina smiled reassuringly.

"It's nothing, Mutti," she soothed, "I was just…just remembering."

Mutti walked over and felt Katharina's forehead.

"Get some sleep, child. Go up and get some rest. Margaret make sure she goes right to bed, and do not keep her awake with your chattering. Tomorrow is another day, and I have no doubt that it will be long enough as well."

Margaret and Katharina trudged up the stairs to the girls' bedroom. As Katharina took off her dress and laid it out in the corner on the chest of drawers to wear again in the morning, she noted that Margaret was placing both of their sets of shoes under the bed in a careful manner. That in itself was not unusual. They placed their shoes under the bed each evening. But Margaret was turning the shoes upside down.

"Margaret," Katharina laughed, "what are you doing? Afraid of mice?"

"Frau Bauer told me last week," Margaret responded defensively, "that putting your shoes upside down under the bed prevents ailments of any sort."

"Oh, Margaret," Katharina responded to her sister, "that is nonsense."

"Well," Margaret shrugged, "it won't hurt, will it?"

Then they both giggled and jumped into bed.

"Let's go to the baths tomorrow," Margaret whispered after a few moments as they lay on top of the blanket in their white shifts. "It's been so frightfully warm."

Katharina, already half-asleep, yawned without answering and then she knew nothing until the first morning light.

"You look much better than you did last night, daughter," Mutti smiled when Katharina came down.

Margaret, who had risen earlier, had gone to the market.

"Do you think that you might visit Frau Schilter for me this morning?" Mutti continued, as she carefully arranged some freshly sliced bread on a platter and placed it in front of Katharina. "She complained to me of a toothache when I saw her two days ago, and I wonder how she is faring. Especially as she is due to deliver soon."

Katharina nodded. Actually she was relieved to have a chore which in some way released her from a conscience which told her to return to Annalein's side.

"Where is Vati?" she asked and, "Did he and Annder come home last night?"

"Yes," Mutti said, "and they said Frau Stoffler's son-in-law came and took over walking with Annalein. Frau Stoffler also returned to the guild hall. The church, it seems, is providing some food and drink for those who are remaining with those who are afflicted with the dancing sickness."

"Poor Annalein," Katharina sighed, looking at the bread lying in front of her with sudden distaste.

She had no appetite at all, but to please Mutti, who was eyeing her rather anxiously, she took a bite. Her mouth was dry and although she chewed and chewed, she was not able to swallow at all.

"Take a drink," Mutti suggested, noting her difficulty, pushing a pitcher of water and a cup toward her, "and when you are done, please put the packet of powdered herbs I have put together for Frau Schilter in your pocket. If she needs them, tell her to mix them with some water and to hold the mixture in her mouth no less than ten minutes before spitting it out. If she does not need it, bring it home again."

"Yes, Mutti."

Katharina got up as she spoke and walked over to where Mutti had placed the packet on the table. She picked it up rather listlessly and slipped it into her pocket.

"You have not finished...." Mutti began, but then stopped.

Yet she could not refrain from adding, "Well, at least take a drink, child."

Katharina poured some water from the pitcher on the table into the cup. She took a long drink, smiled at her mother and wiped her mouth with two fingers. Then she walked toward the door and, turning and blowing her mother a kiss, she was gone.

FRAU SCHILTER LIVED at the south end of Strasbourg. It was not in the direction of the cathedral and consequently, not toward the guild hall where Annalein was apparently still dancing. It both bothered and lightened Katharina that she was walking away from that particular area. On the one hand, her conscience plagued her that she was walking away from problems; on the other hand, her body felt sturdy and alive and glad to be walking out. It was already warm, and she recalled Margaret's words before she had dropped off to sleep last night that they should go to the public baths together. Perhaps this afternoon. It surely would be good to wash all of her body instead of just her arms and face as she had done that morning in the ewer of lukewarm water stationed on the chest in the bedroom.

Few people were about in the street. An air of desolation hung over the cobblestones under her feet. A stray dog passed her, tail between its legs, followed a few minutes later by a shaggy goat who must have escaped his rope in a nearby yard. Ravens flew overhead, making hoarse music as they winged. As well, a cuckoo alighted on a tree and produced such a mournful series of notes that Katharina shivered in spite of the heat. She was not easily spooked, but there was something unwholesome about this morning. This section of Strasbourg was too still. She would even have welcomed—and she smiled to herself at the thought—the sight of a beggar or two, or even a fat priest on his way to conduct a Mass somewhere. But here she reprimanded herself. It was not good to think such thoughts about those who wore the cloth. As it was, there was not a soul about—no one at all.

"Sickness attacks those who are most afraid," Katharina whispered to herself.

They were words she had often heard Mutti say.

FRAU SCHILTER WAS not a wealthy woman. She was a young widow whose husband had been a fisherman, a fisherman who had recently died in a boating accident. Earlier in the year, Mutti had met her as she stood in line buying vegetables at the market and had been impressed by something in the woman's demeanor. Whatever it was, it had moved her to strike up a conversation. Frau Schilter, at that time, was just in the beginning stages of pregnancy with her first child. Mutti had discovered that she took in washing and sewing, managing to just eke out a living without a husband to sustain her. Still, she kept clean and was honest, and Mutti had been looking in on her regularly. While thinking on these things, Katharina reached the front steps of Frau Schilter's small home. Immediately noting that the door was open, Katharina's innate sense of carefulness was alerted. After knocking several times, she walked in.

"Hello! Are you here, Frau Schilter?" she called out and again, "Hello, anyone home?"

There was no answer. Lifting her skirts so as not to disturb the rushes strewn about on the cottage floor, she stepped further into the room, an area which served both as kitchen and livingroom. She had been here once before with Mutti. There was hardly any furniture—just a wooden table and two chairs. Only one other room made up the small cottage, and the door to it was slightly ajar. It was the room in which Frau Schilter slept. Katharina cautiously proceeded toward it. Through a thin crack she could see part of Frau Schilter's straw pallet pressed against the far wall, but beyond that she could see nothing. Cautiously she pushed the door open all the way.

"Hello?"

She breathed the greeting quietly and walked in. There was a sweetish odour. Frau Schilter was lying at the other end of the pallet—a pallet which was stained red with blood. Her eyes were closed, but Katharina could detect her breathing. For a split second, she recalled cousin Ursula and how the blanket covering her had moved up and down, up and down. Frau Schilter seemed to be holding something in her arms. As Katharina stepped closer, she heard a heart-rending, small, mewling sound. In a trice she had reached the mattress, kneeling down in front of Frau Schilter.

"Frau Schilter," she whispered, "can you hear me?"

There was no answer. She gently pulled away the thin blanket covering the woman, for the mewling sound came from underneath. A baby, one who had stuffed some of the straw mattress into its mouth, sneezed in her direction, afterward lifting big black eyes upward to Katharina's face.

"It's a girl."

The words were ever so soft, but distinct.

"I've tried to keep her warm and...."

Frau Schilter's voice was fading, but her eyes were now wide open.

"...and I've fed her too."

"Yes," Katharina said, her eyes held fast by the little body, naked and still covered with meconium.

"I'm so tired," Frau Schilter mouthed and closed her eyes again.

Katharina stayed in her kneeling position, transfixed by the baby's gaze. It seemed that the child had no need to blink. She herself blinked several times.

"She...."

Her eyes went back to Frau Schilter's face. The mother's eyes had opened again—had opened wide. They were dark, like her daughter's eyes.

"She needs to be baptized."

Katharina nodded.

"There are swaddling bands...in the drawer.... Please...."

Frau Schilter's eyes drooped shut once more. Katharina slowly rose and walked toward a small chest of drawers across from the bed. She pulled open the top drawer. There was binding for the baby in it. She knew how to bind a baby—she had done it often when accompanying Frau Bauer at birthings. She also knew how to bathe a newborn. The water in the bowl on the small table next to the drawer, looked clean, as did the towels stacked on the floor next to the drawer. She felt the water with her pinky. Tepid to warm because of the heat, it would do fine. Picking up one of the towels, she returned to the mattress. Bending down, she gingerly disengaged Frau Schilter's clinging arm from the newborn. Lifting the little girl, who was featherlight and who continued to focus her gaze on Katharina's face, she smiled and clucked. Wrapping the towel around the miniscule body, a wonderful feeling of love and compassion enveloped her. What an amazing miracle a newborn child was! She walked over to the far end of the pallet. After laying the baby down, she brought the water bowl over with the intention of cleaning off the meconium and binding and swaddling the little one.

"No."

It was Frau Schilter.

"You can swaddle her, but then you must take her to a priest."

"But," Katharina hesitantly answered, "shouldn't she be washed first?"

"No, she cannot remain unbaptized or she will be consigned to hell."

The whisper was insistent, containing a hint of terror.

"Go, go quickly and find a priest who will baptize her. Please! Should the babe die before baptism, she will be robbed of eternal life."

Frau Schilter wearily closed her eyes when Katharina nodded. The words had tuckered her out. A noise behind Katharina caused her to turn abruptly, taking her gaze away from the mother. A woman dressed in a short-waisted, tight-laced brown gown, stood in the bedroom's doorway. Although she appeared friendly and smiled reassuringly, there was something in her demeanour that Katharina instinctively mistrusted.

"I'm Augusta Papus, Frau Schilter's neighbour. I helped her deliver the baby early this morning, but had to leave to take care of my own children."

"You must go."

Frau Schilter reiterated what she had said and Katharina obediently bent down over the bed to pick up the child.

"Go to the St. Thomas Church. It's closest."

Augusta Papus made no move to enter the bedroom.

"Will you watch Frau Schilter while I am gone with the child?" Katharina asked her.

"I cannot stay," the woman shrugged and spoke simultaneously, "I have several little ones at home and my husband has gone to work."

"Frau Schilter has to be bathed. She needs to be cleaned and she should also be fed some broth."

Instinctively Katharina realized that the woman was not really listening, that she had no intention of helping and that she was simply standing in the doorway to gather gossip. Perhaps if she hurried, she could be back shortly. The St. Thomas Church was close to their home and if she could stop by and tell Mutti what had happened, then either Mutti or Frau Bauer could come and help Frau Schilter.

"Go and get the child baptized. Her name...her name...." Frau Schilter's voice was very weak now. Katharina bent down by the bed, holding the baby carefully in the crook of her right arm.

"I will go," she promised, "but I or Mutti will be back soon. Do you have a name or do you want me to choose a name for the baby?"

There was a grateful smile, a blinking assent to the question, and then the tired eyes closed.

Katharina, quite convinced that Frau Schilter had truly fallen asleep, walked back toward the chest of drawers. She then carefully lay the baby down on the bed in the towel and stretched out the little limbs, smoothing the wrinkles. Quickly swaddling each member separately and thickly, she also put a light binding around the lower stomach. A little cap that had been placed next to the swaddling bands was fit onto the small skull. And all the while the child stared at her, not making a peep. As well, Katharina carefully folded the towel on which the child was lying, around the little form. After all, it would not do to go about carrying a cold child, even if the temperature outside was well nigh hot. All the while Augusta Papus watched her, neither saying anything nor offering any help.

"I shall be back," Katharina said, moving toward the door, sheltering the baby in her arms, "and it would be good if you could keep an eye on Frau Schilter, who is, after all, your neighbour."

"If I had four arms, indeed," the woman said, "then it would be possible, but as it is, I'm already where I ought not to be. The only reason I was able to help early on this morning is that Frederik, my husband, was still home. He urged me to go. Her groans were keeping him awake."

Katharina stared at her.

"And then, she delivered on her own. Before I came in, mind," Augusta prattled on, as if Frau Schilter should have had the courtesy to wait for her.

"Maybe one of your children....?" Katharina murmured.

"They are too young. But," and she tapped the palm of her left hand with the index finger of her right, "perhaps if you were to offer me some recompense...."

The baby stirred in Katharina's arms and she glanced down. She remembered that earlier on in the morning she had entertained the thought that she would welcome even the sight of a beggar. She shook her head at Augusta Papus whom she did not trust and whose greedy eyes ran up and down her pocket.

"I can only offer you," she responded, "the goodwill of our Lady Mary."

Augusta snorted. Turning quickly, she disappeared through the doorway into the street. Katharina sighed. Taking one last look at Frau Schilter, who lay as still as death, she followed Augusta outside through the door and began walking toward St. Thomas Church.

The street was still as empty as it had been when she arrived. Katharina began to speak to the small child in her arms.

"And what shall your name be, little one?" she asked it, "You were born in the early morning, so perhaps Aurora would be a good name."

The baby blinked, and Katharina smiled down at her.

"Aurora means dawn, you know."

Stumbling over a clod of earth, she tightened her hold on the wee bundle, but continued her speech to the child.

"Perhaps Beata would be a good name as well. That means blessed, and you are blessed to be alive and going to your baptism."

After a few more paces, she added, "And what do you think of the name Katharina? That is my name. You would be little Katharina, and I would be big Katharina."

There was a sweetness in carrying this child. Katharina knew not what it was that made her feel so tender and loyal and loving. Perhaps it was the stark contrast with yesterday when she had walked side by side with Annalein. She had not been able to help Annalein, but she could help this little girl.

Chapter XX

Within a block of St. Thomas Church, the wealthiest church in Strasbourg, Katharina saw a young boy loitering at the side of the road. He looked to be a beggarly child, dressed poorly in ragged pants and shirt, with a jerkin overtop that looked fit for a much older lad. She stopped and began to talk to him.

"Would you like to earn a *pfennig*?"

The boy stared up at her, eyes round.

"A *pfennig*?"

"Yes," Katharina smiled, "a *pfennig*. Just take a message to a woman who lives on Johanngasse. Ask someone on that street where Herr Schütz lives. Most people will be able to direct you to his home. Knock on the door and tell Frau Schütz that Frau Schilter has need of her."

The boy continued to look up at her, wonder in his face.

"Will you do it?" she asked.

He nodded.

"But first," Katharina went on, "You must repeat to me what I have just said and also" she added, "you will receive a trencher of stew from me tomorrow if you come by the house again."

He proceeded haltingly, but clearly, to reiterate what she had told him to say. She made him do it once more, then dug into the pocket of her kirtle and gave him the promised *pfennig*. It was her *beichtspfennig*, the penny she normally gave as an offering to the priest who heard her confession.

"What is your name?"

"Hermann."

The boy's grubby hand was hot. She could feel heat and sweat emanating from the palm, and she thought of how it could be little Jacob standing in front of her. But God in his great mercy had given little Jacob a good home. Hermann grinned, and she could see gaps where several teeth were missing.

"Remember tomorrow," she said again.

He bobbed his head up and down with enthusiasm, turned around and ran off in the direction of Johanngasse. The baby fussed and she rocked the child back and forth as she walked on in her quest for a priest.

St. Thomas Church had been used as a place of worship since the sixth century. Once quite an exceptionally beautiful building, it had burned down twice—once in 1007 and again in 1144. The two steeples presiding over the roof towered imposingly and made the church look like a fortress, even though they were not quite as magnificent as the tall cathedral steeple. Yet, nonetheless, St. Thomas Church was quite grand and becoming grander. Presently, workmen could be seen on her ramparts doing more construction, and it was generally projected that there would be a complete renovation of the building in a few years time.

St. Thomas was a hall church, which meant that the nave and the side aisles were of the same height and under the same roof. Entering through a wooden double door, Katharina sincerely hoped that the baby would stay quiet. Standing resolutely for a moment in the apse, she walked on into the nave, pillars on either side. She noted there was a gallery on the left and a chapel on her right, and she turned to the right. It seemed reasonable to assume that a priest would be found in the chapel. A few people were kneeling in the pews and at prayer. The air was cool and pleasant after the humidity and heat of the street outside. She scanned the sanctuary for a priest but could not locate a robed figure anywhere. Memorial plaques denoting benefactors were present on the walls, on the floor and under pews. Glancing upward she noted the high rose stained glass leaded windows. Parishioner wealth was also displayed prominently in the church monuments and furnishings, for St. Thomas was lavishly decorated with figures of saints—saints who seemed to be staring down at her from everywhere, whether approvingly or disapprovingly, she knew not. She was startled when the figure of a woman rose from a nearby bench and approached her.

"Katharina?"

It was Frau Bauer.

"Frau Bauer? I didn't know you came here for prayer?"

Her neighbour smiled, almost wryly, Katharina thought.

"Yes, I do. I still pray faithfully after all these years that perhaps I might...."

She stopped abruptly but Katharina knew within herself what words had been left unspoken—"that perhaps I might...still have a baby.'"

"Do you know where I could locate a priest who would baptize this child?"

Frau Bauer raised her eyebrows quizzically at the bundle in Katharina's arms, and Katharina briefly, in very low tones so as not to disturb those at prayer, explained.

"Who will stand as the child's godparent?" her neighbour asked when she had done speaking.

Katharina had not yet thought about that aspect of the baptism.

"I suppose," she hesitatingly answered, "that I might stand. I have the age and I am confirmed."

"There are several priests here who are very kind," Frau Bauer said softly, "and I dislike them not. They have helped me several times when I had questions. And," she added in a whisper, "most seem not to be money-hungry."

The baby began to whimper, and Katharina mechanically rocked the little one back and forth. Glad of Frau Bauer's presence and help, she watched gratefully as the woman disappeared in search of a priest. She came back almost immediately with a man of medium height and friendly countenance. Indeed, he smiled at her in such a way that it put her at ease.

"I'm Brother Wilhelm," he said by way of introducing himself, "and I understand you would like to have your baby baptized?"

"It is not mine," Katharina answered, blushing as she spoke and went on to explain yet once again Frau Schilter's request.

Brother Wilhelm listened patiently, before commending her on the wisdom and willingness to bring the child to St. Thomas for baptism. He then asked her to accompany him to the baptistry. Frau Bauer stayed close by Katharina's side all the while, and she was grateful for it. When the matter of godparent came up Frau Bauer actually stepped forward, looking askance at Katharina as she did so.

"Would you mind if I stood as godmother?"

The voice carried a plea, and Katharina acquiesced readily. Although being a godparent carried no legal right or ecclesiastical authority to the custody of a child, the godparent was a practical choice to raise the child should the mother die. Frau Schilter was ill. There was a constant, nagging worry at the back of her mind for the woman. Hopefully Mutti had received the boy's message and had gone out to the Schilter's cottage.

The priest made no mention of the fact that the baby was not wearing a white gown, and when he poured the chrism onto the baby's head, it dribbled down mixing with the meconium still present on the newborn body. Remembering the wonderful white gowns her siblings and she herself had worn, Katharina felt almost as if the baby was being cheated. For the girl's name Katharina gave Beata Aurora, liking the sound of it as the priest spoke.

"Beata Aurora Schilter, I baptize you in the name of the Father, the Son and the Holy Spirit."

The ceremony was over and after thanking Brother Wilhelm profusely, Frau Bauer and Katharina walked back down the nave through the apse toward the outside door. After the coolness of the church, the heat outside embraced them aggressively.

"Have you heard any more news about Annalein?" Katharina questioned when they were back on the road.

"No."

Frau Bauer answered rather absently, all the while fingering the fringe on the towel and gazing at the wide-eyed face of the baby. They had turned quite naturally toward the Johanngasse. While still in the church, Frau Bauer had suggested that carrying the child back to her home for a washing might be in order and that it would only take a small while and then they could carry little Beata back to her mother—clean and fresh. Besides that, she had told Katharina that she might have some tiny clothes, which she could give along for the baby—clothes she herself had never used.

"Would you like me to carry her?"

Eager arms took the bundle from Katharina's care, and she again marvelled at the softness in Frau Bauer's face. Why would it be that God had never given this woman a live child?

Little Beata was bathed in warm water. Katharina remained a spectator as her neighbour carefully cleaned the child's nose with a little olive oil, also dabbing a little of the oil into her eyes. Afterward the child, who was beginning to protest with healthy squalling lungs, was swaddled up again with fresh swaddling bands which Frau Bauer also had handy.

"We must go back now," Katharina said, suddenly more uneasy than she had been, "Frau Schilter will be wondering what has happened, and she will be so glad to hear that Beata has been baptized. I hope she will like the name."

Frau Bauer was busy tying the strands of lace on the bottom of the tight-fitting cap and did not appear to hear her.

"We must go now, Frau Bauer," Katharine said again.

"Yes," the woman answered with a sigh, "we must indeed. I think she grows hungry."

The walk back to the Schilter's cottage was uneventful. Frau Bauer carried Beata who continued to wail every few minutes or so. Before they reached the cottage, however, Katharina noted that there were several people grouped in front of its door. She felt a familiar surge of fear. People had also milled about their steps the day little Jacob died, the day she and Barbara had walked up the Johanngasse after that horrible accident. She increased her pace, breaking into a half-run, leaving Frau Bauer and Beata far behind. Reaching the door, she passed the women, for they were all women, and let herself in. She could see her mother straightaway sitting on the edge of Frau Schilter's bed. And she could smell, yes, she could smell, death.

"Mutti?"

It was a question. Her mother turned.

"Katharina. Have you the baby with you?"

"Yes, I do, Mutti. That is, Frau Bauer, who is coming down the street, she is carrying the baby. I met her in St. Thomas Church."

Frau Schilter lay very still and the coverlet over her body did not rise as it should rise with breathing.

"Is...is Frau Schilter...?"

She did not finish the sentence.

"Yes, she is dead, Katharina."

"Were you here?"

"Yes, I was."

"Because she died in childbirth," Mutti went on, "and I could see she was slipping away, I had her confess to me."

Katharina looked at Frau Schilter, hands folded peaceably on her chest, face pale and white, body still, ever so still.

"Frau Bauer," she began softly, "stood godmother for the baby, Mutti."

"She must be buried shortly," Mutti said, almost as if she had not heard Katharina, "it is too hot for the body to stay above ground."

"The bell will toll," Katharina said, "only a few times for Frau Schilter, I think."

"I was allowed to shrive her," Mutti murmured as if she was speaking to herself, again mentioning Frau Schilter's confession, "because I am a midwife. I have delivered many babies."

Katharina sat down next to her on the pallet and put her arms around her mother. "Of course it was all right, Mutti."

"There was no priest," Mutti went on in a low tone.

"No, there was not," Katharina agreed, "but you were here."

Frau Bauer walked in, carrying the baby in her arms. She stopped in the bedroom doorway and leaned against the lintel.

"The poor babe!" she whispered, upon noting the dead woman and again, "The poor babe!"

Mutti disengaged herself from Katharina's arms and stood up. After one last look at Frau Schilter, she turned away from the straw bed.

"You have a goddaughter to raise now, neighbour. May God

guide you in this!"

"Indeed," Frau Bauer replied, very much moved, "Indeed, may he guide me!"

FRAU SCHILTER WAS, the very next day, laid to rest in the consecrated cemetery around St. Thomas Church. Crosses marked its corners and a tall cross stood in its centre. Not everyone was allowed burial in consecrated ground. Suicides were kept out, unless they were known to be insane; those who died in tournaments were disallowed; those who had been excommunicated and never repented were not laid to rest there; and those who were known to have been committing a public sin, such as money lending for profit, were also forbidden a place. Frau Schilter fitted none of these categories and as the Bauers requested that she be buried in their church confines, and were generously willing to pay for the burial, a gravedigger dug a proper pit the very evening of her death. Herr Bauer also paid for prayers for the soul of Frau Schilter for some years to come. Frau Bauer provided a proper shroud, and just prior to the funeral the bell tolled sombrely for the space of a full half hour.

Little Beata, unaware that she had become an orphan the very first day of her life, was fed, that initial night, a pap made of white flour, butter and beer, which was alternated with whole milk. The day after her mother was buried, a wetnurse was found for the child by her godmother—a sturdy pleasant woman who had given birth to a baby boy two months earlier. The woman, who was of peasant stock, had good colour, possessed a strong neck and had firm breasts. According to Frau Bauer, Liesl, for that was the woman's name, also demonstrated good morals and conduct and was not easily given to melancholy, anger or fear—all traits which could be passed on to the baby, traits which could physically endanger little Beata. Liesl's milk, when tested on Frau Bauer's thumbnail, beaded up until the nail was turned downward at which point the liquid ran off smoothly. Frau Bauer claimed this was a sign of sweet and excellent milk.

Later that week Katharina, standing on the stone steps of her home, contemplated all these things. She looked directly up at the Bauer's window and remembered how as a young child, she had often looked up only to see that her neighbour was sitting by the window ready to wave at her and her siblings. Katharina had just been to market for Mutti. Now, as she gazed up at the living quarters of her neighbour, a basket of onions on her arm, she could detect no one, even though she stared for a good long while. At the expense of one death, Frau Bauer, their good and kind neighbour, had now been blessed with a wee one, a little baby to hold and to dandle. Perhaps she was now at this moment, standing by the cradle—a cradle that had been reserved for a little Bauer child for several decades. God's ways were surely mysterious. Mutti said that Frau Bauer had experienced at least six deaths—six little babies who had been stillborn. And yet that woman had continually prayed for more pregnancies, for more chances to be a mother. Katharina could just faintly make out the shadow of someone passing the window. Frau Bauer would have been up last night to change or perhaps, soothe Beata. Or perhaps the wetnurse, who had come to live with them for a season, had gotten up. Katharina sighed deeply and turned, walking up the steps toward the door. The last few days had been strange. Indeed, they had been passing strange.

Chapter XXI

All counted, there were close to 400 people who were dancing in the city of Strasbourg proper; and all seemed to be afflicted with what was now widely accepted to be a dancing plague. It had begun with the solitary wooden movements of Frau Troffea in Stable Street, but with whom, people asked, would it end. Priests had come and sprinkled holy water on those who were afflicted; musicians had been hired to play for the dancers; and two wooden platforms had been erected near the Horse Market to give those caught up in the dancing frenzy a place to recuperate. But these remedies were all to no avail. No one saw much recuperation. Indeed, the mania seemed to continue without any end in sight. The uncontrollable dancing groups were a curious, obscene and fearful sight to beholders. Some of the people acted like animals, jumping about, hopping and leaping into the air without stopping. A number of them in doing so broke their ribs and died; others had heart attacks and simply stopped breathing. But mostly they continued to live—live madly by laughing, screaming, crying and singing, often, it was noted, reacting violently to the colour red.

An edict was enacted by Strasbourg's ruling city council that those with the dancing sickness were to be taken by relatives on wagons and carts to the nearby shrine of St. Vitus at Zabern, or to any shrine they might desire. It would clear the streets, it was argued, making them safe again for ordinary pedestrians who would not have to worry about bumping into bizarre groups who seemed not to note whom they ran down or bumped into.

As well, because it seemed that music actually seemed to be spreading the disease and the disorder, days of quiet and of sober repentance were advised for all the citizens of Strasbourg.

Frau Stoffler had been instructed to accompany Annalein as she travelled with a group of people up to Zabern where the Chapel of St. Vitus was located. But Johanna, Annalein's sister and heavily pregnant with her first child, knocked at the Schütz door the day before that group was to leave. She was a short girl, or rather a short woman, and her shortness was greatly emphasized by the fact that she was presently as round as the wooden barrels that the cooper made.

"Hello," she said timidly, as Frau Schütz opened the door.

"Hello, Johanna," Frau Schütz answered kindly. "Won't you come in?"

Johanna smiled and shifted her bulk over the threshold, standing awkwardly in the hall. She wore a saffron-coloured dress, loosely laced in the front.

"Come into the kitchen, child," Frau Schütz said, shutting the door behind them, "and sit down for a bit. It's so hot outside that I think you might do well with a bit of ale."

"No, thank you, Frau Schütz," Johanna demurred, "I cannot stay, for my mother is waiting for me at home."

"How is she?"

"That is why I am calling on you. You see, she is not very well. Her leg pains her much. It is swollen and I fear...."

She stopped and looked down at the wooden floor."

"Yes," Frau Schütz encouraged, "what is it you fear, child?"

"Well, she cannot...and I cannot...that is to say, neither of us can accompany Annalein to Zabern. And someone, a woman that is, has to...or should, go with her."

Johanna sighed deeply after this long string of words and shyly looked up at her hostess.

"I see," Frau Schütz replied, for she did indeed begin to see.

Johanna sighed again, plaintively rubbing her hands over her belly.

"We did not know," she said, "to whom we could turn but you…you who have been so kind this last week. We had hoped that perhaps Katharina might take mother's place and travel with Annalein to Zabern."

"I will have to ask her," Frau Schütz answered carefully, "for she is not a little maid whom I can command to go here and there, especially to such a place as Zabern with so many ill and failing in health."

Johanna nodded but made no move to leave her place. After a moment of silence between them, she coughed discreetly into her hand.

"Could you," she began hesitantly and then repeated, "could you perhaps ask her now, so that I could go home and tell my mother what reply she gave?"

The baby in the round belly kicked. The saffron-coloured material jumped up. Frau Schütz was moved.

"Are you quite certain you will not come and rest a moment and take some ale?" she asked again.

But Johanna shook her head once more.

"No, thank you, Frau Schütz. You are so very generous. But I have to go back home. I think that my mother is very anxious, and we should like to be settled in our hearts and minds about what is going to happen tomorrow. They are set to leave early. Carts and wagons are being made ready, and Annalein is listed to go in one of the first of these transports travelling out of Strasbourg."

It was another long account and Johanna turned red in the face because of it. Frau Schütz did not reply but walked over to the stairs and called up.

"Katharina, could you come down for a moment?"

They could hear a door open and not too much later Katharina stood by them. She greeted Johanna and asked after her mother. Johanna quietly related to her how her mother was and what it was she had come to ask. Katharina could scarcely take the matter in so quickly and contemplated quietly for a moment. Physically she minded how Annalein's body had felt, stiff and wooden, leaning against her own. She again saw her friend's unseeing eyes, eyes staring out into nothing. What if it was herself who had been so afflicted? Or Mutti? Or Margaret? She felt no great desire to play a heroic nursemaid but how could she say no?

"Yes," she said, looking straight into Johanna's troubled eyes, "of course I shall go."

Mutti made a small noise—a noise that was not a word nor an intelligible sound. Katharina patted her mother's arm.

"I shall be all right, Mutti," she whispered, "and, after all, there will be others. The road to Zabern is…well, it can be beautiful."

She turned her full attention to Johanna.

"So what time tomorrow morning should I be making my way to the Horse Market?"

Johanna's eyes pooled full of tears. She took Katharina's hand.

"At dawn and oh, thank you. Thank you."

"It is nothing," Katharina murmured, "but what I should wish for someone to do for me."

ZABERN LAY TO the northwest of Strasbourg. Situated at the foot of a pass over the Vosges Mountains, the journey toward it entailed seeing some castles along the way. Once there, weather permitting, the great spire of the Strasbourg cathedral would be clearly visible. So she would not be as far away from home as she might be. The great spire would remind her of Margaret and Mutti and Vati, all praying for her. Such were some of Katharina's thoughts as she walked, together with Margaret, toward the Horse Market the next morning. It was another warm day. Not quite so hot as it had been, but warm enough to make one sweat just a little without doing any work.

Katharina wore a light green gown with a white partlet edged with yellow trim. It had a high waist and was trimmed with a belt. A summer dress, the sleeves were slashed open and loose, allowing air to breeze in and cool her a little. Her hair was confined under a linen hood of the same light green shade, and she carried a cape over her arm. She had not wanted to take the cape, but her mother had insisted.

"It will be cold tonight, child. And you will be in the mountains. The mountain air…."

"Yes, yes," Katharina had interrupted, knowing that her mother was quite right, "I know. Only it will be so cumbersome to carry a cape."

"Mutti is right," Margaret added, giving her opinion of the matter, "and you will be so glad when you have the cape, Katharina. It will be like a blanket. And if it is too warm to wear it, why then you can lie on top of it. No doubt the grass will be dirty or wet, or who knows what little creatures will be...."

"Margaret!"

Mutti's voice rang out in warning. Margaret stopped talking, but then continued as another thought occurred to her.

"Can I walk Katharina to the Horse Market?"

"Only if you promise not to talk overmuch."

Katharina laughed out loud.

"That promise may be too much for her to obey, Mutti."

KATHARINA WAS GLAD of Margaret's company. They walked amiably, side by side, Margaret was quite in awe of the fact that her sister was brave enough to venture away from home for a few nights to help the Stofflers. Passing the Franciscan monastery and the Penny Tower Treasury and then the Dominicans' house, they approached the Horse Market.

"Oh, Katharina," Margaret quavered, "you can still be of a different mind. I'm sure that Frau Stoffler would understand."

"But who then," Katharina interposed, "would take sweet Annalein to St. Vitus, Margaret? Would you?"

"No, you know that I would not. But I also know that it need not be you," Margaret answered, "What, for example, of her brother-in-law? Why cannot he take her? He is family. And you...."

"Indeed, what am I?"

"Oh, but it is warm already," Margaret sighed, not answering her sister and waving her right hand in front of her face.

She carried a small basket in which Mutti had packed some bread, sausage and ale. Swinging the basket aimlesslessly about with her left hand, she almost hit a passer-by.

"Be careful," Katharina admonished.

"I shall go to the cathedral after you leave," Margaret promised, "and say some prayers for you and for Annalein."

Katharina stopped and placed a kiss on Margaret's cheek.

"You are a dear sister and I love you."

They had come to the guild hall by the Horse Market. Many people were already gathered about, standing in groups on the street. Working their way through the crowd, Katharina directed them to where she knew the platform had been erected for those afflicted with the dancing sickness. There had been no dancing on the platform, though, not since the city council had determined that soberness was needful and not the sound of music. Thinking to recognize several people, Katharina stopped to ask where she might go in order to find the wagons that had been outfitted to travel to St. Vitus that morning. A burly looking man with a jolly face took her under his wing.

"This way," he said, immediately guiding her by the arm through the dissonance of many people talking at once; past the knots of curious onlookers and well-wishers. With Margaret trailing behind, he led them neatly through the disorder of the noise and unending activity, up to a swath of green grass where three large wagons stood in a row. And in the melee of this very public place, Katharina spotted Annalein. It had only been a few days since she had last seen her friend, but Annalein was so much thinner, her face so gaunt and her eyes so.... Katharina could not find a word for it. Margaret, behind her, gasped. The man let go of Katharina's arm.

"Is there some poor soul here for whom you come?" he asked.

Katharina nodded.

"Well, I give you my blessings, lady," he said, "even as I expect I might like yours. For I also am here to conduct someone and that someone is my poor wife. I would walk her to the grotto even if it was in Spain. For I do so hope that it may help her recover."

"I am sorry," Katharina responded.

"Ah, we are all sorry," he said, "for what is it that we poor citizens have done which can so evoke the anger of almighty God?"

Katharina had no answer.

"These poor creatures," the burly fellow continued, "on their way to St. Vitus, are to be allowed no stringed instruments. Neither are they permitted jewellery, nor beautiful clothes. What laws these town councillors make."

He smiled strangely and continued.

"As if," he said, "as if these poor creatures should want jewellery or splendid clothes."

"Who...." Katharina began in answer, but was interrupted.

The man was anxious to speak.

"The Strasbourg councillors have decided that it is time for a general penance. They seem to think all these folks," and with a broad sweep of the hand he indicated the mass of folk behind him, the twitching, ill-behaving and sad group of people afflicted by the dance, "are prostitutes, ruffians, gamblers and drinkers."

"I don't know...." Katharina began again but was once more interrupted.

"None of us know," he said, "and it seems to me that the 100 lb. candle which the city has ordered as contribution for the health of these unfortunates, as well as the three low Masses to be sung in the cathedral, will be of little benefit."

Margaret tugged Katharina's green sleeve.

"I think I shall return home now," she said, her eyes wide with dread at the figures, the dozens of figures of wooden people around them, some kicking their limbs out and some prostrate upon the grass.

"Yes," Katharina gladly turned her attention away from the man and focused on her sister, "I think that would be a good idea. Tell Mutti I arrived here safely and that I shall take great care."

"You can also tell your Mutti," the burly man intervened, "that I shall watch out for your sister. She need not fear for her safety. Markus Burrmann is the name."

Margaret smiled at him timidly.

"I shall tell Mutti so for you. And I shall pray for you and your wife in the great cathedral, Herr Burrmann, even as I shall pray for Annalein Stoffler and for Katharina, my sister."

Katharina took the basket from Margaret's proffered arm and waved goodbye as the girl disappeared into the crowd.

THE SHRINE OF St. Vitus lay in a cave in the Vosges promontory named Vixberg, or St. Vitus Mountain, west of Zabern. It would be a good day's travel for the three wagons now being loaded full of ill people. There was also an additional wagon, Herr Burrmann pointed out to Katharina, that would carry the healthy caregivers, the custodians. Katharina could see a number of priests climbing onto this additional wagon, as well as women like herself. Men like Herr Burrmann would also board, presumably to serve as help for mothers, daughters and wives. She walked over to the first wagon where she supposed she had seen Annalein being lifted in by two men. The remaining two wagons held those unfortunates who were able to sit upright, but the first wagon appeared to hold only those who were down. She found she had observed correctly and saw her friend lying prostrate on the flat boards in that first long wagon. Between several others also prostrate, Annalein appeared to be sleeping. Her twitching had lessened since Katharina had last seen her.

"Can I climb into the back and sit with them?" she asked the man on the driver's seat. "I am here to help my friend, Annalein. She is one of the women who is lying down in this wagon."

The driver seemed doubtful.

"I don't know," he said, "it has been decided that all custodians should go in the last wagon."

"Please," Katharina said, "please, sir. God reward you for letting me stay close by. She is a very good friend, and I have promised her mother to watch over her."

The man weakened in his resolve and nodded curtly, indicating she could climb into the back and sit by Annalein. Hoisting up her green skirts with one hand, the basket dangling in the other hand, with the added cumbrance of her cape hanging over her right arm, Katharina found it difficult to climb in. The edge of the wagon was high, and she had nowhere to put her foot to give herself a boost up. Suddenly she found herself lifted by the waist and deposited unceremoniously into the back hold. A booming voice accompanied this action, Herr Burrmann's voice.

"Please also keep an eye on the woman lying against the side-board, and I shall be eternally grateful."

"I shall," Katharina promised, smiling at the big man.

He tipped his beret, bowed and strode off in the direction of the last wagon in the row. Katharina, turning her head, could see that he, in spite of his bulk, jumped lithely into the cart making up the rear.

Crouching down on her knees next to her friend, Katharina took Annalein's hand into her own. Her green skirt overlapped Annalein's thinning form. Straw had been deposited on the floor of the wagon. Through the dress, it scratched her knees.

"I am here, Annalein," she whispered, "and will travel with you. Together we shall be banished from the city for a while, but we'll come back. You'll see. We'll come back."

Annalein's eyes did not open. Next to her, on her right side, a woman shook convulsively. Katharina shuddered involuntarily. Looking around, she saw that all of the occupants were women— all sisters, mothers and daughters. What was she doing here? How would she ever be able to help them? She was a mere girl and how.... Her thoughts faltered. Somewhere a bird sang high up in a tree—somewhere. God had made the birds. God cared for the birds, for the sparrow. She had read that in her Bible just last night. And if he cared for the sparrow.... A calm began to descend on her.

THE TRAVEL BEGAN. The wooden carts, or rather the long wide wagons, started their trek toward the St. Vitus shrine. Riding past New St. Peter's Church and across the bridge over the River Ill, they took the road out of the city toward Hagenau. Soon Strasbourg was merely the spire of the great cathedral—the cathedral where Margaret would perhaps even now be praying for her. The road was dusty and every now and then clouds of sand swept up and settled in Katharina's nose making her sneeze. She continued to hold onto Annalein's hand. The bumps on the road made the bodies of those around her shift and slide. Katharina soon grew weary of sitting on her knees and made a pillow of her cape, thankful that she had let Mutti talk her into taking it. Cliffs and crags began to abound on both the right and the left side of the road. It was a slow and laborious ride and did not get easier as they went on.

Stroking Annalein's hand, Katharina had plenty of time for

thought—for deep thought. On the church doors and on the shop doors and on the windows of many Strasbourg homes, there had been papers posted this last year—plenty of papers. She and countless others in the city, had read them—indeed, had read them frequently and had discussed them. They had been written by the monk Luther, that teacher in Wittenberg who was on the tongue of all. The monk who had walked with Annalein during the dancing in the guild hall considered the posters heresy. But the truth was, most of what Luther wrote was well received by the majority of Strasbourg citizens who deemed, even as good Dr. Geiler had deemed, that the clergy was getting away with a sinful lifestyle and that fat and lazy monks should be held to account.

A few of Luther's paragraphs were etched on Katharina's memory. One of them was:

> To hope to be saved by indulgences is a lying and an empty hope, although even the commissary of indulgences—nay, further, the pope himself—should pledge their souls to guarantee it.

Instinctively, Katharina felt this was true. So much then for that piece of paper she had purchased on that long ago day to help poor little Jacob in purgatory. Sweet Annalein had lent her the money to purchase that paper. Actually, much of what Luther said on these posters made sense, good sense, and she knew that Vati felt this as well.

Luther had also written, and she minded it well:

> They are the enemies of the pope and of Jesus Christ who, by reason of the preaching of indulgences, forbid the preaching of the Word of God.... The true and precious treasure of the Church is the holy Gospel of the glory and grace of God.

She was so glad that Vati had given her a Bible; it was her very own. The monk Luther wrote of a free salvation—one that did not have to be bought by indulgences or candles. Katharina thought of the 100 lb. candle that had been purchased by the city for the poor folk around her. Was such a purchase to be despised? Luther said that in order to be forgiven by God for one's sins, one did not need the pope's permission. The power of forgiveness was God's alone. There was a certain sense of relief in this. Katharina felt it keenly. Luther maintained that all his poster words came from the Bible. Did Annalein need forgiveness from God before she could become better? Her hands, in response to this thought, began to rapidly and gently rub Annalein's left arm. Frau Burrmann moaned and made jerky motions as if to sit up. Katharina let go of Annalein's arm and stretched across two other bodies to take hold of Frau Burrmann's hand.

"It's all right," she murmured, "It's all right, Frau Burrmann. Stay down. Stay still."

The woman opened her eyes and looked straight at Katharina.

"So tired," she whispered before closing them again.

Katharina let go of Frau Burrmann's hand and began to sing. She herself, later, could not remember what words she had used. But her clear voice lifted up over the wagon and soared skyward with the birds. She had always loved singing ever since she was old enough to speak words, and she had always made up songs. She praised God for his wondrous creation, and she sang of his love and kindness. The driver turned his head for a moment, but she did not heed his look and continued her paean. And all around her the bodies of the unfortunates lay, some twitching, some still as death.

JUST TO THE west of Zabern, lay St. Vitus Mountain. About halfway up the mountain was a grotto called Hohlenstein. Above the grotto, higher up at the top of the mountain, a chapel had been built dedicated to St. Vitus. It had been stipulated that when the wagons approached Zabern, one of the caregivers or custodians, who rode alongside the wagons on a horse, should be sent ahead in order to obtain the services of several priests. These priests would then be instructed to begin saying Masses for those unfortunates who would soon be with them. It was late in the afternoon when Katharina saw a man on horseback pass her wagon. She stopped her singing. From time to time she had to cease, as hoarseness would overtake her. Taking a drink from the water container Mutti had put in the basket, she crawled on her hands and knees to also wet the lips of those around her. The driver turned his head.

"Don't stop the singing," he said, almost kindly, "for I believe that music and singing ward off the evil that these poor souls must fight."

Katharina smiled at him.

"I must needs rest my voice," she replied, "but thank you for your good driving and your encouragement."

He shrugged and clucked at the two horses pulling the wagon.

The wagons were now climbing a mountain road between the cliffs and the crags. It was slow moving. Small flowers peeped out in small mossy patches, smiling at the passersby in the wagons. Every now and then, a rabbit darted across the road. Katharina also noted deer from time to time, feeding on the grassy leas between the trees. The Hohlenstein grotto was not far off. It had to be passed on the way to the higher chapel of St. Vitus. Would St. Vitus be able to heal Annalein and Frau Burrmann and the others? Or had St. Vitus caused this disease and was punishing those who had not paid enough attention to him? But St. Vitus had died long ago and the Bible reading had taught her....

Katharina stopped thinking and wiped the sweat off her face. She was weary with the long day and with all the caring and all the thinking. Her dress had become dirty from touching the straw-strewn boards of the wagon. Several women had soiled themselves as they slept away the day, and the smell made her feel ill. Annalein moaned and Katharina began stroking her arm again. They would soon arrive at their destination, and she was glad of it. She could already make out the steps to the grotto. It had been told her that morning, that the wagons would stop at the bottom of the steps and the unfortunates would be encouraged to walk up—in groups of six or seven perhaps—as best they could. After stopping for meditation in the grotto, they would continue their walk up to the chapel. Letting her gaze drop on the women prostrate in the wagon, Katharina doubted that this would be a quick process.

The wagon wheels slowed down and then ground to a halt. Dust whirled up but died down just as quickly. The sun was still high above the horizon. It was late August and it would not be dark for quite some time. Herr Burrmann appeared at the wagon's side even before the driver had a chance to jump down from his place.

"I have forgotten your name, Fraulein," he said, "but I thank you for watching out for my good wife during this journey."

Katharina nodded, then courteously put out her hand over the wagon edge.

"My name is Katharina Schütz," she replied, "and it was a small matter. She, your wife, slept most of the day."

"Yes, they say it is good that they sleep."

Herr Burrmann took her proffered hand, drew it to his lips and kissed it gently.

"If you stand up," he then suggested, "I will lift you down. The driver will, no doubt, lower the side of the wagon, and we shall be able to try and awaken your friend and my wife. It is possible that perhaps they can walk up the steps with our help."

Katharina stood up—slowly and painfully. She had been sitting all day and was stiff, dreadfully stiff. Then, as if she were as light as a feather, Herr Burrmann took her waist and swung her over the edge of the wagon. Before she knew it, she was standing on the road. Stretching her limbs, she was aware of the extreme need to relieve herself.

"I…" she began, embarrassed, "I have to.…"

She stopped, blushing profusely. Herr Burrmann laughed out loud.

"The bushes, Fraulein Katharina."

His laugh exposed fine strong teeth, before he pointed to the side of the road, adding, "and I shall keep watch that no one comes to look. You have the advantage of being the first one out of the wagon."

Katharina gathered up her skirt and disappeared, reappearing moments later only to find that Herr Burrmann, with the help of the driver, had already lifted both Annalein and his wife onto the grassy berm next to the road. They were sitting up—both Frau Burrmann and Annalein—Katharina's basket and cape between them. Leaning heavily against a huge fallen tree, the look in their eyes was dazed, as if they had not any idea where they were or why they were there. Katharina knelt down next to them.

"Annalein," she whispered, "Annalein, my friend. Do you know me?"

Smiling hesitantly, the girl blinked rapidly before her gaze again became clouded over with what Katharina deemed sleep. She reached into her basket and brought out the flask with water. "Have something to drink, Annalein," she said softly, "some water will do you a world of good."

Supporting Annalein's head she held the flask to her lips. Surprisingly enough, the girl sipped a little, swallowed audibly and opened her eyes again.

Herr Burrmann returned from the wagon with a third woman.

"She is the driver's wife," he informed Katharina, "and he asked my help to lift her down so that he can walk with her to the grotto. At the grotto, they can...."

"Yes?" Katharina said, waiting to hear what would happen in the grotto.

"Well, I'm actually not sure what is done or what is in the grotto. But it is on the way to the chapel."

"Where is the driver?"

"He has gone to speak with some of the other folks. I'm thinking that a number will stay here overnight. There are too many to attempt the walk up this very evening."

"I have some bread, sir," Katharina said, "would you share it with me? I know not that your wife or that Annalein could eat."

Herr Burrmann smiled broadly.

"But you are a good girl," he answered good-humouredly, "and I would be glad to have something, for my innards are crying out for food."

"You sound like my brother Annder," Katharina smiled, opening the basket again and taking out one of the loaves and a sausage that her mother had carefully packed, "and if you would like to try and give your wife a drink, here is a flask of water also."

Annalein made a sound and both turned to look at her. Her eyes were still open, and she was gazing at the water flask with unmistakable desire. Immediately, Katharina brought the mouth of the flask back to Annalein's lips. This time her friend did not just sip but gulped the water greedily.

"Easy, girl, easy," Katharina said, "not too much or you shall choke."

But she smiled as she said it, for surely this seemed to be a good sign.

It was some fifteen minutes or so before the driver came back. He was a small, wiry man. His wife, unlike Frau Burrmann and Annalein, lay against the log without having stirred once. He spoke to her, prodded her and wet her lips with water, but all to no avail. She remained limp and unresponsive.

"I'm afraid that she will have to be carried, Karst," Herr Burrmann advised, "and I can take turns with you if it so happens that my good wife is able to walk while leaning on me."

Karst nodded sombrely, eyeing his wife with a mixture of tenderness and pity.

"We can begin our journey toward the cave," he said. "The others are about ready with the ones they will guide to the grotto and from there to the chapel. I think it matters that we go now. We will be the first ones to go up."

Herr Burrmann helped Katharina get Annalein to her feet. The girl leaned heavily on Katharina at the first, yet as they stood for a minute or two waiting for Frau Burrmann and Karst's wife, she seemed to regain the ability to balance, shifting her weight to her own two legs.

"We will manage fine," Katharina said, to assure her, "and I am here to help you."

"I slept..." mouthed the girl softly, "for a long time...?"

"Yes, you did," Katharina answered, amazed that she was actually talking to her friend.

"I'm awake now," Annalein said, staring at Katharina, her eyes clearing even as she spoke. The dreadful unknowing trance-like stare she had displayed previously was rapidly receding. Katharina squeezed her friend's arm.

"I think we shall be fine."

"Where...where are we?"

"We're at Vixberg, at St. Vitus Mountain."

Annalein did not respond, but her face was a question mark.

"You have...you are ill, Annalein," Katharina gently said, "and we've travelled to St. Vitus with many other people who are ill as well."

"Ill?" Annalein repeated.

Katharina nodded, noting out of the corner of her eye that Karst had lifted his wife into his arms and that Herr Burrmann had his arm around his wife's waist and was guiding her toward the grotto steps. Herr Burrmann was also carrying her basket and her cape. He was a kind man.

"Can you try and walk with me, Annalein?"

As a response, her friend took a step, first faltering a bit and then, becoming stronger, following Katharina's lead toward the stairs.

It was difficult at first, one stone step at a time, one foot in front of the other. But the grotto was not too high into the mountain's side, and the entrance, after only some fifteen steps, could be plainly seen.

"We will not be long in coming to the grotto," Katharina encouraged Annalein, who was beginning to show signs of weariness.

"Why?" Annalein breathed with difficulty, "Why are we going there?"

"The grotto is thought to be helpful for...for ill people. St. Vitus' water is good, I think. If you are consecrated with it...."

The steps were smooth, but it required careful guiding by Katharina to direct Annalein's way. The girl was once more beginning to lean heavily against herself. Herr Burrmann turned from where he was, only a few steps ahead.

"Are you managing?" he called.

"Yes," Katharina called back. "Thank you."

They slowly advanced to the top of the stairs. The higher they climbed, the cooler it became. The opening to the grotto appeared grimly dark even when they neared the entrance. Herr and Frau Burrmann, as well as Karst carrying his wife, stood at its opening waiting for them. Katharina held Annalein's arm and led her along the steep path toward the black mouth of the cave. A wooden carving, representing the Virgin and the Child, as well as two figures flanking them, within the belly of the cave, could be seen dimly from where they stood. One of these figures was seated in a pot and the whole group was set in what seemed to be the middle of the cavern. A priest, hooded and quiet, stood next to the carvings.

"Welcome, pilgrims," he chanted in a sing-song voice, "welcome to the grotto. Please enter."

The entire cave was about ten elle high, eighteen elle wide and thirty-four elle long. Katharina shrank from the enclosed area, her whole being crying out to remain in the fresh air. But Annalein hung on her arm and could not seemingly move without her. And this was, after all, why they had come, was it not? Herr Burrmann smiled at her and walked in ahead of them.

"Pope Marcellus, who is represented at the right of the Virgin," chanted the priest, "is to be thanked for having invoked St. Vitus as the patron saint of those diseased with epilepsy and other maladies of the limbs."

The dank air of the cave seemingly embraced Katharina. It was an unwholesome embrace. Her green skirt swished over the damp stones by her feet. She trembled and held Annalein's arm tightly.

"And St. Vitus himself is seen in the cauldron."

Katharina stared at the wooden images and remembered Luther's pamphlets condemning images. Was she about to sin?

"Please walk around the altar."

Karst was already halfway around. His wife still hung limp and lifeless in his arms.

"One *pfennig*," the priest chanted, "one *pfennig* to be deposited into the box for a contribution to the church. It will speed healing."

There was some noise behind Katharina, and glancing over her shoulder she saw that more of the wagon people were filing up the steps onto the path behind them. There were those who were being carried and those who were half-walking, half-dancing. Katharina began her circuit around the group of wooden images, supporting Annalein as she went. Herr and Frau Burrmann were directly in front of her.

"A *pfennig*," the priest repeated as they completed the circle.

Katharina stopped a moment to reach down into the pocket

of her kirtle. Vati had given her some money before she left this morning, and she was glad of it now. As well, Johanna had given her a little bag with coins. It also was snug and secure within the pocket of her kirtle. She dropped a *pfennig* into the coffer and then, without giving the priest a single glance or word, slipped by him back onto the path.

Continuing to the right of the cave entrance, up a rather steep path toward the higher chapel, the three couples plodded on. Annalein walked with her eyes shut. Katharina noted it and wondered how indeed she could do so. But Annalein's feet moved and surely once they got to the chapel there would be occasion to rest. It had been told her that food would be provided at this station for the pilgrims, and a little sustenance, perhaps some broth, would do Annalein a world of good. The girl moaned softly and Katharina spoke reassuringly in short sentences. It took some forty-five minutes for the walk and later she marvelled that they had been able to climb so high. For once at the top, in front of the chapel, the world lay at their feet. It was a vista of treetops with glades between and mountains beyond. Birds sang in the twilight and there was a peace and a stillness that crept into your heart.

"Isn't it beautiful here, Annalein?"

Annalein nodded slowly, almost mechanically. Katharina knew that the girl ought to sit and rest. It was nothing short of incredible that they had come this far. She turned from where they were standing and noted that the chapel door was open and that several priests were in attendance at the entrance. Karst, still carrying his wife, was there already, and Herr and Frau Burrmann were just arriving.

"Come, Annalein," Katharine encouraged, "we've only a few minutes to go. And I think you shall be able to sit down in the chapel and perhaps have some food."

Annalein's answer was that she began to walk toward the chapel, sighing pitifully as she did so.

Chapter XXII

t was not until after one of the priests had said a Mass over the pilgrims as they sat in the pews of the small chapel, that they were offered some food. But for this they had to walk to another area, to another room. Katharina asked if there might be broth for Annalein and herself and thankfully, some was provided for them. She was extremely gratified to see that Annalein was able to swallow some of this broth, as well as drink a few mouthfuls of the ale that was served from a large tin pitcher on the wooden table in the anteroom next to the sanctuary.

"Sleep," Annalein whispered suddenly.

They were sitting on a bench by the table and without any warning Annalein lay down her head on the table, narrowly missing her broth-filled trencher.

Alarmed Katharina leaned toward her.

"Annalein," she spoke softly to the bent form of her friend, "you can't go to sleep at table. I'll go and see if there are some rooms we can use. Just wait here.

But Annalein's eyes were shut and she did not respond. Katharina approached the priest who had ladled out the broth. He was a large fellow, a brown cowl hiding half his face. But he had been genial enough when he had served them.

"Sir," Katharina began, "my friend needs sleep, for she has been very ill and has not had much rest these last few days. Is there perhaps a room we might have?"

He looked doubtful.

"Please sir!" Katharina added.

He raised his right hand to his face and began rubbing the smooth, round chin.

"Mmh."

"She really must rest," Katharina continued her plea, "and I could pay some small amount of money if you could find even a small cubicle where we might spend the night?"

His eyes became more lively. Leaning closer in, he began to speak in a low voice, warning her.

"Fraulein, do not let the abbot here know that you have any money, or you will not walk away with much left in your pocket. He is...he is...."

He did not finish, leaving his sentence dangling and incomplete. Katharina spoke again.

"But is there some place, brother, where I can take my friend?"

Of a sudden he winked at her and conspiratorially mouthed the words, "Follow me."

"Wait," Katharina said. "Just wait because I must take my friend along as well. Only I do not know if she can walk. She is so overcome with fatigue."

The priest noiselessly padded over to Annalein alongside her. Herr Burrmann, having eyed Katharina's conversation with the priest and noting Annalein's bent form, strolled over to them.

"Can I aid you, Katharina?"

"Oh, Herr Burrmann. Annalein is so tired and this kind priest is about to show us a resting place. But I do not know if I can get her to wake up and walk."

Herr Burrmann smiled, picked up Annalein as if she were a little child and stood with her in his arms, the girl's head trustfully reclining against his shoulder. The priest nodded, then motioned that they should follow him. Leading the way through a small hallway past several doors, he stopped at the last door and opened it. Inside the exposed miniature room stood a small cot wedged against the wall. A wooden chair beside it faced a miniscule, square window aglow with evening sunlight.

"This is my sanctuary while I am staying here," the priest said, but smiled as he did so.

"Oh, sir," Katharina said, realizing he was sacrificing his own bed for them, "we thank you so very much."

Herr Burrmann deposited Annalein on the cot, bowed to Katharina and left. The priest likewise, after wishing them a good night, stepped back into the hallway. Katharina bent over to check Annalein who had slept through the whole procedure. Straightening the skirt about her legs and stroking her arms, Katharina was satisfied that her friend was resting naturally and sweetly. Walking over to the window to take in the scenery, she was startled a few moments later by a knock at the door. It was Herr Burrmann who carried Katharina's basket as well as her cape.

"I thought you might need these," he said, warmly regarding her before he retired down the hallway.

Katharina smiled at the closed door. How thankful she was once more that she had heeded Mutti's advice and had taken that cape. Setting the basket on the chair, she considered the size of the cot. Annalein lay sprawled out, but perhaps they might both fit. Taking off her linen hood, she placed it next to the basket. Then, carefully moving the girl's arms and legs and turning them toward the wall, she snugly fit her own body next to her friend's. Reaching back for the cape which had fallen on the floor, she spread it over both of them as best she could. Part of her foot extended over the edge of the cot, but this position was certainly to be preferred to resting on the hard floor. Annalein moaned in her sleep and Katharina rubbed her back.

"Sleep well, Annalein," she whispered. "God watches over you, and I am so thankful that you are getting stronger."

KATHARINA AWOKE WHEN Annalein moved her body in an abrupt manner, almost pushing her off the cot. The light falling in through the window told her it was morning—perhaps very early morning. She really had no idea what time it was.

"Where am I?" Annalein whispered in a hoarse tone.

"You are at St. Vitus," Katharina answered soothingly, rubbing her friend's shoulder for a moment, "and you have been ill, Annalein "

Turning, she sat up slowly, swinging her feet to the ground. She felt rather stiff and a little chilled. Annalein turned to look at her.

"Katharina, how long have I been ill?"

"Just a few days, perhaps a little more than a week, dear heart."

"That is a long time," Annalein said slowly, "a very long time. Where is my mother?"

"She is in Strasbourg. She...she could not come so far with you and she asked me to come in her stead."

"Where is this place, this room where we are now?"

"It belongs to a priest, a kind man who has let us use it for the night. I do not know his name."

"What are we going to do now?"

"This morning there will be a Mass, I think and maybe, after that, if you are feeling well enough, we can go back to Strasbourg."

Annalein yawned and stretched.

"I am still tired, Katharina."

Her voice was plaintive, tinged with an edge of fear.

"You will grow stronger, Annalein. And I will help you to get back home to your mother."

Katharina got up from the edge of the cot and reached for the basket.

"You can have a drink before we rise, and I shall see if I can find some water to wash ourselves before we...."

"Katharina, I have to...."

Annalein stopped short of saying that she had to use a privy and indeed, Katharina herself felt the need also.

"I will see if I can find a brother monk to help us," she replied, "just lie here and I shall be back soon."

Smoothing her crumpled green skirt and straightening her hair, she bent down and reached for the green linen hood, which had fallen on the floor.

"Do I look presentable?" she asked Annalein, who lay quietly, watching her friend get ready.

"You look very well," Annalein replied softly.

"Well, then I'm off to find a place where we might relieve ourselves and I shall be back soon, I promise."

Out in the hall, Katharina stopped for a moment to get her bearings. If she recalled correctly, they had turned left down this hallway from the dining room. That meant she should now turn right to get back to the dining room. She began her walk down the hallway, and reaching the end, turned right again. Faint strains of singing could be heard. It must mean that the monks and lay brothers were at matins in the church sanctuary. Perhaps she would not be able to ask anyone for help. Indecisively, she stood in the opening of the first door she had reached. It was not the dining room but the kitchen. Two monks were busy at the table. She could smell fresh bread in an open hearth oven, and her mouth began to water. One of the monks stopped his work and approached her.

"I'm sorry," Katharina began, "but I am rather lost. Would there be a place where I might be able to find some water to wash and to...."

She stopped. The other monk also stopped his work and turned to face her. She was relieved to see it was the monk who had given them the room last night.

"Have you slept well?" he asked as he also walked over.

"Oh, yes," she replied, "and we are so grateful to you."

"I will show you where the reredorter is," he said, "Please follow me."

Leading the way quickly in the opposite direction of where their room was, Brother Thomas, for that is what he said his name was, gave a running commentary as he walked.

"Beyond these walls," he said, pointing to the left, "is where the garden is laid out. And to the right is the chapter house, where the abbot meets with certain priests to discuss the running of St. Vitus Church. And here, to the left again, is the walkway through which you reach the church."

"What is your function, Brother Thomas?" Katharina asked, hard put to keep up with his almost running pace.

"My function?"

Brother Thomas laughed out loud, the sound echoing down the hall, mingling with the rapid clip of their footfall.

"Have you no function?"

Katharina was puzzled. Brother Thomas had seemed so sure of himself in these surroundings and, indeed, had seemed so in charge.

"No, I have no function. I am only a visiting lay-brother. I've come from Hagenau and have stopped here for a few days as the abbot was in need of someone to do some gardening. But this very day I will leave for Strasbourg. I am bound for St. Lawrence Church."

"Today? You leave today?"

"Yes, daughter, today."

Katharina was silent, pondering, thinking quickly.

"And here," Brother Thomas said, "here is the reredorter."

He halted before a doorway and Katharina saw a long room in which a flat piece of wood spanned from one wall to the other. There were several holes in the wood on which one could sit. She blushed and thanked brother Thomas for taking her there.

"I shall go back," she said, "and take Annalein here."

He smiled at her.

"And I shall take a basin of water to your room, so you can wash."

"Thank you, again. You are so kind."

He nodded and walked off.

LATER, ABLUTIONS COMPLETED, the two girls found their way back to the dining room, Annalein still leaning quite heavily on Katharina. The delicious smell of freshly baked bread piqued their appetites as they passed the kitchen. They could see loaves being piled high on platters, and as they entered the dining room, they were greeted by Herr and Frau Burrmann as well as Karst.

"How is your wife, Karst?" Katharina asked, seeing that the man was by himself and sad.

But she was horrified when, as a response to her question, the man spat on the floor, swore and walked away.

"She died last night," Herr Burrmann explained, "and will be buried in the cemetery here later this morning."

"I am so sorry," Katharina murmured, her arm tightening around Annalein.

"Mass will be said in the church sanctuary for those who are ill in about an hour's time," Herr Burrmann went on, "but meanwhile I think we are free to eat the bread that is being carried in and drink some of the ale the abbot is placing at our disposal."

"How are you, Frau Burrmann," Katharina said, noting that the woman also looked better than the day before.

"She seems to be getting well," Herr Burrmann answered for his wife who smiled wanly, "and I am so glad."

"Where are some of the other…other pilgrims? I have seen very few of the people who followed us toward the cave?"

"Only a few made it up to the chapel last night," Herr Burrmann said, "and those who did slept outside in the garden around the church. Most of the other folks stayed down by the wagons and slept by the side of the road. They will likely be arriving soon."

Annalein and Katharina sat down at the table. Katharina broke some of the bread into small pieces for her friend and also offered her some ale. She was gratified when Annalein did actually eat a few pieces and drank thirstily of the proffered drink.

"I think," she said with a smile, "that you are beginning to look and be much better."

Annalein smiled back, and it occurred to Katharina that she probably did not remember much of what had happened the last few days. Brother Thomas walked past their table carrying a platter of more fresh bread in his hands. Katharina made so bold as to tug at his robe as he walked by.

"Pardon me, Brother Thomas," she said and when he stopped, she continued. "Would you mind telling me at what hour you will be leaving here for Strasbourg?"

"Late morning," he replied courteously.

"Would it be possible," she continued, "for me and Annalein to accompany you back to Strasbourg?"

He looked thoughtful. Herr Burrmann stopped eating and began tapping his fingers on the table. Then he spoke.

"Surely, Katharina," he said. "Surely you are not thinking of leaving here already? You have only just arrived and look at how much improved your charge is. She is eating and drinking. The journey has obviously been a blessing to her—as," he added, looking at his wife, "it has been to Erika."

Katharina nodded. She had no wish to offend Herr Burrmann who had been a wonderful helper to her and Annalein. Nevertheless, she was becoming convinced that Annalein might also have improved had she not come on this trip.

"You are welcome to come, child," Brother Thomas said kindly, "if that is what you wish."

"She does not wish it," Herr Burrmann interjected. "She has not thought this through carefully. She is young—too young to be discerning in this matter."

Annalein stopped eating her bread. She turned her neck to the right, a fact which thoroughly convinced Katharina that she had been right in thinking that the girl was well on her way to being healed. For only a few short days ago, her neck had been cramped—almost frozen in position. And now, she was turning it—turning it quite easily and without any apparent pain.

"I would like to go home," Annalein said, clearly and loudly enough for all in the living room to hear.

"She does not know what she wants," Herr Burrmann commented, and then, as if washing his hands of the whole affair, he picked up his tin mug full of foaming ale and took a long draught.

Brother Thomas winked at Katharina and whispered, "I shall wait for you and your friend at the entrance to the grotto close to the noon hour. If you change your minds, do not let it fret you. That will be fine."

After the meal, during which a number of other afflicted people entered the dining room, a solemn-looking priest arrived, inviting everyone to follow him toward the sanctuary. Most of the ill were incapable of walking alone and were guided by either caregivers or by other priests who had appeared to help. Annalein and Katharina were among the last of the group to enter the church, trailing the others through a smaller door on the east side.

It was warm in the church. The nave, a large central area where the sick congregants now stood milling about with their helpers, was flanked by aisles. One of these aisles had a small chapel dedicated to the Virgin Mary and another held a small altar reserved for worship to St. Vitus. One of the monks intoned plaintively through the moaning and commotion of the crowd that all those who were ailing could pause here and pray before, after and even during Mass. Katharina and Annalein took their places behind all the others. The wooden choir screen at the front of the chapel partially hid from view the officiating priest who stood with his back to the congregants. Facing the high altar, his gestures and words were muffled. It was especially difficult to hear what he said because the noise and actions of some of the very ill jumping in front of them was harsh and discordant.

"I think," Katharina whispered to Annalein, pointing to the priest, "that he is the abbot."

Annalein nodded. She sat very quietly, leaning against Katharina and never taking her eyes off the high altar. The white amice hung over the priest's shoulders and was tied at the waist. His chasuble was red. Red, Katharina knew, was the colour of martyrs. Were these ill people dancing around them martyrs? The *Kyrie Eleison* and *Gloria* chants drifted past them through the disturbing noise. Annalein pulled at Katharina's robe. Katharina turned to her questioningly.

"I want to go home," the girl said once more, very clearly.

"We will," soothed Katharina, "later this morning. Brother Thomas will guide us."

"I want to go now," Annalein insisted.

Another monk took a place at the front and began to read from one of the Epistles. At least Katharina presumed it was from one of the Epistles.

"I cannot breathe in here, Katharina," Annalein complained, "it is too crowded. I feel faint."

Worried, Katharina could see that her friend was turning very pale.

"Can you not wait a little longer," she whispered back, although with all the hullabaloo around them, there was really no need to keep her voice down.

Annalein nodded and looking away from the priest chanting in the front, instead began staring down at the floor. She sat quietly like this for a very long time. Around them, the afflicted danced and sprang. They even danced and sprang around the altar. Held by their caregivers, they successfully drowned out the voice of the priest in his reading from the Epistles and his subsequent intoning of the *Vater Unser*. Annalein showed no inclination to join the dancers and for this Katharina was very thankful. Faintly she could hear the choir behind the wooden screen begin singing the *Agnus Dei*. Out of the corner of her eye, she could see another priest enter the sanctuary from the same side door that they had come through. He was carrying something. She strained sideways to see, leaning over Annalein in her curiosity.

"He is carrying shoes," she whispered to herself, "bags full of red shoes."

Fascinated she watched as the rather heavy-set monk deposited the red shoes, and there must have been some twenty-five pairs of them, in front of the abbot who had resumed his post by the high altar. The abbot's server, a younger priest, stood next to him. Latin phrases began to pour from his lips like a well-recited lesson, and Katharina had heard them often enough so that she could hear the words within herself. The abbot then bowed down, kissing the altar, and she knew he was saying those very special transforming words—words that were supposed to change the bread into the very body of Christ. The server rang the bell. She could clearly hear a high tinkle above the hum and dancing noise and above even the strange laughter of the crowd.

The abbot now held the consecrated host in his hand in front of the afflicted, but they paid no attention. Yet it was Christ's body. Or was it, after all, still a mere piece of bread? Certainly after reading many of Luther's pamphlets, she did not know for certain. But tradition was so ingrained in her that she automatically knelt. Pulling Annalein down to the ground with her, the girls were the only ones, aside from Herr Burrmann, his wife and the attending monks, who had sunk to their knees. And Katharina was aware that at this precise moment the Abbot was blessing all who were in the sanctuary.

IT WAS OVER now. Katharina sighed and felt relieved. Perhaps now they could escape this overly full room—this sanctuary beset with affliction—and seek out Brother Thomas. She pulled Annalein up and the girl looked at her, a question in her eyes. But as both edged their way out of the pew, turning toward the door, they were stopped by a priest.

"You must not leave as yet," he said, not at all unkindly but rather as one passing on some information, "for there is the gift of the shoes and the cross."

"The shoes?" Katharina repeated.

"Yes, please follow me."

Annalein made no move to follow and Katharina took her hand.

"Come, Annalein, we will soon be on our way. But we should ...."

She did not finish but pulled her friend along to shadow the back of the heavy-set priest who was clearing a path for them through the sea of dancers. He led them to the high altar where the abbot was busy sprinkling a number of red shoes with holy water, as well as tracing the sign of the cross on the tops and on the soles of the shoes. Having led them this far, the priest smiled at them and left to perhaps solicit the presence of more people to the front. The abbot stopped his work and regarded them sternly.

"Have you come here on a pilgrimage from Strasbourg to recover your health?" he asked.

"Indeed, we have been most blessed," Katharina responded, "for I believe my friend, Annalein, has been healed and that on the way to St. Vitus."

The abbot smiled a slow and small smile.

"Is that so?" he said, "St. Vitus is a powerful patron of this disease and worthy of much thanks."

"Yes," Katharina answered, not knowing what else to say.

Throughout this exchange, Annalein stood quietly, looking down at the floor.

"I have some shoes for you," the abbot continued, "as well as a small cross. These things are most effective, coming from the place dedicated to St. Vitus. If you take them with you, they shall protect against a recurrence of the illness."

Katharina nodded and again, Annalein made no response. Indeed, she began a slow backward walk away from the abbot.

"She is eager to go home," Katharina explained, even as she took the cross and the shoes from the abbot, "Now that she is well, she would fain see her mother soon and feel her embrace."

"There is a coffer at the entrance where you came in," the abbot said, pointing, "and you may put your money contribution into it. I would suggest you be generous, for God is not mocked. And indeed, being blessed so richly in that the disease has been warded off in such a short time period is a miracle. Would you not agree, daughter?"

"God is to be praised," Katharina said, all the while remembering the words of Brother Thomas, words which had warned her about the hunger of the abbot for money.

Herr Burrmann and his wife appeared behind her.

"I am glad to see that you are still here," Herr Burrmann said.

"Oh, but Annalein is better," she responded, "and we shall be going back soon."

Herr Burrmann frowned.

"That is foolish of you, child. However, I cannot fault you for your care. You have been a good friend to your charge and to my wife. I wish you godspeed."

"Thank you, sir," Katharina responded before turning to search out where Annalein had gone.

AT THE DOOR, Katharina felt for the small bundle of money that Annalein's mother had entrusted to her care. It lay deep within the confines of her kirtle's pocket, and she carefully brought it up. Undoing the blue yarn which tied the neck, she stared in amazement at the heap of gold coins clustered together in the bag. Surely Frau Stoffler herself could use this money very well. Feeling the eyes of the abbot sear into her back, she sank her right hand into the pile and took out seven gold coins depositing them into the small wooden coffer. At least twenty or more were left in the bag. Yet seven gold coins were a great deal of money, and would they not please God, or St. Vitus if so it could be that St. Vitus could be pleased, he being dead for such a long time already? If Frau Stoffler wanted to give more, well then, at some point when her leg was better, she could return to this place and donate more with her own hand. She laced up the bag and returned it to her pocket. Through the open door she could see Annalein standing outside in the garden. The girl was looking up at the sky and smiling. Katharina smiled too. Now if they could only find Brother Thomas, they could be on their way.

Chapter XXIII

n the early fall of 1518, when the heat was beginning to ease off just a breath and trees were setting up their easels of autumn colours, Matthis Zell, a new priest, took charge of the cathedral parish of St. Lawrence. The parishes of Strasbourg were nine in all—St. Martin, St. Aurelia, Old St. Peter, Young St. Peter, St. Lawrence, St. Nicholas, St. Thomas, St. Stephen and St. Andrew. Not all were blessed with their own parish church. St. Lawrence met in the transept of the great cathedral, while St. Stephen shared a church with a nunnery.

Normal times had returned to Strasbourg. The stressful weeks of the St. Vitus dance epidemic had died down, and people began to speak of other things. Citizens went about their everyday work. The market square was filled with hustle and bustle on market days, and women's voices called over and back as they sold their wares. Both tradesmen and peasants, as well as servant girls and farmers wives, gossiped and stood before carts, vying for bargains. Sinful human nature was flagrantly displayed out in the open. Those who had been arrested for thievery, or some other sort of mischief, stood in the docks at the town hall often attracting crowds of curious onlookers. Held up to shame for a certain length of time, their misdeeds were read aloud over them. Others, who had been dishonest about selling or buying property, or had been caught promoting the evil vice of prostitution, were publicly expelled from Strasbourg, accompanied by crowds shouting out jeers and howls of derision. Life continued, although it was at a premium. Babies were born—some lived but many died. Old people as well as younger folk were conducted amid the ever tolling bells, to cemeteries. And all under the shadow of the cathedral.

ANNALEIN HAD RETURNED home recovered from the dancing sickness, albeit in a weak state. During these warm autumn days, she regained much of her strength. Frail of body for a season, she soon flourished. Her mother and her sister were extremely grateful for her returning health and lovingly pampered her. And why should they not! There were many who had died of the disease, and there were others who had been disabled in some way. Annalein had seen a young woman like herself who had lost the ability to walk normally and who now had a halting gait. She had beheld others who had stretched the muscles in their necks so severely that they could still not hold up their heads properly. But Annalein lived— and lived normally and joyfully, often holding her sister Johanna's new baby on her lap softly singing to the child.

It was Annalein who informed Katharina that St. Lawrence had acquired a new parish priest—a man by the name of Matthis Zell.

"What does he look like?" Katharina asked, her curiosity piqued.

They were sequestered in the Schütz sitting room, side by side, heads drawn close in conversation. Mutti had left to see Frau Bauer about some cloth for a winter dress for Margaret, and Margaret had gone with her. Katharina rather suspected that both of them actually had a yearning to see little Beata who, if Frau Bauer was to be believed, was the most beautiful baby that had ever seen the light of day.

She poked Annalein, who was dreamily staring out the rectangular-shaped window panes through which the afternoon sun was shining.

"What does he look like?" she repeated impatiently.

"Who?" Annalein asked, almost as if she were waking up, "Whom does who look like?"

"The new parish priest," Katharina said, resisting an urge to shake Annalein. "You just told me that St. Lawrence had a new parish priest."

Forgetfulness was not a vice Annalein had acquired since she had been ill; she had always been rather absent with her thoughts. But Katharina knew that there was not a kinder girl in the whole of Strasbourg.

"Oh, the new priest," Annalein responded, a slow smile appearing at the corners of her mouth, "He seems quite nice, actually. But Katharina, you will never guess whom I saw at Mass this morning. Herr Burrmann and his wife and...."

"I didn't ask if the new priest was nice, Annalein," Katharina patiently replied, "but I asked what he looked like. You know as in: Was he tall? Did he have dark features...?"

"Oh," Annalein said, "is that what you meant?"

"Yes, it was."

"Well, I only saw him from a distance and could not make out his features very well. He was of medium height—neither short nor tall. And whether or not he had a dark complexion...."

She stopped, shrugging a little helplessly and then went on, animation lighting her pale face.

"But Herr and Frau Burrmann had their son with them. He is quite tall and rather good-looking, I think. They remembered me and stopped to speak with me. The son was very kind also. He asked after my health and told me that his mother, like myself, had quite recovered."

During the somewhat rapid flow of words cascading down from Annalein's lips, Katharina observed her friend carefully. Annalein had never had much interaction with men in her life and, as far as she could recall, she had never heard her speak of anyone of the male gender with such praise. Frau Stoffler had kept her rather sheltered.

"What is his name? What is the son's name?"

"It is Reinhart."

"Reinhart," Katharina repeated, adding, "a very noble name."

"Yes, indeed," Annalein agreed, "I did think so as well."

Katharina smiled indulgently, before adding, "So might you see him again?"

Annalein blushed most becomingly.

"Well, he did say that he might call on my mother, just," she added innocently, "to ask about some particular matters with regard to her *heidnisch werk*. He was thinking of buying something for the church because he is so thankful about his mother's complete recovery."

"Oh, I see," Katharina said, "a devoted son. And that is," she added, "the way it should be."

"Indeed," Annalein agreed demurely, hands folded in her lap, "he appears to be very devoted."

Then the girls caught one another's eyes, and they both began to laugh—first softly, but their peals of laughter increased by the moment. Margaret walked in at this moment.

"What are you laughing at?" she demanded, almost beginning to laugh herself because the merry sound that met her was so contagious.

"Oh, nothing," Katharina spoke with difficulty, heaving a big sigh to control the mirth that kept bubbling up.

"Nothing?" Margaret said disbelievingly.

"Well, actually we were speaking of...of the new parish priest at St. Lawrence," Annalein added, trying hard to speak seriously.

"Well, what is so humorous about him?" Margaret asked, "I have heard him preach a few times, and he is quite...."

She stopped. In spite of herself, Katharina was intrigued.

"He is quite what, Margaret?"

"Well, I would say, he is quite stern."

"Stern?"

"His eyes," Margaret said, sitting herself down on a chair opposite the two girls, "his eyes are quite piercing, and when he speaks, you must listen for you cannot look away."

"You have not spoken of him before," Katharina observed, "but it seems that he has made quite an impression on you."

"He carries himself," Margaret went on, "with a quiet dignity and not at all like many of the priests we are wont to see who...."

She stopped, rather at a loss.

"Yes," Katharina encouraged.

"I would not," her sister said softly, "I would not malign those of the church and thus incur...incur...."

"I know," Annalein finished her hesitating words, "you are not eager to incur a lot of disapproval, especially when you will feel bound to confess in the booth to your local priest what you have just said. For he is likely to fine you and give you a week's worth of 'Hail Mary's' to boot."

"Annalein!"

Both of the Schütz girls gasped at her audacity. Annalein placidly stared at them.

"It is true what I said, is it not? I think I am not the only one to scoff at those who preach good works but who steal from the poor."

As the sisters continued to stare at her, she added, "And, from what Margaret has just said, I would like to hear brother Zell preach and not," and here she poked Katharina in the side, "just look at him."

It was Katharina's turn to blush.

"I merely wanted to know what he looked like, so that I would recognize him in the pulpit," she responded with what dignity she could muster.

"As I said, I have heard him," Margaret repeated, noting her sister's blush with interest, "and I do learn from what he says."

"How old," Katharina asked, "is he?"

"I think that he would be in his late thirties, maybe about forty," Margaret said, "quite old really. But not so old as Vati. And," she added as a *non sequitur*, "he has a rather large, longish nose."

Annalein yawned and stood up.

"Reinhart," she said, "has not got a long nose, and he is quite drawn to the new faith—that new heresy of which many people are speaking."

She smiled a little and went on.

"Reinhart spoke of it briefly when we met at the cathedral after Mass. His parents are also, strangely enough, not averse to him conversing on the subject. I thought they were rather adamant that one must be faithful to a fault to the Roman Catholic tenets."

"Yes," Katharina agreed, "I would have thought that also about Herr and Frau Burrmann."

"Who is Reinhart?" Margaret asked.

"He is better looking than your Jergen von Lübeck," Annalein teased.

Katharina laughed. Jergen, who was apprentice to a local gold-smith, had been frequenting their home recently, and it was quite clear that he was interested in Margaret and she in him.

"I must go back home," Annalein murmured, walking toward the door, "or Mutti will worry. And I do not like to worry her."

IT WAS NOT until several months later, in the spring of 1519, that Katharina finally met the new pastor of St. Lawrence in person. In spite of increased Bible reading, Katharina's spirit was still often overcast by a sense of guilt that she was not doing enough to earn her salvation. She daily strove to wipe out that guilt with her ministries to the poor and less fortunate. Almost every day saw her go out with Mutti's basket on her arm to help someone who was ill, to aid some woman who had many children or to provide succour to someone who was dying. Even as she had helped Frau Schilter, so she helped others, and she was much loved and known for it throughout the streets of Strasbourg. But her heart yearned for assurance; she greatly desired to have the gospel speak to her in a personal way. She often read her Bible, sometimes by moonlight and sometimes in the early morning hours, yet she frequently felt like a child reading a book with words that were too big for her to understand.

The parish of St. Lawrence, of which the newly appointed Matthis Zell had become both priest and penitentiarius, was the largest in Strasbourg. St. Lawrence was incorporated under the control of the great cathedral, and Matthis Zell was but a hireling, a paid subordinate, whose contract had to be renewed yearly. His duties were manifold. Together with saying daily Masses, attending baptisms and weddings and taking care of those who were dying, he also had to hear confession and absolve those who had committed sins which only the bishop could usually remit. Men appeared before him who might have faulted in paying church taxes, and women came to him who might not have had enough money to pay the purification fee after a childbirth. The poor are a part of every city, and so it was in Strasbourg. Matthis Zell's heart was a large heart, a compassionate one that ached for people who struggled. Though Margaret had described him as appearing stern, he was not a sombre man by nature, something which the laugh lines next to his eyes and mouth betrayed. Indeed, he liked to laugh and he liked to laugh often, for by nature he was a cheerful man. But when he was on the pulpit, the serious nature of his preaching, something of which he was extremely aware, made him appear stern.

High infant and child mortality were the norm of the age. Some one third of all children born in Strasbourg died before the age of five. A child was at risk before and during birth, as well as during infancy. When the poor came to Matthis, especially in cases where there was a miscarriage or a stillborn child, he tended to absolve them quickly, deeming it inappropriate for the church to exact payment for a dead infant. Word of his love and generosity spread and, consequently, he was often sought out.

ONE FINE DAY in the spring of 1519, Katharina visited a woman whose only son, an eight-year-old, had become ill with a severely swollen stomach. Steadfast at the boy's bedside, the mother had barely had any sleep. The child's stomach was so distended he continually screamed with pain. Purgatives had been administered, but the boy repeatedly vomited them up. Just prior to Katharina's visit, the doctor had concocted a powder that the child had kept down, soon afterward passing a great many worms in his stool.

"May almighty God," the mother whispered, "still grant his grace in letting Kristoff live."

Katharina patted her hand, and then guided her toward a small cot made up in the corner of the boy's bedroom and made sure she lay down. Satisfied when both the mother and child appeared to be sleeping, she went outside into the small yard with a bucket of sudsy water to clean the soiled sheets and blankets. She was thus occupied when she saw a priest approach the dwelling. Because she was aware that both child and mother were trying to sleep, she quickly ran to intercept the man.

"Pardon me," she called, crying out just as he was lifting his hand to knock on the door, "but have you come to visit Frau Freiburg?"

He stopped, hand in mid-air and nodded. Somewhat shy, she went on to explain that she was helping the family, putting her own soapy hands, which held an old towel, behind her back.

"They were sleeping, both she and her child, when I left them some fifteen minutes ago," she finished.

The priest had a rather longish nose and remembering her sister Margaret's comments a few months back, Katharina suspected that it might be the new priest of St. Lawrence parish and bit back a smile.

"Truth be told," she went on, as the man did not respond but simply gazed at her, "the sleep will do both mother and the child a world of good as the boy has been and is still very ill. But you are undoubtedly aware of his illness."

While she spoke, she dried her hands on the towel.

"So I take it," he spoke and his voice was a rich, deep baritone, "that you suggest I not come in."

"Far be it from me," she replied, "to tell you what to do. But, yes, given the severity of the boy's affliction and that he has been but a foot from the grave, I would deem it wise that you not awaken them."

"You are quite right," he smiled, "and I think they have a fine neighbour in you, for you are a Good Samaritan. Would that all the people in Strasbourg were so blessed!"

She blushed, and he regarded her deeply for a long moment, without speaking.

"My name is Matthis Zell," he finally spoke.

"Yes," she responded, "so I thought."

There was another quiet.

"And what might your name be, if I may be so bold as to ask?"

"Katharina—Katharina Schütz."

"Ah," he responded, regarding her with his great brown eyes, eyes that reminded Katharina of a faithful dog.

She experienced a certain amount of regret that she had not worn a better gown, one with, perhaps, elaborately cuffed sleeves. But this man, this priest, did not seem the type of fellow to whom a matter such as dress would be important. Nevertheless, she felt a strange desire to appear pleasing to him, to appear neat, with a hairnet hiding the ever-rambunctious hair strands that always escaped from beneath her cap.

"Well, I must...." Katharina eventually said, blushing as he chose that same moment to also speak.

They both left off words again, and Katharina was quietly contemplating a return to her labours on the sheets and blankets, when they heard an agonized cry come from within the house.

"I think," the priest said, "that we...that you, at any rate...."

Katharina lost no time and bolted past Master Matthis Zell, who stepped aside to let her enter the front door. The wailing that met their ears as soon as the door opened was heart-rending. Katharina ran toward the bedroom. Although she had left both the mother and the boy in slumber, a state of turmoil and disorder met her eyes when she entered the bedchamber. Frau Freiberg was attempting to hold Kristoff down. But he, talking constantly, although not in such a way that one could understand him, was frantically trying to get out of bed. His breathing was laboured and difficult and his eyes were bulging. Katharina knelt down on the opposite side of the bed and attempted to help Frau Freiberg to get Kristoff to lie down again. Matthis Zell stood in the doorway, but then also drew near to the bedside.

"Let me help," he said, "I am stronger. Perhaps if I lift him up and carry him about, he will be more comfortable."

The two women immediately stood up, and Matthis bent over the child, easily lifting the lad into his strong arms. Initially, Kristoff quieted in the priest's embrace, but just as Katharina was about to heave a sigh of relief that a crisis had been averted, the child began to convulse. Within a few minutes, the boy was dead— dead in the priest's arms. Gently he laid the boy back on the bed, closing the wide-open eyes. Then turning to the bereft mother who had fallen down on her knees by the edge of the bed, tightly gripping the blanket in her hands as if by doing that she might hold on to the life of her little one, he laid one hand on her head.

"May God keep Kristoff safe until we come to him!"

"Indeed," Katharina echoed, even as she, coming around the bed, put her arms about Frau Freiberg.

A little cowhide-covered horse stood in the corner of the room. Herr Freiberg, a merchant like Herr Bauer, had brought it back for Kristoff from one of his business trips the last time he had been home. A brown jerkin and some skin-coloured stockings hung over the toy's side. How long ago had it been since the boy had worn them? How long since he had played with the horse? How vain life was! Soon this child, Katharina fleetingly mused even as she patted Frau Freiberg's shoulder, would be buried to the tune of clergy's chanting and the sound of bells would carry his memory away. For who would remember him in the long run? Who would? She was ashamed to admit it, but her own memory of little Jacob was fading.

Later, after Frau Freiberg's relatives had come to be with her, Katharina and the black-robed Matthis Zell went home, walking together side by side for a considerable length of streets. Katharina was somewhat lost in thought, her mind overly occupied with the loss that Frau Freiberg had to sustain. Why did such things happen? It was true, all men had to die—but such little ones?! Hard put to keep up with Katharina's quick steps, Matthis was uneasy. He was impressed by the girl's gentle and yet decisive manner, by her way of helping the family they had just left, but she seemed so far-off with her thoughts now. He studied her profile as she paced next to him. It almost seemed as if she had forgotten that he was there.

"Which church," he began in a low tone, curious about but also genuinely interested in the young woman that providence had placed on his path, "do you attend, Fraulein Schütz?"

She began walking more slowly, suddenly realizing that he was still there and turned her large blue eyes toward him. They were troubled, he noted.

"Which church?" she repeated slowly, "Well we, that is to say, my family and I, always attended Dr. Geiler's church. After he died, his nephew, Peter Wickram, took over the pulpit but Peter Wickram is not his equal in preaching, I am afraid."

He inclined his head to show that he had heard this, but did not say anything else, as he believed it was in bad taste to criticize a colleague.

"You are at St. Lawrence?" Katharina asked him.

He nodded again.

"Yes, I am and I have been given comfortable quarters on the Bruderhof Strasse just behind the cathedral."

He did not know himself why he volunteered this information. Surely the girl was not interested in knowing where his place of residence was.

She smiled, slowing her pace even more, "I am glad for you. It must be difficult to come to live in a new place where you know very few people."

"The ones I have come to know have been kind," he rejoined.

"Where," she hesitatingly went on, not wishing to appear nosy, "are you from?"

"From Kaysersberg."

"Oh, that is where Dr. Geiler was from. It was his home town."

Her face shone now, and he remarked within himself that the smile that transformed her face exposed a sweetness that was very pleasant to behold.

"Yes, I have heard that he was."

"And did you know," Katharina went on eagerly, "that forty years ago Dr. Geiler was on his way to a preaching post at Würzberg when he was waylaid by Peter Schott, who was one of the chief magistrates of Strasbourg, and was persuaded by him to come here instead?"

"I have heard the story," Matthis Zell replied.

"And Peter Schott, who was also curator of the cathedral, had the magnificent stone pulpit built for Dr. Geiler, with its nearly fifty saints, from which he preached for some thirty years to us here in Strasbourg. Perhaps you will also...."

Matthis Zell nodded and smiled as she halted her account.

"I had indeed heard."

Katharina stopped, suddenly embarrassed. Here she was again, dominating a conversation and comparing this man to Dr. Geiler. Perhaps he was intimidated by her words. Indeed, it was perhaps most unkind. Katharina herself did not like to be compared to others. It was sometimes humiliating and oppressing. She began another topic, trying to cover up her enthusiastic endorsement of Dr. Geiler.

"And your parents live there—in Kaysersberg? And have you brothers and sisters whom you will surely miss?"

She stopped again. She was such a waterfall of words and knew herself to be speaking overly much, something Mutti was always warning her not to do.

"I," she continued, suddenly shy and withdrawing her smile, "do apologize for talking too much and for asking such questions as are not really mine to ask. I surely over speak."

"No, indeed," he responded quickly, "too few people are interested. They think a priest is made only of black robes and has not a background of flesh and blood and is not interested in stories and such."

This made Katharina grin in spite of herself, for she knew that there were indeed a great many priests who were very much made of flesh and blood, priests consisting mainly of bellies and greed.

"Why do you smile now?"

Matthis Zell's curiosity was piqued.

"It is just," and she spoke slowly now, not certain as to what she should reveal of her thoughts, "that I have known a great many priests who hid money pouches and slack flesh underneath their robes."

He was quiet for a great many steps, and she was afraid that she had been too bold once more and that she had offended him.

"I am sorry," she began, "I did not...."

But he interrupted.

"No, you need not apologize. I am only too well aware of the iniquities of a great many men of the cloth."

He sighed deeply as he made this statement.

"I am sure that you," she began again, "especially from what I have heard of you...."

He cut off her words.

"Do not listen to what others say, Katharina. It is often only exaggeration and this often leads to disappointment."

Katharina blushed. She knew herself rebuked and stared pointedly at her shoes before reverting the conversation back to the question she had asked him before.

"Do you have family?"

This seemed a safe topic and one that would not lead to controversy. Besides that, inside herself she was for some inexplicable reason so very glad that Matthis Zell came from the very same city in which her beloved Dr. Geiler had made his home, and she wished to hear him speak of it.

"Well, I have a housekeeper, Mey Bäbelli, who was cook to my aunt in Freiburg. When my aunt died, Bäbelli came to live with me and she takes care of me. So she is like family. But, yes, I also have one sister and one brother. My sister's name is Odile."

"Odile," Katharina softly repeated, "that is a very nice name. I know no one by that name. Perhaps some day I will meet her."

"Yes, perhaps you shall," Matthis Zell nodded as he spoke. "As for me, I did not stay in Kaysersberg and have not been back for a number of years except briefly to visit my brother who still resides there."

"Where have you lived then?"

"Well, I served in the army for a short time. And this was the time during which I moved away from Kaysersberg and lived neither here nor there, as the regiment I was with moved about quite a bit. And after serving in the army, I went on to enroll at the University of Freiburg in Breisgau. When I received my master of arts there, I continued with theological studies."

"Why?"

Katharina knew it was another rather impertinent question, and she looked back down at her shoes even as it flew out of her mouth.

But Matthis Zell did not appear to be put off by it.

"Because I did so love to study, and the more I studied the more I loved it."

"You felt not that you ought to study, in order to...? You only did it for the sake of the pleasure of studying? That is to say, you were not motivated by an inward call...?"

She stopped here abruptly. Her speech had consisted of unfinished phrases, and she knew quite well that her words sounded muddled, probably making very little sense to him.

"Motivated by an inward call from God?" he finished her last phrase, noting that her face was clouded.

"Yes," she looked up at him now as she spoke, her blue eyes bright with interest, "for it seems to me that God has a purpose for all people, and it also seems to me that if priests were to take such a purpose seriously we would not see all the vice that is so rampant in Strasbourg today."

A voice within her, a voice that sounded remarkably like Mutti, warned her that once more she had overstepped her oral bounds and had spoken too much and too quickly. After all, she had only just met this man. After all, her words accused the priesthood and the man walking next to her was a priest. She glanced at his face. In profile, his nose seemed longer than it actually was. That nose was now pointing at the ground. It was almost as if the nose was sad.

"I'm sorry," she murmured, truly repentant of perhaps having caused him discomfort.

He had been a source of easement to Frau Freiberg and Kristoff, and the fact remained that she had only heard good things about him. He put her worries to rest by smiling, revealing even, white teeth.

"No need to feel sorry. I'm glad you feel that you can speak your mind to me," he replied.

"What think you of Luther and his views?" she said, blurting the words out rather quickly, for this indeed was a matter that nagged at her often, nagged her at night and in the daytime as well.

"Luther?"

"Yes, Herr Luther. You surely know of the priest in Wittenberg who has written at length about indulgences and who posted but just this last year, some points on the church door of that city."

He smiled.

"Yes, I am acquainted with Herr Luther. I am and have for some time, been reading a number of things that he has written. My parishioners obviously read him, and I ought to be aware of what they are reading."

He smiled as he said this, but she did not smile in return.

"I would know what you think of his charter, of his theses," she said, "for his words do touch my soul."

"As they do mine," brother Zell immediately rejoined, "as they do mine."

"Do you think he speaks the truth?" Katharina asked.

"He is a very courageous man, in any case, to speak as he does. As you may know, he appeared before Cardinal Cajetan at

Augsburg last October. They spoke for three solid days. Initially, I understand, Luther prostrated himself on the floor in a gesture of humility before the cardinal, and the cardinal raised him up as a gesture of goodwill. But Luther refused to take back anything that he said."

"Yes," Katharina very nearly stood still, turning her body toward him, her feet moving at snail's pace, "so I have heard."

They had almost arrived at an intersection.

"He has said," she cautiously went on, "that the person who truly repents, has full forgiveness both of punishment and guilt, even without letters of indulgence."

Matthis Zell looked at her rather quizzically.

"So I have read also," he responded.

"And what thought you?"

"I think that the trafficking in indulgences is shameful," Matthis replied, his eyes serious, "and it grieves me deeply."

She heard that he meant his words and, although she knew the truth of them, was rather shocked by the sentences that followed.

"The public perception of the priesthood is appalling. Nearly all people disrespect the priests. There are so many examples of gluttony, of ambition, of lives of lasciviousness, of harlots being allowed into monasteries...."

He stopped rather abruptly. It was almost as if he had forgotten that she was there. She wished to reply; to say something intelligent, or, at any rate, something comforting, for she gauged that he was lonely. But there was nothing that came to mind.

And his voice, almost metallic now, continued.

"They say that the nearer people live to Rome, the less religious they are. How incredibly strange and despairing is that thought! And I have heard tell that there are those who care not what evil they do, for they say they can always get a plenary remission of all guilt and penalty by absolution and indulgence granted by the pope for four or six or...or whatever sum of money they carry."

The metallic tone in his voice had given way to a tremendous sadness—a sadness which distressed Katharina and which made her want to hold his hand to guide him away from such black thoughts. This she could do with little Jacob, but with a priest? No, of course not. But he did appear so mournful. She swallowed and was about to say something about the weather, when he went on.

"Rome has become a harlot. The church has become blind to all but that which brings monetary gain. And we have so many poor, so many who stand in need of love and help."

He stopped, seeming suddenly to remember that he was speaking with someone and was not alone.

"I am sorry," he said. "I do indeed apologize for speaking so freely."

She shook her head, cautiously replying, "I speak too much and too hastily myself. And what you say is true."

She forgot that but a few moments ago she had sincerely worried about her hair coming undone, about a few stray strands flying about her face, for truly there were so many more important things to worry about.

"I have to turn off at this corner," she swallowed as she spoke, regretting that they were now close to the Johanngasse, "and you will have to keep on straight to reach the Bruderhof Strasse."

"I know," he said, and she bit her lip yet once more for appearing to know the way better than he did.

"Well, Katharina," and he spoke softly, as if to guide her into humility, "I have very much enjoyed speaking with you and hope we can do so again. I think I can tell you a story, perhaps the next time we meet, of an encounter I had with Dr. Geiler when I was but a small boy."

Her eyes widened at this. He had stopped—stopped walking and stopped talking. She did too.

"You met Dr. Geiler when you were a little boy?"

"Yes, indeed. It was only a small encounter, but I should like to tell you about it as I gather you really loved him, this great preacher of Strasbourg. I also hope," he then added warmly, "that you feel you might want to hear me preach sometime."

She vigorously pumped her head up and down, feeling several more hair strands escaping her hair net. In spite of herself, her hands flew up to smooth out and tuck in the rebellious curls, remembering as she did how distraught and messy Frau Stoffler had looked when she had walked toward her through the crowd that awful day in August when Annalein had become ill. Did she look like Frau Stoffler to Master Matthis Zell at this moment? She flushed at the thought of it and her hands dropped down to her sides.

"I would very much like to hear the story of your meeting with Dr. Geiler. And, yes, I would also like to hear you preach, and I thank you for helping Frau Freiberg," she ended the conversation rather lamely, sensing innately she had used a great deal too many 'I's' in these sentences, yet adding, "and I bid you good day, Brother Zell."

He smiled at her and the corners of his mouth, as well as the corners of his eyes, crinkled with the many laugh lines the years had placed there. She was glad of it, for some of the weariness and sadness that had lined his face but a few short moments ago disappeared. Looking into his friendly face, she flushed even deeper before she turned and walked toward the Johanngasse. After staring at her retreating figure for a few moments, Matthis Zell also turned and walked toward the Bruderhof Strasse.

Chapter XXIV

Shortly after Katharina's conversation with Matthis Zell, the festival of Corpus Christi was celebrated in Strasbourg. Always observed on the Thursday after Trinity Sunday, it was generally greeted by good spring weather. This year was no exception. First there was a formal religious ceremony in church, including a special Mass, and from there the festivities moved out into streets warm with sunshine. A procession of clergy, town officials, members of guilds and confraternities followed the consecrated host, which was displayed on a magnificent vessel. This year, however, the procession was noticeably smaller than other years, and the streets of Strasbourg were but sparsely lined with people. Although there were a number of houses decorated with tapestries, flowers and budding branches, the usual interest and enthusiasm was simply not there. As the host passed by, people knelt, but it seemed that they knelt grudgingly.

There were open grievances against the papacy—against the Vatican's systematic looting of German taxpayers, taxpayers of which the citizens of Strasbourg were a considerable number. Businessmen found themselves competing yet again with the monasteries who were exempt from taxation. Strasbourg was not the only German city that grumbled—and grumbled loudly. Half of Germany, it seemed, was critical of the Vatican and many "enterprising," greedy priests were regarded with an unfriendly eye.

Katharina and Margaret were not among those dwindling Strasbourg citizens watching the Corpus Christi procession and neither did they go see the Corpus Christi play—a play which was to be enacted on a platform set up at the Horse Market. Mutti was ill, and the girls were busy nursing her. She had a fever and they took turns watching and sitting by the bed. The doctor had recommended pomegranate sap and pumpkin, or gourd water with sugar and a little camphor. Frau Bauer with her amazing skill of herbs, did not drop by as often as she was wont to do in the past—little Beata now took most of her time and attention. Frau Schütz's recovery took quite a few months. As a matter of fact, it took the whole summer before she was well enough to walk about again. Although Elisabet, who was expecting a baby, and Barbara, who had married Josten Vetter, a Strasbourg glassmaker, in January, often dropped by to help, the burden of the nursing lay mostly with Katharina and Margaret.

Lux came home for a brief visit toward the end of the summer. He had been kept informed, through letters, of his mother's illness and her slow progress back to health. Bringing with him many stories, the one that fascinated Katharina and her father the most was Lux's account of Luther's debate with John Eck in Pleissenburg Castle at Leipzig.

"How came you to be there?" Vati asked as they sat at supper one evening.

Mutti was the only one missing. She had begun to eat with the family again, but tired out, had already left the table to lie down.

"The debate was, after all," Vati went on, "between Wittenberg University and Leipzig."

"I was an observer," Lux replied, "as were many from Ingolstadt."

"What does Luther look like?" Katharina wanted to know.

"Oh, he is not a tall man," Lux responded, "being just a little shorter than myself, and he is quite thin. You might almost say he is emaciated to the point where you can count his bones. But it is not as though this makes him look ill. Rather, he looks quite well, as if he could run a great distance and not be weary."

"And what does this John Eck look like," Margaret added to the conversation.

She was listening avidly, eyes wide, as were Annder and little Jacob.

"John Eck actually was the opposite of doctor Luther in physical appearance. He is a rather heavy-set man, barrel-chested with a loud voice and a rough manner. And his hands, with which he gestured most dramatically, are the hands of a butcher."

"A butcher?"

Katharina and Margaret called out the words simultaneously and Lux grinned at them.

"Yes, a butcher. They were definitely meaty hands, hands that seemed accustomed to handling flesh in a rough manner."

The girls remained silent at this, noses wrinkled in disapproval, and Lux smiled rather ruefully at them before he continued.

"I guess you can hear that I was not taken with Master Eck given that he, comparing Martin Luther to Jan Hus, condemned this brave monk to the stake."

There was quiet around the table, save for the fact that Annder took that moment to take a big bite of his bread, chomping on it with gusto, earning him a long look from Katharina.

"The truth is," Lux went on, "that Master Eck, for so he is called by many, is an extremely intelligent man. Did you know, Vati, that he was a child wonder? He was only twelve years old when his guardian, an uncle, enrolled him in the University of Heidelberg and that he was but thirteen years of age when he transferred to the University of Tubingen. In six months, he had earned his bachelor of arts and, less than a year and a half later, his master of arts. After this he learned an amazing number of things that I can't even begin to enumerate. But, the fact remains, Master Eck was a child prodigy and—even though he is an irritating man—his knowledge hangs about him like a great cloak. Anyone debating him deserves a medal for courage."

"I know of Master Eck," Vati replied soberly, "for was he not ordained a priest in Strasbourg many years back? I recall that a special dispensation from the pope was required to have him ordained because he was underage."

Lux nodded. The others listened.

"Perhaps these early events in his life have made him proud. It is certainly true that he has never been very popular," Vati went on. "His harshness of speech, his rude treatment of opponents and his conceit, have made him very disagreeable to his colleagues. There was also the matter of his defence of those loaning money being able to charge five per cent interest. Such a point of view is not going to earn you favour with people. It was for this reason, it is said, that he moved away from Strasbourg to the University of Ingolstadt. And I thought, by the way, Lux, that initially the debate was to be between Andreas von Karlstadt and John Eck, not between Luther and Eck."

"Yes," Lux replied, his right hand under his chin as he regarded his father, "that was indeed to be the case, and for the first few days it actually was between these two men. However, early on in July, after the debate had been going on for a few days, Martin Luther arrived in Leipzig also—and about 200 students armed with battle-axes came with him. It's strange because Master Eck also arrived with a body guard of seventy-six men."

He paused and Margaret swallowed audibly. Everyone smiled at her and Lux continued.

"An interesting matter happened to Master Eck when he entered Leipzig. One of the wheels of his wagon broke down and he fell, consequently landing in some mud. It was a humiliating and a rather ominous beginning for the man. Such an occurrence not even a bodyguard can prevent. When the debate began, however, the scales were tipped in favour of Master Eck. Von Karlstadt was not doing a terribly great job in answering questions. He is not very quick in responding."

He took his hand out from under his chin before he went on.

"I rather think that John Eck wanted to debate Luther anyway and not Karlstadt. As it was, when Luther arrived both Master Eck and Karlstadt invited him to join in. Eck's gesture included, no doubt, a hopeful notion of catching Luther in some heresy. So the debate went on almost exclusively between Luther and Eck."

"I take it, hearing you speak so highly of Martin Luther," Vati said, looking long and hard at Lux, "that you are convinced that what the man says is true?"

Lux smiled a slow smile back.

"You take it right, Vati. And I am sure that you also do not need much convincing of his...his new ideas. By the way, Hans Bock, Strasbourg's *stettmeister* was also at the debate."

"Are they new ideas then?" Vati pondered.

Margaret, Katharina, Annder and little Jacob all followed the conversation with much interest. They were keenly aware of the talk in the streets, of the flow of the new thoughts expressed in the pamphlets found everywhere in Strasbourg.

"Luther carried," Lux answered his father, "a small bunch of flowers in his hand. Now there is a strange thing, you say, carrying flowers into a debate. I confess it was a rather odd sight, and yet it conveyed to those around him Luther's sense of love for living things, a sense of caring. His voice is melodious and knowledge of Scripture rested at his fingertips, even as the flowers were resting at his fingertips."

"You have not really answered my question," Vati persisted.

"Yes," Lux went on, scuffing his shoe into the rushes under the table, "you asked if these are new ideas? Well, not really, are they? Many years ago Jan Hus brought out similar scriptural truths— and many of these truths are the same as those now being put forward by Luther."

Save for the eating and the clatter of cutlery on the table, it remained quiet in the room for a long while. Even as she chewed her bread, Katharina pictured in her mind a thin monk, a monk carrying a bouquet of flowers, bravely staving off verbal attack.

"What were the main points of the debate, Lux?" she asked, her mouth quite empty, her eyes fixed on her older brother.

"Initially, the debate was on the freedom of the human will— something which Master Eck espoused and which Von Karlstadt denied. But when Luther entered the ring, the talk shifted to the authority of the pope, to indulgences and to the infallibility of the church. Master Eck, of course, maintained that the pope is the successor of Peter, the 'Vicar of Christ' by divine right. And Luther said this was contrary to Scripture."

"The pope is not the successor of Peter?" Margaret whispered, eyes wide, hands round her trencher.

"Luther says not," Lux cheerfully responded, "and he says it very convincingly. You would like him, Margaret, perhaps even more than you like Jergen the goldsmith."

He stopped and winked at his sister. She blushed and smiling shyly looked down at her trencher. Then Lux went on.

"Luther very ably stated that the head of the church is Christ and not a man. Indeed, so many students were convinced by his speech that a great number of them left to study at Wittenberg University afterward. I am also of that mind, Vati, to seek a position there soon, as lecturer. There is a new professor of Greek there—a man by the name of Philip Melanchthon—I think he is younger than I am."

Vati did not respond but sat still, his eyes fixed on some unseen object in the distance. Katharina wondered what Matthis Zell would think of all this, for surely news of the debate travelled quickly and he would have heard it. And it came to her that after all these months, she had not yet gone to hear the man preach.

"In the end," Lux said, as an afterthought, "Luther was condemned by Master Eck, openly and in full hearing of all those present, as a heretical, erroneous, blasphemous, presumptuous, seditious and offensive man."

They were all quiet for a bit, taking in the harsh words Master Eck had used to tar Martin Luther.

"And now," Lux concluded softly, "how will the new emperor, Charles V, judge Luther? I fear that Charles V, heir of a long line of Catholic sovereigns will most certainly rule against a simple monk, a miner's son, with nothing to back him up but his faith in the Word of God. And what will the emperor's judgement be but that Luther be hunted down and burned at the stake?"

"Yes, these are the consequences," Vati said slowly and softly, but not so soft that all his children could not hear him, "and Luther's faith may cost him his life. Rejecting the pope will have consequences for...."

He stopped and all looked at him. He smiled at his children, a tremulous sort of smile and did not finish his sentence and no one dared ask him to finish for all could see on his face that he was not able to finish because of the emotion within his heart.

To be so convinced of something, Katharina thought later that evening as she lay in the great bed next to Margaret, to be so totally sure that something is right that one would be willing to die for it, was a grand and somehow beautiful thing.

Chapter XXV

t was several months later that Katharina was startled to find cousin Margred knocking on the door of their Johanngasse home early one morning in a rather dishevelled state. Her dress was slightly soiled, her skirt badly creased, as if she had slept in it, and her cap askew. The kind plump cheeks were flushed and splotchy underneath her crinkled eyes, as if the least breath might set them off weeping.

"Oh, Katharina!"

The words flew out as if they were birds escaping a cage—birds that had been cooped up so long they knew not where to fly.

"Margred, please come in, dear cousin."

Katharina took her cousin by the shoulder, guiding her into the home as she shut the door behind them.

"Come, dear one," she repeated kindly, "you look as if you could sit by me in the kitchen for a spell and have a drink of some sweet ale."

Speaking gently, Katharina led Margred down the hall into the kitchen. Mutti, who had been feeling quite well that morning, had accompanied Marta on an errand to the market. Margaret was visiting Jergen von Lübeck's family for the day, Annder was at work, little Jacob at school and Vati was in the workshop. There was no one else about.

"Well, Margred," Katharina joked, as she cajoled her cousin toward a chair, hoping to make her laugh, "have you left your sweet spouse, the good Herr Wolfgang Schott? I vow you missed me too much to stay with him?"

But Margred seemed not to hear her words. Despondently sinking down on the chair, she placed her elbows on the table, covering her red face with two trembling hands. She was the picture of despair. Strands of her dark hair, with a few grey threads weaving through, had escaped from her cap. Katharina resisted the urge to tuck them in, even as her sisters were so often wont to do with her own. She took a chair next to Margred and began to stroke her back.

"Now what seems to be the problem, dear cousin?"

"Oh, Katharina!"

The words wailed out again and this time Margred began to cry in earnest.

"Now, now," Katharina said, changing her stroking to patting the round back of her cousin.

"I can't..." came the words, "I just can't be a good...."

"A good what?"

"A good mother."

The last word came out in a half-sob.

"Nonsense, you are a most excellent mother."

"No, I'm not."

Katharina held off replying. There was no point in talking right now. Margred first had to come to rest, and so she merely continued to pat the weeping back all the while making soothing, clucking sounds, even as her mother had done to her when she was a little girl. After a few minutes the shoulders ceased to shake and only a few shudders erupted every now and then. Then Margred sat up, raised a rueful face toward Katharina and blinked tearfully.

"I'm so sorry, Katharina."

"Whatever for," Katharina responded, "I am so honoured that you should seek me out for comfort."

A trembling half-smile now hovered at the corners of Margred's lips.

"You do make one feel loved, cousin. I am so glad you are kin. Indeed, I do not know what I would do without you."

"So am I glad that we are kin," Katharina said, "and now how about that sweet ale?"

Margred nodded. "That would be good."

"And while I am pouring it out for you, perhaps you can try to tell me what has happened to so distress you."

As Katharina rose and walked to fetch the ale from the counter, Margred took her elbows off the table, shifted her position slightly and leaned back. Sighing deeply she began with a voice that was just a bit shaky.

"It is Sebastian."

"Sebastian? Your stepson?"

"Yes."

"Why, what has he done?"

"He is thirteen now and a big lad," came the words, softly and distinctly, "but for all his size, he has always been a good boy. He has ever been kind to me and I can only give words of praise...."

She stopped.

"Well, then?" Katharina prodded as she carried back some ale to the table, "what is the problem?"

"I must first tell you how good the boy is," Margred insisted, "I must do so."

"Fine," Katharina answered, "if that is what you must do, go ahead, cousin."

Margred nodded and went on. "Sebastian is *gern gehorsam*, happily obedient, if there is such a thing. When called on, he answers quickly and modestly. He reads to me from his schoolwork, or sometimes tells me stories from books. He listens attentively and never interrupts. Sometimes, I think that he, out of all the children that Wolfgang has, would have truly pleased Ursula. He is that sweet."

Katharina listened with interest. She knew Sebastian Schott a little but not intimately. He was always away at school when she called. Now she grinned broadly.

"Pleased Ursula? Then he must be as near perfection as children can come."

Margred came close to grinning herself, albeit tremulously.

"It is true," she agreed complacently, "I have thought the same."

"But then what is the problem, dear cousin," Katharina went on,

"If the child is so sweet and good as you say, then what causes you to be so upset."

Margred face fell again.

"Well, it was yestermorn," she said, "I went down to the cellar to fetch some of the wine that Wolfgang bought last month from a wine vender. He bought several vats and we had stored them in the cellar, you see. But when I opened the tap to the one that we had begun to use to take some out, nothing came out except a small dribble of liquid. It appeared that the vat was quite empty."

She lifted a forlorn face toward Katharina and repeated her last words.

"The vat was quite empty."

Katharina nodded to show that she was listening.

"I knew not what had happened. A few days before there had been plenty, and it was a full vat when we purchased it."

"Don't tell me, cousin," Katharina began, a surprised look on her face, "that Sebastian has secretly been drinking the vat empty in the cellar?"

"Well, when I questioned the other children as to who might have been in the cellar the last few days, they mentioned that Sebastian had taken some boys down into the cellar with him when I was out at market."

"Boys?"

"Yes, that is what they said. Ernestine was with me at market and so was Katrina, our maid. Only Liesl and Gretchen were at home."

"So, who were these boys?"

Margred did not respond to this question, but simply kept on with her story, doggedly plodding on.

"So when Sebastian came home from school yesterday, I asked him if he had taken any wine out of the cellar. He would not answer, but turned his face away from me. And when I mentioned the boys that his sisters had said were in our home, he ran up the stairs to his room and shut the door. I followed him as quickly as I could. I knocked at his door and asked him as I was standing in the hallway why he would not speak with me. Then he opened the door and said, 'Mutti,' for he has ever called me Mutti, Katharina, ever since I married his father."

Margred stopped again and looked pleadingly at Katharina, almost as if she was a lawyer pleading the case of a guilty client. Then she went on with her story.

"You know, Katharina," she said softly, "he is a good boy and the only son Wolfgang has."

"Yes, I know," Katharina answered, "and you are a good mother for him, Margred."

"Well, at any rate," Margred said, "the child was honest, for he then told me that the boys were from his Latin school and that they had goaded him into raiding the wine cellar and emptying the vat of its contents. They said that if he did so, he would have proved himself a man and would be able to come with them to the dicing table and that they would teach him how to play cards."

Katharina gasped.

"Oh, Margred," she said, "and so Sebastian allowed these boys to drink and he drank as well?"

"Well, no," she answered, "that is not quite what happened. It seems that they had several buckets with them and emptied the vat's content into these buckets. And then they left."

"So he allowed these boys to steal from his father."

Cousin Margred sighed deeply.

"That is not the crux of the matter. It is not why I am so...so distraught, Katharina."

"Then what is it?"

"It is what he did after he confessed to me."

"What did he do?"

"He went to a priest at St. Thomas Church and confessed his wrongdoing. This particular priest was not...well he was not sympathetic, as of course, he should not be," she added quickly, "But he was so demanding."

Cousin Margred stopped for breath. Her face was turning quite red once more.

"What mean you," Katharina asked, "by demanding?"

"Well, he did not give him a normal penance of 'Hail Marys' or a small fee such as is normal in cases of lapses with young boys."

"What was it he asked of Sebastian?"

"Well, first he asked what his father's name was and then

what it was that his father did. How he earned his living."

"What strange questions," Katharina mused.

"Yes," Margred agreed, "so it seemed to me. But perhaps not so strange, for then the priest went on to say that Sebastian must needs bring his father in to see him and that the sum of money required for the forgiveness of this particular sin would be large—and that it would be a sum which would require his father to meet with him at the church."

"Such a thing is abnormal. It is not usual," Katharina said. "What was the priest's name?"

"I think it was Borst...no Horst," Margred answered.

"Balthazar Horst?"

Margred shrugged.

"I know not his full name. Sebastian was in fear when he told me. He is so deathly afraid that he has caused his father harm—harm of reputation, harm of financial loss and ... oh, Katharina, if I had been home...if I had been there...well then this would not have happened."

"Oh, I don't know, Margred," her cousin said softly, "Sebastian is old enough to choose his friends, and he has made an error of judgement. I think you can safely assume that he will not make such a bad choice again. This is in some respects, a good experience for him. The matter of the wine is not so great, but this matter of a priest exacting a penance in this way...."

She stopped and thoughtfully tapped her fingers on the table.

"I think," she murmured, "that we ought to ask someone else if this is proper; someone who has more authority than this Balthazar Horst who, I hasten to add, has not a very good reputation, Margred."

Margred looked at her, puzzled of face.

"Not a good reputation?"

"No, cousin, do you not recall the priest that came to see Ursula, the priest who gave her the last rites? The man who wanted to have Ursula's money, your money actually?"

A light went on in Margred's face.

"Think you it is the same priest?"

"Yes, I do and I wonder if he knows that Sebastian is your

stepson and if he has, after all this time, held a grudge for not securing more money out of Ursula's death."

"Well, what can we do?"

Margred's countenance was the epitome of helplessness.

"I know just what we should do," Katharina said firmly. "We should speak to and seek the advice of Brother Matthis Zell."

"Matthis Zell?"

"Yes, he is the new priest at St. Lawrence. That is to say, he has been there for a fair while now, and he has a good name. He is a very kind man, Margred, and he holds the special office of penitentiarus. Consequently, he is authorized to levy fines and grant or withhold absolution for sins."

Cousin Margred listened, eyes wide, but her face registered very little understanding.

"How will this help, Katharina?" she questioned her cousin.

"Well, I am certain that Balthazar Horst is not being honest in this matter at all and seeks to line his own pockets; and I am also very certain that Matthis Zell is very honest in matters pertaining to the church and to parishioners and that he seeks to keep the church pure."

"But we are not his parishioners."

"No, but you are citizens of Strasbourg, and he is the sort of man who will not tolerate priests taking advantage of any folk."

"Balthazar Horst," Margred pronounced the name slowly. "Actually, I think I do recall the name now. The truth is that this man has ordered Sebastian to bring his father in to see him this afternoon around four at St. Thomas Church."

"Well, we must be quick then and try to locate Brother Zell."

"Oh, Katharina, are you certain this will help? Last night Sebastian told Wolfgang what had happened. Wolfgang said nothing. He just sat and stared at the boy."

Katharina felt compassion for the woeful face in front of her, a face that seemed ready to weep again.

"Hush, Margred," she said, "it will be all right by and by. Now it seems to me that you ought to go home. Will not the girls be looking for you?"

Margred's face changed from woeful to sudden panic.

"The girls," she called out. "I have been here much too long! Oh, Katharina, you see what a bad mother I truly am! But Katrina is with them, and Ernestine is old enough to look after things. But still, I am in charge. Wolfgang ever says that I am in charge and that he is so proud of me."

The last words were pronounced with just a touch of pride.

"Well, there you are then," Katharina smiled, "and never you mind what Balthazar Horst has said or has threatened. I will see if I can find Matthis Zell and present the matter to him. I am sure that he will help."

Margred got up from her chair, nearly upsetting it in her fervour. Katharina rose hastily as well. Quite running over to the kitchen door, Margred stopped suddenly, turned and almost bumped into Katharina.

"You are ever so good to me," she whispered, before she put out both her arms and enveloped Katharina in a hug, "and I love you so dearly."

"Oh, Margred," Katharina whispered back, "and I you."

Chapter XXVI

The first thing that Katharina did after she had seen Margred out the front door was to make her way to the back of the house to her father's workshop. Standing for a moment in the open doorway, she relished the warmth of the sunlight flooding in through the large window. The smell of wood shavings permeated the room. Vati was busy as always but looked up from where he was sitting in front of his bench and smiled at his daughter.

"Ah, Katharina," he said, "you are home this morning. You did not accompany your mother to market?"

"No, Vati," she answered, stepping in and closing the door behind her, "I did not. But you need not worry. Marta went with her. She is not alone."

"So have you come to help me as you were wont to do when you were a little maid?"

He was speaking absently, even as his frame bent over some paper. She wished at that moment that she truly was a little maid again, having nothing else to do but gather curls of fragrant wood into her arms and deposit them into a cosy pile in the corner where she might sit and watch him work.

"What are you making, Vati?"

"I was trying to make a drawing of your Mutti."

"Of Mutti?"

Never before had she known him to attempt such a thing—that

is to say, never before had he mentioned such an endeavour to her. For a few seconds, curiosity made her forget why she had come.

"Can I see it?"

"Well, it is not very good. I would rather work on it longer before I show it to anyone."

"But why draw Mutti, Vati? Why would you...?"

She stopped. He loved Mutti dearly so why should he not try to draw a picture of her? As she stood in the workshop, she fleetingly recalled that Vati had but recently recounted to her that Dürer, the famous engraver and painter, who loved his mother very much, had drawn a charcoal portrait of her but a few years back in 1514. Dürer had drawn his mother when she was very ill, sketching her just prior to her death. Vati had shown her the picture Dürer had drawn, revealing a woman who was thin to the point of emaciated, and one who appeared rather frightened. Of course drawing your Mutti was different than drawing your wife—but the similarity was that love had stimulated the desire to draw. Dürer's sketch had made her wonder though, wonder and think. Was the man trying to preserve life or draw death?

"Why would he have drawn her so frightened, Vati?" she had asked.

"I'm not sure except that he is an honest man and perhaps the truth was that she must have been afraid to die."

"Hmm," Katharina had murmured, rather puzzled, "and yet you have told me that this woman was a god-fearing lady and that as far as anyone could see she lived a blameless life."

"Someone told me," Vati had answered, "that just before her death, as Dürer was sitting by her bedside, he perceived his mother witnessed a vision—that she saw something fearful at the moment when she passed from life to death."

Katharina remembered all these things in the few seconds that she stood looking at her father bent over the picture he was trying to draw of her mother. The truth of it was though, that you could not really preserve life by drawing someone. You could only create a memory.

"Remember the picture Dürer drew of his mother," she slowly formulated her words, not exactly sure where she was going with them, "and how you told me she was afraid to die?"

"I have heard say," her father said, seeming not at all surprised by the turn of the conversation, neither turning his face toward her, but keeping it down as his hands kept drawing, "that Dürer had a fear of death as well, but that he has credited Luther, the priest of whom your brother Lux was speaking when he was home last, for the peace of mind he now has. If I remember correctly, Dürer has called Luther 'that Christian man who has helped me out of great anxieties.'"

Katharina said nothing in response for a moment, pondering his words. Then she breathed deeply.

"Do you think, Vati," she at length went on, "that Luther has the answers?"

"Perhaps," he smiled, finally looking up at her again, his hands still, "perhaps he does, daughter. And now would you like to tell me why you came to interrupt me at so important a task as I have here—the task of attempting to draw your beautiful Mutti?"

"I'm so glad you love her, Vati," Katharina replied impulsively, "it is a very good thing."

"Someday and someday soon, I hope," he quietly responded, "I pray you will also have such a love, my dear one. And now, please tell me what it is that you have to say so that I can get on with my work."

"Yes," Katharina said, suddenly recalling Margred's problem and that she had come to tell her Vati that she was going to call on Matthis Zell.

Taking up the broom from the nearby corner, she began to sweep shavings. It calmed her and she could think better as she swept. It had always been so, that this act quieted her mind—or so it seemed.

"I'm about to go out," she began, "and I'm going to call on the priest who is at St. Lawrence Church."

Her father nodded at her words. He knew his daughter and was keenly aware that she would tell him of the purpose of her errand much quicker if he did not hurry her with questions.

"Cousin Margred has just left here," Katharina went on, sweeping vigorously, and then she proceeded to tell him all that Margred had recounted.

When she mentioned Balthazar Horst, her father made a derisive sound and almost spoke, but then thought the better of it.

"So I thought," Katharina finished, "that to seek out Matthis Zell, a priest who is known for his leniency in meting out punishment and for his mercy to the poor, would be a wise thing to do. He is the penitentiarus and thus would have the authority to forgive and...well, to deal justly and wisely with this case. If Balthazar Horst has anything to do with the matter, it will, no doubt, end up with poor cousin Margred's husband being robbed of money and even possibly land he owns. What think you, Vati?"

"I think it is a good thing for you to go," he answered, "but simply present the facts, Katharina, do not give your opinion or tell him what to do. That would be unseemly for a young woman such as yourself."

"Yes, Vati," she assented, returning the broom to the corner where she had found it and walking over to him even as she spoke.

Planting a kiss on his cheek, she caught a small glimpse of the drawing. Indeed, she could see her mother's face vividly caught on the page. It was a good likeness.

"Are you afraid of dying, Vati?" she asked on sudden impulse.

"Perhaps I too," the reply came rather quickly, "will have to find out if Luther's words can help me out of that anxiety."

THE PARISH OF St. Lawrence was the largest and perhaps the most notable in Strasbourg. Yet Matthis Zell, reflected Katharina, as she closed the Johanngasse door behind her and began walking toward this church basking in the warmth of the sunshine, was merely, when all was said and done, a hired subordinate of this church, one whose contract had to be renewed annually. Dr. Geiler had not been such a subordinate. He had simply been there all the time as far as she knew and never had to worry about having a contract renewed. Did Matthis Zell worry about his contract renewal? There were fierce struggles among the various members of the clergy in Strasbourg. She knew this for a fact. And she also knew that people much preferred Matthis Zell's preaching to Master Peter Wickram's preaching. He drew ever-larger congregations than Master Wickram, Sunday after Sunday. She herself had been several times now to hear Matthis Zell preach and had been moved by his words—and surprised at the crowds that had come to hear him exhort. So perhaps, because of popularity, Matthis would not have to worry about a contract. She did not know if Matthis was aware that she had been to hear him preach a number of times. Even now, walking along the street, contemplating his figure on the pulpit, she blushed at her own audacity in addressing him as Matthis in her thoughts. He was after all a priest, a member of the clergy and thus demanded respect of address. She thought of his eyes, clear eyes, honest eyes and eyes that seemed to have the ability to gauge what you hid away in your heart. Would he have known that she considered his nose long and somewhat aristocratic? She kicked a stone into the canal alongside which she walked. There was a small kerplunk and then quiet after the stone sank. Matthis Zell had told her he was investigating some of the new teachings of Luther. This was becoming apparent in his preaching. But, oh how good it was to hear him speak! It was like Dr. Geiler's sermons, and yet it was not like Dr. Geiler's sermons. How strange! Whereas both men criticized the lax style of living of the priesthood, Matthis added this to his criticism: such living was against the clear instructions given in Scripture.

She was now nearing the cathedral. The warm, tender sandstone of the massive building never failed to amaze her. The stone had been shipped from the Vosges Mountains in Eastern France and also from the Black Forest in Germany. Almost pink, the stones were *sandstein* as people said. Perhaps they had been chosen to build the church because they seemed to react to light. What you saw when walked down the street to worship in the cathedral depended on luminosity. Some days the cathedral appeared quite dark and on other days, such as today which was full of sunshine, it appeared very light. The portal of the St. Lawrence transept with its stone-faced statues leaning and looking down at the people below, was now directly in front of her.

The sun shone kindly down on her form and she revelled in it. Stopping and lost in reverie for a long moment, she smiled at the thought that she was not at that minute moving forward even as that the great clock inside the cathedral was not moving forward—that ancient clock which had been built in the 1300s, 200 years before she was born. But just because the clock had stopped, it did not mean that time had stopped. It was said that the local authorities in Strasbourg had ordered the constructor of the clock to be blinded after he was done his work so that he could not try to build something like it ever again. Truthfully, it was a rare clock and had a calendar and an astrolabe, as well as some miniature statues. The main statue, of course, was the Virgin Mary holding her baby in her arms. In front of the Lady Mary, every hour, three kings used to step out of their chambers and the music would announce the time. She never had seen the clockwork but Vati and Mutti had, and they had told her how extraordinary this sight had been. The clock had stopped functioning properly when she was but a very little maid.

Shaking herself out of her reverie, Katharina continued on her way toward the portal of St. Lawrence, which was located at the north transept of the cathedral. This transept balanced St. Catherine's chapel on the south side of the church. A half-smile lay on her face as she eyed the smooth stone faces sizing her up as she approached. Pulling open the heavy wooden door she lightly stepped inside, passing between the statues of the three wise men on high at her left and St. Lawrence, accompanied by four saintly companions, on her right. As she passed, she gave St. Lawrence a little wave. How fitting it was that Matthis Zell should serve in a church called St. Lawrence! For the story was told that this second century deacon called the poor the "treasure of the church" and he distributed alms with great generosity. In the same manner, it certainly appeared, Matthis Zell estimated the poor as dear in the eyes of God and seemed to care a great deal for their welfare. Deacon Lawrence, however, had been martyred, and she would not wish to carry the analogy between him and Brother Matthis Zell as far as that.

This part of the cathedral, the St. Lawrence transept, served as one of the seven parish churches for the city. Even though the outside of the chapel was fairly unostentatious, the inside was beautiful. The high vault overhead with its double curved ribs was magnificent, and the stained glass windows at the sides had sunlight streaming through them. Its colours made the whole place light and peaceful. Indeed, although the St. Lawrence chapel was vastly smaller than the main cathedral, and she had been here now a number of times, she found it to be a very personal place of worship.

A bit at a loss as to what to do next, Katharina stood next to one of the pillars and looked about. There was no one here as far as she could see, performing some small task such as sweeping, or polishing, so that she might ask if perchance Brother Zell was in the building. So what ought she to do? What if she could not find him, what then? For a moment she almost rued the fact that she had given cousin Margred some cause to hope for help. And then, as if by divine ordinance, a phrase Dr. Geiler had been wont to use, a side door opened and Matthis Zell himself walked into the chapel. She breathed a great sigh of relief. But now she must approach him, ask him, or rather, tell him why she was here. He seemed intent on prayer for he was heading for one the pews; face down, as if very fastened upon some particular thought. She coughed discreetly and his head turned. A glimmer of recognition flitted across his face even though it had been months and months since she had last seen him.

"Katharina Schütz," he murmured softly.

But such was the height of the ceiling that his voice echoed clearly to her ears. He came toward her and she blushed, though she knew not why. Surely a great many people came to meet him here to ask for advice, to be shriven of sins perhaps and to tell him things. Her blond hair was pinned up and confined under a net. Unconsciously her right hand moved up to make sure no stray hair was escaping. Then the wide sleeve moved down, brushing past her face to hang demurely against the side of her front-laced greyish gown.

"How can I be of service, Katharina Schütz?"

She particularly liked the way he pronounced her name. For a moment she did not answer. Then she collected her thoughts and began.

"I wonder," she began. Her voice sounded a trifle squeaky and she cleared her throat.

The noise sounded and resounded in the chapel.

"I beg your pardon," she went on, "but I crave to have you listen to a story regarding my cousin and her family."

He nodded and indicated that they might sit down in one of the pews. She recalled that years before when she had been but a little maid, she had sat thus with Dr. Geiler in the great cathedral and that he had advised her regarding her grief over Jacob. He had been so very kind. She folded her hands together as she sat down. Grey long sleeves fell half way over her fingers. Matthis Zell waited patiently. She swallowed and nervously looked into his face. What was she doing bringing such a matter to a man who surely had more important things to which to attend?

"This morning," she haltingly began her story and he smiled encouragingly.

"Yes?"

Suddenly she was infused with assurance that he would listen and that he would indeed care to help. The words, which seemed to have been tied up into knots within her, now came pouring out. He never interrupted, save to ask twice the name of the priest who had made free to ask for an audience with Wolfgang Schott. When she came to the end of her story, saying that the interview was for four o'clock that afternoon at St. Thomas Church, he stood up and smiled at her. She smiled back at him.

"In one of his tracts," he said, "Luther states that he will be called a heretic by those whose purses will suffer from the truths that he promotes. And I am quite certain that Balthazar Horst will refer to me in the future as a heretic."

Katharina stared at him, her blue eyes wide.

"I shall be there at St. Thomas Church this afternoon," he went on, "and I thank you for bringing this matter to my attention, Katharina."

She flushed. He had addressed her by her first name and it sounded fine to her. As if he truly cared about her situation.

"I knew not whom else I could confide in," she answered, "and am most grateful, as I am sure my cousin Margred and her husband will also be."

She stood up and bending slightly, smoothed out her grey skirt.

"I will be going back home then," she continued for lack of other words, her eyes still on his face.

"Perhaps," he said, "unless you are in a great hurry, I can now tell you how I met with Dr. Geiler when I was but a small boy. I would like very much to relate it to you."

Katharina sat down next to him once more.

"I would very much like to hear this," she answered, "and I do have some time."

AND MATTHIS ZELL began. His voice was sonorous and rich and Katharina could not help but listen. She minded very much that in this way Vati had often told her a story—she sitting next to him in his workshop and he relating some story or event that had happened in the past.

"I was but a very small boy, I think I was not yet ten summers old when Dr. Geiler came back to Kaysersberg to preach. He was to be the guest of Count William of Rappoltstein in company of Sebastian Brandt who then held an official position at Basle. But that matters not."

He stopped for a moment and went on.

"Dr. Geiler, as well as preaching in the city, was to visit his grandmother who lived in Kaysersberg. Everyone in the city was excited that he was coming. He was much loved, and people were so happy and proud that he was returning to his own city."

Katharina listened. She was spellbound.

"Indeed, the young men of the city formed an honour guard around his carriage as he drove into town toward Count William's castle; others stood at the drawbridge of the castle with flags and pipes and drums. It was a joyful occasion. I was there, Katharina. I stood within the throngs of people and watched."

Within her mind's eye Katharina could see him standing among the crowd. She saw him as a little boy, a little boy with brown wavy hair and a smile on his face. Perhaps he had also carried a flag.

"Did you have a flag?" she questioned, the words out of her mouth at the thought.

He laughed out loud.

"No, I did not. But I remember wishing I had one."

Then his face changed. It became almost sombre. Katharina was puzzled. He had carried such a happy countenance but a moment before.

"There were beggars that day—a number of them. You see it was a day of festivities, and they thought a few pennies might drop into their hats, into their hands...."

He stopped for a minute, searching for words. Katharina waited.

"There was one beggar in particular. He was blind, not a very old fellow, just barely in his twenties, I would venture to guess thinking back. He was not only blind, but also dreadfully disfigured from the pox. Pits grooved and ran across his face. He had, for a guide, a small black dog that was tied to him by a string. Now this beggar's manner of living was to sing. For God had gifted him with a wonderfully melodious voice."

Katharina thought of the beggars she passed daily in Strasbourg. She did not often think of how these poor souls lived day by day. It made her glad every now and then to give one or another some small pittance, but she had never heard one sing.

"This blind beggar, whose name was Fritz, also had a lyre, and he played as he sang. The dog led him about, and these two were a fixture in Kaysersberg."

Katharina was much moved and looked down at the church floor as she blinked back tears. She was being a silly child, she thought to herself, to be so moved by a beggar who was likely dead by now and whom she had never met.

"Now there was a boy standing near me, who with a small knife ran over to Fritz and cut the string by which the dog was attached to Fritz. This was before Dr. Geiler's arrival. The crowd, somewhat tired of waiting for Dr. Geiler, was moved to jeers and mocking laughter at seeing Fritz stumble about, trying to find his dog. He bumped into everyone and was pushed around. The dog, faithful friend that he was, came to his blind master and tried to get him out of harm's way by pulling at his pant legs. But the beggar fell and hurt his leg."

"Oh, how dreadful!" Katharina cried out, now feeling the tears sting behind her eyelids. "What happened?"

"Well, someone helped Fritz up and supported him to a barn

not too far away. There he was given a bed of straw. He was quite distraught, as he had hoped to obtain an audience with Dr. Geiler and to implore him for his help. For not only was the young beggar blind, but he also helped support a poor mother who looked to the pennies he collected to help feed his younger siblings."

"Oh," Katharina sighed and went on softly, "you know this because you spoke to the beggar?"

"I did," Matthis Zell affirmed, "for I followed.... The dog as well would not leave Fritz and stayed by his side."

"Then what happened," Katharina asked, much interested.

"Fritz was fed by the owner of the barn. I went home before long, and the next day I heard Dr. Geiler preach. I remember well that his sermon was on Matthew 25. "Inasmuch as ye have done it unto one of the least of these my brethren, ye have done it unto Me.""

He was quiet for a moment. There were no other people in the sanctuary. It was very still and Katharina could hear Matthis breathe in and out a few times before he continued his story.

"I will never forget that Dr. Geiler said that God did not command us to build churches and convents while at the same time suffering the unfortunate among us to languish. He said that we do not read in the Bible that Jesus will say at the last judgement 'Come ye blessed of the father, inherit the kingdom prepared for you from before the foundation of the world because you have built churches and monasteries.' But Dr. Geiler said that Jesus did say, 'I was hungry and ye fed Me; I was naked and ye clothed Me; I was sick and ye visited Me....'"

Katharina sighed and sighed deeply. How strange that Matthis Zell should be telling her these things!

"Dr. Geiler went on to stress that we should not do the one and leave the other undone, for love is the first and greatest commandment."

There was quiet for a bit, and at last Katharina asked, "And what of the beggar? What of poor Fritz?"

"Dr. Geiler heard the story of poor Fritz and asked someone to take him to the beggar's side."

"And were you that someone?" Katharina exclaimed impulsively.

"I was actually one of several in a group, Katharina," Matthis answered, "and you will be surprised to learn that the child who cut the string by which the dog was attached to Fritz was also there. Indeed, he had been so moved by Dr. Geiler's sermon that he was filled with remorse."

Again when Matthis fell silent at this juncture, Katharina asked, "What happened then?"

"After the child had confessed his crime and had sobbed earnestly a good while asking for punishment, Dr. Geiler told him that his sin was forgiven him for Jesus Christ's sake, because Jesus bore his punishment for him on the cross. The boy stopped crying and asked Dr. Geiler if he was sure that he was forgiven. 'As sure,' Dr. Geiler replied, 'as I know that angels in heaven rejoice over your repentance. But you must also tell Fritz that you are sorry.' This the boy did."

Katharina's hands folded and unfolded on her lap. It was such a beautiful story and such a wonderful tale to hear about Dr. Geiler—*her* Dr. Geiler.

"And what happened to Fritz?" she asked at length.

"Dr. Geiler promised him assistance, this I heard him say with my own ears. But I left before I found out what that was. And that," Matthis Zell said, "was how I met Dr. Geiler, and it is a memory I cherish and often dwell on when I deal with others."

"It is a good memory," Katharina agreed, "and now you have let me share it."

She stood up and stretched out her hand.

"Goodbye, Matthis Zell. I thank you."

He stood up as well and, taking the proffered hand, held it for a moment.

"Goodbye, Katharina Schütz," he answered, "it was a pleasure to speak with you again. God go with you."

"And with you," she softly replied.

Chapter XXVII

I t was but a few days later that a bubbly and very thankful cousin Margred called at Johanngasse once more. She told Katharina, and indeed the whole family, of the events that had transpired since Katharina's visit to the St. Lawrence parish priest, Matthis Zell.

"He was there, Katharina, even as you said he might be," she blurted out even before she was seated at the kitchen table in the Schütz home, "and he was so very kind. Wolfgang is so grateful, and so are we all. We don't know what would have happened had Balthazar Horst been allowed to proceed with whatever wicked scheme he had in mind to extract money from us."

She stopped for a breath of air before she resumed her streaming dialogue.

"When Wolfgang arrived at St. Thomas Church with Sebastian that afternoon, Brother Matthis Zell was already seated in one of the pews. He was not in the front of the church, but concealed at the side. What I mean when I say that he was concealed is that he was not in full view of whoever entered the church, if you understand what I am trying to say."

Katharina nodded. She did understand. Indeed, she could picture Matthis quite clearly sitting in one of the side pews while he was waiting for Balthazar Horst and Wolfgang and Sebastian.

"And then what happened, cousin?" she asked.

"Well, Wolfgang and Sebastian walked past him toward one of the side chapels to the right of the apse. That's where Balthazar Horst had told Sebastian they were to meet. And Balthazar Horst was there almost immediately upon their arrival. Dark cowl around his head, he was gravely faced, Wolfgang said. That is, he was of such a countenance that you would think Sebastian had murdered his grandmother."

Vati, who was also sitting at the kitchen table, chuckled.

"Such a crime," he commented, "would mean that he would not be permitted in church, cousin Margred, but would likely be sitting in a jail cell awaiting sentence by the civil authorities."

"Well," cousin Margred shrugged away his objections, "the truth is that such was Balthazar Horst's face, that looking at it you would conclude that a death sentence awaited poor Sebastian."

"What happened next?" Katharina interjected. "I am most anxious to know."

"What happened next was that Brother Matthis Zell stationed himself behind Wolfgang and Sebastian. He appeared so silently that it shook Brother Horst's speech and conduct. He had been about to lead Wolfgang and Sebastian into a private chamber, a chamber off to the side of the nave, but he stopped mid-sentence and simply gazed at Brother Zell. I think that he knew who Brother Zell was and that his was an overlapping authority."

Mutti spoke next. "What then, cousin Margred?"

"Well, Brother Zell asked in a very calm but clear voice whether or not he could be of any assistance. The almost humorous response was," and cousin Margred smiled at all of them as she continued, "that both Wolfgang and Balthazar Horst answered him at the same time with Wolfgang saying 'Yes, he could' and Balthazar Horst answering, 'No, thank you, all was well.' Nevertheless, Brother Matthis Zell persisted in saying that he was out visiting the various churches of Strasbourg and that he was quite interested in what the particular problem at hand was and could Brother Horst indulge him and just explain the matter."

The kitchen was quiet for a moment. Even Marta was listening intently as she slowly stirred the pot holding the noonday meal.

"It was Sebastian who, after a moment, explained what had

happened. And Wolfgang said that he explained the situation extremely well."

There was no doubt that there was pride in cousin Margred's voice as she related this.

"Balthazar Horst tried to interrupt Sebastian several times, but a look from Brother Zell stopped him short, and he, becoming very red of face, was discomfited. At the end of the story, Brother Zell asked Balthazar Horst if this was how events had occurred and whether or not the boy had, of his own volition, come to confess to him."

"I warrant," Katharina interjected, "that Brother Zell was checking my story against Sebastian's story."

"The priest had to admit," Margred blithely continued, with a smile at Katharina, "that Sebastian had come of his own volition. At this point Brother Zell asked Balthazar Horst if the boy was not to be commended for coming freely of his own will to confess a sin? And did Brother Horst now mean to congratulate the father for having such an honest son, and is this why he had called both of them in for an interview, for surely to come together for penance was not practice?"

Katharina and Vati grinned simultaneously. Margred also continued to smile, a great sunny smile, before she took up the thread of her story once more.

"Balthazar Horst stuttered something which no one understood and then, very calmly, Brother Zell turned to Sebastian and said, 'My boy, you were wrong in permitting those unruly boys to come into your house to take your father's wine. I think you are quite aware that this was a grievous error. But I leave it to your father to punish you, as punish he must, and I warn you not to let such a thing happen again. Now go home and make sure you confess the matter to our Lord, and ask him to forgive you.'"

"That is what he said?" Katharina asked incredulously.

"Yes," cousin Margred triumphantly crowed, "and it is surely a wonderful matter, is it not?"

All nodded, and then Vati inquired, "And what is the punishment that Wolfgang has meted out to Sebastian?"

"That he must, every day for a month, work for two hours in

the printing shop doing whatever chore is given him by his father or by the journeymen, in order to pay back the price of the wine."

"That seems reasonable," Katharina said, and cousin Margred nodded.

"And now I must be off," she added rather suddenly, "for this evening we are having Brother Matthis Zell over for supper. And I mean to have a very good supper for the wonderful courtesy which he has extended to us; I cannot put it into words. I think I could speak all day and still not sufficiently do credit to the kindness that he has shown."

"For supper?" Katharina parroted.

"Yes," cousin Margred smiled at her, "he has been so very kind that I sent an invitation to his quarters in the Bruderhof Strasse. And he responded immediately that he would be glad to come."

Katharina stared at her. Perhaps they could also, at some time in the future, invite Matthis Zell to the Johanngasse for supper. And they could speak of many things—things that bothered her —things to which she did not know the answer—and things....
Here her thoughts stopped. Cousin Margred was already at the kitchen door. She stood up hastily.

"Farewell, cousin Katharina," cousin Margred called out, "and I thank you again for coming to our aid. Perhaps," she added, the idea striking her suddenly, "you would also like to come to sup with us this evening?"

There was nothing Katharina would have liked better, but she had already promised her sister Elisabet that she would come for a visit.

"I cannot," she answered regretfully, plucking at the light green sleeve of her dress, "but perhaps some other time."

"Some other time then," Margred sang out cheerfully, and then she was gone.

ELISABET AND HER husband had bought a house in the heart of the Rossmarkt, an area northwest of the cathedral. A few hundred years ago the Rossmarkt, the Horse Market, had not been walled in, but now it was properly situated within the city walls and much business was conducted here. Initially sparsely populated, it presently held quite a number of homes surrounded by court-yards and gardens. But it was an uncobbled area, subject to ruts and bumps. Katharina cautiously picked her way around the numerous piles of horse manure. A great number of horses were sold here each year. And this was, of course, the very place from which Annalein and all the others ill with the dancing sickness had been sent to Zabern. It was strange, she was today wearing the self-same dress that she had worn that day—her light green gown with the white partlet edged with yellow trim. She did not really envy Elisabet living here. But then, she reflected wryly, Elisabet would be happy anywhere as long as Michael was with her. And now that they had a little baby boy, young Michael, Elisabet was twice as happy and content. Katharina felt a small stab of jealousy in her heart. Sighing deeply, she mulled over her intention to stay unmarried. Her sisters laughed at her, as did her mother, but she had ever thought that she would like to remain as she was; each day helping others who were in need of nursing, of encourage-ment and of a listening ear. Was not this what Dr. Geiler had ever recommended as even the story which Matthis Zell had told her had born out? And there were truly so many in need. Frau Bauer had taught her the names of herbs and their efficacy for various ailments, and Mutti knew how to concoct many broths and soups for disease as well.... Her thoughts broke off as the door to the house she was about to pass opened and Elisabet called out to her.

"Katharina, you goose, were you going to pass us by without even so much as a glance?"

She laughed as she called out, and Katharina, startled out of her daydreaming, laughed as well.

"You must have been watching for me, sweet sister."

Katharina turned toward her as she spoke, and Elisabet clapped her hands in the air in assent.

"Indeed I was. I have been looking forward to your visit all day. So come into my house, for you are most welcome."

"Well then, here I am. And how is your beautiful baby?"

"Little Michael is well, but I do want to speak with you about some concerns I have."

Elisabet beamed when she spoke her son's name, and Katharina envied her sister again, even as in her thoughts she had envied her but a few moments earlier. While they were conversing amiably, Katharina climbed the steps, reaching out to her sister for a hearty embrace.

"Oh, Katharina, I'm so glad you're here," Elisabet murmured in her ear. "Mutti Schwencker calls often, and I've been afraid to let her change little Michael's cloths because he has a such a rash. I just know she is convinced that I'm not the perfect model of motherhood."

The sisters walked, side by side, into the foyer of the home.

"Nonsense," Katharina answered, calmly responding to her sibling's self-deprecating statement and beginning to take off her cape, "you are the best mother in all of Strasbourg."

"You goose," Elisabet said, smiling broadly. "Oh, I am glad that you are here for I know you are ever well-versed in Frau Bauer's remedies. How is little Beata?"

"Little Beata is well and growing bigger each day. When he is home, Herr Bauer struts about the street with the child in his arms and I vow he is as proud of her as if she were his own flesh and blood."

They walked through the hallway together with Katharina commenting enthusiastically on Elisabet's dress. Indeed her sister was looking very much the tidy, well-groomed and capable *hausfrau*. She wore a simple white bodice with front lacing, a bodice which had the skirt pleated into it. The skirt was a rich, dark green colour, and it majestically trailed numerous pleats onto the floor. The dress sleeves were puffed, and its material matched that of the skirt. A small cap perched on Elisabet's hair. It sat immaculately and was stitched all over with small reddish flowers. Katharina greatly admired it and inadvertently her hand stole up to her own cap. Not much to her surprise, she felt it had sagged over to the right side of her head, and a great many loose hairs were undoubtedly peeping out on the left. Elisabeth, seeing the gesture, laughed out loud.

"Oh, Katharina," she exclaimed, even as they walked into the sitting room, "you look very well also, and your cap is about as neat as I have ever seen it."

But even as she spoke, her hands straightened her sister's headgear, stroking her sister's cheek when she finished. She recalled ever so clearly how she had often straightened Katharina's cap when she was but a little maid.

"Come," she commanded, "I've got little Michael resting in the cradle in the front room. Mutti Schwencker has told me a number of times that this is not proper, but I do so love to watch him sleep. We waited, as you know," she added softly, "for this little son for a number of years, and he is so special. Besides, we have two cradles, and I can always carry him to the other one if we have company. Or, if I see Mutti Schwenchker coming down the street. You," she added at the end with a smile, "are not real company."

Katharina smiled at the waterfall of words her sister gushed out, who appended her speech with a non sequitur by saying, "And I've also got some very good ale which we can drink while we are having a conversation."

"Whatever you have for me to drink will be fine," she answered.

"But what I have is wonderful," Elisabet sat down as she spoke, patting the seat next to her, "even Mutti Schwencker has mentioned that she believes my ale is quite amazing."

Katharina laughed out loud, sitting down next to her sister.

"You know pride is one of the sins Father Geiler ever addressed."

"But it is true, Katharina," Elisabet pouted, "I add mint, marjoram and sage, the same that Mutti adds to her ale. But then I also put in cumin, ginger and anise. I had heard tell by some merchant in the market that this makes ale very tasty. So I experimented. And that, I think, gives mine the distinctive flavour that it now has. Michael has grown quite fond of it, and I don't know if I mentioned it but Mutti Schwencker has asked me what special ingredients I put in."

"And I am sure, being the good daughter-in-law that you are, that you have apprised her of all the ingredients?" Katharina questioned, with an impish look in her eye.

"No," her sister readily took the bait and lowered her voice, "for this is what makes her respect me in a way that she did not do before."

"Oh, you are the silly goose now," Katharina retorted, "for if you share the recipe with her I think this will not only make her respect you, but also love you."

"Yes, I suppose you are right," Elisabet blushed as she spoke and moved the cradle with her foot to rock it slightly.

"Of course I am right. I am always right."

"Now you are being prideful," Elisabet rejoined, "and the truth is that Mutti Schwenker's ale often tastes sour, and then she spices it with nutmeg to make it palatable. But it is not easy on the stomach."

"Well, you must help her then, and I vow she will appreciate you more."

Elisabet smiled at her sister.

"I thought our Barbara was always the little moralizer. But you certainly have it in you also, and…I suppose that you are right."

"Now do you want me to look at little Michael's bottom?"

"Oh would you, Katharina? It would make me so much happier to have your opinion. I do worry so, and he is quite red. Perhaps there is something in his diet…I know not. As I said, I am ashamed to ask Michael's mother, and Mutti has not been by of late."

As she spoke, she rose from her seat and lifted the little baby boy out of the cradle. He yawned with his eyes closed and then wrinkled them in a rather unhappy facial expression, making as if to begin crying.

"There, you see!" Elisabet said, rather distressed, "I'm sure he is in pain, Katharina."

She laid the child on the table and proceeded to take off the damp cloth swaddling his bottom. The bottom did appear very red and Katharina winced when she looked at it. No wonder the little fellow was fussy upon waking.

"I have pulverized myrtle to lay on the skin," she said, "and will have Marta bring some to you tomorrow. As well, after you bathe Michael, you should rub him with some olive oil."

"Do you think it will help?" Elisabet asked, even as she put a dry cloth around Michael's inflamed little bum.

"Well, I saw Frau Bauer use it on Beata when she first came to her and it worked like a charm. So I imagine that it has a good chance of also helping Michael."

"You are a wonderful sister," Elisabet exclaimed.

She gently laid Michael back in his cradle. He whimpered a wee bit, but then closed his eyes and went back to sleep. Elisabet came over and planted a kiss on Katharina's cheek. She could not help but whisper another sweet sentence into her sister's ear.

"At one point, you will also marry and have a child," she averred, "and you will be a wonderful mother. You will charm some man off his feet and…and…. "

Katharina laughingly pushed her sister away. The evening sunlight stole through the window and the room was a pleasant place. Fleetingly her thoughts travelled to cousin Margred's where she knew Matthis Zell to be visiting.

Elisabet brought out some ale and some cake, and the two sisters sat companionably for a while, chatting as they ate. Katharina vividly recounted the drama that had occurred in the life of cousin Margred and her husband Wolfgang and how caring a mother cousin Margred had proven to be to Wolfgang's children.

"This Matthis Zell," Elisabet asked, "I've not heard him preach as yet, but I think I will go and hear him. Michael has been to St. Lawrence a few times, and has been very impressed."

Katharina could not help it, but she blushed and indeed, she did not know why she was blushing. Hoping her sister would not note, she looked down.

"Last Sunday," Elisabet continued, "this was his theme, for so Michael recounted it to me. 'If God has given us his Son, has he not given us all things with him?'"

"Why Elisabet," Katharina said wonderingly, "how well you remember. I do not recall you ever speaking of a sermon theme previously."

"Well," Elisabet responded, "Michael does explain things so very well. And he said that Matthis Zell spoke in this way. That it is reasonable to assume that going on a pilgrimage makes one a pilgrim. But going on a pilgrimage does not make one a Christian; that fasting makes people who fast. But fasting does not make one a Christian."

Katharina was looking at her sister with amazement. It was not that Elisabet had never professed her faith in so many words, but the fact that she spoke with such enthusiasm. It must be that

Michael infused her with this.

"And," Elisabet continued, "entering holy orders makes Franciscans and Dominicans, such as we have in Strasbourg, but entering holy orders does not make one a Christian."

She was red now with the exertion of remembering what Michael had told her. Obviously it was important to her.

"And," she laboriously went on, "then Matthis Zell said that Jesus Christ teaches in the Holy Bible that only spiritual things make one a Christian. No outside thing can do it. No works can make one a Christian."

She stopped for a moment catching her breath before adding a question.

"What think you, Katharina?"

Katharina shook her head slowly and felt her cap once more slide a bit to the side.

"Well," she answered slowly, "in spite of the fact that I bought one many years ago, I think I know now that indulgences do not have any merit. As for pilgrimages, you know that I went to Zabern with Annalein and she did get better. But I am quite convinced that she would have recovered had she *not* gone to Zabern. As for the Franciscans and Dominicans, I cannot really say. I do know that a great many of them disregard the poor here in Strasbourg, and I often wonder where all the alms and gifts go. If you would cut open the fat stomach of a brother monk, I vow that gold coins would roll out."

Elisabet grinned and nodded vigorously. The baby sputtered a bit. His eyes were open now, and he blew a bit of a milk bubble out of the side of his mouth. She bent over him to adjust the coverlet, at the same time responding vigorously to what her sister was saying.

"Indeed, this is exactly what Michael says. And that is why he so enjoys going to hear Matthis Zell. He says Brother Zell is different from the others. He says...."

The baby cooed up at her, and Elisabet left off speaking. Katharina got up and stood next to her and both contemplated the baby with something akin to adoration.

"Have you heard," Elisabet said at length, "that Tilman von Lyn, the director of the Carmelite monastery here in Strasbourg, has been preaching...."

She stopped, searched for words and then shrugged.

"I am not always able, as you know, dear sister, to put matters into words as ably as you or Michael. But what I understand is that von Lyn has been saying that priests should marry."

She laughed out loud for a long minute before she went on.

"There are many who would not like a corpulent monk for a spouse. I for one...."

She left off and her laughter peeled out again.

"I think," Katharina spoke clearly above the gaiety of her sister, "that there are those who might make very good husbands.... There are some who...who are serious and kind and would make excellent...just like your Michael. Besides, and this is the most important of all, no person is bound to vows invented by human beings. The Bible does not teach it."

"What does it not teach?" Elisabet asked, distracted by another milk bubble her little Michael was blowing.

"It does not teach that people should not marry."

She stopped and looked down at the floor.

"But of course," Elisabet agreed, a smile still hovering over her face, "the idea of monastics marrying is not new. Indeed we have heard it before, have we not, from the tracts that doctor Martin Luther has put out? And I do truly think it makes sense that God has made men and women so that they can marry one another."

Katharina nodded.

"Tilman von Lyn agrees with you. Monks and nuns should be allowed to leave cloisters is what he openly advocates and preaches off the pulpit. And he adds this to his sermons, that the government should provide assistance to former monks so that they can marry and learn how to provide for themselves."

"I don't know what will happen," Elisabet sighed, stroking small Michael's downy scalp, "but I fear that Tilman von Lyn might not only be forbidden to preach but will also be removed from Strasbourg."

"Do you?" Katharina said, her face troubled and wistful. "Yet I fear he is not the only one who holds to such opinions."

"Indeed, I do," Elisabet responded, her hands now fluffing the boy's blanket, "for Michael has said so, and he knows a great deal."

Katharina could not help but grin at this statement and playfully poked her sister in the side.

"And if Michael said that fish danced every Thursday at midnight, you would believe that too?"

"Oh, Katharina! How could you understand? You are not married."

"No, indeed," Katharina replied, slowly repeating, "No, indeed."

Chapter XXVIII

I t was well-known by virtually everyone in Strasbourg that the monk Martin Luther, whose tracts were being read with so much favour and enthusiasm, had been summoned to appear before Emperor Charles V at the Imperial Diet. The Diet, which had begun in January 1521, was held in the city of Worms. Luther's summons to it was for April. The citizens of Strasbourg differed in opinion as to whether or not there was any wisdom in the monk's obeying the emperor's summons. The emperor was, after all, the same Charles who had recently been crowned at Aix-la-Chapelle, the same Charles who had sworn at his crowning in the presence of princes, dukes and archbishops that he would keep the Catholic faith and protect the church against such heretics as Dr. Luther. In short, the emperor was a fervent Roman Catholic and the pope's loyal vassal. It followed, therefore, many people in Strasbourg reasoned, that because the pope had excommunicated Luther and would like to burn him at the stake, that the emperor would be of the same mind. This Diet of Worms was the first major event in the reign of the new emperor. It was an event in which he could display power, an event in which he could flex his imperial muscles.

Vati was morosely unhappy about the whole issue. Totally persuaded that Dr. Luther, as he was referred to by most people, should not go, he was thoroughly convinced that the good doctor would never return alive from such a meeting.

"They will burn him and reduce his body to ashes, as they did with Jan Hus," he predicted dolefully.

Lux, home for a short visit, disagreed with Vati. He was of the strong opinion that Dr. Luther should attend and defend the new teachings, insisted that the man would live because of the safe conduct the emperor had promised and that he himself would go to watch.

"Why must you go and watch?" Vati asked him.

"Luther's books were burned last year in Rome's Piazza Navona," his son replied, and when Vati did not answer but looked at him rather blankly, he added one word to the sentence.

The word was "Savonarola."

Vati smiled a slow smile in response, but it was a troubled smile.

THE MONTHS PASSED by rather peacefully. But by the middle of May, Strasbourg was again abuzz with gossip. It was being reported in the marketplace that the brave monk who had travelled to the Diet of Worms, had disappeared. Though he had apparently left the Diet in good health after giving a wonderful testimony of his faith, no one knew where he presently was. Surrounded by a group of companions, all of whom were accounted for, the monk himself had seemingly vanished. After he had presented his testimony, the emperor had given Dr. Luther three weeks of free conduct to return to Wittenberg, after which time he would be treated as an unrepentant heretic. But somewhere along the way back to Wittenberg, perhaps close to the Black Forest, he had been lost to human view. Was he dead? It was thought by many that he was. Surely it was a puzzle. Vati averred that disappearance from public eyes was perhaps a good thing to have happened, for it was crystal clear in his mind that the emperor meant to tie Dr. Luther's body to a stake. There were snatches of news from various folks who had been present at the Diet, folks who professed to have vague notions at best to what might have occurred. But, truth be told, no one had any credible evidence as to where the man was. Lux had not as yet been home to report on what he had seen and heard.

Matthis Zell came for a noon meal during this time and afterward, still seated at the kitchen table, fell into deep conversation with Vati about the matter of the disappearance of Dr. Luther. He had become a frequent caller since the incident with cousin Margred and her family, and the Schütz family had grown to enjoy his companionship and opinions very much. Vati especially, was very much impressed with Matthis' point of view and often engaged him in long and serious conversations. Katharina was often privy to these conversations and thoroughly enjoyed them.

The conversation Vati and Matthis Zell were having continued after the noon meal. It was lively and gave Katharina much on which to reflect. Trying to work diligently, at the same time listening to the men still seated at the table, she was barely able to keep her mind on stirring the medicinal potion that Mutti had put together for a sick neighbour. When the smell of burning reached her nostrils, Mutti sighed and gave Katharina another errand, taking over the stirring herself.

"Frau Bauer," she said softly, to Katharina, "has seemed poorly lately and could very likely use a visit and some encouragement."

Katharina, albeit blushingly, obeyed Mutti. She was certain Matthis Zell had heard the soft-spoken rebuke she had been given and that he had smelled the burning potion. Dragging her feet a little, her heart and mind staying behind in the kitchen, she left the house, crossing the street toward her neighbour's home.

Although she had half-expected a pale and perhaps tired-looking woman, a healthy and cheerful Frau Bauer bouncing Beata on her hip answered her knock on the door. Had Mutti known? The truth of it was, Frau Bauer appeared delighted with Katharina's call. Perhaps it gave her a rare audience on whom she could expend her ever-increasing knowledge of a toddler's care.

"A child's external actions, manners and expressions," she commenced immediately after greeting Katharina and even before the girl had crossed the threshold, "are very telling as to his or her innermost character."

Beata, at this particular juncture of wisdom, put out her tongue, grabbed her surrogate mother's cheek with one chubby hand and pinched it hard. With her other hand she took hold of Frau Bauer's hair, pulling with all her might.

"Indeed," Katharina said, much amused and following her

neighbour inside, "and does this particular action on Beata's part tell you something about her innermost character?"

"Well," Frau Bauer answered, loosing the child's grip on both her jowls and her hair, "it tells me that she is most free in showing that she loves me."

She smiled indulgently at the child she carried and continued to speak as they slowly walked up the stairs to the Bauer's' apartments, "I have been reading Erasmus, Katharina, who seems to be an expert on child-rearing. Have you read him? He is a most excellent author."

"No and I did not know that Erasmus was an authority on child-rearing," Katharina replied, bemused that Frau Bauer should be studying the writings of the man known as the 'prince of humanists' and went on, "neither was I aware that Erasmus had any children."

Frau Bauer snorted derisively.

"Well, just because he has no children does not mean that he cannot have insights into the rearing of them. He is known to be very clever, Katharina. For example, and I think this is a pearl of wisdom, he pays special attention to facial features in children. Facial features, he says, reflect the true qualities of a child."

Beata continued to stick out her tongue over her mother's shoulder as they were walking up the stairs and Katharina stuck hers out as well. The child giggled and Katharina began to feel rather cheerful, rather as if the whole business of being sent away because of a burning potion was miles and miles away.

"A child's cheeks," Frau Bauer went on as they entered the kitchen and as she offered Katharina a chair by the table, "should maintain natural colour and placement; if cheeks are puffed out, they indicate pride."

Katharina couldn't help it, but upon hearing these words she puffed out her cheeks. It was an action that made Beata squeal with laughter, laughter into which Katharina heartily joined.

"Indeed, Katharina," Frau Bauer reproved, "sometimes I think you are still a child and years away from...."

She stopped short.

"From what?" Katharina demanded.

"Well, from marriage and from being able to manage a household. Although," she added quickly, "I do mind that you helped your Mutti a great deal when she was ill. But Erasmus holds forth that laughter without cause is the mark of either a fool or a mad man."

"Mad woman," Katharina interjected, beginning to smile once more.

"And, young lady," Frau Bauer went on mercilessly, "at no age is it proper to laugh so uproariously that one's body shakes, something I saw you do just one moment ago, for this reveals a lack of inner control. Neither happiness nor joy should ever overcome you to the point that you lose facial composure; if laughter overwhelms you, disguise such defeat with a hand or a cloth."

She spoke perfunctorily, as if reciting a lesson. Katharina was not offended by her speech. She knew Frau Bauer was ever kind and was presently most likely very intent upon bringing Beata up properly.

"And you learned all this from Erasmus?"

"Indeed I have, and much more."

Frau Bauer was eager to share.

"For example, the disciplined child's mouth should be clean and circumspect. It should be rinsed every morning...."

At this point, Beata, who was still being dandled on her mother's hip, let loose a volley of gassy burps. It was extremely quiet in the kitchen for a long moment after the sound died away. Katharina tried desperately to control her urge to squeal out with laughter once more. She concentrated hard on a crack in the kitchen wall.

"What is it the learned doctor says about such...eh, such eruptions?" she finally managed, her eyes fixed on the wall. "Has he ever dealt with them in his writings?"

After she spoke, Katharina felt silly laughter bubbling up within her again. Indeed, she was now quite glad that she had come for the jocularity of the situation made her relax. My, but it felt good to pause for the ordinary things for a brief moment. When she felt her mirth sufficiently under control, she looked up at Frau Bauer—only to discover her neighbour was smiling as well, and this smile was spreading into a huge grin that suddenly burst forth into a howl of merriment.

"Oh, Katharina," she managed, "I'm such a fool at times. Why do you put up with me?"

Beata, all arms and legs with excitement, hugged her mother.

"Having the child has been such a blessing for me," Frau Bauer said a few moments later, "and I can never thank you enough for letting me stand godmother to her. Indeed," she repeated, "this has been such a blessing to me."

Katharina's eyes travelled through the kitchen. There was a walking bench in the corner with a harness stretched out overtop of it. It had held Beata up when she was learning how to walk. She was much past that stage now. A rattle lay on the table and several shirts and embroidered caps were haphazardly hanging over the edge of a chair. Tiny red shoes, leather shoes, stood by the door. Everywhere there were signs of little Beata's presence.

"And my husband, my dear Eucharius, he is so fond of...he loves Beata, as if she were his own flesh and blood."

"I know and I'm so very glad," Katharina responded.

And she was glad. Vaguely in her mind, she could see herself as a child standing on the front steps of her home, looking up—looking up to ever see the shadowy figure of Frau Bauer. Frau Bauer had often been alone at home. Her husband was usually away on business trips. But she had always been willing to help, always been willing to minister to the needs of others. The others, though, had always been someone else's family and someone else's children.

Katharina left after an hour of visiting, an hour of talking about children's aches and how to combat rashes and head lice. Beata had fallen asleep on Frau Bauer's lap as they spoke. Later, back down in the street, Katharina contemplated on the odd ways God managed lives. If she had never run into Frau Bauer in St. Thomas Church that day, then it was very likely that Beata might have been placed in a nunnery as an orphan. But such had not been God's will. In deep thought and contemplation about how paths are determined, even paths of newborns, she crossed the street back to her own home.

"Excuse me, Fräulein Katharina?"

It was the voice of Matthis Zell. She had almost bumped into him because she had not been watching where she was going.

"I'm so sorry," she murmured, "I was thinking of other matters and did not see you."

He smiled.

"I've had such a good conversation with your Vati and was sorry not to have you participate in it. It would have been a fine thing for me to hear your opinions on where Dr. Martin Luther is, and I would greatly enjoy telling you what a friend has recently told me about the Diet of Worms. He was present when two guards were escorting the good doctor to his lodgings after the Diet. It appeared he was in good hands at the time and quite safe."

"You have a friend who was present at the Diet?"

"Yes, a Master Stauper, a merchant who travelled to Worms to encourage Dr. Luther. There are a great many people who travelled to Worms. I would that I might have done so myself."

"What has this friend, this Master Stauper, told you?"

"He has told me a great many things. I hardly know where to start, for there are so many things. I also very much enjoyed our conversation in the church a good while back. I have thought about it a great deal. It was good to tell you about my meeting with Dr. Geiler. I hope you were blessed by the hearing of that story."

"Oh, yes, I was," Katharina responded, her face aglow, "and I would very much like to hear about what your friend has said about the Diet. But I think it must wait, as I promised Mutti I would be back directly after I visited with Frau Bauer."

"I know," Matthis said, "but just this one small story I will leave with you before you go in. Dr. Luther was sent a silver jug with Einbeck beer by Duke Eric of Brunswick while in his lodgings in Worms."

As Katharina regarded him somewhat blankly, he went on to explain.

"The Duke, who was a very old man, but obviously favourably disposed toward Dr. Luther, was one of the papal members of the Diet. Actually, he died shortly after the Diet. But on his death-bed he asked one of the pages at his bedside to read to him from the Bible. And the page, opening the Bible, read these words: 'Whosoever shall give you a cup of water to drink in My name, because ye belong to Me, verily I say until you, he shall not lose his reward.'"

Katharina stared at Matthis face. She could literally see an old man, leaning back on his pillows, listening to words of Scripture being read to him.

"Was he comforted?" she asked softly.

"Yes," Matthis answered, "so the story goes in any case. It is said that when the duke's spirit was fading, he was given, not a silver jug, such as he sent Dr. Luther, but a gold cup and that he drank from the Water of Life."

"Oh," Katharina said and drew a breath to say more.

But she stopped short. Mutti had strictly enjoined her to come back home when she was done at Frau Bauer's.

"I must go back home," she continued. "Mutti is expecting me. Perhaps...we could speak again some other time?"

"Actually," and he smiled down at her, "your Mutti was so kind as to invite me for dinner next week. Your Vati and I had not time to cover all the matters in which he was most interested. Perhaps you will be able to sit down with us and partake in the conversation. And I can relate all other matters pertaining to Dr. Luther's defence of his faith."

She nodded and looked up into his grey eyes. There was so much good in learning and in speaking about what one had learned; there was so much comfort for the soul in this.

"Till next time, Fräulein Katharina."

The laugh lines crinkled around his eyes as he spoke. She curtsied, flushing slightly and smiling simultaneously.

"Till next time, Master Zell."

Chapter XXIX

"The chapel of St. Lawrence is much too small for the number of people that attend services," Katharina said to her father, "and I know for a fact that hundreds of citizens have petitioned that Master Zell be allowed to use Dr. Geiler's pulpit in the cathedral."

"The chapel of St. Lawrence is full because Matthis is preaching through the books of the Bible," Vati answered, "and the people are hungry to hear the actual Word preached. But I fear, daughter, that I have heard that this petition has been denied by the bishop and that the stone pulpit is closed to our friend."

"I cannot understand that," Katharina sighed, "for his preaching teaches everyone so much."

It was Saturday morning and Katharina and her Vati were on their way to his workshop at the back end of the house. She had promised to clean the workshop as Vati had requested this of her the previous night, complaining that he had been quite busy and unable to find time to do it himself.

"What have you been working on, Vati?" she asked him.

He stopped and sighed deeply, passing his right hand through his thick bushy beard, but did not respond.

"Well, Vati," Katharina persisted, "is it a secret?"

"You haven't been down to the workshop of late, daughter," he said by way of an answer, his eyes twinkling as he opened the door.

"No, I...," Katharina responded quickly, beginning to make a list of excuses about running errands for Mutti and about visiting sick neighbours. But, she was stopped short in her apologies by the strange sight she beheld in the middle of her father's workshop. Clasping her right hand in front of her mouth, she stared. What met her eyes was a sizeable wooden platform and next to it a pulpit and a small ladder by which, she ascertained, one might ascend the pulpit.

"What?" she exclaimed, slowly walking up to the crafted structures, touching them with her fingers, stroking them with her hands, repeating, "What is this, Vati? And for whom is it? Have you made them for Master Zell's use?"

And all the while Vati stood in the doorway, smiling at her surprise.

She went on wonderingly, repeating, "Is it for Master Zell's use that you have made these things?"

"Yes, it is for Master Zell's use, yet it is for the benefit of all of us," her father spoke the words gently, and she turned to face him.

"You did not tell me."

"No," he agreed, smiling. "You have been busy. So I am telling you and showing it to you now."

"But," she said, not fully comprehending what her father's plan was, "why and how...."

"Tomorrow the Joiner's Guild will pick up this pulpit and carry it through the streets of Strasbourg to the cathedral. They will place this pulpit in the centre of the sanctuary, next to the great stone pulpit. So even though Master Zell cannot preach from the great stone pulpit where we were wont to hear Dr. Geiler preach, he will still be able to preach in the large sanctuary. And great will be the number of people that will hear him expound the Word of God."

"Oh, Vati," Katharina exclaimed, "that is wonderful!"

"Yes," he agreed, "only do not mention it to him, for he knows nothing at all about the matter."

So it was on the first Sunday of Advent in 1521, when Matthis Zell entered the chapel at St. Lawrence to preach a sermon, that he found the sanctuary empty of congregants. He puzzled over this but was helped out of the dilemma by a messenger from the

Joiner's Guild who guided him over to the cathedral where his congregation was waiting. It was very quiet when he walked in, the only noise being the sunlight pouring through the rose-coloured windows. The approximately 3,000 people gathered to hear Matthis Zell preach sat silent as he, head bowed, slowly passed them. Led to the wooden pulpit, which had been placed right next to Dr. Geiler's stone pulpit, he solemnly ascended the platform and stepped behind the lectern. The cathedral was crammed full of people and Katharina, who sat with her sisters and their husbands in the middle pews, could not help but reflect upon the time when she had come here and indulgences had been sold and bought. How worried she had been and how ignorant! And now...now there was true preaching from the Word of God, in this very same place, true preaching for all of Strasbourg to hear. She could see the back of the chief magistrate's head a few benches ahead of her. She had beheld the aged humanist writer Wimpfeling pass through one of the aisles on the arm of Jacob Sturm, Strasbourg's *stettmeister*, as they made their way to a front pew. As well, she noted the presence of many monks, canons and priests who seemed not at all happy to be present. Although they stood quietly enough against the side walls of the great cathedral, there were frowns on their faces. And yet, happy or not, all were gathered and would hear the Word of God proclaimed.

After Matthis Zell ascended the small ladder to reach the wooden pulpit, the first thing he did was to fall on his knees in prayer, robe billowing about his person. Afterward he stood up and offered a fervent prayer of supplication for the people. He mightily entreated God that the words which would be spoken might honour God and that the hearts of all those listening might be opened. Then he proceeded to preach. He preached Advent. That is to say, he focused on the coming King, the Lord Jesus Christ. And as his words fell into the hearts of those listening, it was so quiet that Katharina could hear the beating of her heart.

"Christ came," the words rained down earnestly upon the packed audience of the cathedral, "seeking his own. He was not chosen by the crowd. Rather," Matthis Zell emphasized, even as he continued to gaze about the cathedral, "He chose his own."

A child coughed somewhere in the back pews and the sound reverberated. Katharina shifted her position so that she could better see Matthis and listen more attentively.

"You do not find Christ," Matthis voice resounded, "but he finds you."

All eyes were fixed on the man in the wooden pulpit. All ears were tuned to what he spoke. And he kept on speaking.

"If you are his followers, you must recognize his love and magnify his grace. His followers were and are only made holy through him—through faith in him."

You could hear a pin drop. And then he went on.

"All good works done in Christ's name are meaningless unless they begin in Christ and flow out from the grace that he gives."

Katharina noted that her breathing had become shallow. She swallowed. And all the while she listened, as indeed, everyone in the cathedral was doing.

Afterward, when he had descended, the pulpit parts were dissembled by members of the Joiner's Guild and carried out of the cathedral to be kept in a special place in the St. Lawrence Church until the next service.

THERE WERE A great many services that followed, but it was not until 1522 that there was a backlash against Matthis Zell by the bishop of Strasbourg. Everyone spoke of it and Vati was greatly angered by it.

"The bishop has threatened to remove Matthis Zell by placing him on furlough, by not renewing his contract to preach."

"How can he do so? The people love him."

Katharina was seated at the kitchen table and spoke to her father who was standing in the doorway, about to leave for a meeting.

"The bishop says that Matthis Zell preaches Luther and that alone, today at any rate, is akin to heresy."

"Oh, father, heresy?"

"I support Matthis Zell, Katharina. You know I do. As a matter of fact, I have asked him to come and dine with us this evening."

"Oh," Katharina said and again, "Oh."

Then Vati was gone and she was alone—alone with her thoughts and her feelings. For feelings and thoughts she had aplenty. Ever since she had begun to listen to Matthis' preaching regularly, there had grown such a peace within her. It had come gradually; it had entered softly. The voice of her conscience, ever condemning and reproaching her for not doing enough, for being inadequate, was growing duller and sometimes it was almost gone.

THERE WERE SPECIAL tarts and sweetmeats with the evening meal. Little Jacob, who was truly not so little any more, and Annder especially relished the treats but were given severe reprimands by Mutti for eating too heartily and too greedily. Annder even received a kick under the table from Katharina who let him feel, by the pain in his shins, that she felt his manners were unbecoming.

"All right," he muttered, and pushed his chair away from the table, resigning himself to not eating any more but simply listening.

"Now you must tell us," Vati said, after he had wiped his lips, "how matters stand for you, Matthis?"

It had become a normal thing that Vati called Matthis by his first name as the preacher was invited more and more frequently to the Schütz household. It was so that he was beginning to look upon the preacher as a dear friend, as an older son.

"Well, things stand this way," Matthis began, first looking down at his trencher and then pushing it away from himself to the middle of the table. "I am accused of having read Luther. To be sure I *have* read him. Who in Strasbourg has *not* read Herr Luther?"

They all nodded in agreement, from Mutti and Vati down to little Jacob.

"Indeed, how is a shepherd supposed to know where to pasture his sheep if he has not tried out the pastures? Even if Martin Luther were guilty of some mistakes, I would conclude that this does not make him a heretic. Were any of the church fathers free from all error?"

Matthis' strong tenor increased in strength as he spoke.

"Men say that Luther's language is too rough. I agree, but the question is not whether his language is too rough or too gentle but whether he is right or wrong. He is being read all over Germany, and am I alone to be forbidden to read him? Besides this, I follow

Luther only insofar as Luther follows the Bible. What a shame it would be to be ashamed of the Word of God!"

Margaret, seated next to Katharina, put her hand in her sister's hand. Katharina squeezed it comfortingly. She knew such talk made Margaret nervous.

"There are those who preach badly," Matthis went on, warming even more to his subject, "those who spend more time hunting and gaming than in truly searching out the Word of God. But I would say this, though the pope issues a thousand bulls against sincere preachers who are today searching out the Scriptures and preaching according to what the Scriptures say, the Word of God will prevail."

"Amen," Vati agreed, a smile on his face, and Katharina felt as if she had been privy to a great and wonderful moment.

Her eyes were riveted on Matthis face, a face glowing with animation as he spoke of his love for preaching, of his love for God. She was so thankful for him and for other preachers that were also proclaiming God's Word in the same manner.

THERE WERE SERMONS and more sermons and more sermons. And the people of Strasbourg grew and grew and grew in listening, even as the Holy Spirit opened their hearts to hear wonderful and age-old truths. There were clear trumpet calls to the authority of Scripture as well as the repudiation of what Matthis Zell termed 'legends.' One such very popular legend in Strasbourg was that Mary, the mother of Jesus, had been born without sin. Matthis Zell underlined that there was far too great an emphasis on Mary and that, although she should be honoured as being the Lord's mother, indeed, she was not sinless.

"There is not a word about this in the Bible," Matthis repeated again and again, "not a word."

As well, he criticized pilgrimages to Marian shrines where people went to ask forgiveness of sins through her, rather than through Jesus Christ alone.

"Such pilgrimages are not mentioned in the Bible," he was wont to exclaim from his wooden pulpit, adding, "and no grace can be obtained from the Virgin Mary. This can only be obtained through Jesus, our Lord."

Matthis Zell also questioned the doctrine of purgatory. In the fall of 1522, the parishioners coming to the cathedral for the feast of St. Matthew heard a forceful sermon from his lips.

"Human fear," Matthis said, leaning his arms on the wooden pulpit, his piercing eyes encompassing all the people sitting in front of him, "human fear comes from an imperfect trust in Jesus Christ. If one firmly has his eyes fixed on Jesus, then the gates of hell cannot hurt him. The Bible says nothing about purgatory— nothing at all! Belief in purgatory comes from certain 'revelations' that people say they have had. But the only revelation you and I can trust is the Bible. Paying for prayers for the dead to be delivered from purgatory only makes fat the pockets of greedy clergy."

The learning went on; hearts were opened. And Katharina Schütz who, from the time she was a little maid, had struggled to make peace with God by her good works—by her fasting, her self-denials, her frequent attendance at Mass, her service to the poor—now began to understand that Christ had lived a perfect life and that he had lived this perfect life for those who believed in him. His yoke was easy and his burden was light; and his salvation, Katharina knew, was hers freely through grace by faith.

Matthis saw that Katharina's face, almost like a budding flower, began to turn toward the light of redemption. He noted thankfully, that it had begun to shine with a great love for her Redeemer. There was much talk between the two, even though Matthis was some twenty years her senior.

IT WAS DURING the early summer of 1523, that a former Dominican priest by the name of Martin Bucer arrived in Strasbourg. A former monk turned Lutheran, he had pastored the church at Wissembourg and had tried to make that city a Protestant city. When Roman Catholicism had prevailed, he had been forced to flee for his life. Penniless and excommunicated, Martin Bucer did not arrive in Strasbourg by himself. He came with a wife—a former nun by the name of Elizabeth Silbereisen—whom he had married that previous summer. The couple was homeless and friendless, and Matthis opened his house in the Brüderhof Strasse to them.

Perhaps it was the arrival of the Bucers that opened a conversation between Matthis and Katharina—a conversation that had been long in coming.

"I have spoken with your Vati," Matthis said one evening as they walked together toward the Schütz home after supper with cousin Margred and Wolfgang.

"Oh," Katharina answered, "and what did you speak about?" thinking perhaps that it was some matter dealing with theology or such.

"It was about you," Matthis said.

The manner in which he spoke these words made her stand still.

"What do you mean," she faltered, "it was about me? Have I done something? Have I said something?"

She stopped.

"No, indeed," Matthis replied quickly, raising his right hand to his forehead, wiping it as if he were greatly troubled.

"Well, then," she said, "what was it you spoke about?"

"You see," he went on, and it appeared to her that he was having difficulty swallowing, difficulty enunciating his words, something she had never before known him to have trouble with. "I have been watching...watching the Bucers, Martin and Elisabeth. You know, I think...that they will have a child soon."

Here he paused. Katharina, quick to surmise that she was needed, jumped into the pause.

"Oh, you need not worry," she smiled up at him, "I shall be most happy to come and help at the birth. You need only...."

"No," he interrupted and interrupted rather sharply, "No, I do not mean...."

He wiped his forehead again. She looked down at her feet. Again she heard Mutti admonishing her, as she had been wont to do when she was a little maid, "Katharina, Katharina, don't speak over much. Wait for others."

"I'm sorry," she whispered. "I talk as much as a sparrow chirps. Surely I offend...."

"Oh, Katharina," Matthis whispered back, "what I spoke to your father about was not that you offend. Not that at all."

There was a long quiet but she durst not speak, and she began to fear that she had said quite the wrong thing once again. Finally, she could not bear it any longer and whispered.

"What then did you speak to him about?"

Her curiosity was piqued, but she was also nervous. Shadows danced about them. Stars were beginning to light the sky above them. It was nigh on autumn, and the early winter chill made Katharina shiver and long for the fire in the hearth.

"We are both body and soul," Matthis spoke solemnly now, his nose pointing toward the setting sun, "and with the breath of God, we became alive."

Katharina stared at him. Was he teaching her some new truth? She tried hard to listen and not to think of the goose bumps forming on her arms.

"We are unique in this. We are part of creation but...."

He halted, seemingly groping for words. She wished that she could help him, but she knew not what it was that he was going to say.

"The Bible says," he went on with difficulty, once more wiping his forehead, "that you and I, man and woman, were created in the image of God. Now with regard to marriage...to marriage...."

Katharina became warm. She felt her face flush and her heart began to race.

"Now with regard to marriage," Matthis doggedly repeated, "there is the word 'helpmeet.' This is not a derogatory word. It does not mean assistant. The word helpmeet is used many times in the Bible in reference to God himself.

"Yes?" Katharina encouraged, feeling as if she were being lifted up as high as the gables overhead.

"In Psalm.... "

"Yes?" Katharina encouraged again.

"I've forgotten the Psalm I wanted to quote," Matthis said lamely.

Several people emerged from a house close by where they were standing. Katharina pulsed with a sense of expectation. The people passed them, and when they were some distance down the street, Matthis commenced once more. They had not moved from their spot the whole time.

"The word helpmeet stresses Adam's inadequacy. It does not

stress Eve's inferiority. It does...."

It began to rain. Softly at first, the drops hit the cobblestones, wetting them down and painting them clean.

"What did you say to my father about me?" Katharina probed again, curiosity getting the better of her.

"Oh, Katharina," Matthis' voice rang through the increasing raindrops, "I asked his permission to marry you."

"*Marry me?*"

"I know that I am older and not, perhaps, what you are looking for in a husband. But truly, I need you. I look on you as my helper."

"Need me?"

"I love you, Katharina."

It had begun to rain harder, but Katharina did not feel it. All she felt was the wonderful and intense look with which Matthis was regarding her; all she felt was the need to lay her head on his shoulder. Indeed, she felt so incredibly thankful to God that she burst into tears.

"Katharina?"

But she could not speak for the sobbing, and Matthis could not help but put his arms around her.

"Is it such a bad question that you must weep because of it?"

She shook her head 'no' and turned her face toward him. It was a wet face, shining with both rain and tears.

"Indeed, it is not good for a man to be alone," she answered, "and I would be honoured to be your helper."

Epilogue

T his book is a work of fiction in which I delved into what I knew about the character and life of Katharina Schütz Zell. Having said that, however, many of the events taking place on its pages did, in fact, occur and many of the people mentioned were real people. The dancing plague, for example, really happened, and there is a good chance Katharina was involved in aiding those afflicted. Katharina lost her older brother, Jacob, at some point in her youth, and an indulgence could well have been bought by her when Tetzel visited Strasbourg. The names of her siblings and their spouses are correct, and her father was, indeed, a wood craftsman. Katharina was sent to learn *heidnisch werk* when she was young, she did have family members in the beguinage, and Dr. Geiler von Kaysersberg was a beloved pastor of the city. The historical data wound around her days is all correct and, without doubt, encompassed her thinking. The book stops at the time of Katharina's marriage to Matthis Zell. The following is a bit of a closure on her life. If you want to know more, there is always the future meeting in heaven.

KATHARINA WAS THE first woman of Strasbourg to marry a priest. After her marriage on December 3, 1523, she described herself with joy as "a splinter from the rib of that blessed man Matthis Zell." He, for his part, referred to Katharina as "his helpmeet" and his "wedded companion." There was slanderous talk in the beginning. Rumors were circulated that Matthis beat his wife and that he contemplated having an affair with a maid. To reprove the gossip Katharina wrote:

> There has never been a single quarter hour...that Matthis and I have not been united. I have never had a maid. I have had the help only of a little girl, too young for that sort of thing, and as for thrashing me, my husband and I have never had an unpleasant fifteen minutes. We could have no greater honour than to die rejected of men and from two crosses to speak to each other words of comfort.

Devoted to one another, God was pleased to give them two children. Then, in his strange providence, God took these children to himself again. This was a very sad time for both Katharina and Matthis, as they would have loved to bring up some little ones. Katharina devoted her life to helping her pastor husband. She was a faithful housewife and a hostess to many refugees who fled to Strasbourg from persecution in Roman Catholic cities. It caused Matthis to refer to her as "mother of the poor and refugees." At one point she bedded down eighty in the parsonage and fed sixty of them for three weeks.

In 1525, shortly after Katharina and Matthis were married, the Peasants' War broke out. Katharina, along with Matthis and one other pastor, visited encampments around Strasbourg, pleading for peace. In the end the peasants were massacred and some 3,000 survivors flocked into Strasbourg. It put a great strain on the economy of a city only designed to facilitate its population of 25,000. Katharina was at the forefront of those providing relief. The emergency lasted for six months. Then the war subsided, and the families could return to their homes.

In the late 1530s, Calvin was expelled from Geneva. Arriving in Strasbourg, he was taken into the home of Katharina and Matthis Zell and treated with great kindness. Katharina and Matthis themselves, at one point, traveled some 600 miles to visit Luther and Melancthon at Wittenberg.

During her married life, Katharina wrote many pamphlets,

speaking out for the truths of the Reformation. She penned, for example, a booklet defending the marriage of priests. She also wrote a meditation on the Lord's Prayer. As well, she was instrumental in editing a hymnbook for the people of Strasbourg, she said:

> This is not just a hymn book but a lesson book of prayer and praise. When so many filthy songs are on the lips of men and women and even children, I think it well that folk should, with lusty zeal and clear voice, sing the songs of salvation. God is glad when the craftsman at his bench, the maid at the sink, the farmer at the plough, the dresser at the vines, and the mother at the cradle break forth in hymns of prayer, praise and instruction.

Katharina and Matthis were filled with a spirit of compassion toward other Christians. They devoted their income to meeting the needs of those who came to their door. Katharina consequently criticized religious leaders of Strasbourg for intolerance toward Christians of other traditions. She said:

> Anyone who acknowledges Christ as the true Son of God and the sole Saviour of mankind, is welcome at my board.

Much beloved by many people of Strasbourg, Katharina visited prisons, nursed people with the plague, carried out the dead, housed poor students, was a frequent visitor of one who lived in quarantine because of leprosy, and so on. She greatly mourned Matthis' death in 1548. But he encouraged her on his deathbed by saying:

> You will remain after me awhile, and will also see much against yourself, lies; do your best and be comforted, God will be with you. You are still heretofore Master Matthis' wife; he will be now taken from you. If you do not sing to please everyone there will be trouble, but do not fear; God has given you enough, more than to other women; that he will not take from you.

Permitted to remain in the manse just over two years, Katharina did keep up the work. At one point she hid two ministers in her house—two ministers who had been exiled from Strasbourg for preaching in a manner deemed too controversial. Pastors Bucer and Fagius remained with Katharina quite a few weeks. Upon their departure, they left behind two gold pieces for her and from their safe haven in England, sent her a letter of thanks. She reponded to the gift of the gold pieces by writing to them:

> You put me to shame to think that you would leave money for me, as if I would take a heller from you poor pilgrims and my revered ministers. I wish I could have done better for you but my Matthis has taken all my gaiety with him. I intended to return the two gold pieces with this letter, as Joseph put the money in the sack of his brother, but a refugee minister has just come in with five children, and the wife of another who saw her husband beheaded before her eyes. I divided the one gold piece between them as a present from you. The other I enclose. You will need it.

Later in life, Katharina moved into the hospital for syphilitics with a nephew who had contracted the disease. She was appalled by the bad conditions in the hospital and wrote a letter to the town council:

> The manager and his wife live in luxury and neglect the patients. Beds rot. Water is not heated for baths. Tough and sometimes wormy meat is served indiscriminately, whereas some require a soft diet. There is no religious instruction and some patients do not know the Lord's Prayer. The manager mumbles a grace so that one cannot tell whether he may not be swearing. The mercury cure martyrs the patients. There should be a dedicated couple in charge. The number of maids should be reduced. The fewer, the less quarrelling. Get rid of the savage dog which mangles all the cats. Give up swine and goats in favour of a hundred hens.

Have religious instruction every morning while the heart is fresh. For medication use only guyac.

Her recommendations were accepted and changes came about. She then moved out of the hospital.

Katharina died in 1562.

Glossary

Agnus Dei—a prayer that begins with the words *Agnus Dei* (Lamb of God).

amice—oblong, linen cloth tied at the waist and worn by a priest during Mass.

apse—a semicircular projecting part of a building, especially the east end of a church that contains the altar.

astrolabe—an early instrument used to observe the position and determine the altitude of the sun or other celestial bodies.

atelier—an artist's studio or workplace.

Ave Maria—a prayer to the mother of Jesus:

> Hail Mary, full of grace,
>> The Lord is with thee
>
> Blessed art thou among women
>> and blessed is the fruit of thy womb, Jesus
>
> Holy Mary, mother of God, pray for us sinners
>> Now and at the hour of our death. Amen

baptistry—the area of a church used for baptism.

beguinage—a number of terraced houses within a courtyard enclosed by walls. Women living here were under restricted monastic rules but they could leave and choose to marry.

bolster—a long, often cylindrical cushion for a bed.

burin—sharply pointed instrument used in engraving.

burse—a flat case used for carrying a special linen cloth for celebrating Mass.

Cardinal Cajetan (1468–1534)—a Roman Catholic theologian and spokesperson for Catholic opposition to Martin Luther.

cassock—a full-length black robe worn by priests.

chasuble—large bell-shaped priestly vestment.

confraternity—a Roman Catholic organization of people dedicated to special good works of Christian charity or piety.

cowl—the hood on a monk's cloak.

dabber—a leather-covered wooden tool used to cover a cut out wood design with ink.

Diet—formal assembly for discussing or acting upon public or state affairs.

dropsy—an abnormal build-up of fluid between tissue cells.

durst—old form of dare.

Dürer, Albrecht (1471–1528)—German painter, engraver, printmaker, mathematician and theorist.

elle—a measure of length, now little used. Distance between elbow and fingertip, often a little over a foot.

excommunicate—to cut off from the sacraments and fellowship of the church by ecclesiastical sentence.

Frau— German equivalent of Mrs.

genuflect—bending the right knee to the floor and rising again, as a gesture of respect.

Gloria Patri—The following prayer:
Glory be to the Father and to the Son and to the Holy Spirit,
As it was in the beginning, is now and ever shall be,
World without end. Amen.

gouge—an instrument used in digging out wood when sketching a design on wood.

hausfrau—a housewife.

Herr—German equivalent of Mr.

jerkin—a sleeved coat or jacket.

kirtle—a long gown or under-gown.

Krotten Stein—a toadstone.

Lehrhäuser—private schools in Strasbourg, dating back to the late fourteenth century, headed by a Lehrmeister or a Lehrfrauen (male and female teachers), which gave elementary instruction in the basics of German. In the fifteenth century, this instruction was extended to girls as well as boys.

matins—morning prayer.

meisterin—the formal title of the woman in charge of a beguinage.

Mentelin, Johannes (1410–1478)—pioneering German book printer and seller, who in 1466, printed the first Bible in the German language.

Michelangelo (1475–1564)—Italian sculptor, painter, architect and poet.

novena—in the Roman Catholic Church, the recitation of prayers for nine consecutive days to achieve a particular purpose.

nave—the long central hall of a cross-shaped church, often with pillars on each side, where the congregation sits.

Orate pro Jacob Schütz—Latin for, "Pray for Jacob Schütz."

penitentiarius—a confessor. A major penitentiarius was authorized to pardon murderers and outlaws, allowing such criminals to become monks.

partlet—collar.

pfennig—a small, lightweight monetary coin used in Germany, worth about a penny.

portal—an entrance to an important building.

purgatory—in 1439, the Roman Church Council of Florence formally authorized this dogma that provided a sort of 'half-way' house where souls would have a second chance to work out salvation and possibly move on to heaven. Based on salvation by merits, it has no foundation in Scripture.

pyx—container in which consecrated wafers for communion are placed so that they can be taken to those who cannot leave home.

Raphael (1483–1520)—Italian artist.

reredorter—medieval word for communal toilet facilities.

shrive—to hear someone's confession of sins and give the person absolution.

sandstein—sandstone.

snood—a woman's hairnet.

stettmeister—the ceremonial head of the ruling body of Strasbourg, burgomaster or mayor.

stoup—a basin for holy water.

Strasbourg—the name is of Germanic origin and means 'Town (at the crossing) of roads.' *Stras* comes from the German *strasse*, meaning street, or Latin *strata* (paved road), while *bourg* (French for town), is like the German word *burg* and the English *borough*, meaning fortress.

Strasbourg Cathedral—This building, begun in 1176, took centuries to complete. Its spire reached as high as a 45-storey skyscraper, and it stood as the tallest building in Europe until the Eiffel Tower was built.

strasse—street.

St. Vitus Dance—also known as choreomania, was possibly caused by a fungus called ergot, which grows on standing corn and rye in wet summers. Anyone eating from this infected flour was liable to be afflicted with violent spasms and mental derangement. Victims were wont to dance, as the exercise seemed to help ease their suffering. Europe saw as many as ten dancing epidemics before the one in Strasbourg in 1518.

surplice—a white flowing garment, like a smock, often with flared sleeves, worn by priests.

transept—a section of a cross-shaped church that runs at right angles to the long central part.

thurible—censer.

Trinity Sunday—the first Sunday after Pentecost.

Bibliography

Belloc, Hilaire. *Characters of the Reformation: Historical Portraits.* Rockford: Tan Books and Publishing, 1992.

Blackman, E. Louis. *Religious Dances.* London: George Allen and Unwin, 1952.

Brady, Jr., Thomas A. *Ruling Class, Regime and Reformation at Strasbourg.* Leiden: Brill, 1978.

Brady, Jr., Thomas A. *The Politics of the Reformation in Germany: Jacob Sturm (1489–1553) of Strasbourg.* Atlantic Highlands: Humanities Press, 1997.

Carter, R. *Tales from Alsace, or, Scenes and Portraits from Life in the Days of the Reformation.* New York: John Wilson and Son, 1869.

Chrisman, Miriam Usher. *Lay Culture, Learned Culture: Books and Social Change in Strasbourg, 1480–1599.* New Haven: Yale University Press, 1982.

Hanks, Merry Wiesner, ed. *Convents Confront the Reformation: Catholic and Protestant Nuns in Germany.* Milwaukee: Marquette University Press, 1996.

Hutchison, Jane Campbell. *Albrecht Dürer—A Biography.* Princeton: Princeton University Press, 1990.

Marshall, Edith, ed. *Women in Reformation and Counter-Reformation.* Bloomington: Indiana University Press, 1989.

McKee, Elsie Anne. *Katharina Schütz Zell.* Leiden: Brill, 1998. 2 vols.

McKee, Elsie Anne. *Reforming Popular Piety in Sixteenth-Century*

Strasbourg: Katharina Schütz Zell and Her Hymnbook. Princeton: Princeton Theological Seminary, 1994.

McLaughlin, R. Emmet. *Caspar Schwenckfeld, Reluctant Reformer—His Life to 1540*. New Haven: Yale University Press, 1986.

Nohl, Johannes. *The Black Death*. London: George Allen and Unwin, 1926.

Oberman, Heiko. *Luther—Man between God and the Devil*. New Haven: Yale University Press, 1982.

Ozment, Steven. *Magdalena and Balthasar: An Intimate Portrait of Life in 16th-Century Europe Revealed in the Letters of a Nuremberg Husband and Wife*. New York: Simon and Schuster, 1986.

Ozment, Steven. *The Bearing of Children*. Cambridge: Harvard University Press, 1983.

Ripley, Elizabeth. *Dürer—a Biography*. Philadelphia: J.B. Lippincott & Co., 1958.

Roper, Lyndal. *The Holy Household*. Oxford: Clarendon Press, 1989.

Rose, Mary Beth, ed. and intro. *Women in the Middle Ages and the Renaissance: Literary and Historical Perspectives*. Syracuse: Syracuse University Press, 1986.

Russell, Frances. *The World of Dürer (1471–1528)*. New York: Time Inc., 1967.

Schultz, Selina Gerhard. *Caspar Schwenckfeld von Ossig, 1489–1561*. Pennsburg: The Board of Publication of the Schwenckfelder Church, 1977.

Shahar, Shalamith. *A History of Women in the Middle Ages*. London: Routledge, 1983.

Stafford, William. *Domesticating the Clergy—The Inception of the Reformation in Strasbourg 1522–1524*. Missoula: Scholars Press, 1974.

Strauss, Gerald, ed. and trans. *Manifestations of Discontent in Germany on the Eve of the Reformation*. Bloomington: Indiana University Press, 1971.

Tillmans, Walter G. *The World and Men around Luther*. Minneapolis: Augsburg Publishing House, 1959.

Deo Optimo et Maximo Gloria
To God, best and greatest, be glory

www.joshuapress.com

www.ingramcontent.com/pod-product-compliance
Lightning Source LLC
Chambersburg PA
CBHW030639020726
47493CB00006B/1791